ASSUMPTION CITY

ASSUMPTION CITY

TERRENCE MURPHY

iUniverse, Inc.
Bloomington

Assumption City

iUniverse books may be ordered through booksellers or by contacting:

iUniverse
1663 Liberty Drive
Bloomington, IN 47403
www.iuniverse.com
1-800-Authors (1-800-288-4677)

ISBN: 978-1-4759-5659-7 (sc)
ISBN: 978-1-4759-5660-3 (hc)
ISBN: 978-1-4759-5661-0 (e)

Library of Congress Control Number: 2012919388

Printed in the United States of America

iUniverse rev. date: 12/06/2012

To my wife, Betty,
my loving partner in so many ways.

Acknowledgments

Jan Schreiber saw merit in my original idea and generously guided me at every step of the process.

Rev. Frank Silva provided invaluable insights into the workings of the Church and saved me from making some whopping errors.

The late Dr. Vernon Pais walked me through medical procedures central to the story.

The late Monsignor Thomas J. Daly helped me envision "Little Rome" and "Saint Luke's Seminary."

Rev. John L. Sullivan gave me an insider's view of seminary life.

Jim Wood introduced me to the world of vintage cars and explained how you pull the engine of a 1951 Studebaker for a rebuild.

Jack McClellan taught me what I needed to know about hospital power grids.

Dan Gauvin helped me imagine what the "voyage of the *Nerses*" would have been like.

Catherine Hutchison recreated Faneuil and Egg Rock in her maps.

Many read the story and gave me helpful advice. They include Ruth Aaron, Dr. John Brusch, Patricia Brusch, RN, Madeleine Corcoran, Polly Herz, Dr. Emilie Hitron, Frances Nason, Diane Paterson, the late Leo Smith, and John Welsh.

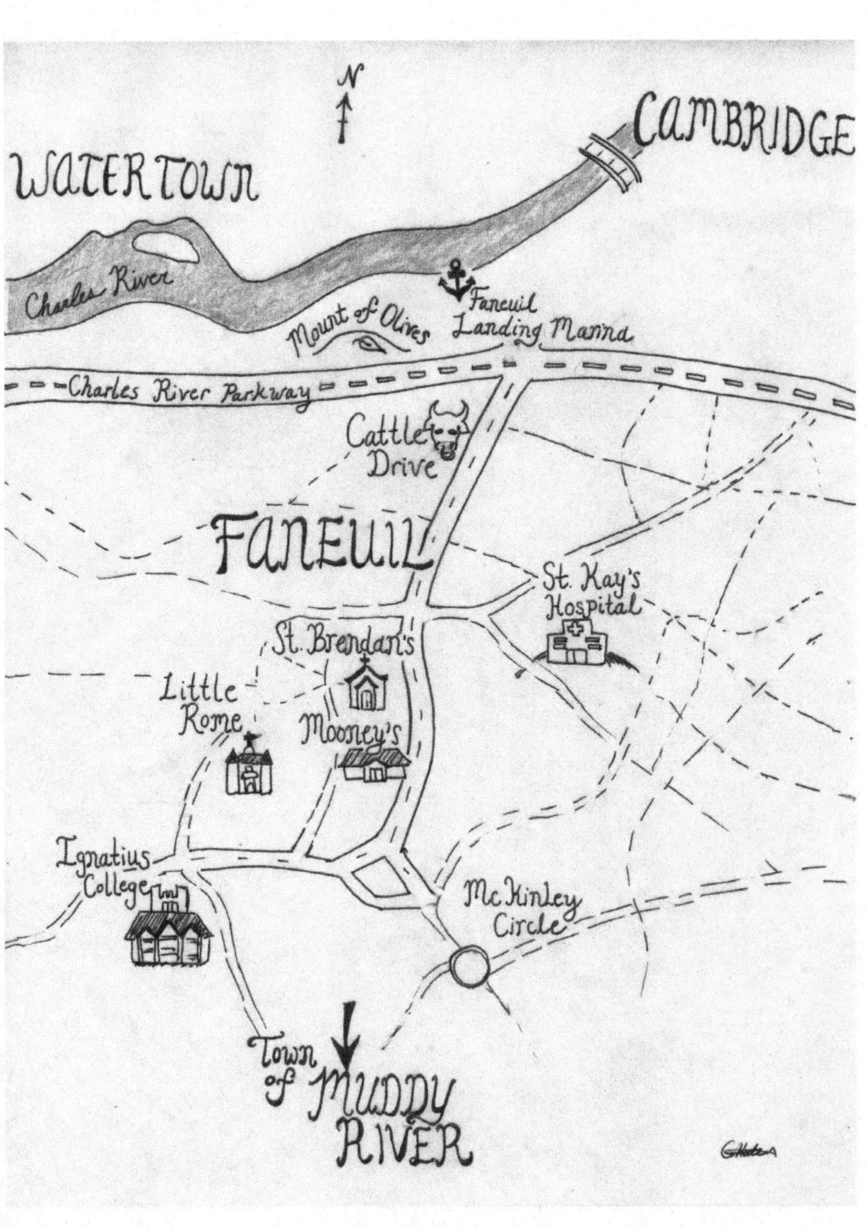
N
WATERTOWN
CAMBRIDGE
Charles River
Faneuil
Landing Marina
Mount of Olives
Charles River Parkway
Cattle
Drive
FANEUIL
St. Kay's
Hospital
St. Brendan's
Little
Rome
Mooney's
Ignatius
College
McKinley
Circle
Town
of
MUDDY
RIVER

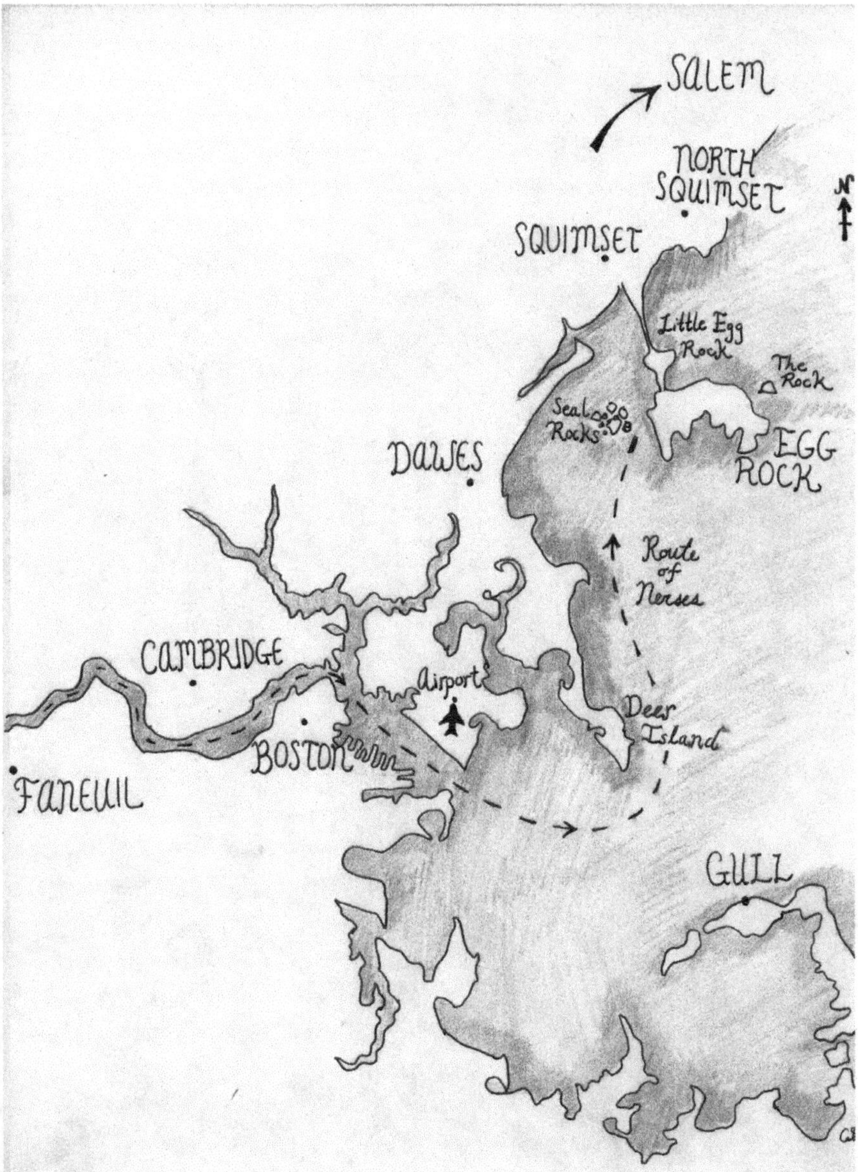

SALEM
NORTH SQUIMSET
N
SQUIMSET
Little Egg Rock
The Rock
Seal Rocks
EGG ROCK
DAWES
Route of Nerses
CAMBRIDGE
Airport
Deer Island
BOSTON
FANEUIL
GULL

The Mulcahy Family

Vincent Mulcahy
His children:
Father Frank and
Portia

Dr. Leo Mulcahy, Vincent's nephew
Claire, Leo's wife
Their children: Francine and Sam

The Cronin Family

Dr. Eddie Cronin
Kitty, Eddie's wife
Their children: John,
Lawrence, Ambrose, Ita,
Fabian, Charles, Irene,
and Anthony

Eunice Rafferty, Kitty's mother
Bridget, Kitty's sister
Buzzy, Bridget's husband
Bridget's children: Brian and Sean

The Rowley Family

Dr. Thomas Rowley
Helen, Tom's ex-wife
Thomas Rowley Jr. (died 1994)

Saint Kay's Hospital

Gert Kleindienst, Eddie Cronin's secretary
Pat Kaminski, chief of security
Raymond Stanton, security guard
Gene Autry, hospital attorney, trustee
Dr. Harold Nalbandian, Leo's partner
Geri, Harold's wife
Veronica, Leo and Harold's receptionist
Father Guido della Chiesa, hospital chaplain
Dr. Nina Nichols orthopedic surgeon
J. J. Rideout, drug rep

The Church

Archbishop Sebastian Quilty
(Sean Cardinal O'Rourke, former archbishop of Boston, died 1944)
(Edmund Cardinal Campion, former archbishop of Boston, died 1997)
(Father Malachy Dunn, missionary and pastor in Egg Rock, died 1999)
Father Dan Skerry, Quilty's secretary
Father Joe Maguire, Quilty's junior secretary
Auxiliary Bishop Louis Fannon
Archbishop Giuseppe Sarto, Papal Nuncio
Sister Philippe, cook and manager of household for Archbishop Quilty
Father Richard Mears, seminary professor
Father Gregory Tally, pastor of Saint Brendan's

Others

Corinne Caruthers, TV news reporter
Michael and Eiko Mooney, funeral directors
Lavern "Spike" Birdsong, VP, American Pharmaceutical Enterprises

DECEMBER 1994

It was weird to see the Mount of Olives parking lots so empty. Even on those rare days when he got there early, the only spaces left were in the second lot, behind Pius XII Auditorium. Tommy considered parking near the half-dozen cars in the first lot but settled on putting the old Volvo behind a couple of yellow school buses in back of the building.

He felt much better. Now that he had a plan, the panicky feeling was gone, and he was thinking clearly.

The wind kicked up some leaves that the grounds crew had missed. A dusting of snow overnight coated the ground, but coming as it did a couple of days after Christmas, it didn't much matter. He remembered one of those TV weather guys saying that Boston gets a white Christmas only once in seven years. Tough on the little kids who needed to believe in Santa and his sleigh. They could burn through a whole childhood without the reassurance of snow on the roof.

His father was sure to be at the hospital by now, screwing around with his petri dishes and incubators. Dr. Tom Rowley loved his little lab on weekends, when folks didn't mess with him. And last night, Tommy heard Ma talking to one of her friends on the phone about the after-Christmas sales. They'd be cruising the Charles River Mall by now.

The patch of woods between the parking lot and the ball fields was bare and lifeless except for a few scattered evergreens. Their history teacher called this area a "copse," and the kids all laughed.

"Did he say corpse?" one of the kids stage-whispered, and everybody laughed again.

He pulled the early admission letter from his parka and smoothed it carefully before unfolding it and studying it for the hundredth time. He loved the way the college seal was embossed on the top of the page. He closed his eyes and ran his finger over it like a blind man reading a message in Braille.

We are pleased to offer you …

He folded the letter, slipped it snugly into its envelope, and placed it on the passenger seat, where it wouldn't get soiled.

He peered into the rearview mirror and realized that he hadn't really looked at himself for a long time. With his contacts in, he looked totally un-nerdy. Studying his deep-set eyes and strong chin, he decided he was good looking. He flashed a winning smile, as if on camera.

The all-American boy.

It was time to step out into the cold.

Clouds skittered across the sky, making the sun flicker and making it feel colder than it was. Father Guido would call this a "high-pressure day." On their walks, back when they talked about so many things, they decided that they both preferred low-pressure days when the air was calm.

Father Guido … God knows this isn't his fault, Tommy thought.

He pulled up his collar against the wind and walked into the woods. On cue, the memory loop in his brain kicked in, just as it did at least once every waking hour.

It was the day before Thanksgiving break, and the whole school was in holiday spirits. Two jocks from the football team were walking past him outside the cafeteria, when one of them (he wasn't sure which) stuck his foot out and tripped him. By the time he retrieved his books and picked himself off the floor, they'd disappeared.

Meanwhile, the hallway was wall-to-wall with kids and a scattering of teachers, but no one seemed to notice.

He had to act quickly, before he changed his mind.

He eased the old man's .45 from his parka, rubbed it with his hands to get it warm, and leaned his forehead against the muzzle.

Then he closed his eyes and listened to the wind in the trees and the cars whizzing along Charles River Drive below the ball fields for a few seconds before tightening his finger on the trigger.

AUGUST 2002

MONDAY

1.

Dr. Edward Cronin was already half shaved when he heard his cell phone bleeping from the bedroom. As the president of Saint Katherine's Hospital (which just about everyone called Saint Kay's), his cell was on 24/7.

Kitty jumped out of bed and answered the phone.

Cronin feared it might be another call from Archbishop Quilty. The archbishop of Boston loved to call early in the morning or late at night to talk about what was on his mind, never asking whether it was a bad time to call or whatever. Apparently, Cronin wasn't alone. The archbishop's secretary, Father Skerry, once confided that the Boss needed no more than four hours' sleep and was driving the chancery staff nuts.

Then he remembered that the archbishop was on retreat.

Kitty put her hand over the receiver. "Eddie, Pat Kaminski is calling from the hospital. He says it's an emergency."

"Sorry to trouble you so early, Dr. Cronin, but I need to tell you about what's happened here overnight. Actually, at 5:01 this morning."

"What is it, Pat?"

"The power went down all over the hospital."

"Did the emergency generators kick in?"

"Perfectly. As you know, the backup system was updated in '99, at the time of the millennium computer crisis."

How could he forget the two-hundred grand he threw away for the threatened computer shutdown that never happened? All he ended up doing was lining the pockets of those nerdy little computer wizards!

"Auxiliary power kicked right in for the emergency department, in-patient areas, and the operating room."

"Are we still on backup?"

"No, sir. Boston Edison got power back at 5:43. We were down for forty-two minutes and thirty-four seconds. Edison says that a transformer at the foot of the hill failed, and they were able to reroute the grid around the problem. They anticipate no further difficulties."

"Is everything back to normal?"

"Yes, sir, technically."

"Technically? What the hell is that supposed to mean?"

"No more problems with the power, sir. All the computers have surge protectors, so no data was lost. The clocks all over the hospital stopped, of course, and need to be moved ahead manually the forty-two minutes and thirty-four seconds, but that's a minor headache."

"So what's the problem?"

"Well, sir, something really out of the ordinary is happening."

"A power outage is out of the ordinary enough. What else?"

"One of my men reported some unusual lighting on one of the windows at the medical office building."

"I'm not in the mood for riddles, Pat."

"No, sir."

"Well then, what do you mean by 'unusual lighting'?"

"I guess you could say, a lighted image, one that looks like the Virgin Mary."

"The Virgin Mary? Like in Jesus, Mary, and Joseph?"

"Yes, sir."

"Have you looked at this 'image' yourself?"

"I'm standing underneath the window now. I thought you'd want to know about it right away."

"So what is this? Somebody's idea of a joke?"

"I really don't know, sir. By the time I drove in from home, the power was back on. I was on the phone in my office with the Edison guys when Raymond, our night supervisor, burst into the office to tell me about the window. I was sure this was going to be some kind of a crock, and I figured someone would have to point the window out to me. But when I walked around the corner, the window was *glowing.* I'm not much for religion, you know, but the window really shook me up. Looks like the outline of the Virgin Mary just like I remember in my old missal when I was a kid. Dr. Cronin, I was over at the medical office building yesterday afternoon, and the windows looked normal then. Something must have happened overnight."

"Look, Pat, I'm ready to leave. Keep one of your guys over there to keep order. We don't need this to turn into a circus. Just make sure you're in my office at seven thirty sharp."

"No problem, sir."

2.

Dr. Tom Rowley had finished reading about the Red Sox's dismal weekend and was working on his second cup of coffee, along with his eggs, when a nurse at the next table leaned back in her chair and asked him if he'd heard the big news.

"There's some kind of apparition on a window over at the MOB," she confided, using the familiar initials for the medical office building.

"The kids on nights say it's an image of the Virgin Mary, if you can believe it. We're headed over there before the shift begins. Want to come along?"

Tom smiled when he heard about the "kids on nights," since most of the third-shift nurses would never see fifty again. But if these old hands, who had seen just about everything, were impressed, he'd better take a look for himself.

Putting down the newspaper and mopping up the last of his fried egg with the remaining corner of toast, he thought of Helen. She was the one who taught him to eat his eggs like that.

God knows she was always practical. The evening he got home and found that she had taken off, he saw the *Better Homes and Gardens Cook Book* and *The Joy of Cooking* on the kitchen table along with her note. On Post-it notes, Helen had designated the first book for "Every Day" and the second "For Special Occasions." And with little tabs she must have swiped from the library, she'd marked the recipes for his favorite dishes.

In the months before she finally walked out, she made a real campaign of getting him to do some cooking. "How about you doing the cooking one night a week?" Some nights, she'd give him little chores like mashing potatoes, warming leftovers in the microwave, anything to get him comfortable in the kitchen, but he resisted.

"It can't be that different from the work you do in the lab," she'd argue.

Once the house was sold, he had found a neat one-bedroom apartment on a leafy side street at the foot of Hospital Hill. It was an okay place, second floor with a sunny exposure, but he just couldn't get around to moving in completely. He was still living out of packing boxes, with *Faneuil Movers* printed on the side, even though he'd been in there for a year.

He let Helen have most of the furniture, including the stuff from Tommy's room, because he couldn't bear looking at it anymore.

Furniture can be cruelly evocative.

Walking over to the MOB now, he wondered if anybody noticed his limp. The weight he had gradually put on over the years was not helping matters, as his orthopedist pointed out. He'd need his hip replaced soon and worried about the convalescence now that he was all alone. He thought about his living room with the packing boxes and how he'd need to explain them to the visiting nurse and the cute physical therapist who'd come by post-op.

He and his nurse friends carried on with their usual banter as they passed the main entrance where the young Hispanic guys who ran the valet parking concession were greeting their first customers, mostly anxious old-timers with hovering spouses, overnight bags in hand, arriving for their same-day surgery.

He and Helen used to talk about growing old together, helping each other through the hard times.

A small group was clustered under the window, aglow in orange. At its center stood the Virgin Mary dressed in blue, holding the baby Jesus in the crook of her left arm, gazing down on them.

The chit-chat among Tom and the nurses ended abruptly as they took in the sight.

The world suddenly became quiet.

In the distance, he could just make out the low hum of cars turning into Hospital Drive at the bottom of the hill.

He closed his eyes, trying to compose himself, but in place of the window he saw Helen and Tommy sitting at the dining room table, laughing.

"If I had a rock, I'd smash the fuckin' window," he said under his breath.

He finally looked up again and found the Holy Mother gazing directly at him, comforting him, welcoming him, understanding him. She must have overheard him, but it didn't seem to matter. He could swear she was smiling.

And for the first time in years, Tom Rowley felt like smiling too.

3.

Irene was standing in the upstairs hallway when Eddie Cronin exited the master suite. Not quite two and a half, she seemed older. Her little girl's gaze was both appealing and spooky while she took everything in. If she were prattling like a normal two-year-old, she wouldn't look like such a genius. The seven others had all been babbling away at this age, but the pediatrician said that, yes, Irene was a little late, but it was too soon to be worried. In his opinion, she simply chose not to speak; she would do so when she was good and ready.

Mindful of his surgical incisions, he bent down carefully. But before he could give her a hug, she made a head-fake to the left before darting right, directly through the open door to find her mother.

Eddie staggered a moment but righted himself before taking the main staircase and making his way outside.

Eddie had expected less pain from the vasectomy, especially on his third post-operative day.

He had snatched Gilchrist, the new urologist, from a teaching hospital in Baltimore. Cronin couldn't quite match Gilchrist's salary down there but sweetened the deal with a six-figure no-interest loan toward the purchase of a new house. The Saint Kay's board didn't know it, but they voted for the loan, which he inserted into the Psychiatry Department's operating budget, after slipping the chairman the exact amount, in cash, from the hospital pension fund.

Unlike some of the old guard on the hospital staff, like Leo Mulcahy and his pals who spent most of their energy gunning for the hospital president, Gilchrist knew who was running the show and acted with appropriate deference. He went so far as calling him Edward, a name Eddie hadn't heard since his mother died.

"Call me Eddie, Gilchrist. Everybody else does." But he rarely did.

Gilchrist had done the vasectomy off-site on Friday, at a house Eddie had the hospital buy through a straw and convert into a satellite office. If he'd opted for the minor surgical suite at Saint Kay's, it might as well have been broadcast on the hospital's in-house channel, preempting the usual selections from the Catholic Evangelical Network, reruns of the hospital chaplain's daily Mass, and Eddie's own twelve-part pep-talk series about the hospital's mission statement.

When they toured the satellite surgical suite on Gilchrist's first day on the job, Eddie had explained the arrangement.

"We can't risk doing vasectomies on hospital property."

"But isn't this still hospital property?"

"Legally it isn't, Gilchrist, and that's all that matters."

That wasn't the only hurdle Eddie had to clear with Gilchrist. The urologist urged him to discuss the vasectomy with Kitty first, but Eddie wasn't that crazy!

"In Kitty's world, contraception is a mortal sin. My problem is that we have eight kids already. You'd never know it from looking at her—she's still gorgeous. But any more visits from the stork, and I'll be building a frigging wing on the house and paying college tuitions with my Social Security checks. The only way we're going to solve this little problem is to keep my wife in the dark."

"What about the rhythm method?"

"Christ, Gilchrist, your resume says you graduated from medical school. You've gotta know more about human reproduction than simply writing out Viagra prescriptions. The rhythm method is about as effective as saying a dozen Hail Mary's before climbing in the sack."

It was good to see Gilchrist blush.

"As a matter of fact, we did try the rhythm method. Kitty has never been regular, but she insisted. She took her temperature every five minutes for weeks and kept track of it on a big chart taped to the refrigerator. And thanks to the Church's meddling in an area they don't know shit about, we have Irene!"

More kids would be bad enough, but if it got out that the president of Saint Katherine's Hospital had a vasectomy, it would take about five minutes for the archbishop to be on the horn demanding his resignation. And Kitty would be kicked off the Mount of Olives Board of Trustees five minutes after that.

But as long as Eddie Cronin remained discreet and Gilchrist kept his mouth shut, the archbishop would look the other way.

He glanced back at the house now as he made his way to the garage. A classic, white, center-entrance colonial, he and Kitty fell in love with it the first time they saw it only weeks after he became president of Saint Kay's.

He thought about taking the Harley when that cute weather girl on Channel Six, the blonde with the push-up bra, predicted a high of seventy-five, but tooling up Hospital Drive on a motorcycle wasn't going to happen. Not with the image he needed to convey—and his incisions.

Punching in the code on the garage's security pad, he decided on the Lincoln Town Car. Not too flashy but commanding. It didn't hurt that his favorite vanity plate was on it, too. "MD/CEO" would send the right message.

Cars were Eddie Cronin's passion and his stress-relievers. And he'd collected enough of them for every day of the week—and then some.

He could feel the tiniest pull in the groin as he eased himself into the driver's seat. No pain really, just a reminder.

While the automatic door was purring to the open position, he thought of calling his friend at Channel Six. Then he caught himself. Corinne Caruthers, with all her contacts, probably learned about the window before he did. He'd wait for her to call him.

He leaned on the horn to get an elderly couple out of the passing lane, and they pulled over in front of Mount of Olives Academy, just in time for him to fly by them along Charles River Drive.

Saint Kay's was particularly impressive when approached from the west. Built on the crest of Faneuil's highest hill, it never disappointed Eddie on his morning commute. Its largest building, the Cardinal O'Rourke Pavilion, was dominated by a rather squat, yellow brick tower containing air-conditioning condensers and elevator motors. Its plainness troubled Eddie for years, before he could do anything about it. The building was just one of scores of a similar boxy structure the archdiocese erected in the boom years following World War II. All of these eyesores were built with the same signature yellow-to-beige brick, making them instantly recognizable as Catholic institutions.

The original hospital building, Saint Benedict's, comprised the whole enterprise when it was built in the 1840s. The hospital flourished throughout the nineteenth century, expanding constantly to keep up with the waves of Irish immigrants. A half century later, Saint Ben's was replaced by the nursing school, which lasted until the 1970s, only a few years before the current nursing shortage. If the school had held out, it would be turning a handsome profit by now. *But God works in strange ways*, Eddie thought. With any luck, the Virgin-in-the-Window would more than make up for the financial loss.

The point was that once the nursing school was razed, the modern medical office building, now attracting such attention, was erected on the site.

Within weeks of becoming hospital president, Eddie ordered a forty-foot Plexiglas cross to be affixed to the front of the Cardinal O'Rourke tower, and he had the ugly yellow bricks repainted red. The giant cross quickly became a landmark, like the Citgo sign near Fenway Park. Visible for miles, it was especially impressive at night, when its imbedded fluorescent lighting gave it a cool, otherworldly look.

Eddie loved the big, white cross on winter mornings, still lit as he made his way to work before sunrise.

Once the cross was in place, Eddie told the board that it would be "a beacon of hope for the sick, the frightened, and the poor," the Statue of Liberty of health care. He added that it was "the best fifty thousand dollars we've ever spent."

But only a few board members knew the truth.

The cross cost three times that.

Most of the board couldn't distinguish a financial statement from a racing form, since they weren't familiar with either. They were the window dressing, whose pictures would appear regularly in the *Saint Kay's Newsletter* and the *Faneuil Chronicle.* He was able to pack the board with a bunch of do-gooders. There were a couple of senior doctors from the hospital, selected more for their loyalty to the institution than any particular skill; three priests, two of whom were retired (for good reason); and a handful of "community activists." They all seemed content with their monthly meeting in the auditorium, full breakfast included, featuring a neat, meaningless agenda and the usual platitudes. He was able to keep each little interest group among them happy with a simple formula. Mention was made at each meeting about "quality initiatives at the bedside" for the doctors, "spiritual outreach" for the priests, and "green initiatives" for the rest. Every few months, the language would change, but the message was the same. The "bedside" would become the "laboratory" or the "operating room"; the "spiritual outreach" would become "pastoral support" or "faith in our core values"; and "green initiatives" would become "diversity awareness" or "community empowerment."

The idea was to mention "core values," "mission statement," "vision," "principles and ideals of Catholic health care," "emergent strategic themes," "strategic focus," "renewed energy," and "talented and committed staff" as many times as possible without saying anything new or meaningful.

The strategy worked smoothly most of the time. The hand-picked doctors and priests never made trouble, but occasionally community activists would get all heated up, and a member of the executive committee would need to sit down with them and straighten things out after the meeting.

After pulling into his reserved space now, he took off for the medical office building to see what all this craziness was about.

Tom Rowley almost collided with him along the walkway between the hospital and the office building. Rowley was rushing in the opposite direction as fast as his limp would allow.

Eddie wondered whether the hip problem was related to Vietnam. He once asked Rowley about the Purple Heart he saw on a visit to his office. He'd been wounded when his battalion aid station was attacked by the Viet Cong.

At the MOB, about a dozen people were camped out, every one of them looking up at a forty-five-degree angle.

No one bothered to look in his direction. Instead, all eyes were on a brightly lit window in Leo Mulcahy's office. He looked up at the window, but he could only come up with a round, dark area the size of a cantaloupe on top of one or two larger, somewhat rounded, dark areas. It looked like a photographic negative of a snowman.

Right away, he started on his game plan, counting the points with his fingers. "First, it must be a chemical reaction … from a leak in the Thermopane. Second, it's a perfect press opportunity."

He could see Corinne Caruthers, his friend the newscaster, doing a remote at the window.

"Third, protect the asset." He needed to be sure his own people kept their hands off of it. If those clowns from maintenance got involved, they'd break the seal and—*poof*, his little profit center would be only a memory.

"And fourth, leverage this stroke of good fortune into a windfall."

Eddie looked at his Rolex. If he didn't get moving, he'd be

late for his meeting with Pat. But first he needed to take a look at the window from the inside. Then he'd have Gert track down Leo Mulcahy, on whose window this commotion was taking place.

4.

Dr. Leo Mulcahy sat waiting for the traffic lights at McKinley Circle to turn green. The Circle marked the boundary between home and work. Behind him was the town of Muddy River, surrounded on three sides by the city of Boston.

Faneuil, Boston's westernmost neighborhood, was just beyond the lights. Muddy River's brick homes on half-acre lots gave way to a tawdry commercial area catering to the students at nearby Ignatius College, and single family homes gave way to apartment houses.

Faneuil was named after Peter Faneuil, a seventeenth-century businessman who built a home in that part of town. His great claim to fame, of course, was Faneuil Hall, downtown.

The easiest way to spot a newcomer was when they pronounced Faneuil, "Fan-yool" or "Fan-you-ell" since the locals pronounced it more simply, like "flannel" without the first l. A newly hired reporter on one of the TV outlets made the "you-ell" error recently and had to apologize later in the broadcast.

"Last night, the Department of Homeland Security raised the terror alert level from yellow to orange, because of increased Internet chatter about attacks on national monuments." The radio announcer went on to say that no information was available as to the timing of such attacks, but with the first anniversary of 9/11 looming, officials were being extra-vigilant.

Then, just as the light turned green, Leo looked up to see a red Mazda cut in front of him, abruptly pulling him back to the present.

The weekend sign-out last night could have been a lot worse. Three of his patients were in-house, and one more was in the ICU (where the staff down there did most of the decision making). Two of his "frequent flyers," as his secretary Veronica called them, telephoned the answering service on Saturday, asking to be seen "first thing" this morning. One bit of good news: two patients cancelled their office appointments, neutralizing the two add-ons, at least for the moment.

Another weekend had flown by.

The Sox dropped the Friday night game to Minnesota in the seventh, five to four. Again, the bullpen didn't come through, and they had no offense for the last three innings. After that, he couldn't bear to watch any more of those heartbreakers for the rest of the weekend.

But baseball, and any other distraction for that matter, was always preempted by "date night." Ever since they first met, he and Claire made Saturday night their special time. They needed to compromise at times—if Leo was on-call and spent the evening with a patient in the emergency room, or when Claire was immobilized in the last days of a pregnancy—but they still made it special. This past Saturday night, Leo boiled lobsters for the two of them in the big enamel pot handed down from his grandmother, and they ate by candlelight. Then it was early to bed with plenty of time for love-making before dropping off to sleep.

On Sunday, he managed to read the papers and watch the morning talk shows for the first time in weeks. Claire got herself off to church and didn't pressure him to go.

When she got back home, she joked that she had fulfilled two obligations in one. The Mass counted as both the customary Sunday obligation and that due for the Feast of the Assumption, a holy day of obligation.

Actually, she explained, it was more complicated than that.

She'd talked to Father Frank about the holy day situation the night he was at the house for dinner, but he said that her explanation was "99 percent" correct.

"The holy day wasn't 'moved' to Sunday. It's still celebrated on Monday this year, but the obligation part is dropped when it falls on a Monday or Saturday," was the way Frank put it.

"Oh, that really clears things up," Leo commented at the time. "How's the Universal Church coming along with the big question?"

Cousin Frankie waited for the inevitable punch line.

"How many angels fit on the head of a pin?"

At the Commonwealth Avenue lights, the traffic was held up by a Green Line trolley lazily making a left turn through the intersection. Its wheels made a screech like fingernails running down a blackboard. And the "motorman" was a young black woman, who gave Leo a friendly smile as she inched by.

The sun streamed across the road horizontally, making the apartment buildings throw off giant shadows, creating a checkerboard of light and dark up ahead.

Just as the trolley cleared his lane, Leo's beeper burst into song.

This new high-tech model was his partner Harold's idea. Harold fell in love with the Ultrapager when the saleswoman brought it to the office. Of course the fact that she was a knockout in a well-cut business suit didn't exactly hurt her chances for a quick sale.

As he tried to unhitch the sucker from his belt, the trolley finally got clear of the line of cars, and the driver behind him, at the wheel of a Teutonic sports coupe with a piercing claxon for a horn, let Leo know that he was holding up traffic.

As he told Claire, he'd get rattled because he never knew what kind of problem was waiting at the other end. It could be anything from an anxious patient awakening Leo in the middle of the night for an Ativan refill, to someone going into cardiac arrest.

He could never be sure.

An unfamiliar hospital extension flashed on the little screen. The fluorescent green characters were the color of crocuses as they poke through the just-thawed earth of a spring garden.

"Urgent message from Dr. Cronin's office."

After one ring, he heard Gertrude's baritone.

"President's office."

"Hello, Gertrude, it's Leo Mulcahy. I was paged."

Without replying, she transferred the call, and Eddie Cronin himself was on the line in a nanosecond.

"Leo, where the hell are you?"

"I'm passing the old monastery gate and should be on the other side of Hospital Hill in a couple of minutes."

"Come to my office before you think of doing anything else."

Gertrude Kleindienst, heavily made-up as always, was reading something when Leo arrived. Without looking up or saying a word, she lifted her right index finger and pointed at the door to Dr. Cronin's private office.

Eddie was at his desk talking to Pat Kaminski, the chief of security, when Leo stepped inside.

"Don't just stand there, Leo. Come over and have a seat next to Pat."

He felt like a schoolboy summoned to the principal's office.

"Leo, Pat here called me at home about an hour ago to report something unusual over at your office."

Pat told Leo the story, and every time he got bogged down in unnecessary detail, Eddie would pick up a ballpoint pen from his desk and begin clicking.

Without warning, Eddie stood up and came around to the front of the desk, signaling that the meeting was over.

"On your feet! We're walking over to the MOB. I was over there before you showed up, Leo, but I need to see the window again. I already took a look from inside your office and couldn't find anything suspicious. Remember that the window is hospital property, inside and out. Look—but don't mess with it!"

The trio burst out of Eddie's office, and before Gertrude could react, Leo saw that she was thumbing through a copy of *Playgirl.*

5.

Father Frank Mulcahy counted half a dozen extra faces at the Saint Gabriel's morning Mass. The extras probably didn't get wind of the new arrangement and mistakenly thought that today was the Feast of the Assumption, a holy day of obligation.

He preferred things the old way, when the rules were unbending, and everybody knew it. Traditionally, the Feast of the Circumcision, Ascension Thursday, the Feast of the Assumption, All Saints' Day, the Feast of the Immaculate Conception, and Christmas were holy days of obligation unless they fell on a Sunday.

Frank's friend Professor Richard Mears said the new method reminded him of summertime in Indiana. Out there in the farm belt, each county decided whether or not to adopt daylight savings time, meaning you never really knew what time it was.

The Vatican would deny it, but it relaxed the rules because no one was showing up. There was simply too much going on in people's lives, and almost nobody had a clue about what the holy days of obligation signified anyway. Ask a parishioner about the meaning of the Assumption, and you'd likely be met with a shrug.

Frank himself remembered how confused he was with the "A" words as a kid back in Sunday school. For the longest time, he couldn't keep Assumption separate from Annunciation, and to complicate matters further, Ascension, Affirmation, Absolution, Abstinence, and Apocalypse entered the mix from time to time.

After a long period of decline, Saint Gabe's weekend Mass attendance was better but still had its ups and downs. A few raindrops, which would never interfere with any other activity, would keep people away. But the recent trend was positive. Frank saw new faces all the time, and the church hall was getting busy again with Sunday school, parish council, AA meetings, even a knitting group. Still, they had a long way to go.

Weekend collections hadn't covered expenses for years, but the gap was closing. Receipts from bingo and parking-space rental helped, but without the summer fair, he'd still be operating in the red.

The pencil pushers at archdiocesan headquarters in Faneuil Heights (known affectionately as "Little Rome") took a hard look at the numbers. In a burst of creative activity, they took the totals for Mass attendance, baptisms, weddings, and funerals for each parish—added, subtracted, and multiplied them—and came up with something they called the "sacramental index." Saint Gabe's sacramental index must have been in negative territory when Frank started out, but it was creeping up. Not all trends were positive, however. He often thought of Saint Gabe's as an old ship, prone to springing leaks.

One such leak involved golfers with early tee times crossing town for the "quickie" seven o'clock Mass at Saint Monica's. "In and out in twenty-nine minutes," he heard. Father Cornelius, the pastor at Saint M's, reportedly flew through the Creed without taking a breath. One witness said it was like watching the priest swim the whole length of an Olympic pool without coming up for air. And it didn't hurt that Saint Monica's was two blocks from the golf course.

To make matters worse, Father Cornelius was screwing around with his sacramental index, upping the weekly attendance and the number of weddings and funerals, each group by just a few souls, making the bottom line double. Frank's secretary, Jane, heard about Father Cornelius's cooking the books from her cousin, who happened to be the secretary over at Saint M's. The cousin offered incriminating photocopies, but Frank had no taste for espionage.

He was convinced that if he could keep the momentum going and keep things totally on the up-and-up, Saint Gabriel's would survive and, in the quaint language of the Church, avoid being "suppressed."

In this Monday morning sermon, he referred to the Assumption, the day Mary was received, body and soul, into heaven, and how that event revealed to all of us the Blessed Mother's closeness to God and her willingness to intercede with her Son on our behalf.

Then, as he sat for a moment of reflection, he felt terribly weary and sad.

He didn't believe a word of what he had just said.

He often thought of the Church as a house of cards, like the ones he and his sister, Portia, used to build on the kitchen table back in Egg Rock. The Feast of the Assumption, for example, would have formed part of the front wall. If he withdrew the card, so carefully that he held his breath, the structure would shudder for a second but then steady itself. But if he removed any another card, even with the utmost care, the house of cards would collapse.

How different he had felt as a newly ordained priest!

As he thought about it, he'd never been asked to stand up and defend the faith, since everyone believed in those days. The church was always filled for Mass, with latecomers standing in the aisles. The parish was a 24/7 operation with its innumerable sports teams, clubs, social events, and service projects. And the rectory door was always open for anyone who rang in the middle of the night with an emergency.

He was reminded of where he was by a discreet cough and the subtle shuffling of feet. Since he didn't know how long he had left them waiting, he sped up the last half of the Mass to make up for lost time.

6.

Archbishop Quilty, who kept careful track of such things, had told Father Dan on the ride out to the monastery that this would be his twentieth retreat there—and Dan's fifth.

As in past years, the Boss scheduled himself for five full days in August, including the Feast of the Assumption on the fifteenth.

The monks' day, devoted to work and prayer—in complete silence—was exactly what the archbishop needed. Almost as beneficial was the fact that he'd be cut off from the outside world, with no access to newspapers, radio, or TV.

He referred to his annual retreat as Assumption Week, although, as far as Dan knew, no such official term existed.

Father Dan took up residence in a nearby guesthouse, getting a retreat of his own. Like the Boss, he observed the rules of silence and isolation. However, since the archbishop required a channel to the outside in case of emergency, Father Dan kept his cell phone on his person at all times, careful to switch it to vibration mode during morning and evening prayer.

Back when Quilty was a mere monsignor and then auxiliary bishop, others could cover for him when he went on retreat. That all changed, of course, when he was elevated to archbishop.

In past years, Father Dan never received a call, and he expected the streak to continue.

Dan was pouring himself a second cup of coffee when his luck ran out.

Father Joe Maguire, the archbishop's second (and brand-new) secretary, was calling. Dan had never heard the young priest so wound up. He was talking so fast that all Dan could make out was repeated references to the Blessed Mother and a windowpane.

Finally he got on his feet.

"Start back at the top, Joe, and for the love of God, take it slow."

After Father Joe's second recitation, Dan had the basics. At dawn, a security guard at Saint Kay's Hospital noticed an image on a window that resembled the Virgin Mary. The press had the story within a couple of hours, and the "Virgin in the Window" was already dominating the TV stations and the Internet.

Joe hadn't seen the window himself, but he thought it looked "awesome" on TV.

Work at the chancery had ground to a halt except at the switchboard, where both day operators were so swamped that they called in backup. Media from all over the world were calling for comment; pastors from all over the archdiocese were checking in, seeking advice on how to respond to questions from the faithful; and officials from the governor's office to the mayor of Boston (who got on the line himself) wanted to speak with the archbishop personally. Minutes earlier, Joe had spoken with a fellow named Dr. Edward Cronin, the president of Saint Kay's.

"Do you know him, Dan?"

"Yep. Whenever the Boss visits Saint Kay's, Cronin magically appears. And he's a big publicity hound. He hogged the camera during Mother Teresa's visit a few years back."

"I remember. I was still at Saint Luke's then and watched her visit on TV with the other seminarians. The guy with the terrible comb-over?"

"That's the guy. I bet he wanted to talk to the archbishop, too."

"Sure did. Actually, he demanded the Boss's cell phone number. When I told him that would not be possible, he assured me that he'd be talking to the archbishop about my attitude the first chance he got. Then he got friendlier, telling me that the image of the Virgin was very realistic and might well be the Miracle of the Century, right up there with Lourdes and Fatima, and that the archbishop should know about it right away. He added that he'd assist the archbishop in building a permanent shrine to Our Blessed Mother on the hospital grounds. He left his private number. Want it?"

"Hold on to it, Joe. We'll be seeing plenty of Dr. Cronin after we get back."

"I'm counting the hours, Dan."

Father Dan then put in a call to the Saint Kay's page operator and asked her to beep Father Guido della Chiesa, the hospital chaplain. Guido was, in the Boss's words, "no Thomas Aquinas," but he was the archdiocese's man on the scene. It took several minutes to locate him, and when he finally got on the phone, his voice was barely above a whisper, and he sounded uneasy.

"I'm sorry, but I've been advised by Dr. Cronin not to speak to anybody about this."

"Look, Father Guido, I'm not calling for just anybody. I'm calling for the archbishop of Boston, your spiritual leader and the guy who signs your paycheck. Dr. Cronin may be the president of Saint Kay's, but he doesn't own you. I'm going to ask you two simple questions, Father. And speak up. I'm having trouble hearing you. First, have you seen this window yourself?"

"Three times since just after dawn, when she first appeared."

"And what do you think?"

The chaplain's voice was no longer querulous, and it was now loud enough for everyone in the nursing station (for that's where he said he was when he picked up the page) to hear. "Our Holy Mother is standing there, filling one of the windows over at Dr. Leo Mulcahy's office. She's radiating all sorts of colors and is holding the baby Jesus in her arms, looking directly at us. Her gown is a magnificent bluish green, and she's wearing a gold crown. Her smile could melt a stone. I feel so blessed to witness this ... miracle. I keep praying that she'll speak to us."

Father Dan felt his heart racing. "Thank you, Father Guido. I'll relay your impression to the archbishop."

Before hanging up, Guido had the last word. “This isn’t an ‘impression,’ Father Skerry. I have no doubt whatsoever about what I’m seeing. I want the archbishop to understand that.”

Right then, Father Dan made his decision. He would handle this distraction himself.

7.

As soon as the trio rounded the corner of the MOB, Pat Kaminski pointed to the third floor, but by then, Leo was already staring at it.

The window was filled by a full-length figure. Using a little imagination, Leo was reminded of traditional depictions of the Virgin Mary, standing, holding the baby Jesus in her arms. Over her head was an ill-defined object that could have represented a crown or perhaps a halo. The baby Jesus was a simple, rounded lump, jutting from the left side of the figure, suggestive of a baby’s head. The Virgin appeared to be standing on a rock or pedestal, below which he could barely make out a curved outline.

“You see, she’s standing on the earth,” Pat whispered, “the Queen of Heaven.”

Leo was struck by the figure’s vivid yellow and blue highlights but knew that others would see much more. His red-green color-blindness put him at a disadvantage.

Only then did he notice the clusters of people looking up at the window. Some stood frozen in place, a few were on their knees, and one woman was clutching a rosary. There had to be at least fifty there, and more were arriving every minute.

In spite of that, the place was as silent as a church.

Eddie Cronin, who had found a spot away from the crowd, was looking up at the window like everyone else, but he had broken into a grin, an expression he tried to avoid in public because of the wide gap between his upper teeth.

To Leo, he looked like the big winner watching his Megabucks numbers flashing on a Jumbotron. He was wearing one of his spectacular custom-made suits. This number was a medium gray with a subtle lighter stripe, wide lapels, and tailored—Leo felt—a bit too severely for a pudgy, middle-aged hospital executive. The overall effect might have been one of affluence, self-assurance, and a touch of daring if it weren't for his ridiculous haircut.

Eddie was still smiling when Leo ducked inside, took the stairs two at a time, and speed-dialed his home number as soon as he reached his desk.

After five rings, enough time for him to catch his breath, his daughter, Francine, answered, sounding sleepy and annoyed.

"Frannie, is your mother still there?"

"Oh, it's you, Dad. I think I hear the shower. I'll go check."

Claire was on the line in seconds.

"I'm dripping all over the rug, but Francine said that you sounded strange and that I'd better talk to you right away."

So much for congratulating himself on sounding matter-of-fact!

8.

Father Frank rode his bike from the Saint Gabe's rectory to his father's house in Egg Rock every Monday, year-round, weather permitting. Being assigned to a church near the family home made Frank's life easier. A couple of nights in Egg Rock each week allowed him—for all practical purposes an only child—to keep an eye on his aging father.

It took the parishioners some time to get comfortable with

the shepherd of their flock tooling around the neighborhood on a mountain bike, but just about everybody came around eventually.

From the look of the weather, this would be the best Monday of the year to make the trip. He ran upstairs to change into civvies, like a kid ready for a day at the beach. In fact, he now owned more civilian clothes than clerical, the reverse of when he started out. During his first assignments, the priests dressed like priests except, as his friend Father Richard Mears liked to put it, when they were taking a bath.

But nowadays, the Roman collar had become a lightning rod.

Frank loved bikes from the day his dad taught him to ride a two-wheel J. C. Higgins in the driveway of the house in Egg Rock, with his mom and his sister, Portia, watching from the kitchen window.

He always had a bike handy, except during his first week at Saint Luke's Seminary, where it was prohibited. Since the bike rule made no sense to him, he went to the dean of students to discuss it. The dean declared that bikes were prohibited because they always had been and that he saw no compelling reason to change the rule. Frank tried to make a distinction between articles of faith, where rational thinking must be suspended, and practical matters, like bikes in dorm rooms, where rational thinking was a good idea. Without a word, the dean escorted the young seminarian to the door.

Frank began to call that Bike Lesson #1: don't rock the boat.

Instead of pressing the point further, he quietly kept the bike in his room and went out for a quick ride whenever he could find the time.

That led to Bike Lesson #2: be discreet. If you disobeyed a rule, which was absurd to begin with, but did so discreetly, the Church would look the other way.

The seminary bicycle rule was never rescinded. Doing so would have acknowledged that it had no merit in the first place and that rules, even very old ones that take on legitimacy simply on the basis of age, could be challenged.

At one of their recent dinners, his friend Father Richard pressed him on the "paradox" of his bicycle and house of cards theories.

"According to your house of cards theory, you must obey all rules, no matter how silly, or the house will collapse. But then you 'discreetly' disobey the rules according to your Bike Lessons. You can't have it both ways."

"But the Church accommodates both approaches, side-by-side, every day."

"That doesn't make it right."

"Perhaps not, Richard, but that's the reality."

At the crest of Gallows Hill, where witches were once executed, he was rewarded with a stunning view of the whole North Shore, from Cape Ann to the north, followed by Squimset Neck and North Squimset, to Massachusetts Bay with the two islands making up Egg Rock and the rock itself, for which the town was named, dead ahead, to the arc of the Squimset shoreline and the Egg Rock causeway to the south. Further south, the Boston high-rises beckoned, their glass walls reflecting the morning sun.

He just made it to the shoreline when his cell phone rang.

"Frank, it's Leo. Are you in Egg Rock yet?"

"Halfway. What's up?"

"There's an image of the Virgin Mary on my office window."

"Just who thinks it's an image of the Virgin?"

"Not me, but I can see why folks are making the connection. There's a big crowd outside, gazing, kneeling, and holding rosaries. Eddie Cronin has been here twice this morning, looking like he's hit the jackpot."

He could see the story, with Eddie playing the lead and the Virgin Mary getting a bit part. Back when he was Cardinal Campion's secretary, Frank dealt with Eddie when Mother Teresa visited Boston. She wanted the visit to be low key, visiting the sickest patients, thanking the nurses, that kind of thing. But when she arrived, Eddie was there at the front entrance with cameras, lights, and worst of all, a female newscaster in a clingy dress ready for an interview. Thanks to Frank's intervention, the interview never happened, but a very fatigued Mother Teresa looked at him reproachfully, as if to say, "You let me down, Father."

"Leo, once I get to the house, I'll change back into uniform and drive into town for a look. Then I'll come upstairs to your office, and we can talk."

"That's good, Frank. This thing … I don't know what to call it … is upsetting. I hope you can make some sense out of it."

From his seminary days onward, he considered these "miracles" one big headache for the Church. They were impossible to prove or disprove, attracted fringy people, and diverted energy from the Church's core beliefs and its social mission.

The Squimset shoreline curved gently to the south-southwest until it met the causeway leading out to Egg Rock, where it veered sharply southeast. Two hundred years before, crowds gathered there to get a glimpse of the famous Egg Rock Sea Serpent offshore, the Loch Ness Monster of its time.

Not so different, he thought, *from what's going on at Saint Kay's this morning.*

9.

Leo felt better when Claire promised to hurry over to the office. He then decided to check exam room #3, just inside the suddenly famous window. To insure privacy, its window had been covered as part of the office "build-out" before Leo and Harold's internal medicine group took over the space.

As Eddie had reported, the wall covering the window from the inside appeared untouched, as did a small writing desk affixed to it.

Above the desk was a white laminate cabinet containing the usual supplies—bandages, blood-drawing equipment, extra thermometers, tongue depressors, and ammonia ampoules for the unlucky patient who might get woozy during a blood draw. Leo opened the doors of the cabinet and found nothing out of place. Then he ran his fingers slowly over the wall's surface.

The wall was cool to the touch, but he wouldn't have been surprised if it had burned his fingertips. In the space directly above the desk, a plastic stick-on calendar, courtesy of Ameripharm, was intact. There wasn't the smallest dab of fresh paint or a mote of sawdust—no indication that the area had been tampered with.

The trash had been emptied and the surfaces cleaned in the usual manner, undoubtedly by the cleaning crew Friday night.

Leo could picture all those eyes fixed on the image only inches away from where he stood. For many, it was a miracle.

He knew exactly what he'd be doing if the window was at the house in Muddy River and not, as Eddie put it, "hospital property." He'd be taking it apart piece by piece to see what was really going on.

Leo had plenty of personal experience praying for miracles, but no divine personage swooped down in the jungle as he tried to patch up boys hardly old enough to drive. Where was the Holy Mother when he was powerless to do more than keep saying, "It's okay, kid, you're going to make it, you're going to be fine" while he waited an eternity for the Medevac chopper and the little fellow coughed feebly and then stopped breathing just as Leo heard the helicopter clear the tree line. If she existed and really loved mankind, she would have shown up then.

And what was the Virgin Mary doing when his own parents needed her? Was she on a celestial coffee-break while his mother was saying her rosary for the last time, with the 707 spiraling into the sea?

10.

Vincent Mulcahy scanned the sky as he walked through his yard, waiting for Frank to arrive for his morning of gardening. It promised to be a spectacular late-summer day, and if the forecast held, Portia would be seeing Egg Rock at its best. The only possible complication was a tiny tropical depression that might move north later in the week, but from what he could see, upper-level winds didn't favor development, and a blocking high over Bermuda would deflect it if it got that far.

Of course he had no idea how long his daughter planned to stay, if she actually showed up in the first place.

He had a pretty good night, up only three times to pee, but each time he got back under the covers, he wanted to reach out and touch his wife. After twenty-eight years without Maddie, he shouldn't feel like she just got up for a minute and would be right back.

He was amazed that he was sleeping at all, with Portia scheduled to fly from California in twenty-four hours. About a week ago, he picked up the phone, and there she was. Although he hadn't heard her voice in years, he recognized his daughter instantly.

She wanted to come home for a visit and was anxious to "catch up on what's been going on in our lives."

Portia had taken off on a beautiful morning much like this, in August of 1974, four months after her mother's death, leaving no note or any hint of where she was going. In the following weeks, he was convinced she'd come home any day, but every time he got back from work, the house was empty. He ran to the phone every time it rang, expecting her to be on the other end. Friends seemed to know nothing, and the police expressed little interest in pursuing a runaway. Frank, in the seminary by then, agreed with his father. Portia just needed time.

Then, about a month later, Vincent's brother and sister were killed in a plane crash while on vacation in Greece, and he was caught up in the horror of their violent deaths and news that their plane was brought down by a terrorist bomb.

When Thanksgiving came and went without a word from Portia, Vincent and Frank felt they had waited long enough, and Vincent hired a detective.

It turned out that Portia had spent time in New York and Santa Fe, and ended up in San Francisco. She was working in a library by then and seemed to be in no trouble. Feeling she was safe, Vincent stopped his inquiries and slowly made peace with the fact that he had lost not only his wife and brother, but his daughter as well. And with his son on the way to becoming a priest, it felt as if his whole family had been wiped out.

Then, on the fifth Christmas Eve after she disappeared, the first card arrived, postmarked Oakland, California. It was a simple Christmas greeting, signed "Love, Portia" and nothing else—no note, no return address. But it was by far the best Christmas gift Vincent had ever received.

The cards began coming regularly after that—Christmas cards, birthday cards—sometimes with a little note like "Greetings from California," but little more. He stored the cards in the bottom drawer of his desk at home, in chronological order. When they first started arriving, he tied them with a blue ribbon from a Christmas or birthday present. Recently, he started to worry that the bundle was getting too large for the ligature.

Down at the water line, while the dog busied herself with a deposit of seaweed, Vincent followed a 767's graceful approach to Logan, slowly pivoting as it passed overhead. A big part of forecasting during the war was to study the skies, so it was only natural that he could recognize the silhouette of any aircraft overhead. And as newer planes appeared over the years, he added them to his repertory.

He didn't see many 707s anymore, since they'd been phased out in favor of more fuel-efficient planes. But whenever he did spot one, he'd stand at attention with his hand over his heart, to honor the memory of his brother, Wally, and sister-in-law, Patty.

He was still daydreaming when Frank rolled into the yard on his bike.

"Well, Dad, the weeds will have to wait. Leo called me as I was riding over. Saint Kay's is in an uproar. An image of the Virgin Mary has appeared on your nephew's office window, and he wants me to go into town and have a look. Want to come along?"

Vincent didn't answer right away.

"Dad, did you hear me?"

"I couldn't have heard you correctly. Some image on a window? What's the world coming to?"

Frank filled him in on the details.

"Thanks anyway, but I'm expected for cards this afternoon at the Vets Club and don't want to disappoint the guys. Anyhow, it sounds more like a priest kind of thing, not for us lawyerly types."

"The lawyer part will come later, Dad."

"It always does."

11.

Leo went out front to speak with Veronica, the practice's receptionist.

"Have you seen her, Dr. Mulcahy?" She looked radiant, more alive than he had seen her in months.

Now it's her, not it, he thought.

"Yes, Veronica. And I've called Claire and Father Frank. They'll both be here soon."

"Thanks be to God," she said quietly.

Leo had the best view of the city from the Saint Kay's campus. Beyond the front entrance and the road leading up Hospital Hill, he could take in the Back Bay, the downtown office buildings, a bit of the harbor, the tower at Logan, and aircraft taking off and landing in the sky to the east.

Now he was stunned to see that the area below him, usually tranquil, was packed with hundreds of people, while traffic was stalled on the entrance road.

Minutes later, Claire arrived, followed by Harold.

"Claire tells me you guys are going to stick around for a few days." Harold looked relieved as he shook Leo's hand.

Claire gave her husband a wink.

Leo didn't know how it started, but he and his partner had been shaking hands every morning for years. Claire commented on it once.

"It seems European."

But Harold was as local as you could get. He was born at Saint Kay's and brought up in the Faneuil projects down the street from the Cattle Drive restaurant.

For Leo, the morning handshake was a welcome ritual.

Harold was worried. "I doubt it's occurred to our friends in the executive suite," he gestured in the general direction of Eddie Cronin's office, "that patients aren't going to put up with this circus. You know what happens to the schedule when the TV guys hype a few flurries like it's the blizzard of the century. The patients all stay home once they've stocked up on candles and bottled water. This will be worse. If the patients don't come, we don't eat—but never fear, the hospital administrators will continue to get their paychecks."

Harold promised to track down Pat Kaminski, to see if administration had a battle plan.

Looking out at the crowd massing below, Claire spoke first. "I stopped at the window before coming in."

"I was watching, but I couldn't pick you out of the crowd from up here."

"Leo, I have to tell you, what I saw sure looked like the Virgin Mary."

"It must be a chemical reaction. You know they covered the window from the inside when we moved in, what is it, five years ago? And the inside of the window is intact. It doesn't look like anyone tampered with it."

"Actually, you moved in six and a half years ago. We had Francine's sweet-sixteen party on the same weekend."

Not for the first time, Leo was amazed at how different his and Claire's brains were wired. It was all a matter of associating. With momentous events like 9/11, everyone remembers where they were and what they were doing when they got the news. Claire did that too, of course, but was able to associate more personal events in the same way.

"Leo, honey, this is a big deal. I don't understand what it's all about, and maybe nobody ever will, but I know it's big."

"It's a big deal for Eddie."

"It's a big deal for all of us, including you, dearest."

12.

Frank borrowed his father's Buick to get into the city. It was a good thirty years old, but he kept it in mint condition. He went so far as to buy an aerosol that promised a "new car smell," and amazingly, it worked. Vincent inherited it from his brother, Walter, after the plane crash and spent whole afternoons tinkering with the engine and keeping the deep blue finish nicely polished.

Frank flew past the strip malls in Squimset and Dawes and was gunning the Buick out of the Boston exit of the Ted Williams Tunnel when the 11:00 a.m. headlines came over the oldies station. Thankfully, there was no mention of the Virgin Mary on a window, just a water main break in Somerville and a tropical depression east of the Windward Islands. Frank wondered again where the Windward and Leeward Islands were exactly and silently vowed (again) to look them up in the atlas. In fact, he really needed to straighten out, once and for all, the difference between the Windward and Leeward Islands, and the Greater and Lesser Antilles … and a million other little details he could never get straight.

He found an empty reserved space and squeezed the Buick between two SUVs, put his clergy placard on the dashboard, and got to work. The grounds were jammed. If only he could transport these people to Saint Gabe's for Sunday Mass, he thought, he'd give his best sermon ever. The collection baskets would be overflowing, and his church would be saved.

The walkway in front of the building was blocked by guys hauling equipment out of a Channel Six truck. On its roof sat a white satellite dish, and stenciled on the vehicle's side was an idealized likeness of their star anchorperson, Corinne Caruthers, and their famous slogan, "The News Masters" (or "Trash Masters," as his old boss, Cardinal Campion, liked to call them in private). Channel Six (or "Sex" as many called it) had the largest viewership in New England.

He joined the group in front of the window and surveyed the scene. He was tempted to look up right away but was determined to slow things down by getting a feel for where he was.

Some of the more devout were on their knees while others were taking pictures, but most of the hundred or so spectators were simply gazing upward. In front, watched over by a security guard, were flowers, cards, photos, and handwritten messages scattered on a grassy patch and attached to the base of a tree.

A little shrine was already taking shape.

Earlier, biking the beach path and then driving into town, he had it all figured out. This "apparition" would turn out like all the others—either the product of an overheated imagination or an out-and-out fraud … or something in between.

He couldn't put his finger on why, but he felt different now.

He closed his eyes and bowed his head. "Merciful and ever-loving God," he whispered, "please let me see without prejudice and help me understand."

Then, instead of looking up, Father Frank turned away. The crowd was growing by the minute, filling the space to capacity. More security people were on the scene, cordoning off the shrine area with yellow tape.

Crowds never bothered him before, but right then he felt he'd suffocate. Squeezing by the new arrivals, he made it around to the back of the building and took a deep breath before reaching for his phone. Father Richard Mears, his old professor, needed to be in on this as soon as possible. After three rings, the answering machine clicked in.

"Richard, in case you haven't heard, you have a new Marian apparition to investigate, on an office window at Saint Kay's. I'm over there now and am sure you'll be fascinated. I'll pick you up, you can take a look, and we'll grab some dinner."

The hospital lobby was jammed with people lined up at the information desk, and the chapel, where he expected to find space for quiet reflection, was overflowing.

"What's the use?" he said to himself, before pointing himself in the direction of Cousin Leo's office.

Veronica greeted him warmly. "Have you seen her, Father Mulcahy?"

A smile was all he could manage, but she seemed satisfied. Then he raised his eyebrows and pointed to the inside door.

"Oh, Father, by all means go right in. Dr. Mulcahy is expecting you, and Mrs. Mulcahy is in there, too." After all these years, she still referred to Leo formally, even to family.

Once beyond the reception desk, he came upon a fellow busy stacking medications in an open closet.

"Good to see you again, Father Mulcahy. How are things up at Saint Gabe's?" he asked pleasantly as he proffered his hand to the priest. Frank noticed a jeweled pinky ring as the younger man shook his hand.

Frank had an excellent memory for faces (one couldn't survive in a parish without one), but he had no idea who this guy was. He was certainly distinctive looking enough to remember. He was no more than thirty, heavyset, an inch or two shorter than Frank, with blond hair cut in a pageboy. He vaguely resembled an older, stockier version of the boy pictured on a can of house paint. The kid looked like he knew his way around the office, making Frank assume he was a new hire.

"Things are fine up there, thanks," he answered as he disappeared into Leo's inner office.

13.

J. J. Rideout took his sweet time checking Dr. Nalbandian's drug boxes. It was like having a ringside seat.

He watched that silly skeleton of a woman, Veronica, bubbling over with excitement, darting in and out of Leo Mulcahy's office, rearranging his schedule. Unlike Harold, so absentminded and sweet that he never suspected that J. J. would eavesdrop, Leo and Claire (who was in there with him now) kept the door shut and their voices down.

He was rewarded with more gossip here than anywhere else on the hospital campus, and he loved the way Cronin would gobble up any tidbits J. J. threw his way.

They were having quite a pow-wow in there, the three of them, now that Priest Mulcahy had arrived. He wondered if they were spending all their time on this apparition thing.

Strange word, apparition. It made him think of *Poltergeist.* He and his pals saw the movie at the old Capitol Theatre in Squimset when he was in the eighth grade—and it scared the crap out of him.

That Priest Mulcahy looked puzzled when J. J. greeted him. *It's always cool to know more about people than they know about you. From the puzzled look on his face, maybe he got worried that I was a kid he fondled during Sunday school or whatever these perverts do for kicks,* J. J. thought.

Just as he was packing up his stuff, he heard the girls out at the desk talking again. This time, the file clerk, who usually only talked sports, spoke up. She'd heard that Cronin had undergone a hush-hush after-hours surgical procedure, but the others laughed it off, since, as crazy a place as Saint Kay's was, that was too far-out to be believed.

That was one piece of intelligence J. J. wouldn't be sharing with the hospital president.

14.

Father Richard Mears was pleased to hear Frank Mulcahy's message on his machine in his quarters at the seminary. Frank had been one of his best seminary students and was now his best friend.

It would be more accurate to say that he was happy that Frank left a message, but he had mixed feelings about the message itself.

In one respect, this would be like every other Marian apparition he'd studied. It would bring out into the open the borderline people who spent most of their lives in the shadows and ended up being another embarrassment for the Church.

Every religion had them.

The archbishop had the good fortune to be on retreat, cut off from all worldly distractions. Otherwise, the Boston media would already be in his face.

The newspapers were sure to be flooding the chancery switchboard with inquiries by now, and he could picture TV people setting up their campsite on the far side of the trolley tracks, in front of the archbishop's residence. The TV trucks were out there for weeks when the sex-abuse story broke.

He hoped that Dan Skerry, out on retreat with archbishop, was keeping the Boss in the dark.

After replaying Frank's message, he was able to press the erase button with barely a trace of his tremor. His tremor always seemed to get better when his brain went into high gear.

15.

Frank and Leo Mulcahy could pass for twins—no surprise since their fathers were brothers, and their mothers were not only twins, but identical.

When Frank was in clerical garb, there was absolutely no question of who was who, but when they were casually dressed, it got trickier.

Claire was one of the few who could tell them apart.

For her, their haircuts were usually the key. Frank tended to wear his hair shorter, but if Frank was overdue for a trim, and Leo had just come from the barber, the hair could be misleading, especially since they were both beginning to gray at the temples, in eerily similar patterns. When necessary, she'd focus on subtler distinguishing features. Frank's nostrils were more flared, and Leo had a subtle cleft to the chin that was easy to pick up when his face caught the light from a certain angle.

The fact that Leo had a sizable dimple on his left buttock wasn't helpful, since she'd never find out whether Frank had one or not.

Frank walked into the office and gave Claire a peck on the cheek, while Leo pulled out a chair for his cousin.

"Well, Frank, was it worth the trip?"

"Definitely."

Frank stood at the window and looked down at the crowd below.

Claire, who'd been silent all this time, finally spoke up.

"You've been down there, Frank. What did you think?"

"I honestly don't know what to think."

Leo got up to have another look for himself. Putting his arm around his cousin, he said, "It's nice to have an open mind, I guess, but you're letting us down. I hoped that the priest in the family could give us answers."

"Some questions don't have answers."

16.

J. J. had just left the medical office building when he got a call from Cronin's office. Gert, Cronin's secretary, was on the other end.

"Dr. Cronin wants you in his office ASAP. Use the private entrance."

The evening right after New Year's, when Dr. Cronin handed over a key to his office, J. J. knew he'd arrived. He had just gone over the details of the AP399 deal with Dr. Cronin.

"Now that I have this little arrangement with your company, J. J., I plan to keep our deliberations private. If the board, the medical staff, or the archbishop's people got wind of what we're up to, I'd be through. No details by e-mail or phone, and we'll be holding some of our meetings in secret."

Cronin instructed him to use the key only when he received a message to do so. Then the hospital president showed him how it worked. Behind a towel rack at the back of Cronin's private lavatory was a tiny door that reminded J. J. of an illustration out of *Alice in Wonderland.* He eyed the opening warily, worried about squeezing his husky frame through, when Cronin patted him on the back. "Don't worry J. J. Once you get the shoulders through, the rest will be easy."

The storybook door led to the top of a fire escape, with steps leading down to the service road. Cronin mentioned that the fire escape was a vestige of the old chapel.

"Those preservation nuts wouldn't let me take the sucker down, so I made good use of it. The only problem is the state inspectors. I need to remove the lock before they show up, but I have friends who give me advance notice."

From the road, the fire escape was camouflaged by a stand of tall pine trees, probably as old as the hospital itself. Just as well, since it was an ugly structure, covered in steel lattice work, giving it a cage-like appearance. At the bottom was a locked gate.

"The key is for the locks on the little door and the gate below," Cronin explained.

J. J. had been wondering if he'd ever get the call.

He looked both ways now to make sure the coast was clear before stepping behind the evergreens and unlocking the gate, and thirty seconds later, he was inside the lavatory. He was a little winded from the brisk walk, scooting up the fire escape, and squeezing through the door, but when he scrutinized himself in the mirror over the sink, he knew things could be worse. His forehead was beaded with sweat, but thankfully, the profuse underarm sweating he felt advancing hadn't penetrated his poplin sport jacket. Not yet, anyway. He nearly grabbed one of the monogrammed towels but thought better of it and wiped his brow with his handkerchief.

Then he decided to do some research. The medicine cabinet was crammed with the usual items. Next to Cronin's shaving materials was an unmarked glass bottle with a bulb atomizer at the top. The only place you'd normally see such a contraption was at the cosmetic section of a department store.

J. J. gave the bulb the tiniest of squeezes and smiled when he detected the unmistakable smell of Dr. Cronin's cologne.

Just as he was about to ease the mirrored door closed again, another object caught his eye. The familiar screw top of a plastic container was just visible behind a couple of spare bars of hypoallergenic soap.

It was one of his sample bottles of AP 399. The seal had been broken, and half the pills were missing.

Finally, he sucked in his gut and examined himself again in the full-length mirror mounted on the door to Dr. Cronin's office, before turning the knob.

Inside, Dr. Cronin was pacing back and forth.

What a room! The floor was covered with a huge Persian carpet with the deepest pile J. J. had ever walked on, and he was sure that the double-pedestal mahogany desk would look just fine in the Oval Office. To one side was a leather sofa and inlaid teak coffee table, for informal discussions. Opposite sat a highly polished conference table for formal meetings and an occasional meal. The one dinner he ate there was catered. Even if he'd missed seeing the caterer's truck in the driveway, he didn't need to be Martha Stewart to know that the lobster salad with tarragon hadn't been whipped up in the hospital kitchen.

The office walls were covered with one of those grassy coverings that must have cost a mint and high-end ink drawings of the usual Boston landmarks, signed and numbered by the artist.

A large color photo of Dr. Cronin, flanked by Archbishop Quilty and the Holy Father himself, sat in a gilt frame on an end table. The two religious leaders looked solemn, but Cronin was smiling. The picture must have been retouched, because Eddie's tooth gap was gone, and his closely cropped hair was neatly combed.

The windows looked out at the back of the hospital, the power plant with its massive chimney, and the service road. As far as J. J. was concerned, the view was the only drawback. If he was boss, he'd evict Leo Mulcahy. An office like this with Mulcahy's view of the city would impress the pope himself.

Cronin stopped pacing for a moment and pointed in the direction of the conference table.

"Take a look at that FedEx and tell me what you think of it."

J. J. read through the three pages slowly and then read them again.

Cronin started clicking his ballpoint pen, indicating that time was up.

"Well, sir, the first page looks like an abstract of a scientific paper. I see that Dr. Gilchrist is the first author, meaning he probably did a lot of the work. It describes a simplified method of performing a vasectomy."

"What about page two?"

"It says that you shouldn't use birth control. Is it some kind of a church document?"

"It's a passage taken verbatim from *Humanae Vitae*."

"Is that in the Bible?"

Dr. Cronin looked at J. J. as if he'd taken a crap on his beautiful carpet.

"Hardly, J. J. It's a decree from the pope, called an encyclical. It came out in the late sixties and comes down hard on abortion and all kinds of birth control. Okay, do you recognize page three?"

"Never saw it before. It looks like an old newspaper article about sugar cane, from 1965. I don't see any connection."

Dr. Cronin resumed clicking his pen, only faster.

"You should, J. J., since it was written about the founder of American Pharmaceutical Enterprises, the folks who pay your freight."

J. J. wanted to say that Cronin was also a recipient of APE's largesse but held his tongue.

"I'm afraid that whoever sent this thing is on to our little business arrangement."

J. J. didn't like the way this conversation was going.

"J. J., do you have any idea who might have sent this?"

"Leo Mulcahy is the first name to come to mind."

"I had the same thought, but with that crazy practice of his, I doubt he'd have time to do the research. Besides, I can't see him quoting a papal encyclical. He despises the church."

"What about Rowley? It's no secret that he's a wacko."

"I can see him looking up an old scientific paper, but not old newspaper articles and Vatican documents."

"Isn't his wife a librarian?"

"His ex, and I know for a fact that they had a nasty divorce and hate each other's guts. How did you know about the wife?"

"Market research. The more I know about my clients, the better I can serve them."

17.

After Claire left for home, Leo continued his phone calls and saw three patients who couldn't wait.

By then, Harold was finished for the day, and Leo signed out his in-patients, five in all including the new admits, who would be seeing Harold while Leo was on vacation—not in Maine, but at home in Muddy River, ready to come over if things got out of hand.

Leo asked Harold if he'd called Pat in the security office about crowd control.

"Pat was as pleasant and talkative as always but apparently hadn't thought the problem through. He did promise to bring it up with Eddie Boy tomorrow morning when they're scheduled to meet with Northeast Security."

"Northeast Security?"

"An outside contractor."

"You and Geri are coming for dinner tomorrow night?"

"Claire said six thirty. We'll have plenty to talk about."

"When don't we?"

18.

Out in Egg Rock Vincent visited his late wife on his way to the Vets Club for his scheduled card game. Evergreen Cemetery sat a short block behind the club, making it a cinch to drop by to fill her in on the latest news. He never tired of looking out from that rise with a stand of blue spruce behind him, with Short Beach and the old coast guard life-saving station in the distance. And he made a point of getting there every day, weather be damned.

The day Portia's first Christmas card arrived set the standard. He shoved the envelope in his pocket that afternoon, power-walked the half mile in a snowstorm, and hadn't missed a day since.

He stood before the granite marker and began talking to his wife as he had done every day they were married. He kept his wife up on the everyday stuff she always enjoyed. That included weddings and babies and gossip and politics (the Egg Rock variety, especially). He usually started with the latest weather conditions, just as he had done every morning when he'd trudge back into the kitchen after checking his instruments.

He didn't risk telling anyone about these monologues, although Frankie and the guys at the club knew about his visits. He was embarrassed, honestly, and suspected that if the others learned about it, they'd think he'd gone soft.

"Honey, our little Portia is finally coming home." He touched the cool top of the granite as he spoke.

19.

Father Guido della Chiesa had every reason to be dead on his feet. What else would he expect—going on sixty-five and running nonstop since dawn?

But he felt twenty-five again.

Stepping off the elevator on Cardinal O'Rourke Seven, the hospital chaplain glanced at the portrait of the medical floor's namesake. The prelate stood there, life-size, in full Prince-of-the-Church regalia. His chin was tilted ever so slightly upward, with his eyes hard and unforgiving, and his lips pressed together to form a perfect horizontal line.

Years back, the very day Mother Teresa visited Saint Kay's, he'd walked by the portrait with Father Frank Mulcahy.

"What a disdainful look!" Father Frank had whispered.

Guido felt Cardinal O'Rourke looked dignified, and there certainly was no harm in that. He passed the portrait every day on his hospital rounds and made a point of looking at it each time. On some days, the cardinal looked more distant and unapproachable, but he always looked dignified.

"Disdainful" was the wrong word, though.

O'Rourke had been Boston's first cardinal, and since then, each new archbishop was sure to get a call to Rome to receive his red hat within a couple of years. Everyone figured that Archbishop Quilty, now in office almost five years, was seriously overdue.

Father Guido lingered another moment in front of the portrait before saying what was on his mind.

"Your Eminence, what do you make of Our Lady's visit?"

It lasted only a moment, but Father Guido saw it—he was sure of it. The old cardinal's horizontal slit of a mouth arched upward at both ends, forming a subtle smile.

After Pat rapped on his door with the news in the morning, he had dressed quickly and hustled over to the medical office building, not knowing what to expect. But from the instant he saw Our Lady, he had no doubt whatsoever that he was witnessing a miracle. He wasn't frightened, not for one second. Instead, he felt energized, as if he'd had a big dose of caffeine.

He ventured back to see and be seen by the Blessed Mother several times during the day. She changed as the sun crossed the sky. When he first visited just after dawn, she literally glowed, and the color of her face went from orange-red in the morning to porcelain at high noon. And as the day wore on, the image of the Christ child became more distinct, lovingly held in the crook of His Mother's left arm.

With each visit, he recited the words, "Believe in me, and I will lead you to my Son."

Father Guido had been summoned to Dr. Cronin's office in midmorning and was informed that the hospital administration would handle all the logistics. He should just carry on as usual, visiting the sick, providing the sacraments, and saying Mass. He wouldn't need to trouble himself with the press either, Dr. Cronin said. As the president of the hospital, the doctor would be the "voice of the hospital family," so that the media wouldn't be getting "mixed messages."

That's why the call from Father Dan Skerry threw him off balance for a while. Dr. Cronin had already been in touch with the chancery, of course, so Guido figured he didn't have to speak to anybody. Father Guido never enjoyed speaking to the folks up there anyway.

More often than not, His Excellency the Archbishop and his entourage would show up at the hospital without warning. Whenever he told his sister, Marilena, about those unannounced visits, she'd get annoyed.

"They should have better manners than that. They can swoop down anytime, but just try to pay them an unannounced visit up at their place. If you walked in on them up there, dear Guido, they'd call the police!"

"It's really not a problem," he answered, "because Dr. Cronin always shows up just in the nick of time and takes over."

"Dear Guido, you're out of the loop."

"That's fine with me, sis."

Anyway, once he got over the shock of getting that phone call, he was able to tell Father Skerry that a huge miracle was taking place. That was all that mattered.

The TV at the nurses' station was tuned to the six o'clock news. Dr. Cronin was being interviewed by the newswoman Father Guido saw outside the office building during the afternoon, the one with the tight-fitting blouse.

She should be showing Our Blessed Mother more respect, he thought.

"Joining me outside of Saint Katherine's Hospital in Faneuil is the hospital's president and CEO, Dr. Edward Cronin, with tonight's top story.

"Dr. Cronin, thank you for taking time out of this very busy day to speak with us. How does it feel, Doctor, to have this, er, apparition …"

A shot of the window filled the screen for a moment.

"… if that's what we should be calling it, appear here at the hospital?"

Guido winced. *She's not taking this seriously*, he thought.

"Well, Corinne," (Guido winced again) "this has been a very special day for the entire Saint Kay's family. I have visited Our Lady several times, and I must tell you and your viewers" (with that, he spread his arms, the way Guido remembered the pope doing it) "that my overriding emotion is humility."

The newscaster nodded solemnly, at least as solemnly as one can in such a short skirt.

"I am humbled that our Blessed Mother has chosen our little place of healing for this holy and miraculous event. And, you know, Corinne, I see this visitation by Our Lady as a tangible sign of favor on the men and women of the Saint Kay's family who live out our core values and mission every hour of every day."

"Dr. Cronin, have you been in touch with the archbishop?"

"Not directly, Corinne. His Excellency is out of town on official Church business but is due back on Wednesday. Of course, I expect to speak to him immediately upon his return, if not before. I know the archbishop well and can tell you that he is a man of great faith, and when he visits the site of this miraculous appearance here on the grounds of Saint Katherine's Hospital, he will be profoundly moved."

He spoke more eloquently than Father Guido ever could, but the tone and the setting just didn't seem right.

Still, he knew that Dr. Cronin would have made a great homilist. With all his years of practice, Guido never failed to break into a sweat and rush through his text. And whenever he looked up, he could see eyes glazing over as if anesthetic was leaking into the chapel from the operating rooms downstairs.

If he had half of Dr. Cronin's self-confidence, he could really get his message across.

20.

Frank Mulcahy picked Father Richard up as planned and dropped him off at the hospital. The traffic was so heavy that a simple drive down the hill and back looked like it would give the professor plenty of time to scout out the window.

Father Richard had little trouble working his way through the crowds. Folks stepped back when they saw him and let him pass when they saw the clerical garb and the cane, making him feel like Moses parting the Red Sea.

Afterward, he was pleased to find Frank, still mired in traffic at the foot of the hill, and climbed in. They had agreed to hold off any discussion of the apparition until they were settled at the Cattle Drive. They spent the short trip from Saint Kay's in silence.

There were no tables available when they arrived, but they found a couple of stools at the huge horseshoe-shaped bar that dominated Cattle Drive's main dining room.

From their seats, they had a partial view of the "archbishop's booth," tucked in a corner next to the swinging doors leading to the kitchen. Every week or two, Quilty and his secretary, Dan Skerry, would enter and exit through the kitchen and dine there, out of sight of most of the other customers.

Once the drinks were ordered, Father Richard got started. "People at the hospital are sure that the window was clear yesterday?"

"That's what my cousin Leo told me."

"I really expected that it or she or whatever term we come up with would be a chemical reaction, but now I'm not so sure."

"That's Leo's opinion, too, that it's chemical."

"I'm happy to have Leo's opinion, Frank, but I'd prefer yours."

"I don't have one."

"This doesn't sound like the Frank Mulcahy I know, the class skeptic."

"I didn't look."

The professor drained his glass and set it down with such a bang that the bartender looked over to see if everything was okay.

"I stood there, prayed for guidance, and then turned away

without looking. I don't really know what came over me. I guess you could say I chickened out."

Just then, the waitress set down their plates, and each priest said grace silently before digging in, effectively suspending the conversation.

Frank looked up to see the bartender switch from the ESPN baseball highlights on the big screen to "Six at Six," Channel Six's evening news.

"Team Six takes you live to the Miracle in Faneuil. We have several reports on this breaking story." The hum of conversations quieted down instantly, leaving only the occasional clatter of meals being served and tables getting cleared.

"Turn it up!" some guy shouted from a booth in the back of the big room.

The screen was filled with a live shot of the medical office building, followed by a zoom in to the third-floor window. In the long shot, the entire hospital campus was packed with onlookers, and in the close-up, Father Frank saw the apparition for the first time.

After a series of ads and a quick review of the "day's top stories," including an armed stand-off by a post-office employee in Memphis and mention of a tropical depression expected to reach tropical storm status before grazing the Virgin Islands, "Six at Six" switched back to their remote standing by at Saint Kay's.

Corinne Caruthers was ready with an update.

"The crowds are growing by the minute as news of this sighting of the Virgin spreads. Traffic Copter Six is overhead and reports that the streets around Saint Katherine's Hospital are gridlocked. Police urge motorists to use alternate routes.

"I spoke to the president of Saint Katherine's, Dr. Edward Cronin, about an hour ago. Here's the tape of his remarks."

The priests put down their forks and listened.

By the time coffee arrived, ESPN was back on, and they got talking again.

"Was there much difference between what we saw on TV and what you saw in person?"

"TV doesn't capture the lighting, the *luminosity* of the window, and in person, the image is more three-dimensional. One other thing: you don't get a feel for the setting on TV."

"Meaning?"

"In spite of the crowds, there was an atmosphere of reverence and awe in front of that window."

"I felt it too, and I think that's why I turned away. I was afraid of breaking the spell."

"You didn't want the moment to be spoiled by discovering that you were looking at an out-and-out fraud?"

"Probably. After all that's gone on—scandal, lies, cover-ups—I don't want to be let down again."

"Fair enough."

"I'm no chemist, Richard, but don't you think it's a stretch to have the window go from normal to having this image or whatever, overnight?"

"I have no idea. Maybe it's intentional."

"Intentional?"

"Let's say a pretty talented artist worked on the window during the night while nobody was around …"

"But both Eddie Cronin and Leo checked the inside of the window for any signs of tampering and found nothing."

"I remember. Anyway, breaking into the window and then painting, or inserting an image, in such a public place without detection seems farfetched. Then you need to account for the lighting. The window is lit up in all kinds of colors. I guess there are lots of smart and devious people in the world, but if this is a hoax, it's a damn good one."

They took the river road back to the seminary in order to avoid the traffic jam up by the hospital. A couple of rowers were guiding their sleek shells home before nightfall. They were cutting it close, since the riverbanks were dark.

"So, Richard, about Ms. Caruthers and her telecast …"

"I thought you'd get around to that. Think she'll get an Emmy?"

"She shouldn't be throwing the word 'miracle' around like that."

"Agreed, but we both know that the more sensational they make things, the better the ratings. By the way, Frank, your old nemesis Eddie Cronin must have said 'miracle' ten times during his interview."

"Yep. Old Eddie hasn't changed since my secretary days."

"Uh-huh."

"Okay, so miracle is out. What word would you use?"

"Phenomenon. Something big is happening up at Saint Kay's, that's for sure. Whether it's religiously significant is an open question."

"*The Faneuil Phenomenon*. Yeah, it sounds more neutral, less weighted than miracle."

"Without the baggage that miracle carries. Avoid the *M* word and you don't get into comparisons with Lourdes and Fatima and all the rest right out of the gate."

"It's also alliterative, which should appeal to the press and be noncommittal, which should appeal to the Church."

"That's the old Frank Mulcahy! I was afraid you'd lost your edge."

"I'm on the mend, Richard."

"I'd advise using 'phenomenon' in any press release the Boss may ask me to advise him on."

"You sound ready to get involved."

"Not until the archbishop wants my opinion, Frank. This Saint Kay's business needs more study—and prayer. Then, God willing, I'll be ready for the Boss's call."

"You're confident he'll call?"

"As soon as he's back from retreat, if not before."

The houses lining the street outside the seminary gate were all lit by the time they arrived, throwing off a warm domestic glow that always made Richard lonely. They drove into Little Rome, where the park-like grounds were dominated by the archbishop's residence at the top of a rocky promontory.

The residence had been built in the 1920s by Cardinal O'Rourke in the style of a Florentine palazzo, financed by the owner of a string of burlesque houses. Its origin might have been sketchy, but the building was an architectural masterpiece.

He drove past the chancery, where the business of the archdiocese was conducted, toward Saint Luke's Seminary, located in a quiet corner of the property at the foot of the hill. The topography suited the seminary perfectly, allowing the students and faculty to slow down and learn to separate themselves, at least on some level, from the comings and goings of the outside world.

The campus was deserted, hardly surprising in the middle of August, with the seminarians on summer break and much of the faculty and chancery staff on vacation.

They passed old Cardinal O'Rourke's mausoleum. Most of O'Rourke's predecessors were interred in a crypt at the cathedral downtown, but he chose Little Rome, where he expected his earthly remains to repose until the end of time as we know it.

The mausoleum backed onto the remnants of an ancient apple orchard. While still seminarians, Frank and his friend Greg Tally were strolling up the same hill and came upon two of their classmates emerging from the orchard, adjusting their cassocks. Watching them retreat, Greg made a crack about apples and temptation.

"Enjoyed dinner. Want to call me in the morning, Frank?"

"How about later in the day? The parish summer festival is Saturday, and we have a meeting in the morning, and the tents go up right after lunch."

"Great timing!"

"And my sister, Portia, is flying in tomorrow."

"And I thought I had a lot to think about!"

The old professor stopped by the seminary chapel before turning in. The oak pews were stacked stadium-style, perpendicular to the altar, so that half the congregation faced the other half. It was much more intimate than the usual church arrangement, where all you see are the backs of the heads of the people in the row in front of you.

Morning and evening prayer were held there when seminary was in session. Psalms were sung antiphonally by the student body, evenly divided in the pews on both sides of the nave. When the seminarians really got into it, Father Richard felt transported to one of the great European monasteries.

He was grateful to be alone in this great space. He walked to the altar, genuflected, and took a seat up front. Thomas Merton's Prayer for Discernment was one of his favorites, and he knew it by heart. He recited it aloud.

My Lord God,
I have no idea where I am going.
I do not see the road ahead of me
Nor do I really know myself,
And the fact that I think that I am following your will
Does not mean that I'm actually doing so.

But I believe that the desire to please you
Does in fact please you.
And I hope that I will never do anything apart from that desire.
And I know that if I do this,
You will lead me by the right road
Though I may know nothing about it.

Therefore will I trust you always though
I may seem to be lost and in the shadow of death.
I will not fear, for you are ever with me,
And you will never leave me to face my struggles alone. Amen.

Sitting back, he glanced up at the circular mural high above the altar depicting the Pentecost. The Virgin Mary stood in the midst of the disciples, watching the dove coming down from heaven. The artist had placed tongues of fire over the heads of the group looking up at the sky, signifying the power of the Holy Spirit.

Then he got up, turned out the lights, and sat again in the darkness.

He'd come to the right place.

Later, he lingered in the wide corridor outside the chapel. The walls, lined with portraits of seminary rectors going back over a hundred years, held his attention. The men in their stiff collars stared back at him.

How would they have reacted to the spectacle at Saint Kay's?

Without thinking, he fished in his pocket for the key to the library, and once inside found himself walking toward the archdiocesan history collection. It took him three trips upstairs to carry all the books he'd need for the night.

Washing the dust from the oldest volumes off his hands, he made a startling discovery. His tremor was nearly gone.

In gratitude, he made the sign of the cross, made a cup of tea, and got down to business.

TUESDAY

1.

It was well after midnight when Father Richard Mears finally hit the jackpot. In volume II of the *History of the Boston Archdiocese*, he happened upon a description of a hilltop grotto dedicated to the Virgin Mary. It was built in 1860 to commemorate the recent apparitions of Our Lady at Lourdes.

What really got his attention was the location of the grotto. The hilltop was "some five miles west of the Old Town" of Boston, near the "stockyards and slaughterhouse of Faneuil Village, but high enough to be free of their noise and smell."

Stories circulated at the time that the Virgin herself appeared at dawn before a group of pilgrims gathered at the site. She stood at the top of the stone grotto, radiant in a blue-green gown.

"I am the Immaculate Conception," she said, just as she had to Bernadette. But the rest of her message was directed to the faithful of Boston.

She acknowledged the persecution Catholics had endured, with riots, the burning of churches, the sacking of a large convent, and new laws aimed at stripping Catholics of their citizenship.

"Keep the faith," she continued and promised to intercede with her Divine Son to protect them so that they might flourish.

With that, she began to rise slowly, stretched out her arms before them, and promised that she would return to this very place sometime in the future when Catholics would again be under siege.

He went over the text again to make sure he had all the facts straight. Finally satisfied, he eased himself into his reading chair and, once his tremor subsided, reached into his bookshelf for his book of Marian prayers. The earliest known prayer to the Virgin, *Sub Tuum Praesidium* was on the opening page. Discovered in a Greek papyrus dating to circa 300, it seemed a good start.

We turn to you for protection,
Holy Mother of God.
Listen to our prayers
And help us in our needs.
Save us from every danger,
Glorious and blessed Virgin.

After that, he dozed off and slept until dawn.

The early light drew his attention to the window and the seminary grounds spread out below. A pair of squirrels chased each other across the freshly mowed lawns. In another season or two, these creatures would be only a memory, as would he.

This might be his last investigation, and he wanted, more than anything else, to make it his best.

2.

Eddie spent the night on the sofa in the family room downstairs. That way, he wouldn't disturb Kitty while he tossed and turned.

The sound of Kitty's footsteps from the bedroom upstairs awakened him near dawn.

He decided to use the shower downstairs before going up to shave. Anyway, Kitty would be working on her hair in the master bath by now, and Eddie didn't care to be quizzed about the Blessed Mother's appearance anymore.

He always felt uncomfortable using the downstairs bathroom, but who wouldn't with the statuette in there? Since there was no way they could lug it around Europe on the train, Kitty had it air-freighted. The night they got back from their honeymoon, the oversized package was waiting for them on the front steps.

Only a foot and a half tall, it fit perfectly on the counter to the right of the sink.

At Lourdes, they saw so many people on crutches and in wheelchairs, making their way to the grotto where Bernadette had her visions of the Virgin Mary. At the grotto, Eddie did a double take when he saw ordinary spigots dispensing the healing waters by the gallon. Pilgrims were lined up with plastic containers of all sizes, each imprinted with the image of the Virgin and Bernadette.

The more Eddie saw of these people making fools of themselves, the more he longed to be on the next train out of this stink hole. But Kitty was happier than he'd ever seen her.

That night, Kitty was propped up on pillows saying her rosary when Eddie climbed into bed. She was easily the most gorgeous pilgrim he'd ever seen, with her honey-colored hair loose around her shoulders.

She was also the best mind-reader. She looked up from her beads and announced that there was no way that she was going to have sex here, near the spot where the Blessed Virgin appeared some eighteen times! His options narrowed, Eddie drifted off to sleep trying to get his mind around the real miracle: how this pathetic little village in the Pyrenees was transformed into a boom town by a teenage girl's fantasies.

The more he saw, the more he marveled at how smoothly the worlds of religion and commerce blended in the streets. Peddlers swarmed over the sidewalks, almost assaulting the tourists with statuettes, pictures, rosaries, medals, and booklets. Proprietors of crappy hole-in-the wall shops stood out front, luring passersby inside for shirts, jackets, caps, calendars, paperweights, trays, cups and saucers, trivets, tea cozies, shot glasses, and all other manner of schlock.

No one seemed to take offense while thousands of francs and dollars changed hands. The pilgrims all wanted to take a little of Lourdes and Bernadette back home with them, and the natives were only too happy to oblige.

It was in a narrow airless alley where Kitty found Bernadette. Most statuettes available depicted the Virgin, with Bernadette kneeling at her feet, but this was an exception. This figurine of Bernadette, standing alone, was displayed on a dusty table. An ancient woman, dressed head-to-toe in widow-black, hovered nearby, as if she'd be waiting for Kitty to show up.

The transaction was completed in minutes.

Just why Bernadette ended up in the downstairs bath was a mystery to Eddie. But since it was Kitty's property, what she did with it was her business. He had enough trouble watching over all the "sacred objects" scattered around his hospital. Actually, he'd been able to get rid of the more objectionable ones (such as a crucifix over every bed) and cash out some of the high-end pieces like the old chapel windows.

Now with this Virgin-in-the-Window opportunity, he'd be rethinking his strategy, starting with the cross up on the Cardinal O'Rourke tower. It would need to be replaced by larger versions, four of them this time, one for each direction of the compass. He'd also need to crank up the candle power, so they could be seen from all over greater Boston and from airplanes making their approach to Logan.

Saint Kay's would be the New Lourdes.

The hot water felt great on his scalp, shoulders, and back, and the pounding of the power spray got the cobwebs out of his head. He always liked the water really hot, but when he turned and exposed his surgical site to the spray, it burned like hell.

He had Gilchrist look at the wound when he was in the office (after Eddie locked both doors in case Gert decided to pop in), and he said it looked fine. But Eddie was still nervous.

While toweling off in front of the full-length mirror, he could see that his scrotum was double its normal size and the color of an overripe plum.

Without warning, the door opened, and Kitty let out a gasp.

"Sorry, Eddie, I didn't know you were in here!"

He tried to cover himself up, but the damage was done. She closed the door as quickly as she opened it, and he could hear her footfalls fade as she headed for the kitchen.

3.

J. J. went over his call to the home office in Mobile last night. Good thing they were in Central Time down there. That usually gave him a chance to talk to Spike before closing. But last night was an emergency call, and old Spike sounded a little ticked off when he finally got on the line.

"I was just headin' out for a little sail on the gulf before supper, ol' buddy. Is this all that important?"

It was. And Spike chucked the phony "aw shucks" banter when he heard about the FedEx Eddie had shown J. J.

"Listen up, J. J., I want you *livin'* over at St. Kay's until this problem blows over. The home office will get your other clients covered. If Eddie Boy farts or Gilchrist burps, I want to know about it. AP 399 is our golden goose. And one more thing …"

"What's that, Spike?"

"Don't fuck this up, ol' buddy, or you'll be flipping burgers back in Squimshit."

"It's Squimset, Spike. Spike?"

Only then did it dawn on J. J. that the line was dead.

J. J. didn't like being treated like a buck private again, but what with all the perks of the job, listening to Spike blow off steam once in a while was worth the aggravation. After all, life was pretty sweet for a kid who nearly flunked out of Squimset Community College.

The four years he spent in the army as a pharmaceutical technician paid off big-time. After basic, he was lucky to get assigned to Walter Reed Army Hospital, in Washington DC, where the training was first-rate. He barely made it through the basic pharmacology, but he hit his stride when they got to the nonscientific stuff. Reed was modernizing its pharmacy services, and he was assigned to the team that educated the medical staff about the new computer system. In this assignment, he discovered that he was a good communicator and an even better salesman.

In fact, one of his instructors said that J. J. could turn a profit selling *Just For Men* to chemo patients!

His next assignment changed his life. Landstuhl, Germany, was the largest American medical facility outside of the United States. Although the Gulf War had just ended, Bosnia was still providing the hospital with plenty of business.

One of J. J.'s buddies at Landstuhl was also a pharmacy tech, but not quite standard issue. "Spike" (his given name was Lavern) Birdsong was an Alabama boy whose father happened to be the CEO of American Pharmaceutical Enterprises (APE). The old man, who had transformed the company from a handful of retail drug stores in Mobile to the country's tenth largest pharmaceutical company, had been a pharmacist's mate in the navy during the Korean War. He figured that Spike could use a little "maturing" in the service, just like he did, before coming back to senior management of APE. Besides, Spike had had a little trouble with the law, something about a girl, but he never got too specific. Anyway, Mobile was a small town, and the old man felt that Spike should get away for a while.

Their friendship paid off. After J. J. got back to the States, he telephoned Spike, and before he knew it, he was in Mobile himself, attending APE's six-month training program for its drug reps.

4.

Claire walked into the kitchen to find that Leo had already put the coffee pot on, retrieved the morning paper from under the azalea bushes where the kid had tossed it, and brought a yellow hybrid tea rose in from the garden.

Leo looked up from the paper and turned it around so his wife could see the headline: CROWDS FLOCK TO HOSPITAL WINDOW.

A photo of Eddie Cronin, looking like the happiest of men, took up a quarter of the front page. It was a close-up shot, leaving only a tiny bit of the hospital visible behind him.

"Where's the window?"

"Inside. On page three."

"Should he be smiling like that, Leo? We're not talking about the dedication of a new wing here."

"He's grinning because the Virgin Mary is going to make him a boatload of money."

"What about the archbishop? Shouldn't he be weighing in?"

"He's out of town and not expected back till late tomorrow. The papers expect a statement, of course, but no one seems to know when that will happen."

"If you ask me, he should be here now getting things under control."

"Claire, we both know how things will play out. The archbishop will resume his previously arranged schedule as if nothing out of the ordinary has taken place. Acting precipitously will only give the 'miracle' more standing, the last thing he wants to do. Then he'll try to run out the clock. The longer he can wait before issuing a statement, the better. Given enough time, he can better judge what others are thinking. And if he can wait long enough, something might happen to the window, and his problem will go away."

"What a shame! When Quilty got elevated to archbishop, I was thrilled. Rising through the ranks, he looked like a reformer and a communicator. But as soon as he got the job, he seemed to lose his edge."

Leo handed her the front section. They were quiet for several minutes while Claire caught up on the news and Leo scanned the sports pages.

He was still reading about the likelihood of an all-California World Series when she broke the silence.

"Leo, when I got to the window yesterday, I felt …"

"It's so unusual for you to hesitate like that."

"That's just it. I can't express the sensation I had."

"What did you see exactly?"

"Nothing. I mean that I didn't see a literal picture of a mother and child, or of anything else really. An abstract image, I guess, like a work of art. But at the time, it seemed like something more than that—a spiritual moment is the best I can do."

Leo pulled his chair to Claire's side of the table and gave her a kiss on the cheek.

"But this morning, seeing what's happened—crowds, traffic jams, Eddie Cronin on the front page, our AWOL archbishop—I wish it never happened."

Their conversation turned to the week's plans. Here it was Tuesday, the day before their vacation up at the cottage in Maine, and nothing was going as planned.

"That's another thing, Leo. I'm so disappointed that we can't get away, and I'm angry that this whole 'event'—or whatever I should call it—has gotten in the way."

Leo refilled their mugs and sat back on his side of the table.

"I know you'll feel better once you've made the phone calls."

She had planned to call the rectory in Bangor to cancel her brother Paul's anniversary Mass. Then she'd ask Father Guido to dedicate his Friday noon Mass at Saint Kay's to Paul instead.

Leo turned and looked squarely at his wife. Claire's auburn hair and dark, long eyelashes contrasted beautifully with her fair complexion. For the first time in weeks, her Bell's palsy was obvious. Ordinarily, the fact that the left side of her mouth didn't move like the right side didn't register, but this morning, with the light coming in through the kitchen at just the right angle, the defect jumped out at him. Perhaps Paul's anniversary and, on top of that, this insanity over at Saint Kay's were making it even worse.

Claire was the opposite of most people, who went through their day with a neutral look or perpetual scowl on their faces, smiling only in response to something funny or heart-warming if at all. Claire's baseline expression was a smile; her facial palsy only enhanced it, making it look crooked and zany.

She wasn't smiling this morning.

The first time he laid eyes on her, she was smiling.

Leo was assigned to Saint Francis of Assisi Hospital in Portland for his third-year medical rotation.

The students worked every third night in those days, and on the first night, he saw her. He was paged to the emergency room to admit an old-timer with dehydration and pneumonia. Maine was in the middle of an August heat wave, and this fellow was one of the casualties.

Claire Beauregard was the patient's ER nurse. The patient was upset, but she settled him down, all the while plugging him into an IV, drawing blood into Vacutainer tubes, and packing his meager pile of clothes into one of those plastic bags emblazoned with the hospital's logo. Smiling, she chatted with him in this "we'll take care of this together" tone. She didn't use the saccharine-laced language that some nurses employ, and the patient knew he wasn't being patronized. He seemed genuinely sorry to leave his pal in the ER when Leo helped the orderly roll the gurney to the elevator.

"What's the nurse's name, Doc?"

"Claire. Claire Beauregard."

"She's a catch, boy. Don't let her get away."

It took Leo until Thanksgiving to ask her out, even though they saw each other at the hospital a couple of nights a week. He figured that a girl like this must have a boyfriend, and he didn't care to risk the embarrassment of being turned down.

Their first dinner out was at a little Italian restaurant on the waterfront.

Over coffee, Claire looked him up and down before declaring that he looked older than a typical med student. Yes, he'd enlisted in the army after high school, he admitted, putting him a few years behind his classmates. When he added that he'd been a medic in Vietnam, her face lost all its color, and she stared at her half-eaten dessert. It took minutes for her to regain her composure. After a sip of the wine remaining in the bottom of her glass, she took a deep breath and again looked squarely at him.

"My brother, Paul, was a medic, too," she finally managed to say.

It turned out that Paul had been killed when his platoon took on enemy rocket fire just south of Danang. Like Leo, Paul enlisted in the army right out of high school. He was eleven months and one week older than his sister.

"Mom and Dad loved to call us their Irish twins, even though we were French Canadian."

Later, when her father got cancer, he had only one request.

"Bury me next to Paul."

Claire reached into her pocketbook and pulled out her wallet.

"I have his picture here."

The snapshot showed the young soldier standing next to a little Vietnamese girl, her arm in a sling.

"A buddy mailed this to us after the funeral. He said that Paul spent the little downtime he had working with the children."

One weekend in February, Claire invited Leo to her family's cottage on South Haven Island, up the coast.

US 1 was plowed and sanded, but snow drifts had narrowed the road, and it took four hours to get to the ferry in Rockland. Theirs was the last car on the last run of the day.

They brought food and drinking water with them and heated snow on the stove for washing and bathing. They made love by the fire and slept in an ancient four-poster with the thickest afghan Leo had ever seen. They explored the island on snowshoes (a first for Leo) and marveled at the brilliance of the stars in the jet-black night sky.

By the time they took the ferry back on Sunday, they knew. They were formally engaged over Easter and married just after Leo's graduation, fourteen months later.

"Leo, dear, you're daydreaming." Her smile was back, crooked as ever.

Leo gazed out at the yard, already alive with birds.

"I was thinking about Maine, too."

5.

After coffee, Vincent Mulcahy and his pal Echo went out to the point for their daily check of the meteorological instruments.

Vincent had been fascinated by the weather since early childhood, but it was the great Hurricane of '38 that made him into a lifelong weather nut. Already a careful observer, he was disciplined and knowledgeable enough to appreciate what was happening. Over and over, he told himself to take it all in, since he would never see anything like this again. He wrote down his observations in a notebook, describing the gray-black clouds, the eerie calm when all the sea birds took off and headed inland, and the grayish-greenish hue of everything just before the storm hit.

The storm itself was thoroughly terrifying, with trees down, power lines ripped from their poles, horizontal rain, and then the calm minutes as the eye passed over and the sun shone briefly, followed by even more savage winds roaring in from the opposite direction, finishing off much of what had been left barely standing a half hour earlier.

His most intense memory, however, was the thrill, a feeling deep inside that made him shiver. It was a mixture of exhilaration and fear. He'd only feel something like that again on the beach at Okinawa, during the last months of the war.

Although Vincent spent his working hours in law offices and courtrooms, his heart remained outdoors. The son and grandson of fishermen, his home on the edge of the sea and his fascination with weather connected him to his roots in ways that he recognized more and more as the years went by.

The rain gauge was empty—no surprise since it had been sunny and cloudless for days. Still, he double-checked the gauge and recorded 0.00 in his log book.

The anemometer was motionless, as he expected, and the barograph and thermograph showed routine patterns of atmospheric pressure and temperature over the past twenty-four hours.

Once back in the kitchen, he poured himself a second mug of coffee and opened the morning paper to the weather section. On cue, Echo curled up at her master's feet.

6.

Portia Mulcahy was already a wreck, and that was before she saw the lines to security snaking out to the sidewalk.

The taxi driver had seen it all before.

"Some dude probably cut through security without getting checked. Then they have to screen everyone who's been through all over again. It's just part of doing business nowadays."

She had flown only a handful of times in her entire life, and every flight had been torture. She simply couldn't rid herself of the image of the plane spinning out of control and catching fire.

To make matters worse, this would be her first flight since 9/11.

Anxiety was as much a part of Portia Madeline Patricia Mulcahy as her freckles, her nearsightedness, and her love of Italian food. She looked back at her childhood as a series of panic attacks and hyperventilation episodes. Of course, she didn't remember any of the details until her therapist helped her recover her memories.

The therapist enlisted the help of a psychopharmacologist who prescribed Paxil and Xanax to get her through the panic attacks, which intensified every time she and the therapist turned over a new stone from her childhood and watched what came crawling out.

When she left home at seventeen, she swore she'd never set foot in Egg Rock again. Her mother had been her best friend, and after she died, there was no reason to stay. But as her therapy progressed, she learned that things were much more complicated than that. Soon it was clear that her therapy would not succeed without going back. Only then would she find closure.

She was grateful for the therapy, but it was her work that saved her life. Without the library, she would have become another sad California statistic, turning on the gas jets or jumping off the Golden Gate Bridge.

She'd been lucky to land a job as a librarian's assistant soon after moving to the West Coast. She took the job chiefly because the union at the state university had secured a mental health package for its employees. The only problem was that it was the library for the engineering school. When she started, she couldn't tell the difference between a T-square and a teapot, but she absorbed the new technical language and concepts with ease.

Soon she was assisting grad students with their research projects, locating hard-to-find articles and compiling bibliographies with the help of the library's new computer system.

The therapy came along only after Portia had tried just about everything else. In California, getting therapy was a badge of honor, evidence that you were getting in touch with your inner child, becoming a whole person.

The therapy sessions (with the little pills) and her work at the library kept Portia on an even keel, but she soon found that it was meeting and relating to other victims that gave her life purpose. "Meet" was probably not the right word, since she didn't actually, physically "meet" anyone. The beauty of the Internet was that you could relate to others without going through the messy part. The keyboard and screen were germ-free and didn't carry the burdens of eye contact, bad breath, and unrehearsed moments.

Her therapist concluded that she was too much of a "loner" and encouraged her to socialize more. Since she'd always enjoyed singing and had been a member of the Squimset High Chorus, she auditioned for a local choral group. Unfortunately, she had an attack during the audition and was not asked back. After that disaster (requiring a temporary increase in her medication), she limited her social contacts outside of work to her Internet friends.

She soon learned that the key to minimizing direct contact with the human race was a well-timed siesta. After work, she got in the habit of napping for a couple of hours. That way, she could go to the supermarket late at night when there were more employees restocking the shelves than customers at the check-out counters. And she could slip into a late movie, sit at the back, and have the place pretty much to herself.

While the cab driver jockeyed for position in front of the terminal,

Portia felt the familiar metallic taste in her mouth and a hint of fluttering in her chest. An attack could come on any minute.

But she knew she could get through it. It would be worth it in the end, if she could carry out the plans she'd made online.

After giving the guy a nice tip, she joined the line that snaked its way to the security checkpoints inside the building. A woman passenger up ahead was loudly telling anyone who'd listen that someone had bypassed security, forcing hundreds of passengers to go through the process all over again.

By now, she needed a glass of water so she could down another Xanax, carefully wrapped in a Kleenex in the zippered outer compartment of her handbag.

Once the line got moving, the whole process didn't take long. She made it through the screening machine without alarms going off and was asked to remove her shoes for inspection, as she had expected. The security people were most pleasant in a distant, professional sort of way that put her at ease. Once free of the scanners, however, she dashed into the ladies' room and swallowed the Xanax.

7.

By Kitty Cronin's count, this was the sixth phone call she'd gotten from her mother in the last twenty-four hours. Eunice reported again and again how "ecstatic" she was about the miracle over at Saint Kay's. She reported that she sat up "all night" praying to Our Lady and downing several cups of her best Irish tea. Since her caffeine level had to be in the stratosphere, it was no surprise to Kitty that her mother was, by her own account, "pacing the floors at 2:00 a.m."

No call was complete without the question, "What does your Eddie think?"

At first, Kitty said she wasn't sure, but she finally had to make something up to keep her mother from calling back every fifteen minutes.

"Eddie (not 'my Eddie') feels it's a miracle" was the best she could do, but Eunice seemed satisfied.

Eunice had an all-or-none approach to everything, and the miracle at Saint Kay's was no exception. For her, the Holy Mother's appearance was a given, no questions asked.

To be honest, Kitty was almost as excited as her mother. When the news broke on TV Monday morning, she felt more agitated than anything else and immediately called her old friend Father Guido, to see what he thought. When he got on the line, Kitty wasn't sure for a moment that it was really him. There was a mixture of authority and serenity in his voice that she had never heard before.

"Yes, Kitty, I've already been outside to visit with Our Lady three times."

Instead of calming her down, Father Guido succeeded in making her more jumpy.

Next she tried Eddie's private line at the hospital, but Gert intercepted the call. He was at a meeting, and she would give him the message.

Kitty never heard back from Eddie directly. Instead, Gert called later with a message. Eddie wanted Kitty to record the three network newscasts at 6:30. She could skip PBS because they were so anti-Catholic that any story that they might carry would be tongue-in-cheek. Before hanging up, Gert insisted on walking Kitty through the process of setting the timers, et cetera, on "Dr. Cronin's orders."

Eddie himself finally called around nine Monday evening. He sounded rushed, but he did promise to give her all the details of the Virgin's appearance when he got home. Kitty told him that Eunice needed to speak to him in the worst way, and he promised to give his mother-in-law a call when he got a chance.

Eunice had moved into an assisted living facility called Cosmas House the year before, soon after Kitty's father died. The building had formerly been a convent, and several sisters stayed on to work for the new enterprise. She was on round-the-clock oxygen for her emphysema by then and was able to get checked regularly by the staff.

Kitty and Eunice had settled on a plan. Kitty would pick Momma up at Cosmas House at ten o'clock sharp. Eunice was waiting in the lobby at the appointed hour, and they drove over to Saint Kay's. In the car, Eunice seemed too pumped up, talking nonstop about the miracle she was about to see. Concerned about her mother's rapid breathing, Kitty asked if her oxygen was flowing correctly.

"I'm fine, Kitty. It's just that I'm so excited."

The traffic slowed down as they approached the hospital, and Kitty noticed that the street just outside of the hospital boundary was lined with vans and trucks offering just about everything a pilgrim might require. Eddie had done his work well. Signs on or in front of the vehicles offered rosaries ("blessed by the Holy Father"), pictures of the Virgin, prayer books, votive candles, medals, scapulars, and holy water in "individual vials" or in larger amounts "for tour groups, at reduced prices." Other vehicles offered nonspiritual nourishment, such as snow cones, cotton candy, and fried dough.

Over breakfast, after that embarrassing moment when she walked in on him in the downstairs bathroom, Eddie hadn't been very talkative. Kitty had counted on getting his version of the miracle Monday night but fell asleep before he got home. She had to ask him about the Virgin's appearance a couple of times before getting any kind of response. Finally, he put the newspaper down.

"You and Eunice are going; see it for yourselves."

Kitty tried one last time, before Eddie buried himself in the newspaper again.

"Eddie, is she beautiful?"

"Who do you mean, Kitty?"

She bit her tongue.

Kitty pulled her minivan into the administrative space that Eddie had saved for her. In no time, she had Eunice settled in her lightweight wheelchair and hooked up the portable oxygen tank.

"Are you feeling better, Momma?"

"I felt fine before, and I feel fine now."

They had some difficulty navigating the hundred feet from the parking garage to the window on account of the crowds.

What a sight! The usually tranquil hospital grounds were packed with people who looked as if they were at an amusement park. Kitty and her mother dressed for the event as if they were going to Mass, but many of the revelers were in shorts and tank tops. Kitty noted a dozen or so T-shirts with the message:

I Survived the Pilgrimage.
The Marian Sighting at St. Kay's
Boston, 2002

Kitty was forced to say "Excuse us" as she tried to push the wheelchair toward the office building. And at one point when that didn't work, she heard herself bellow "Coming through!"

"Atta girl, Kitty," Eunice offered as they got on the end of the long line.

The window was brighter by far than the other windows in the building and filled with an unmistakable likeness of the Blessed Mother.

Kitty placed her hands on her mother's shoulder and immediately felt Eunice's tiny body shaking, as if she'd caught a chill. Then she heard her mother, in a voice barely above a whisper, begin her favorite prayer.

Hail, holy Queen, Mother of Mercy!
Our life, our sweetness, and our hope!
To thee do we cry, poor banished
Children of Eve, to thee do we send
Up our sighs, mourning and weeping
in this valley of tears.
Turn, then, most gracious advocate,
thine eyes of mercy towards us; and
after this our exile show unto us the
blessed fruit of thy womb Jesus;
O clement, O loving, O sweet Virgin Mary.

Pray for us, O holy Mother of God

That we may be made worthy of the
Promises of Christ.

Kitty continued to rest her hands on Eunice's shoulders while she looked up at the Blessed Mother, who returned her gaze. For what seemed minutes, she stood there, filled with a sense of peace that she had experienced only once before … back in Lourdes on her honeymoon.

Without warning, Eunice's breathing changed.

"Momma, are you okay?"

"I feel a little dizzy, that's all. It's probably all the excitement. Isn't Our Lady just beautiful?"

"Yes, Momma. She is." Eunice had lost all the color in her face. "How do you feel now?"

"About the same, but I'll be fine. Maybe we can get inside and out of the sun. The heat's probably getting to me."

It didn't feel hot to Kitty. In fact, there was a cool breeze.

Kitty maneuvered the chair back through the crowd, shouting "coming through" again and "I have a sick woman here" when people failed to move out of the way fast enough. Finally, they made it into the hospital lobby.

By then, Eunice looked wretched. She was pale and breathing like she'd just chased a bus.

Kitty gestured to a security man nearby. He wasted no time as he took hold of the wheelchair and said, "We're taking a little trip to emergency. I hear they need a little business down there." He made it sound like they were going to a sale at Bloomingdale's.

Eunice motioned for her daughter to lean down so she could hear.

"Kitty, I'm having a heart attack."

Kitty began to object, but her mother narrowed her eyes, a look Kitty knew meant "Be still and pay attention."

"I'm at peace and can accept whatever happens. Now I know that Our Lady is watching over me."

A woman in a shocking-pink volunteer smock escorted Kitty to a small waiting room reserved for families of the Emergency Department's sickest patients. Once alone, she tried to fix her attention on the TV up on the wall. Contestants in an inane game show were taking turns spinning a massive wheel covered with numbers. With no remote in sight, she climbed up on a chair and switched off the power.

Standard prayers were out.

"God, I need you to get me through this. Momma's dying in the next room …"

Then she remembered what her mother always said when little Kitty was sad: "Think of the good times."

Easter was always a big deal at the Raffertys', right behind Christmas and tied with Thanksgiving.

Kitty's sister, Bridget, and her family were expected from Rhode Island. Except for Christmas cards, this was their only contact with that branch of the family all year. Kitty's little nephews, Brian and Sean, who had been adorable toddlers, had morphed into hyperactive five-year-olds the previous Easter, and she didn't look forward to seeing them again.

This was going to be the family's first chance to meet Buzzy. Ever since Bridget and Buzzy got married, he had made excuses for not coming, but he agreed to show up this year.

Father Guido from Saint Kay's was also invited.

Counting Eddie, there would be nine at the table.

The Rhode Island contingent pulled into the driveway around noon with Kitty's sister Bridget's new husband, Buzzy, at the wheel and the boys having a wrestling match in the backseat.

Bridget had remained a single mom until she married Buzzy a year ago New Year's in Vegas. Eunice got the announcement in the mail.

After grace, Eunice addressed her son-in-law.

"Buzzy, can you tell us about your business?"

"What's to tell? We make badges."

The boys put down their forks.

"We've got tons of neat badges."

"How big is the business?" asked the usually silent Kevin.

"We have six full-time employees and a couple of other part-timers who come in when we get a big order. Not quite General Motors yet, but growing. We're up from four full and no part-timers a year ago."

"Mom works for Buzzy," the twins volunteered.

"With *me, guys. She's management."*

Kitty remembered that all this began with Bridget answering a want-ad.

"I was desperate," Bridget had told her at the time. "You have to eat."

Kitty looked up when the door to the waiting room opened and Father Guido and Leo Mulcahy appeared. Without a word, the priest sat down and took her hand.

"Eunice is dead," Leo said quietly.

Looking a little shaken himself, Leo asked what he could do.

8.

Father Guido was shaken, too, but he had no choice but to gear up for the noon Mass. His little chapel promised to be jam-packed, since he could hear people filing in and there were still fifteen minutes to go. Since Monday's noon Mass was filled to capacity, he planned to keep the door to the lobby open this time so that those who couldn't get in could at least hear the liturgy.

This was his biggest crowd by far since 9/11, and in the thirty-plus hours since the Blessed Virgin appeared, the little chapel hadn't been empty one minute.

He was reminded of the old days, when his original chapel would fill up routinely every Sunday.

He would never get over losing the old chapel, which was gutted to make way for the new administration building. For hours, Father Guido stood out in the rain, watching the men in their steel helmets tear his old home apart.

The shell of the church was retained in compliance with its designation as a historic site, but the building's innards were transformed into a modern office building. The old priest's quarters above the sacristy (known as "Guido's penthouse") became Dr. Cronin's executive office, and the chapel itself provided space for the hospital's four vice presidents and their staffs.

Father Guido had the job of overseeing the de-sanctification of the old chapel in a process quaintly referred to as "relegating to profane use."

Originally, "profane" simply meant anything extra-ecclesiastical or outside of the church. The Latin literally means "in front of the temple." Today, the word makes people think that the building was converted into a dance hall. Father Guido prayed that the Church would find a less unseemly term.

He'd arranged to have the stained-glass windows put in storage and incorporated into the new chapel. He loved the rose window over the entrance and the scene of young Jesus speaking in the temple, but his favorite was the scene of John the Baptist, paradoxically aristocratic in his camel skins, pouring water over Our Savior's head.

Then came the call from Gertrude at Dr. Cronin's office. The windows would be too large for the new chapel, she said, and would be going to a parish "someplace down south." As usual, she was very businesslike and was off the phone in less than a minute.

Later, Dr. Rowley told him that the windows ended up in one of those megachurches you see on cable TV, Baptist or something, but certainly not Catholic. He also said that Dr. Cronin got $150,000 cash for them.

The annual doctors' dinner dance had been held in the church hall downstairs as long as anyone could remember, but the final one was probably the most memorable of all. The medical staff put on a costume ball to raise money for the medical library. Leo and Claire Mulcahy were a sensation as Bonnie and Clyde, but the hit of the night was Dr. Harold Nalbandian, dressed as old Archbishop Campion.

During the course of the evening, everyone in the hall got around to greeting "Archbishop Harold," and a couple of junior surgeons, well oiled by then, tried to kiss his ring.

Just when the band was about to play its last set, Father Guido sensed a commotion at the doorway and, like everyone else, began applauding when he saw what was happening.

Archbishop Campion, the genuine article, entered the room with his secretary, Father Frank Mulcahy, at his side. The applause intensified and became rhythmic while the archbishop navigated around couples frozen in place on the dance floor and greeted Harold with a smile and a hearty handshake.

At least everyone could tell them apart, Father Guido thought at the time, since Campion arrived in full crimson regalia, whereas his imitator settled for the less formal black suit and pectoral cross, topped, however, by the crimson skull cap or "zucchetto" of a cardinal.

By then, the band got into the act, cranking out "Camptown Races," as if it were the cardinal's theme song.

Three days later, the wreckers came.

Sister Agneta touched Father Guido's arm, her usual signal to stop daydreaming. She had been his assistant at Saint Kay's for years, and as he often put it, had him "all figured out."

"Oh, right, Sister. I guess it's time to get started."

Sister Aggie led the small procession, followed by a seminarian, who carried the lectionary upright in his outstretched hands. Father Guido followed three paces back.

9.

After shaking off the aftereffects of his nap, Father Richard tried to concentrate on the apparition.

Here I am, the "apparition expert," but I can't get to first base on this one, he thought, as he smoothed out the bedspread on his cot.

As a child, Richard Mears knew he'd grow up to be a professor. But he had no idea that he'd become a Catholic priest. Back in Virginia, where the pope was only one step below Hitler and Mussolini, such a trajectory was unthinkable.

After a well-received series of scholarly works on the nineteenth-century popes, his publisher urged him to write a book for a more general audience. The result, *Is the Pope Really Infallible?*, hit the best-seller lists, and the trickle of royalties still coming in just about covered the cost of his weekly food and drink at the Cattle Drive.

Meanwhile, the nineteenth-century papacy led him in another direction—to Lourdes.

In 1858, a peasant girl named Bernadette Soubirous reported seeing the Virgin Mary in a grotto in the French countryside eighteen times. Soon people with every kind of ailment found themselves cured by the waters, and Lourdes became famous overnight.

Once Father Richard delved into Lourdes, he looked into other reported sightings of the Virgin—and his papers pulled no punches.

His quiet academic life was turned upside down when one of his most controversial cases made it into the newspapers. A family in San Antonio, Texas, discovered an image of the Virgin on the hood of their truck. He was attending a conference in Corpus Christi at the time and drove up to San Antonio in his rental car to have a look. Arriving unannounced around dawn, he happened on a couple of men "touching up" the image with a paint brush.

The *New York Times* quoted him commenting on the irony of such a "fraud" taking place in the city whose patron saint was the great miracle worker of Padua.

The public reaction was frightening. There were angry letters, some with threats, but they were tame compared to the Internet. Dozens of Marian websites called his work satanic, while one French group went so far as calling him Professeur Merde.

Since he was making no headway, he thought about driving back to Saint Kay's to have another look at the window, but when he thought about the crowds and the fact that his friend Frank wouldn't be waiting for him with his car, he changed his mind. Besides, when he was there on Monday afternoon, he checked things out as best he could; he doubted that another visit would give him more information.

He headed for the Charles. Perhaps a walk along the river would get his juices flowing.

He turned left in front of the Faneuil Landing Marina and, to his amazement, pulled into the last available space in the parking lot. On any other Tuesday morning, the lot would be empty.

A dozen technicians in white jumpsuits were milling around, waiting for equipment to get offloaded from tucks.

"Another oil spill, Father, our third one this year. Looks like another underground tank gave way."

Just then, he was startled by a flock of Canada geese, honking as they swept by in their customary V-formation. He turned to follow their flight path upriver, past Mount of Olives, on their way toward Watertown.

Mount of Olives.

He'd been up to the school for a lecture once, years back, but never got around to making a return visit. The view from the top, he remembered, was spectacular.

Why not? he thought as he grabbed his cane from the backseat.

The driveway up to the school turned out to be a lot steeper than he remembered, and trees on both sides blocked any possible view. In fact, he was about to turn around, more from frustration than fatigue, when the road suddenly opened up at the summit of the "Mount" with the Piersall mansion dead ahead.

Rose Piersall's conversion and bequest was a hot topic when Father Richard was a young professor, and an off-color joke about what the cardinal had to do to get the property made the rounds.

The mansion, in beaux arts style, was dwarfed by a nineteen-sixties-era monstrosity attached to its left flank. The Pope Pius XII Auditorium, with its flat concrete walls, unadorned but for slit-like vertical windows, bore no resemblance to the Piersall family home. The newer building had darkened unevenly, giving it a sooty look. Sponge-like, it seemed to have absorbed all the impurities of the surrounding air.

A bust of Pius, studious and detached, with his high forehead, hooked nose, and steel-rimmed glasses, surveyed the scene from an alcove above the auditorium's entrance.

An obvious coincidence occurred to him. Pius XII was the pope who declared the Feast of the Assumption a holy day of obligation back in 1950. Father Richard had written at length about that edict in his book on papal infallibility, since it was the last act of any pope that invoked that principle. Then yesterday, on the feast day itself, the "phenomenon" on the widow appeared.

The fact that he hadn't made such an obvious connection before this troubled him. He worried, as he did so often these days, that he wasn't as sharp as he used to be. He needed to get off his feet and think awhile.

Since the view of the city that impressed him on his other visit, years ago, was from the east side of the hill at the ball fields, he set out in that direction. The uneven dirt path through a little thicket separating the parking lot from the football field gave him some difficulty, but the cane kept him steady. Finally he found a shady spot at the bottom of the grandstand.

From there, he was high enough to appreciate the river's turning on itself, snakelike, as it made its way to Boston Harbor. The Back Bay skyline and the State House dome on Beacon Hill dazzled in the afternoon heat.

Father Richard was soon on the driveway again, and at the first turn, he nearly collided with a golf cart coming up the hill. A burly guy in an official-looking uniform was at the wheel. Northeast Security was stenciled on the hood, and the wheels looked small enough to fit a lawn mower.

"This is private property. Can't you read?"

Minutes later, he was back in his car, shaking so hard that he could hear his teeth chattering.

10.

Portia relaxed a little when she found the window seat she'd reserved online still empty. A twenty-ish woman with short, spiky, magenta hair had already claimed the middle seat. She sat motionless while

Portia negotiated the carry-on into the storage compartment and climbed over the girl's outstretched legs to get to her seat. She had her earphones on and had that far-away look that young people get while listening to music. Happily, it didn't look like she'd intrude on Portia's very limited personal space.

She learned that the flight was overbooked when the attendant got on the intercom, offering a free ticket to anyone willing to postpone their flight to Boston until afternoon. A pair of college kids jumped out of their seats and collected their bags from the overhead compartment. Portia figured they'd hang around a couple of hours for a later flight and then have tickets to Honolulu or Tahiti or Timbuktu. She envied their flexibility and enthusiasm. Even at their age, she was never like that.

She adjusted her seat into the upright position, made sure the tray table wouldn't come loose at take-off, and clicked the clasp on the seatbelt a couple of times before she could settle down. Then she was able to close her eyes and focus on Egg Rock.

She figured she'd slip in without being overheard, but while she fumbled with her keys, the front door opened from the inside.

"Whatever happened to my little Portia?" His voice was slurred. "Do you remember the little girl who'd sit on my lap while I read her bedtime stories?"

"She grew up."

"Speak up. You're mumbling."

He was shouting by now.

"Where ya been?"

"Dad, I told you I was going out with friends."

He leaned forward to hear her and rocked forward. Before she knew what was happening, he had his arms around her. Her breasts were pressed against him so hard that they burned. Thankfully, she broke free right away. If she hadn't, she feared that he would have assaulted her, and she panicked.

A couple of drags on the joint that was passed around and the kiss that one of the boys gave her in the backseat just minutes ago were giving her enough to deal with already. What she had to do was make an end run around the lecherous old man swaying in front of her, get up the stairs safely, and lock herself in her room.

At that moment, she heard a voice, clear and self-assured.

"I have only one regret."

"What would that be, may I ask?"

"That you aren't the one taking up residence at Evergreen Cemetery."

It took Portia a moment to comprehend that the voice was her own. By then her father had come into focus, looking down at his hands and shaking his head. And she could swear that a bee had stung her left cheek.

She broke for the stairs and was up in her room in a flash, the door bolted.

Thanks to the Xanax, Portia drifted off to sleep soon after the flight attendant cleared away the tray. That little bottle of Chardonnay didn't hurt, either.

She was awakened after her time in la-la land by mounting pressure in her ears.

The punk girl in the next seat remained motionless, staring off in space, like a suicide bomber listening to instructions over her headphones.

The flight attendant walked through the cabin, picking up the remaining cups and napkins while Portia studied the familiar arc of the North Shore unfolding below. The plane had just bisected Boston Harbor from the southwest, made a U-turn off Squimset Neck, and was straightening out for the runway at Logan.

Just when the flaps went down, the original Egg Rock came into view first. She'd always assumed that the town later borrowed the name, but she couldn't be sure it wasn't the other way around.

A mile off East Beach, the huge boulder was bathed in late afternoon sunshine. Its eggshell color, she remembered, was due to the tons of guano dropped by sea gulls over the centuries. The rock had once been topped by a lighthouse, which looked pasted on in an old photograph her father hung on the wall of his study, like an amateur piece of trick photography.

She assumed that the rock was named for the gulls' eggs that hatched there every year, but it sure wasn't egg-shaped. Instead, its shape reminded her of a baked potato, opened, with a dollop of sour cream on top.

The town then swept into view under the plane, its two islands connected by a thin, gray isthmus dominated by the red-and-white lifesaving station. The coast guard manned the building when she was a kid, but budget cuts closed down the station years ago.

She was grateful that no one had torn the building down yet. In California, it would have long since been replaced by a fast-food restaurant with a hundred-car parking lot.

The sun was low enough to cast long shadows, causing every object on the ground to stand out in unnatural relief. The land was a rich green, like a billiard table, a color she forgot existed in nature. You just don't see that shade of green in California.

Seconds later, the gently curving causeway leading to Squimset and the rest of the world came into view.

11.

The Saint Gabriel's steeple never failed to impress Father Frank when he crossed the North Squimset Bridge into Salem. From that distance, it looked fine, but about a block away, anyone looking up would quickly lose count of the gaps left by the bricks that had fallen out. His first priority as the new pastor had been to get the steeple repaired, since it would be an inauspicious start for him if the steeple were toppled by a nor'easter or a falling brick clipped a passerby.

The inspector sent up from the chancery in Faneuil pronounced the steeple safe but estimated that it would take $30,000 to restore it properly.

And that was only the steeple!

Frank's predecessor, Monsignor Lawrence Flynn, had spent the parish savings account down to a few hundred dollars. It was clear that the Sunday collection hadn't covered expenses for years.

Larry Flynn had been the pastor of Saint Gabe's for twenty years and had run the place without an assistant for the last five.

When the monsignor failed to show up for Mass one morning, the sexton found his body, still seated at the kitchen table, with a bowl of uneaten Cheerios and a cup of coffee in front of him.

A week later, the Reverend Francis X. (Frank) Mulcahy, the late cardinal's secretary, was made Saint Gabriel's new pastor.

When he went downstairs to check out the rectory basement, he found the old coal bin filled with hundreds of empty vodka bottles.

About a week after he arrived, the utility bills arrived in the mail. It was a miracle that the lights were still on, since the electric bill was two years overdue and totaled $18,000!

In the five years since taking over, Father Frank fretted about the finances more than any other item, but with his "Please dip extra deep this week so we can pay the oil bill" appeals from the altar, the weekly bingo games in the church basement, cake sales, and the annual summer fair, he was finally running in the black.

Miss Shanahan and her crew of volunteers were chatting outside the basement entrance when he pulled into the parking lot. The four women would have the parish hall converted into Bingo Central in an hour.

Father Frank's introduction to bingo came during his first

parish assignment after ordination, at Saint Eulalia's in downtown Boston.

On his first night of bingo duty, the pastor gave him some advice.

"Frank, being the new kid, so to speak, you'll be asked the same question time after time: 'Father, would you bless my cards?'"

"How do I handle that?" Frank asked, really put-off by the notion.

"Just say, 'I'd be happy to bless you, dear, but not your cards.' Count how many times you're asked."

It turned out that five people asked that night. Frank added that to the growing list of things they never taught you in the seminary.

Monsignor Flynn, the former pastor at Saint Gabriel's, hosted the most popular bingo games on the North Shore. Before long, he was a local celebrity, earning the nickname "Lucky Larry." Players were driving down from New Hampshire because the prizes had grown so large.

Bingo night kept growing during Father Frank's time at Saint Gabe's and was second only to the summer fair as the parish's revenue source. Without it, he knew, the parish would quickly be back in the red.

Jane opened the rectory door. "Father, there's a gentleman on the phone who needs to speak with you. He wouldn't give his name but said it was urgent."

Father Frank quickly greeted his bingo crew before following the parish secretary into the office to take the call.

He was stunned when Gertrude Kleindienst introduced herself on the phone, but with that husky voice, it was easy to understand why the parish secretary told him there was a man on the other end.

He had never met her but knew her by reputation.

"Look, Father Mulcahy, I need your help. Your sister, Portia, told me what a good priest you are. Could you find a way to meet with me tonight?"

She sounded distraught. This was not the time to quiz her and upset her further.

"It's already pretty late, and I do have a commitment here at Saint Gabriel's."

"I'm really desperate, Father."

"Let me see what I can do."

12.

Portia's driver likely had never had the misfortune of traveling north out of Logan, instead of south, into the city, as nine out of ten cabs did. Stopped at a traffic light, he turned to her and smiled, while Creole music played softly on the radio.

She sat back and watched a succession of air freight companies, rental car lots, fast-food outlets, and auto supply stores roll by. After passing two racetracks, one for horses and the other for dogs, her driver navigated a terrifying traffic rotary with vehicles pouring in from every angle.

The only time Portia had ever driven a car was in driver's ed, when she came close to sideswiping the instructor's car in the school parking lot. She continued the classes only because Vincent insisted but never took the driving test. Looking back, she had absolutely no regrets.

As a teenager, she already had the notion that the world would be a far better place if the internal combustion engine hadn't been invented and oil fields had never been discovered.

A mile or so north of the rotary out of hell, they drove over the drawbridge spanning Sachem River, skirted downtown Squimset, and approached Egg Rock.

The house she grew up in looked much smaller than she remembered. The veranda on which she and Frankie played kickball on rainy afternoons had shrunk to half its size. Once the taxicab was on its way, she set her bag in the front hall and made a quick inspection of the first floor.

Nobody was home.

Although her mother died twenty-eight years ago, the place looked like she just stepped out to do a little shopping and would be back in time to put the meatloaf in the oven. It was apparent that her father didn't have the heart to make the most trivial of changes.

The kitchen was frozen in time, the only addition being a bowl of water, apparently for a dog, in the corner by the stove.

In the pantry, all the china, glassware, and serving dishes were untouched and pristine. It reminded her of the Kitchen of Yesterday she once saw at Disneyland.

Turning to leave the pantry, she froze. Her mother always kept her favorite calendar on the inside of the door, a Nantucket calendar with scenes from the island corresponding to each month. Aunt Patty never forgot to give her sister this calendar at Christmas, in memory of happy vacations the two couples spent there, way back, before children complicated their lives. It was a kind of ritual. Mother acted as if she had no idea what was inside the gaily wrapped package, feigned excitement as she struggled with the ribbon, and invariably uttered an exclamation of surprise once she got it open.

The yellowing calendar showed daffodils blooming in window boxes on Federal Street, and the page was dated April 1974!

She began rooting in her bag for a Xanax when a car turned into the driveway.

She watched from the kitchen window as an old man stiffly worked his way out of the driver's seat, straightened out his tall body, and then opened the rear door of the sedan to let a dog out. He was doing all this in slow motion, like the old people you see in the supermarket, blocking the aisles with their carts and taking forever to read the label on a box of raisin bran.

It took her a minute to be absolutely sure this was her father, not a friend or a long-lost relative she didn't recognize. But when he began walking, she knew.

Old as he was, Vincent Mulcahy still walked with the precision and formality of a military man. And he still had a soldier's haircut.

She imagined surprising him and stabbing him in the heart with one of those bone-handled carving knives her mother always kept in the drawer beside her. They'd still be lying in wait after all these years, clean, polished, and ready for the deed. The dog would be a problem of course, as would all that blood, and her therapist would certainly be disappointed.

She could see it—the look of surprise, then horror, and finally comprehension on Vincent's face before he'd fall lifeless to the carpet with the knife jutting out of his chest.

She could get through the trial okay and at times enjoy it some. It would be a sensation, front-page stuff, and would finally put peaceful, innocent little Egg Rock on the map!

Her team of lawyers would advise her that the abusive father angle was her only chance for a reduced sentence or even escaping the electric chair, but she wouldn't allow that. She would never tell them, let alone the rest of the world, what her father had done to her. She'd choose to remain silent and would refuse to take the stand.

The old man and the dog were already on the landing when Portia's mind went blank. She had been preparing for this reunion for years and had rehearsed her lines thousands of times—and now, at zero hour, she had nothing to say.

She managed to get the front door open before Vincent could turn the knob, and they stood there motionless for a minute. Then he reached out, gently took his daughter's hand, and drew her toward him. They embraced silently while the dog circled them approvingly, brushing their legs at each turn.

13.

The supper crowd in the hospital cafeteria was buzzing about Dr. Cronin's mother-in-law, Eunice Rafferty. While visiting the hospital with her daughter to check out the window, she got overexcited, had an MI, and arrested in the emergency room during the afternoon. Apparently, Eddie Cronin and Leo Mulcahy got into a big argument while the staff was trying to stabilize things. As the woman's primary care physician, Leo was trying to carry out her decision not to take heroic measures. She knew that her lungs were so bad that if she got hooked up to a breathing machine, she'd never get off "the damned thing."

Cronin apparently burst into the treatment room and said something like, "What the hell are you all standing around for? Get an endotracheal tube in her and start her on a vent. I know what she would want. I'm authorized to speak for her."

Although she was struggling for air and becoming more than a little blue around the edges, the old girl looked up at Cronin and raised her hand like a policeman stopping traffic.

"Back off, Eddie. Leo's in charge," she managed to gasp before passing out.

Tom Rowley couldn't disguise his glee as the nurse finished her story. "Well, the old girl went out with guns blazing, something I'd like to do."

The table fell silent.

14.

Once she and Eddie told the kids, Kitty picked up the phone and called her sister down in Providence. After a long silence, followed by what sounded like a sob, Bridget cleared her throat.

"We'll be up tonight," she said, in Eunice's no-nonsense tone of voice. Kitty had never appreciated how much her sister sounded like her mother until then. "With Brian and Sean out of the house, we can throw a couple of things in a suitcase and be on the road in a flash. That's one of the many advantages of the empty nest. If you get the kids fed, we'll bring Chinese. Just so there's no confusion, Kitty, Buzzy and I will be staying until things settle down."

They pulled into the driveway less than two hours later, and when Bridget hugged her sister, Kitty broke down and cried for the first time.

She had gone through the emergency room nightmare without shedding a tear. And when she and Eddie got the kids together in the family room and told them the terrible news about Grandma, she had been perfectly calm.

When Bridget got there, Kitty quit being the comforting mother and the supportive wife (you'd think it was Eddie's mother who just died, from the way he was acting) and became the kid sister again—at least for the few minutes Buzzy was outside, getting the suitcases out of the car.

Eddie had already rushed back to the hospital to be on hand for an "important shipment from Latin America" relating to the Virgin Mary's appearance. Perhaps he told her more, but things were moving so fast that Kitty couldn't remember half of what he said.

Bridget spent time with each of Kitty's eight children, and after a hug, she whispered something to each one, and each time the child nodded solemnly.

At supper, Kitty knew that another word about what had to be the worst day of her life would make her break down completely. There would be plenty of time in the morning to tell the whole story.

Meanwhile, Eddie dominated her thoughts.

Everything seemed to start and end with Eddie.

Bridget must have sensed this when she steered away from the obvious questions and launched into an update on the twins and the badge business instead.

Brian and Sean were living apart for the first time in their lives. Brian was working for an advertising firm in New York and living in the East Village, while his twin, Sean, was in Providence helping his father in the badge business, which had really taken off.

"We've expanded into holograms," she enthused, adding that they recently landed a hologram contract with one of the credit card companies and had to open a new factory to accommodate the new business.

"And I don't have to tell you that you're a major stockholder."

Kitty wasn't likely to forget.

Eunice had Kitty accompany her to the lawyer's office for the reading of Kevin Rafferty's will. Only then did Kitty learn that her father had divided his estate evenly between her mother and her without leaving Bridget a penny.

On the way home, Kitty confronted her mother.

"Your father and I could not condone her running away and divorcing and marrying this—"

"Momma, Richie ran out on Bridget and the kids for another woman."

"The wife is responsible for keeping the family together. She must have driven Richie away."

Kitty didn't speak to her mother for weeks. Finally, she confided in Father Guido, who suggested that Kitty split her inheritance with her sister. Before long, Kitty and her mother were on speaking terms again, talking about everything under the sun except Kevin's will and Bridget's disinheritance.

Days after Kitty mailed her sister half of her inheritance money, a large manila envelope postmarked Providence arrived. Inside was a short note: "Dearest Kitty, Buzzy and I will never forget your courage, generosity, and love. Keep the enclosed in a safe place. Someday it will be worth a lot more than the paper it's written on."

The certificate was for five thousand shares of the Buzz Craft Badge Company.

"The price is $342.50 a share as of this morning, and we're expecting a four-to-one split. Doing the math, your interest in the company comes in at a shade over 1.7 million!"

Getting back to the twins, Bridget said that they talk on the phone for hours, and that it was only a matter of time before Brian would come home.

"We miss him like crazy, and I know he's homesick, but it's the twins' need to be together that will bring him home."

Kitty nibbled on an egg roll and downed a little fried rice, surprised that she had any appetite at all. Then she sat back and filled her sister in on her clan.

"It's hard to believe, but John is driving. I sat in the backseat for his driver's test and couldn't open my eyes for the whole trip. Lawrence is mowing lawns to pay for a new drum set, and Ambrose is going to computer camp. Ita and Fabian are home with Charles, Irene, and Anthony while I'm shuttling the older kids around. I don't know how I survived so long without an *au pair*."

Buzzy, who had been content to listen to his wife and sister-in-law during the meal, looked at Kitty.

"How did you and Eddie come up with your kids' names?"

"Saints' days."

"I don't understand."

"We named them for the saint who shares their birth date. You see, John was born on the feast of St. John the Baptist, Lawrence on the feast of St. Lawrence, and so on."

Bridget took over. "Buzzy, dear, I may be a lapsed Catholic—"

"Who married a Jewish guy from Woonsocket."

"Buzzy, the Jewish part was easy. It was the Rhode Island part that took some getting used to. Lapsed or not, I do know a little about saints' days. You see, that's how *I* was named."

"Cool. I didn't know that."

15.

The great thing about having Harold and Geri Nalbandian over for supper was that Claire didn't have to fuss. They expected to be treated like family and would have been puzzled if Claire trotted out her mother's good china or baked a fancy dessert.

They walked in on the dot of six thirty. Geri plunked down a bottle of merlot on the kitchen table and wrapped her long arms around Claire.

Gerarda Rossi Nalbandian was a big woman. She stood nearly a foot taller than Harold and was "big-boned," as Leo's mother liked to describe such people. Leo said that they better never have a fight, because Geri could tuck her husband under one arm and toss him out the nearest window. In Claire's experience, large people were more or less sedentary, but Geri was an exception to the rule. Even at rest, some part of her was in motion. She was a finger- and toe-tapper, keeping time to some fast-paced song that played in her head.

"Give me a job."

Since saying "we're all set" wasn't an option, Claire asked her friend to put the salad together while the guys got the grill started out on the deck. Geri needed no further instructions, since she knew Claire's kitchen almost as well as her own.

They ate at the kitchen table after being chased off the deck by the mosquitoes. The boys had cooked the steaks just right, with just a sliver of deep red sandwiched between layers of pinkish meat, nicely blackened on the outside.

Harold passed the platter around offering seconds, which everyone but he declined. Claire was always astonished by the amount of food Harold could shovel into his minuscule body. He hadn't put on a pound since he and Leo went into practice. And she still wondered if he bought his clothes in the kids' department.

She knew plenty of people who'd kill to have his metabolism.

"Geri walked up the hill to have a look at the window and hitched a ride over here with me," Harold said.

"What did you think, Geri?" asked Leo. "From the way Eddie tells it, Saint Kay's is going to be more famous than Lourdes, Fatima, and Medjugorje all rolled into one." Claire gave her husband a knowing smile.

"Don't mind Leo, Harold. His bark is worse than his bite."

"You're telling me? I have lunch with the guy every day."

They all turned to Geri.

"That business up at Saint Kay's got me thinking about going to church with my mother when I was a kid in New Haven. I would get this tightness in my chest just about every time I walked in and saw the big altar, Jesus nailed to the cross, and all those candles. Back in those days, Italian churches like ours were really big on candles! Harold and I think I was hyperventilating …"

Harold nodded.

"… but the odd thing is that I started getting the old chest tightness yesterday—for the first time in years."

Leo refilled the wine glasses and brought another bottle to the table.

"So, this afternoon I went up to the office building to have a look for myself …"

"And?" asked Claire.

"I didn't know exactly *what* I was seeing. The colors were amazing—vivid and bright in an unearthly kind of way. I wondered if it was a chemical reaction. Halide oxidation can give off that shade of green, and a tiny bit of cobalt, under the right conditions, might look blue like that."

Leo broke in. "So you think it's a chemical reaction?"

"I just don't know."

"Okay."

"If my mother were still around, she'd accept what she was seeing without question. I'm afraid that I'm not wired that way, but I'd love to have her certainty."

"So you're in neither camp."

"I don't think there should be 'camps,' Leo. But since you brought it up, which camp are you in?"

"The skeptics' camp."

"I guess I'm between camps."

"No man's land."

"Yes, Leo, no man's land."

"But where do you draw the line between what you do and do not believe?"

"I don't like the idea of drawing lines around my beliefs. The whole process is more complicated than that."

"Or fuzzier."

"What's fuzzy for some is open-minded for others."

Harold broke the tension by giving everyone an update on his latest boat. Over the years, he'd owned a series of pleasure craft, the newest always a few feet longer than its predecessor. Fresh out of his residency, he purchased his first boat, a brand-new twenty-four-foot Grady White Walk Around. He could never have afforded it without a generous uncle and a less-than-generous loan from the Faneuil Center Savings Bank.

That was "four boats ago."

In the spring, he'd sold the boat he'd owned the longest, a thirty-three-foot Tiara Open Express, which he bought ten years before, and immediately graduated to a secondhand thirty-five-foot Cabo Express.

"This one's the keeper. They'll have to bury me in it."

"Before that happens, Harold, I'd like to get a good look at Egg Rock from the water."

"No problem," Harold replied. "The four of us will get up to Egg Rock before the season is out."

Over coffee, Geri got back to their earlier conversation.

"Leo, I hope I didn't come off too holier-than-thou."

"Don't worry, dear," Harold broke in. "Leo and Claire know how grounded you are, and it's no secret that you have issues."

"Issues? You mean like how sick this whole priest-pedophilia stuff is? And the cover-up? I've got issues all right."

Geri took another sip of wine.

"Of course the same guys who covered up the abuse are making birth control sound like the crime of the century. Those bishops should drop by and see the girls in our school who get pregnant every year. Harold knows that my list of grievances with the Catholic Church is very long."

"I don't get it, Geri. You still go to Mass."

"I do, maybe not every week, but I do."

"I don't see—"

"Why I don't walk away?"

"Precisely."

"Like everybody here, I was brought up Catholic—"

"Except me."

"The Armenians are close enough, Harold. Anyway, you converted. Let me finish."

"Okay, dear."

"For better or for worse, being Catholic is part of who I am. So instead of trying to be something I am not, I work on the basics—forgiveness, the dignity of every person, nonviolence, and most of all, the recognition that we are here for a reason and should make the most of our lives."

Leo brought the coffee pot to the table. "I envy you, Geri. I really do."

"Maybe I'm making the process sound easier than it is, Leo. There are days when I'm so ticked off that I feel like chucking the whole Catholic thing and becoming a Unitarian. But the feeling passes."

16.

Father Guido had just exchanged shoes for slippers when his beeper went off. His heart sank. He was looking forward to watching the Sox's new starter, a lefty brought up from their triple-A franchise over the weekend.

Hopefully, this wouldn't take too long.

The number on the tiny screen looked like the gift shop's extension. The gift shop closed at six, and it was already past seven thirty. The page operator must have made a mistake.

But he dialed it anyway, just in case, and the party at the other end picked up at the first ring. Strangely, it turned out to be Gertrude, Dr. Cronin's secretary who answered.

"Father Guido, Dr. Cronin wants you here at the gift shop right away." As always, she didn't wait for a reply and hung up.

He was astounded. Kitty's mother was dead only a few hours, and Dr. Cronin was back at work? He shook his head in admiration. He wouldn't have the strength to put his personal grief aside like that.

His feet began to ache again as soon as he stood up. They were a little swollen, and the imprint of the shoes he'd been in all day was still obvious when he took off the slippers. He should get up to Leo's office to get his blood pressure checked.

Since his quarters and the gift shop were in the same wing, it took him no time to get down there. Through the open door, he could see packing boxes stacked practically to the ceiling and remembered that when he was there earlier for a Snickers bar (Leo wouldn't be happy), there was no clutter.

Dr. Cronin emerged from behind a large carton with *Articulos Religiosos* stenciled on the front. He was in his shirt sleeves, the end of his tie tucked in. "ECC" was monogrammed on the pocket, and gold cufflinks shaped like half dollars glimmered under the fluorescent lights.

He was about to ask how Kitty and the children were coping with their tragedy, but Dr. Cronin looked too businesslike for a personal conversation.

"Father, we received a large shipment of rosaries, scapulars, and pictures of Our Blessed Lady late this afternoon. In addition, five hundred commemorative T-shirts that I special-ordered arrived about an hour ago. The pilgrims who have been visiting Saint Kay's since yesterday have been asking for such mementos, and I felt that we needed to fulfill their wishes."

In his thirty years in the priesthood, Guido had never seen so many religious goods in one place.

"I want you to bless them."

Guido had no problem with the concept of blessing rosaries and other religious objects, even in bulk. That happened at the Vatican all the time. If the Holy Father had to bless each rosary individually, he would need a hundred hours a day to get the job done.

"I can bless the religious objects, Dr. Cronin, but I'm troubled by the T-shirts."

"If it makes you feel better, we'll skip the shirts. But you know as well as I do that everything gets blessed these days. Every spring they expect the archbishop to hightail it up to Gloucester to bless those rust-buckets they call fishing boats. And one of those yuppie parishes in Back Bay holds cat and dog blessings in order to keep the place from going belly-up."

"Needless to say, the items will be free of charge."

"Actually, Father, we plan to make them available at the gift shop and at a kiosk we're constructing on the grounds, at cost. Obviously, shipping and handling need to be covered as well."

"If I bless them, you are prohibited from selling them at any price."

"Begging your pardon, Father, but I'm the one who makes the decision whether or not they're sold, and at what price. I happen to know that such business decisions are not in the hospital chaplain's job description, since I drafted the damn thing myself."

"It's not me we're talking about, Dr. Cronin. It's the Church. Do you remember the term 'simony'?"

"I believe the term refers to illegal payments to the Church."

"You're on the right track. Simony is the act of *selling* spiritual things. If the Church sold tickets and charged admission to Mass, that would be simony. Blessings are not for sale. If I bless these items, the Church forbids you from selling them, even 'at cost.'"

For reasons known only to God, Dr. Cronin was first in line when red bulbous noses and pink cheeks were handed out. Father Guido understood that such a face was a heavy cross to bear, the more so because Dr. Cronin was nearly a teetotaler. After the simony comment, the doctor's face deepened a few more shades, the way it did when the nurses picketed the hospital a few years back. Anyone could be excused for thinking that he spent most of the time in a barroom.

"Forget about the blessing, Father."

With that, Dr. Cronin turned back to the packing boxes as if the priest no longer existed.

Minutes later, Father Guido was upstairs again, snuggled in his lounge chair, shoes off and feet up.

He picked up his Bible and turned to the passage about Simon Magus in the Acts of the Apostles.

Simon observed that it was through the laying on of hands that the apostles conferred the Spirit, and he made them an offer of money with the request, "Give me that power too, so that if I place my hands on anyone, he will receive the Holy Spirit." Peter said in answer, "May you and your money rot—thinking that God's gift can be bought!"

Finally, the priest picked up his remote and got back to the ballgame.

The Sox had runners at the corners with one out, and their new lefty had given up only two hits over three innings.

17.

Eddie Cronin knew the feeling well: face burning and temples throbbing. With Gert now on the scene, he could get the hell out of the gift shop before he lost it.

"Gert, keep an eye on the place and don't let anybody—and that includes security—in here. I'll be back in a few minutes."

"I won't let the marines in here."

The courtyard was deserted, and the cool evening air was calming him a little. He thought back to Guido.

Now, suddenly, this fat little priest who couldn't put two words together for a decent sermon was a canon law expert on simony. But that wasn't all.

Guido the Meek had turned into a pit bull.

He took in his surroundings. Dead ahead, at twelve o'clock, was the open end of the courtyard, with the power plant in the distance. At two o'clock stood the old, two-story chapel, now converted into offices. He admired the subtle lighting he had installed in his executive office on the second floor. Opposite his office, at ten o'clock, was the research wing, with Dr. Rowley's office and lab taking up the ground floor. For all he knew, that creep Rowley was inside the darkened lab, watching him this very minute.

Then he stood, turned to six o'clock, and looked straight up. The O'Rourke Building towered ten stories, topped by the west-facing cross.

Back at the gift shop, he found Gert was finishing a candy bar from the rack beside the counter, a telltale smear of chocolate visible on her lower lip.

"All quiet here at the front, Dr. Cronin."

After sending his secretary home for the night, Eddie got back to the task at hand, unloading and arranging his treasure trove of religious articles.

18.

Vincent decided on spaghetti and salad, Portia's favorites when she was a kid. While her mother's big kettle was heating up, Portia set the table the way she always did, and afterward, they did the dishes together, Vincent rinsing off the plates and Portia doing the drying.

Later, they took a drive around Egg Rock, with Vincent at the wheel of the old Buick. The village looked just as Portia had remembered.

Portia knew what was coming next when Vincent pulled into the Vets Club lot. She and her therapist had spent weeks getting ready for this moment, including having another Xanax at the ready.

"Would you like to walk up to the cemetery and visit your mother?"

Minutes later, they were standing in front of Madeline Mulcahy's granite marker.

She looked up to see her father standing before her, arms outstretched, as if he was about to sum up a case for the jury.

"Portia, I've been anticipating this moment for years. I want to apologize to you right here, in front of your mother."

He looked at his daughter directly.

"I'll never forgive myself for striking you. My own daughter! I never ever struck anyone in anger, before or since."

"I believe that."

He turned his head, as if to check that they were alone. The cemetery was deserted.

"And I'm ashamed of the way I treated you during your mother's illness and in those awful weeks after she died. I was too caught up with my own problems."

Portia nodded.

"I've thought about this every day since you left."

"So have I, Dad."

Evergreen Cemetery, Saint Lawrence Church (before it was demolished), and the James J. Deveau Jr. Post #215, better known as the Egg Rock Vets Club, formed a triangle. It was only fitting, Portia thought, since they were so intertwined. Her mother, now lying at the Evergreen, was baptized, confirmed, and married at Saint Lawrence's. Maddy Mulcahy kept the wedding album in the living room bookcase, where Portia studied the pictures hundreds of times as a girl. They were black-and-white snapshots, many with crenellated borders so popular back then, and held on to the page with black triangles at the corners. In one photo, the two couples—Mom with her twin, Patty, and Dad with his almost twin, Wally—stood at the top step of the church, looking straight into the camera, as if the lens held their future.

From there, on that breezy June afternoon, so breezy, Portia's mom said, that the brides had to hold on to their veils with both hands, they made their way across the road to the reception at the Vets.

The cemetery had fared the best, with its manicured grounds, its majestic pine trees, and view of the ocean. But it was full. According to Vincent, the town planned to turn the old stone quarry behind the Vets Club into an "annex," encouraging inurnment over interment at the new location. The church closed upon the death of its pastor, Father Malachy Dunn (whose last name was rarely used), who had run the parish singlehandedly for thirty-three years, and who, according to Portia's mother, was "a living saint." Maddy had spoken from experience, since he officiated at her wedding, baptized her children, and encouraged her only son to become a priest himself.

Portia recalled that kids all called him Father Malarkey.

"What happened to Saint Lawrence's?"

"You know how slow the church is about making decisions."

Portia nodded.

"Well, not this time. Father Mal was barely buried a year when the church was torn down and replaced with those townhouses, and, as you can see, the rectory was converted to condominiums. We couldn't believe how fast it happened."

The streetlights were coming on one by one as they walked back to the car, but even in the twilight, Portia could see that the Vets building needed a coat of paint.

"When I was a kid, you guys had all kinds of money. I remember you and Uncle Wally talking about how to spend it."

Post #215 was a shadow of the hot spot where Vincent and Walter Mulcahy were first welcomed when they got back from the war. The crowds were long gone, and the Saturday night dances with girls venturing out from Squimset for a good time were just a memory.

The Vets Club was on life support, eking out an existence by renting out office space to local nonprofits and its parking spaces to neighbors, while converting its front lawn to an off-season dry dock for local pleasure craft.

"The Saint Lawrence affair taught us all a lesson," he added as they climbed back into the car. "No one's going to fight your battles for you. We sat around and felt sorry for ourselves when the church closed, but we'll fight to keep the Vets open."

19.

Gertrude Kleindienst had already commandeered a booth at the Cattle Drive and was working on a drink and a cigarette when Father Frank sat down. She was wearing a red blouse, just as she'd said on the phone. Frank wondered whether the choker with the little gold cross was her standard attire or picked specially for the occasion.

Before he was able to get settled, she started in.

"Let's get the ground rules straight. I want our little chat protected, like a confession."

From the way she had sounded on the phone, distraught was the word he thought of at the time; he didn't expect such a frontal assault.

"If you intend to make a confession, we should get out of here."

"No, I just want to tell you some things in confidence, just between the two of us. Like old friends."

He worried that wait staff or passersby might overhear them.

"I guess we can talk here, Ms. Kleindienst, but keep your voice down."

She ordered a couple more manhattans and puffed away half her pack of cigarettes while she told her story. Each time she ordered another drink, he had another cup of coffee.

It turned out that Gert ("You can call me Gert if I can call you Frank," she said), Frank's sister, Portia, and another woman who lived in Faneuil had all become connected over the Internet.

Actually, she and Portia never communicated directly. They each sent e-mail messages through the third woman whom they met on a website for survivors of teenage suicide.

"Why didn't you communicate with each other directly?"

"Because the third woman recruited us."

"I don't understand."

"She had a plan for righting some wrongs."

Frank raised his hand.

"Whoa, Gert! You're talking in riddles. Who's this third woman?"

"Her name doesn't matter, but she's a librarian here in Faneuil."

"Why are you telling me this? Is Portia planning to hurt somebody?"

"I don't know, Frank, but I think you ought to talk to her. I'm not going to tell you the whole story, only enough for you to understand why I'm here."

"Did Portia ever try to hurt herself?"

"You'd need to ask her that."

"Where do you fit in?"

Gert shifted her gaze upward and took a deep breath before looking Frank squarely in the eye.

"My son, my only child, died suddenly at age seventeen."

"I'm so sorry."

She raised a finger to silence him.

"He had a drug problem, but we were optimistic that he'd be getting the help he needed at Saint Kay's. Instead, he jumped off an outside staircase and landed in the courtyard seven floors down."

"How horrible!"

She showed no emotion but took a long pull from her glass and signaled the waitress for a refill before going on.

"My life fell apart. My husband and I went through a divorce, and I started seeing a shrink. Finally, I pulled myself together well enough to get a job. Just in time, I might add, because my former husband made a habit of skipping the alimony checks. I had been a secretary before and was able to land a job at Saint Kay's."

"I'd think that would be the last place on—"

"The job was perfect. You see, I became Dr. Edward Cronin's personal secretary."

"But why—"

"I decided to meet the devil head-on."

"Was Dr. Cronin involved in your son's medical care?"

"Of course not. He hasn't touched a patient in years. But he was the hospital president, and that was good enough for me."

Father Frank still couldn't understand why they were having this conversation.

Again, she seemed to know what he was thinking.

"The reason I'm talking to you is because I planned to do something terrible to Dr. Cronin, but I've changed my mind. And your sister, Portia, provided technical support."

Father Frank sat silently for a good minute, trying to get his mind around this information.

"Ms. Kleindienst—"

"It's Gert. Call me Gert."

"All right, Gert. What do you mean by 'technical support'?"

"Your sister works at an engineering school. We needed some engineering work done, but I'm not getting into details."

"What made you change your mind about harming Dr. Cronin?"

"It took me awhile, but it finally dawned on me that Eddie Cronin isn't some evil genius. He's a pathetic little man who's in way over his head."

Gert got up to go.

"Listen, Frank, can you give me absolution?"

"No, Gert, but I could pray for you."

"I guess that will have to do."

20.

Vincent couldn't find a comfortable position. As a rule, getting to sleep wasn't the problem. Most nights he dozed off in his chair with the newspaper in his lap. He was accustomed to waking up in the middle of the night and not getting back to sleep, but tonight he was too cranked up to fall asleep in the first place.

He looked at Maddy's side of the bed.

Nobody was surprised when the two couples became engaged a couple of months after the boys came home, and got married six months after that.

They had the first double wedding ceremony in Egg Rock in memory. And it was the first time that twin sisters married brothers that anyone in the town could recall. The nuptial Mass was celebrated by Father Malachy Dunn, the reception was held at the Egg Rock Vets Club, and the three hundred guests danced till dawn.

It was only with the war that any kind of romantic feelings between the brothers and the twin sisters emerged. Once the boys were bound for the Pacific (Vin) and Europe (Wally), they turned their attention to the girls with double dates to the Capitol Theater in Squimset and one memorable night at the Pleasure Island amusement park down by Squimset harbor, with its tunnel of love.

The boys were gone almost four years, and by the time they got home, they felt they had gotten to know their wives-to-be rather well through the scores of letters that they exchanged.

Vincent finally sat up in a chair by the window. He didn't go back to bed until he saw the sweep of Frankie's headlights across the lawn as he turned into the driveway.

Everybody was in for the night.

21.

When Buzzy crawled into bed and turned out the light, his wife rolled toward him and gave him a kiss.

"Good. I was afraid that you were already asleep."

"No, dear, I'm wide awake."

He put his arm around her and drew her close.

"Now maybe you can tell me a little about Saint Bridget. I've been waiting all night."

"I can tell you one thing."

"What's that?"

"She didn't hang around with guys, especially big horny ones."

He drew her even closer.

22.

Father Frank was relieved to find no lights on in the family home. When his assistant priest suggested that Frank spend the night with his family, he was grateful. Now he knew he had no choice.

He sat down at his father's desk in the darkened study and, as he had done so many times, picked up the binoculars. The scattering of lighted windows in the high-rise condos over in Dawes looked like a giant crossword puzzle. Behind them hovered the Boston office buildings, between which he could see the three-quarter moon nearing the horizon, while to Frank's far left the harsh mercury lights of the Deer Island water plant sent the message that it was a 24/7 world out there.

Finally, he picked up the receiver and dialed Father Richard Mears' private number.

The professor picked up right away and greeted his friend Father Frank like it was the middle of the day.

After hearing about Frank's meeting with Gert, Richard advised caution.

"I wouldn't confront Portia directly. Better to nibble at the edges, ask a couple of leading questions, see if she's willing to talk. Push too hard, and she'll clam up."

"Should I go to the police?"

"With what, Frank? Some vague ramblings over drinks?"

WEDNESDAY

1.

The numerals on Father Guido's digital alarm clock slowly worked their way to midnight while he lay there, going over what happened in the gift shop.

He knew he'd done the right thing but couldn't for the life of him understand where he got the courage to stand up to Dr. Cronin the way he did.

Around one, he eased himself out of bed, dressed, and went outside to pay Our Lady another visit. He hoped that a few quiet minutes in her presence might settle him down, but instead of finding peace and quiet, he encountered a noisy Japanese TV crew. The director, a Chaplinesque mustachioed fellow, kept running back and forth, gesturing wildly, while another man stood in front of the Virgin's window, script in hand.

One of the security guys, a new hire whom Father Guido had never seen before, said that they were getting ready for a live remote.

The kid had an old-fashioned crew cut, the kind that in Guido's high school days required a touch of butch wax to make the front stand up sharply. He was happy that young fellows had their hair cut short again, but nowadays it was usually a buzz-cut, flat in the front, the kind the marines made you get at basic training. Without a defined forehead, that style reminded Guido more of a bulldog than a young man. Fellows with the genuine crew cut with its high front brush, like this security guard, were clean-cut and attractive.

Kevin Sheehan, one of Guido's classmates at Holy Trinity High, had a crew cut, too.

Kevin was a skinny kid with bad skin who had no clue about Guido's interest in him, and Guido had no intention of ever letting Kevin (or any other human being) in on his secret.

After graduation, Guido never saw Kevin Sheehan in person again, but he knew more about the man than anyone could guess.

Kevin went on to UMass, where he majored in business. After college, he enlisted in the army and served in Korea during the last months of the war. After discharge, he went to work for a start-up high-tech firm outside of Boston, got married, bought a house in the suburbs, and had three children, two girls and a boy. Then, in 1990, he died suddenly of a heart attack, age fifty-nine.

Father Guido had kept track of Kevin Sheehan for forty years but never intended to meet him face-to-face. If Kevin ever walked toward him on a sidewalk, he'd have run the other way.

He managed to collect biographical data on his subject from a variety of sources.

One time, he drove out to the university in Amherst. At the library, he got his hands on the class of 1952 yearbook and located Kevin's graduation picture with its accompanying mini-biography. This led him to photos of Kevin on the JV hockey team and with the Kappa Sigma fraternity. Then he carried the book to the men's room and cut out the pertinent pages with the scissors from the Swiss army knife he'd brought along.

That was the only time Guido had ever purposefully damaged or stolen someone else's property, and he prayed for God to forgive him for this sin every day since.

Once he became Saint Kay's chaplain, he got in the habit of scanning the Metrowest Chronicle, *Kevin's hometown paper, during his weekly visit to the Faneuil branch of the Boston Public Library and photocopied everything he could find, no matter how trivial. He went so far as to copy a story mentioning Kevin's daughter at another kid's birthday party.*

Since he was frequently copying other material anyway, no one at the library seemed to notice.

He told Leo Mulcahy about Kevin at a time when he was feeling anxious, years ago, and Leo recommended returning the yearbook pages to the library, anonymously of course. That was the only time he'd been upset with Leo, who sensed that and let the subject drop.

No one else knew, not even his sister, in spite of the material sitting right under her nose down at the family home in Gull, locked in the bottom drawer of his desk.

Father Guido watched as lights were switched on and the reporter adjusted his necktie one last time. Then he turned to the security guard.

"Who's going to be watching this in the middle of the night?"

"It's already tomorrow for a big chunk of the world, Father. This is for the evening newscast in Tokyo. It's two in the afternoon there now."

He caught a glimpse of the Blessed Mother before heading back to his quarters, and that was when it hit him. The Virgin Mary was so much more than an image on a window. She had been right there with him in the gift shop, opening his eyes, giving him a backbone—and letting him see Dr. Edward Cronin for the first time.

2.

Early morning was the best time for Helen Rowley to catch up on her e-mail. Most of the librarians she knew weren't morning people, since libraries don't usually open at the crack of dawn. But years married to a doctor who was at his office hours before everyone else had made her an exception.

Besides, the computer required more of her time nowadays.

Once the laptop was booted up and emitted that cheerful "da-da-

da-dah" before asking her for her password, she thought about how fortunate she was to be computer-savvy. Many of her contemporaries were intimidated by computers, even parents with kids who could have taught them.

Being a librarian made it happen.

Library science (she remembered how Tom would sneer at the term) embraced computer technology early on. When she reentered the workforce the year Tommy entered kindergarten, the staff at the Faneuil Branch taught her what they knew on an ancient Atari 800. Her first assignment was to help transfer information from the 3x5s in the card catalogue onto floppy discs. Before long, she was learning about the Internet, already being used by libraries to share resources.

She was e-mailing at work long before it became fashionable.

Then, each night after doing the dishes, she sat down with Tommy and taught him everything she learned on Tom's Apple II.

She scrolled down the list until she found what she was looking for. She opened the message from "eggrocksurvivor."

hi Helen. my trip was smooth and uneventful.
i forgot how ugly the road to egg rock
was with the oil tanks and strip malls. vincent
is older but otherwise unchanged. he seems happy to see me.
look forward to tour of the fan library
& seeing you friday
hope the weekend plans are working out.
portia

3.

Over breakfast, Bridget announced that she wouldn't be helping with the funeral arrangements.

"I'll do anything else, Kitty, but funeral homes and undertakers and caskets and all that are out. Besides, we both know that Momma wouldn't want me to be involved."

Kitty hadn't counted on her sister to work on the arrangements, anyway. Just to have her and Buzzy there for emotional support was help enough.

"Don't worry about it, Bridget. Remember, I went through this with Daddy's funeral. Besides, the best way for me to deal with things right now is to be busy."

Kitty knew enough not to count on Eddie, since he went AWOL when her father died. Eunice would have pitched in, but she was already too disabled by then. It was a blessing in a way that Eddie's folks died before she met him, or she would have taken care of their arrangements as well.

Tuesday evening, minutes after they spoke with the kids, he was at the door again, explaining that the apparition was taking up all his time. "I won't be back till late," he said as the door closed behind him.

She waited up anyway but must have fallen asleep with the light on, since she never heard him come in.

She did hear him get out of bed before six, but then she drifted off again. When she awoke a short time later, he was gone.

He must have been in a rush, since he hadn't taken his customary shower.

Then she remembered walking in on him in the downstairs bathroom and seeing the bruises. They were a lot more impressive than she thought they'd be.

Buzzy broke the silence. "Bridget will stay here to help with the kids, and I'll be your chauffeur."

"Thanks, Buzzy. If Bridget doesn't mind, I'd like that."

4.

Frank was the first one up. He tiptoed past Vincent's and Portia's bedrooms, took the stairs in his bare feet, and slipped on his sneakers at the kitchen table. Echo awoke from her spot near the stove and wagged her tail in anticipation of an early outing.

There would be enough time to get some serious weeding out of the way before breakfast.

He decided to work in his mother's rock garden, which needed the most attention. Vincent never spent any time working the garden but clearly enjoyed looking at it. Madeline and her twin sister, Patricia, next door had been the family gardeners (and each other's critics), comparing their irises and lilacs in the spring and their hollyhocks and sunflowers in late summer.

The funeral guests were getting their coats when Frank looked out at the garden.

"An awful thing, to die in the spring, just when the earth is becoming alive again," he said to Aunt Patty and Uncle Wally, who were carrying dishes over to the sink. "Mother tried so hard to hold on until the azaleas came out."

On that day, the garden became Frank's domain, with his Aunt Patty serving as consultant that first spring. About a month after the funeral, he showed up to cut the grass to find Aunt Patty working in her yard next door.

"Frankie, dear, it's time to pull out the bulbs and get marigolds started in the bed outside the kitchen and impatiens in the bed around the flagpole" were her instructions.

He regretted not taking notes, but who would have guessed that she'd be at the bottom of the sea halfway around the world before the hollyhocks were finished blooming?

He carried the tools out of the garage, looked at his watch, and figured it was only 4:00 a.m. on the West Coast. With any luck, his jetlagged little sister was still asleep upstairs.

Gert, sitting in that booth at the Cattle Drive with her manhattans, choker cross, and attitude, was like a bad dream. As for dreaming, he'd had another of his Cardinal Campion dreams during the night. Campion was dead five years now, but he intruded on Frank's sleep like clockwork every week or two.

The dream went something like this:

Worried about the Boss's reaction, Frank waited until the last minute to break the news. In Edmund Cardinal Campion's world, just about the last place a priest should be seen was on a bicycle.

Up until the night before the charity bike ride, the cardinal knew only that his secretary was going to take a few days off. In those days, AIDS was rarely mentioned in the Church.

Father Frank needn't have worried. After Frank told him about his trip to New York, the Boss moved slowly to his desk.

"I'm envious, Frank. I'd like to think that if I were younger and unburdened by my position, I would join you."

He pulled out his checkbook.

"I'm writing the check to you, Frank, because I don't have the courage to write it directly to AIDS Action. I guess there'll be a little money laundering involved."

The check was for a thousand dollars.

Sensing that Frank was daydreaming, Echo sauntered over and gave him a nudge with her cold nose. He got back to work but wasn't able to shake off thoughts of the old cardinal.

Father Frank stood at the foot of his boss's casket before the cathedral's altar, watching the mourners file by. A woman he recognized from the bike ride gave him a smile. She was helping a man in a wheelchair who was so weak he could barely sit up.

"My brother and I came to honor Cardinal Campion," she whispered after viewing the body.

Then Father Frank remembered his indiscretion. At a pit stop somewhere in the Connecticut hills, they got talking. She looked a bit surprised when he told her what he did for a living.

"What's your cardinal think of this?" she asked archly.

"He's bankrolling me."

Echo returned to a spot on the lawn warmed by the early sun and dozed off again.

Frank and his cousin Leo had been talking about gardening over their monthly dinner earlier in the summer.

Both acknowledged that they could never keep up with the weeds, the insects, and the need for watering, fertilizing, and trimming, but they enjoyed trying. Unlike their chosen professions, gardening offered clear goals and tangible results. Being a doctor or priest was far more complex, ill-defined, and frustrating.

"Flowers don't talk back," Leo said, making Frank worry that his cousin was burning out. Leo suggested, half-joking, that they open a landscape business after retiring.

"I'm afraid you'll have to do it by yourself."

"Come on, Frankie. You love to garden as much as I do."

"That's not it, Leo. It's that by the time I get to retire, I'll be in no shape for a second career. I know guys still out there running parishes in their eighties! When I entered the seminary, I never dreamed that every class after us, year after year, would be smaller and smaller. Now there's no one left to take our place."

Father Frank was halfway through the rock garden when Vincent appeared at the kitchen door.

"Hey, you two! Your sister is in here having her breakfast, in case you're interested."

Echo made it to the door first.

Portia jumped up from the breakfast table, wrapped her arms around her brother, and planted a big kiss on his cheek.

She was wearing faded jeans and a red-and-yellow top with one of those unmistakably southwestern zig-zaggy, abstract designs on the front. Her salt-and-pepper hair was cut severely, giving her a boyish look, and her freckles, over her cheekbones and nose, were just like he remembered. But she had her mother's eyes, set slightly too close together and the identical gray with flecks of green. He wondered how his father was coping with this uncanny family resemblance.

The thing that struck Frank the most, however, was her composure. She appeared totally at ease, as if she'd never been away from home.

Gert, downing drinks at the Cattle Drive, was like a bad dream.

Vincent couldn't keep still. He kept jumping up to get more coffee, juice, and offered to make more toast until Portia spoke up.

"Dad, please sit down. I don't know about Frankie, but you're making me nervous as hell. We can fend for ourselves."

Chastened, Vincent joined the conversation. The three of them caught up on their lives. Portia was especially interested in hearing about Leo's family, since she had never met Claire, Francine, or Sam.

After trying to clear the table and being shooed away by his daughter, Vincent took the leash down from its hook next to the door. The dog was on her feet in an instant.

"We old timers are going out for a walk while you two continue to catch up on your lives."

After they left, Portia got up from the table to get them more coffee.

That was when he saw his sister's wrists, both of them, crisscrossed with horizontal scars. They were shockingly red, so much so that they didn't look real. It was as if Portia had drawn the lines with crimson nail polish. He only hoped Vincent hadn't noticed.

"Portia, I met Gertrude Kleindienst last night."

"Who?"

"She told me you met online and gave her some kind of technical support—"

Portia interrupted him. "Oh, that. I'd almost forgotten who she was. The whole thingamajig was totally innocent. Believe me."

"What she said was very upsetting. Are you planning to hurt someone?"

"Frankie, you have to believe me. I wouldn't hurt a fly."

5.

Leo was disappointed that the kids weren't coming to Egg Rock.

Francine was taking the T into Boston to meet up with friends from the conservatory. Without a musician in either his or Claire's families, Leo considered his daughter's musical talent a happy genetic mutation.

Sam, as usual, was upstairs in his room on the computer. Although he had lobbied hard to commute from home his freshman year at MIT, his parents insisted that he live on campus.

"That's the best part of the college experience," Leo argued.

"I don't give a shit about the 'college experience,'" Sam grumbled. "I just want to learn stuff."

In the beginning, he spent every weekend back at the house, but his home visits came to an abrupt end once he met up with Beatrix, another computer whiz, during his second semester.

Leo joked that Francine got the social gene and Sam the antisocial one.

The bottom line was that getting either of them to come along to meet their Aunt Portia wasn't worth the fuss.

Leo lowered his window and drew in a deep breath as they exited the Squimway for the mile-long causeway. Whenever he tasted that air, he knew he was home.

"The paper said that the tides will be extra high over the weekend, with the full moon."

"That's why they built the sea wall." Leo pointed to the flat-topped concrete barrier between the road and the harbor. Just then a seagull, soaring the height of a six-story building, released a clam from its talons. The shell crashed on the top of the wall as they passed, and Leo watched through the rearview mirror as the graceful bird swooped down for its lunch.

"When I was a kid, high tides would spill over the road once or twice a month. The highway department would be out with their pumps, and then they'd push the sand off the road with a snowplow. I'm sure that's an expense the town is happy to be rid of."

At the end of the causeway sat Little Egg Rock, the smaller and steeper of the two islands. Little Egg sported all the accoutrements one would expect in an up-to-date town. High-tech engineering allowed buildings to be stacked on its cliffs, precisely angled to catch the best view. Most bristled with satellite dishes, roof decks. SUVs were squeezed into tiny driveways.

Once clear of Little Egg, they came to the smaller causeway connecting the two islands. On the ocean side of the road sat the abandoned life-saving station, its windows covered with plywood.

The rock itself sat a mile off shore, its off-white top reflecting the morning sun.

They passed the brick town hall with a huge white flagpole in the middle of its front lawn, its flag hanging limply in the late morning calm. The scene resembled a golf course laid out for giants.

"Strange to see the flag not at half-mast," Claire murmured.

"You're probably thinking of Memorial Day."

Claire came to the parade to please her new husband. Leo was handsome in his uniform as he strode by, and the high school band was terrific. But as she watched the happy, young families cheering groups of Brownies and Sea Scouts who marched by with the scoutmasters barely keeping them in control, she couldn't get her brother, Paul, out of her mind.

The night before he went away, she and Paul stayed up, talking about everything. They sat at the kitchen table with its ancient oil-cloth covering, drinking coffee, while snow filtered down outside the big picture window overlooking the Penobscot. That was when he told her about how much he wanted a family of his own.

Paul Beauregard got the shaft in a war people chose to ignore, these same people who were having such a grand time. She wanted to dash up to the reviewing stand and scream at the top of her lungs, "Hey, you guys, in case you forgot, this is Memorial Day, not the Fourth of July!"

Leo never asked her to attend the parade again. For her part, Claire understood Leo's need to participate, making sure that he could go every year, rain or shine. He tried to stay home the year both kids had the chickenpox, but she insisted that he march.

"You need to do it, and Paul would want you to go."

"But, sweetheart, Paul never met me."

"Through me he has."

They drove by the ivy-covered library, the cemetery, and the run-down Vets Club before reaching Eighty Steps Beach at the eastern-most point of the island. It was Leo's favorite place on earth. From there, the rock looked huge. The beach sat far below the shore road and was flanked by two jagged outcroppings. It had been named for the number of steps down a wooden staircase from the road, but over the years, erosion had required twenty additional steps to be built.

As they gazed at Eighty Steps and the Rock itself looming off shore, Claire asked him what more she should know about Portia.

"She left home after her mother died. Frank never told me directly, but he hinted that his sister and father had an argument, and she ran away."

"I remember all that, and the fact that she began to write her father some time later."

"Years later. Do you remember Uncle Vincent showing us a letter from her?"

"Sure. We were just married then. I was grateful that he let me see it. That made me a member of the family. What was she like as a little kid?"

Leo thought a minute.

"Do you know the Gettysburg Address story?"

"No. Did she recite it?"

"Yep, when she was in the sixth grade. It was a big deal to be chosen for the Memorial Day recitation, so the whole family showed up to cheer her on. Uncle Vinny and Aunt Patty stood right up front. Frankie and I were Sea Scouts and watched with our troop."

"You must have been cute, you two, in your little uniforms."

"My mom and dad were there, too. My mother didn't get to the parade as a rule, because she was always getting lunch together for the whole gang.

"Father Mal started with the invocation, and once he sat down, it was Portia's turn."

"Father Mal? I never met him."

"He was strictly old school, the 'pray, pay, and obey' type, but there was something odd about him. Kids have some kind of sixth sense about grownups—who's okay and who isn't—and the kids I hung around with were wary of him. My mother and aunt felt that Mal should be canonized on the spot, and Vincent, who felt that Portia was kind of a wild child, believed that Father Mal could make her more disciplined through religious instruction."

"What about the Gettysburg Address?"

"Well, Portia started off with great confidence. Once she got through 'Now we are engaged in a great civil war …,' however, she stopped cold. She stood there for what seemed an eternity, just staring, and the crowd, which had been pretty quiet, became absolutely silent.

"Finally Father Mal stepped forward, and Portia seemed to come to. She waved him off, took a deep breath, and resumed the address from the exact spot she'd stopped, flawlessly."

"It sounds like she had a petit mal."

"Yep. Anyway, the priest gave her a hug, and the whole place erupted in applause and cheers."

"Did she see a doctor or anything?"

"Your guess is as good as mine. We didn't talk about stuff like that back then."

Uncle Vincent's house came into view on the island's westernmost point, and Leo slowed to make the turn.

As always, he gave his old house next door a glance on the way in.

6.

Dan was pleased to see Father Joe Maguire drive onto the monastery property at the scheduled time, alone, without the press in pursuit. Since he had the overnight bags ready, it took no time for the Boss to wave good-bye to his hosts and climb in.

Once underway, Dan finally told him what he knew about the apparition.

The archbishop listened quietly, palm under chin in what Dan called his "Thinker" pose, and then gazed at the passing countryside before responding.

"Danny, thanks for keeping me in the dark. You understand how much I needed this time for reflection. I would have been upset if you'd interrupted that."

Father Joe volunteered that nothing new had happened since he'd spoken with Dan around midnight.

On the interstate, Dan was happy to see Joe blend into the flow of traffic in the middle lane, letting the more aggressive drivers fly by. He thought about Joe's first day on the job.

"What about that nickname of yours?"

"Cowboy? Oh I got stuck with that in high school 'cause I liked to drive fast. But those days are over, Dan."

Dan was surprised to see the archbishop napping, especially after five days away from it all. Whenever they traveled by car, the Boss would pull papers out of his briefcase and catch up on work.

Perhaps it had something to do with not seeing the Boss for a while, but the archbishop looked older and frailer. For a moment, he worried that it might not be a nap, but something more ominous, but the Boss's regular, relaxed breathing reassured him.

Dan remembered a remark Frank Mulcahy made over dinner a couple of weeks earlier about "glorified babysitters." He said that Dan had been babysitting longer than most, but nowhere near Father Frank's record.

"How long have you been at it?"

"Seven years and two months."

"You know I was Cardinal Campion's secretary for close to ten years."

"Everybody knew that you were setting records. We were calling you the Hank Aaron of secretaries."

"Looking back on it, I stayed too long. Of course, the job was exciting, meeting all sorts of people and traveling all over the world, but …"

"You don't feel like a real priest."

"Exactly, Dan. It may sound corny, but in this job, you never shepherd your own flock. And that's what being a priest is all about. Everybody in the job gets to feel that way sooner or later. It's no different for the auxiliaries. They feel honored to be named bishops, as they should, but sooner or later, they miss being real priests."

That conversation convinced him that it was time to go. He only needed the right moment to sit down with the archbishop to request a transfer to a parish, but now he'd need to hold off until this Virgin-in-the-Window problem blew over.

Being the archbishop's secretary juiced up his *curriculum vitae* all right, but he would never rise in the organization without running his own parish. At an earlier dinner, Frank Mulcahy had likened parish work to military combat experience.

"Pentagon desk jockeys rarely make general," was the way he put it.

Being the pastor of a busy parish would be a smart career move. With that added to his CV, he'd have a shot at making bishop himself someday.

7.

Father Guido watched the hospital chapel fill up a good half hour before the noon Mass. This was the kind of crowd he could only have dreamed of before the Virgin's appearance, and with overflow already filling up the hospital lobby, they were on track to double Tuesday's attendance.

Just then, the door between the sacristy and the hospital courtyard opened, and Dr. Cronin walked in.

He shook Guido's hand like an old friend, as if their confrontation in the gift shop never took place.

"What a stupendous turnout, Father! I have already arranged for large screen TVs in the lobby and courtyard for tomorrow's Mass. I can guarantee that all the pilgrims witnessing this miracle can share the Eucharist with you."

With that, he shook hands with Sister Agneta and the seminarian and exited for his reserved seat in the front pew.

Ordinarily, Guido spent Wednesday and Thursday nights at

the family home in Gull, to recharge his batteries and give his sister, Marilena, a chance to fuss over him. Besides, her cooking was always a welcome respite from the steam table at the hospital cafeteria.

This week was hardly ordinary, but he needed to get away for an overnight. As usual, Father Tally from Saint Brendan's in Faneuil Center would cover for emergencies.

The crush of people elbowing each other to get a better view of the window, the mini-cams thrust into his face without warning, and the theme-park atmosphere were all getting to him. He'd logged only a few hours of sleep since Monday, and he felt that eight peaceful hours in his bed at the beach house could get him through the rest of the week.

Then he thought about the archbishop. Father Dan Skerry, who looked more like a wrestler than a priest, told him on the phone that the archbishop would be back this afternoon. If Father Skerry did as he asked and explained to the archbishop how *real* the Holy Mother was, Guido had done his job.

8.

The family ate lunch on the screened porch off the kitchen, with its view of Madeline Mulcahy's garden. Echo, banished to the yard, gazed covetously at the cold cuts and potato salad on the table.

Vincent, in the role of patriarch, began the conversation.

"Leo, your cousin here took a course in meteorology and another in astronomy at that college she works for. And I thought California was all movie stars and hippies! I asked her whether the course was astronomy or astrology, and she assured me it was the former."

Portia smiled indulgently at her father.

Leo had pictured her as tiny but had expected her to get a little taller or at least fill out a bit. But take away the salt-and-pepper hair and she looked just like the little girl who recited the Gettysburg Address.

The humans were too busy to notice the sky cloud up, but Echo was already scratching the screen door before the first thunder clap. Once Vincent let her inside, she shot upstairs to hide under Vincent and Maddy's big four-poster.

With that, a lightning bolt struck something out on the point, and the crackle of thunder followed a split-second later.

Everybody scurried into the kitchen just as the skies opened up.

As the rain pounded the roof, Leo helped his uncle go from window to window, making sure each was closed tight, while Portia ran upstairs to secure the second floor.

"This is the first good storm we've had all summer. I was afraid we'd miss out."

Later, while rinsing the lunch dishes, Portia asked Claire if she'd ever heard the story about the Gettysburg Address.

"Funny you'd ask. Leo told me the story this morning."

"What did you think, being a nurse and all?"

"It sounds like you had a petit mal seizure."

"That's what it was, all right. Friends kept telling me about 'spells' where I'd just go blank for a few seconds, but I figured it was just some quirk I'd grow out of. I had no idea that they were serious until I had a full-blown seizure one day while walking down a street in San Francisco and woke up in the hospital. Now I take medication every day and haven't had any kind of spell since."

"You must be relieved that your condition is taken care of."

"Yes and no, Claire."

"I don't understand."

"It won't be completely taken care of until I understand what brought the condition on in the first place."

"I don't think that anyone can explain most seizures."

"Psychological trauma can cause the problem."

"Really? I've heard of stress making seizures more frequent, and I understand how a physical injury can cause a scar on the surface of the brain that can cause seizures. I never heard about psychological trauma being the cause."

"Believe me, Claire. I'm living proof."

Claire, feeling that she'd asked enough questions, invited Portia to join her outside, where Leo was getting the car ready for the trip home and Vincent was showing the kids his flower beds.

The rain had stopped as abruptly as it had started, and the wet grass, the garage roof, and the puddles in the driveway were steaming under the August sun.

Claire turned to Vincent.

"Can you and Portia make it to Paul's memorial service on Friday? Father Guido will celebrate the Mass at Saint Kay's. I reserved a private room at the Cattle Drive for lunch afterward."

Vincent looked at his daughter before answering.

"Absolutely! While we're at it, Portia and I will get a look at the window—see what the fuss is all about."

9.

Guido never tired of the water taxi. During the summer, he'd leave the car down in Gull and use the water taxi every week, and in winter, he'd make the voyage if it wasn't too stormy. He was a regular, and the fellow collecting tickets at the end of the ramp recognized him.

"Father, looks like you picked the best day of the year to make the trip."

The two o'clock boat was only a quarter full, giving Guido his choice of seats topside where he could get a 360-degree view. As the craft threaded its way through the harbor islands, the Boston skyline dwindled behind him, and he strained his eyes to catch the earliest glimpse of Gull.

The water treatment plant at Deer Island dominated the east horizon once the craft got past the airport. But after Deer Island, the view north opened up all the way to Squimset and the town of Egg Rock.

A mass of inky clouds sat directly over Egg Rock. He hoped that their storm was traveling out to sea. Otherwise, he'd get soaked walking up to the house from the ferry landing.

He thought about the Mulcahy clan, proud Egg Rockers, who never missed an opportunity to tell people where they came from. Leo kept a replica of the rock itself on his office desk as a paperweight.

"Carved out of a piece of the rock itself," he said proudly during one of Guido's checkups.

Minutes later, the catamaran slowed as they approached Gull's tiny harbor.

The della Chiesa family cottage was downtown, right behind the seawall that was rebuilt after the blizzard of '78. The basement flooded during the storm, and they had to wait days before the fire department got around to pumping them out. Mama was in her early eighties then, and they kept her bundled up in front of the fireplace until the power came back on.

He studied the hundred-year-old Victorian as the vessel approached the weathered pier. Guido and his sister had the "gingerbread" detail along the roof line restored right after Easter, and it looked great from the boat.

Their grandfather had bought the run-down summer cottage during the Great Depression and spent the rest of his life getting it winterized and up-to-date. In recent years, Marilena occupied it year-round, although the deed was in Guido's name. It was ideal for her, with only a short commute for her job at a nursing home two towns away, and a perfect refuge for him.

On his last overnight, the two of them got talking about the old house after dinner. Since they had no close relatives, they talked about leaving it to the Church as a retreat house.

"After all, that's what it's been for me all these years," Guido had said while drying the dishes.

Refreshed by his ride, he walked the two blocks to the house without slowing down. At the door, he was thrilled that for the first time in ages he wasn't short of breath and his feet didn't ache. Once inside, however, his euphoria vanished when he saw a blue-and-orange FedEx envelope on the floor beneath the letter slot.

He couldn't think of anybody who'd be sending him something like this.

The FedEx contained three sheets of paper held together by a single staple in the upper left-hand corner. The top sheet consisted of a photocopy of Kevin Sheehan's death notice. It looked identical to the copy Father Guido kept with Kevin's other papers. It was centered neatly on the standard office-size sheet, and under it someone had typed the date, July 5, 1990. Father Guido already knew that Kevin had a heart attack at a July 4 cookout that year and was pronounced dead on arrival at the hospital. He started reading, in spite of remembering every word. "Sheehan, Kevin J., suddenly, on July 4, husband of …"

His heart was beating so hard that he thought his chest would explode. He rushed across the room to check his desk. Thankfully, nothing looked disturbed, and the drawers were locked.

He took a deep breath and turned to page two. Centered on it with the same geometric exactness was a copy of another death notice, this time for Thomas Rowley Jr. It, too, had the date neatly typed below: 12/28/94. "Unexpectedly, December 27, in Faneuil, son of …" Father Guido understood that the euphemism "unexpected" was often the journalistic code for suicide.

He felt physically ill. His heart wasn't pounding quite so hard, but he felt just like he did one time when he made the ferry trip to Gull in a fierce winter storm. That episode ended with his leaning over the rail and heaving up his breakfast.

To steady himself, he sat at his desk and focused on the mementos he'd placed there. He knew that Marilena dusted everything carefully a couple of times a week but never really *touched* anything. There had never been a conversation about it, but his sister knew that the desk was the only place in the house that was his private domain.

He studied the Chelsea clock with the inscription.

Father Guido
Always there in our hour of need

It had been given to him by the Saint Kay's medical staff at the time of his silver jubilee. Next to the clock sat a framed picture of him, flanked by Marilena and his dear mother the day he was ordained.

The nausea slowly resolved.

Finally, he was ready for page three. The format was identical, with another death notice centered on the page and the date typed below.

"Unexpectedly, in Gull, August 17, the Reverend Guido della Chiesa, son of the late Mario and Concetta. He is survived by his devoted sister, Marilena. Late Catholic chaplain, Saint Catherine's Hospital, Faneuil. Full notice in tomorrow's editions."

Unexpectedly.

He looked back at the date, but it still took minute for it to sink in.

"Sweet Jesus," he whispered, "that's today!"

His heart kicked into overdrive again, but he was still able to fish the key out from under his shirt, bend over the desk, and unlock the top drawer. The key and his Miraculous Medal shared a chain around his neck and clinked together as they always did whenever he changed position.

The only time he took the chain off was when he showered and the day he went through the airport security on his trip to Aruba with Marilena last winter. His heart quickened like that when the plastic tray containing the chain disappeared under the scanner for a few seconds.

He was relieved to find the Kevin papers neatly stacked inside the desk, just as he had left them. But that gave him little comfort when he read the FedEx again.

Whoever sent him the three obituaries might just as well have rifled through his desk, scattered his personal papers all over the room, and turned the house into a crime scene.

Before things could get any worse, he walked across the room to the bay window overlooking the harbor. The view always managed to calm him. He watched the sailboats lining up for the opening in the breakwater and tried to organize his thoughts.

He could not have been more discreet about Kevin Sheehan. His occasional news gathering ceased back in 1990 when Kevin died, and the materials he had collected amounted to the yearbook pictures he had stolen years back and a total of ten newspaper articles. The only times they saw the light of day were when he'd look at them and then only when Marilena was out of the house. He'd take them out of the drawer and lay them on the desk for a few minutes before putting them back and locking them up again.

The way he saw it, Kevin himself, who never really met Guido and probably never knew he existed, was never harmed. In fact, the only person harmed was Guido himself.

But now that someone else was in on the secret, everything changed.

He glanced at the FedEx again and turned to page two.

He wondered, as he had so many times in the past, what must have been going through Tommy Rowley's mind at the end.

He remembered every detail of that cold December morning. It was gray and raw, with the wind whipping through the few remaining leaves on the trees. Gusts blew the leaves on the ground into the corners of the hospital buildings where they arranged themselves into tiny cyclonic funnels.

He was back in his room after morning rounds when Pat Kaminski knocked on his door and gave him the news. It looked like the Rowley boy had shot himself up by the Mount of Olives ball field. "They're going to need you up at the school, Father. I can have one of my men drive you over."

He spent the day at the Mount, counseling and praying with teachers and students who drifted up there hour after hour. The school was officially closed for Christmas break, but that didn't seem to matter. Then he celebrated an impromptu Mass in the Pius XII Auditorium late in the afternoon. There was no formal announcement, but word got out, and the place was jammed.

He had first met Tommy Rowley three years earlier when Guido was filling in for the school chaplain, who was recovering from prostate surgery.

The freshman had sought out the priest to talk about the Holy Spirit. Times had changed for the better since Guido's childhood, when the last thing on earth you'd do would be make an appointment with a priest to discuss anything. Besides, when he was a kid, the Church still called the third member of the trinity the Holy Ghost, and nobody wanted to spend time on such a scary subject.

Right away, the boy announced that he really came by to talk about entering religious life. He wasn't trying to "pull a fast one," as he put it, by changing the subject, because he could feel the Holy Spirit guiding him in that direction. Guido had certainly thought about becoming a priest when he was fourteen and saw much of himself in the youngster. Tommy asked lots of questions about seminary life and the joys of being a priest, and Father Guido enjoyed talking about his teenage years when he was going through the same process of priestly formation.

They met again soon after, for a walk along the Charles, chatting about whatever came into their heads—theology, priestly life, even celibacy.

Just before the last day of school, they visited the seminary, where Guido had arranged to have lunch at the rector's table, followed by a leisurely walk through Little Rome.

But Tommy Rowley was a different person when they met again in the fall. Pale and subdued, he sat and looked down at the floor for what seemed an eternity.

Guido sat and waited.

When Tommy finally spoke, his voice was deeper. He was a full-fledged adolescent now.

"We can forget about what we talked about last spring. The Holy Spirit has lost interest in me. I'll never be a priest." He spoke quietly, but his eyes flashed with anger.

"Can you explain?"

He answered mechanically, as if reading a paragraph from a textbook.

"I'm attracted to boys."

After swallowing hard, he went on.

"I looked up my problem in the new Catechism *in the library."*

He pulled a sheet of paper from his backpack.

Guido raised his hand.

"You don't need to read it, Tommy. I've read the words 'grave depravity' and 'intrinsically disordered' more times than I can count."

He retrieved the box of tissues from the top drawer of his desk. While the boy blew his nose, Guido sat back in his chair and tried to pray, but no prayer came.

What kind of a priest was he? The boy was waiting for him to say something, but no words came.

Tommy Rowley, God bless him, was not about to spend his life pretending. This kid had the guts to speak up. Guido suppressed the urge to embrace the boy, just as the boy's father might, and tell him that everything would be all right.

Instead, he walked around the desk to where the boy was sitting and shook his hand as if they were finishing up a routine meeting.

Then he opened the door and said, "Thanks for coming in today. Come back again and we'll talk more."

Weeks and then months passed, but Thomas Rowley Jr. never came back.

Whoever sent the FedEx made the wrong assumptions but came to the right conclusions.

Father Guido never broke his vow of chastity, but he had known for years that he had done something far worse.

He'd turned his back on this boy who desperately needed his help … in order to keep his own secret hidden.

Caring for all the cancer patients on earth would never atone for what he didn't do for Tommy Rowley.

He picked up the Chelsea clock with its inscription about "always there in our time of need," carried it out to the back of the house, and tossed it over the seawall into the ocean.

Then he made his way to the garage.

10.

Tom Rowley let out a hearty belch. The Saint Kay's braised beef must have been the culprit. The server, Dotty or Dolly, he wasn't sure which, gave him extra because she remembered it was one of his favorites.

How Helen hated it when he let out a belch like that!

He belched again, not so forcefully this time, switched on the desk lamp, and surveyed his tiny office. Unlike the apartment, he had this place totally organized. His desktop was spotless, his in-box was emptied, and all his files were up-to-date.

His PC sat on a small table to his right, the screensaver showing bacteria as big as Tootsie Rolls dividing contentedly.

The bookcase behind his desk held reference books in general medicine, infectious disease, and microbiology. On the bottom shelf were medical journals stacked in chronological order, the most recent on top.

He glanced at the Purple Heart, sitting snugly in its glass case on the top shelf.

Next to the door to his personal lab, he kept his tularemia notes locked securely in an unobtrusive, brown metal cabinet. A third door on the inside wall led to an exam room where he saw an occasional private patient.

The only adornment in the office was a photograph of Dr. Edward Francis, the man who put tularemia on the map.

He remembered Claire Mulcahy studying the sepia photograph in its black lacquered frame, like the ones traditionally used for diplomas. He had just hired her as his nurse practitioner.

"Who's that, Dr. Rowley? One of your teachers?"

"My favorite, Claire, my absolute favorite."

His love affair with tularemia started only weeks after he'd completed his training and joined the Saint Kay's medical staff. He made a difficult and rare diagnosis of tularemia on a critically ill patient, probably saving his life. Soon, other cases popped up, and before he knew it, young Tom Rowley was dealing with a full-blown epidemic—and had become Boston's tularemia expert overnight.

Then, without warning, a team from the CDC in Atlanta swooped in and took over without much more to say than howdy.

Tom felt like a small-town police chief who singlehandedly tracked down a serial killer only to be upstaged and outmaneuvered by the FBI. The CDC froze him out and took all the credit for managing the crisis, allowing their young investigators to advance their careers. As a final slap in the face, Tom's original work on the index case wasn't even given a footnote in the official reports of the outbreak

And after all these years, he was still royally pissed.

11.

Father Guido looked at his watch. Marilena wouldn't get back from work for another two hours.

He walked quickly into the garage and pulled the overhead door down behind him. He had never physically rehearsed what he was about to do, but he'd thought about it enough to make him feel as if he had.

After taping the lime-colored garden hose to the tailpipe and placing the other end inside the car, he sat in the driver's seat. He started to buckle the seatbelt and actually laughed out loud when it dawned on him that the restraint wouldn't be necessary for this trip.

He slipped the key into the ignition as if he were heading out on an errand, but then his fingers froze. He needed a minute to think about what he was doing, to say a final prayer.

"… Holy Mary Mother of God, pray for us sinners now and at the hour of our death. Amen."

He lost track of the number of Hail Marys he recited, but as the prayers piled up, things got clearer.

It dawned on him that Marilena would be the one to find the body, slumped over the steering wheel. Simply imagining that kept him from turning the key. Meanwhile, he kept on praying and thinking.

Whoever sent the FedEx expected that he'd go away quietly!

He'd receive a good Catholic funeral at the little church in Gull. If he was lucky, the archbishop would send one of his auxiliaries down to concelebrate the Mass, but since there'd be a hint of scandal, no one might be sent from Little Rome. Of course, even if the pope himself said the Mass, the rumors wouldn't stop.

He could hear the nurses: "Who would ever have guessed that our little Father Guido was a pervert?"

Before long, Marilena would hear.

His hands were shaking, but he was able to unhitch the hose and put it back with the rakes and snow shovels in the corner of the garage.

Once in the house, he was shaking all over, the way he did once when he got the flu. He pulled his afghan out of the closet, sat in his favorite chair, pushed it to the recline position, and covered himself to get warm. After that, he wasn't sure whether he dozed off or not.

But there was no question of what he saw. Our Lady appeared right there in his picture window. She looked much like she did up at Saint Kay's, only larger and more distinct. The light reflected off her gold crown and surrounded her entire figure. She smiled at him just like she did up at Saint Kay's. Then she spoke.

"Father Guido, I am answering your prayers. You have been a good and faithful priest and have honored my Son by caring for the sickest and most vulnerable of the human family. He is most pleased."

"But, Blessed Mother, I turned my back—"

"Dear Guido, life is more complicated than that. I can tell you that Tommy did not feel rejected by you. Others were responsible for his death."

Before he could ask where Tommy was now, she smiled again and rose high over the harbor before disappearing in the clouds.

Just then, the telephone rang, and Father Guido sat up straight in his recliner.

12.

Like most Bostonians, the archbishop had a love-hate relationship with Channel Six. He disapproved of their "tabloid, police-blotter journalism," but when there was important local news, it was the channel he chose to watch.

During his first year as archbishop of Boston, he told Dan that he was thinking of Channel Six in particular while preparing one of his most forceful sermons.

It was the first Sunday of Advent, the time of anticipation and preparation for the "good news" of Our Savior's birth, and the first Christmas season for the new archbishop. Little did he know that his sermon about "good news" would *make* news.

"Our airwaves are cluttered with graphic violence, hate language, and the comings and goings of celebrities, leaving little space for the 'good news' that happens every day. My plea to the TV, radio, and newspapers of our city is to review their priorities and restore balance. Take the Church's social outreach programs to our most needy citizens, for instance. No one ever hears about that. The 'good news' of what good people do is drowned out by sensationalism. It's time for our friends in the media to take their eyes off the almighty dollar for a minute and reclaim their social conscience." The response to the sermon was swift and frightening. Newspaper editorials accused the archbishop of meddling with a free press. Overnight, media executives serving on the boards of Catholic Charities, Saint Kay's Hospital, Saint Luke's Seminary, and the archdiocesan Secretariat of Education all threatened to resign. Bankers and CEOs were next in line.

The impact would have been catastrophic, since these trustees gave not only their time and expertise to the Church, but they and their corporations kicked in millions every year. Only by pleading with each board member personally was the archbishop able to avert a disaster. Lesson learned, he toned down public utterances from then on, but the damage was done. When the sexual abuse crisis erupted a year later, the media was relentless.

And ready to get even.

"Danny, it's almost six o'clock. Would you tune in 'Six at Six'?"

The lead story, of course, was the "Faneuil Miracle."

"Good evening from Saint Katherine's Hospital." It was that woman reporter, in a business suit for a change.

The archbishop told Dan that maybe it was a miracle after all, since Corinne Caruthers had changed out of her provocative attire for the occasion.

"This is day three of the appearance of the Virgin Mary on a large window here at Saint Kay's, and the crowds of pilgrims just keep getting bigger and bigger. Tour buses with license plates from as far away as Michigan and Indiana have been spotted on Hospital Drive, and every parking space within a two-mile radius of the hospital is filled. We have with us here a couple who drove all night from their home in Louisville to witness the miracle for themselves."

Sister Philippe, the archbishop's housekeeper, was setting down their supper of tomato soup and grilled cheese sandwiches when an older couple resembling George and Barbara Bush appeared on the screen.

The woman spoke for both of them, while her husband, a wiry fellow wearing a *Jesus is Lord* baseball cap, looked on.

"We're running on pure adrenaline now," she explained, shaking an overgrown mane of snow-white hair out of her eyes. "All I can say is that everyone on the face of the earth should come to see the Blessed Virgin. Tell her your troubles, and she will see to it that your prayers are answered."

The archbishop got up from his seat and switched off the set. Father Dan reminded himself to get the remote fixed.

"Eddie Cronin must feel like he's died and gone to heaven. Next thing we'll hear, he'll be selling tickets."

"I spoke to Father Guido about an hour ago, Archbishop. He was down at his house in Gull for the day. He told me that he needed to have a night away from the media circus up at Saint Kay's."

"I can understand that."

"I think I awakened him from a nap. I already told you about my telephone conversation with him on Monday."

"Yes, Danny, when you told him that Eddie Cronin didn't own him."

"Archbishop, Guido has been transformed. Instead of hemming and hawing, he's speaking his mind. I never imagined I could be so persuasive."

"Believe me, Danny, you can be when you put your mind to it."

"Guido tells me that Eddie is, as you put it, selling tickets, or the next best thing.

"He bought a car-load of rosaries, medals, scapulars, pictures, and even T-shirts from a wholesaler and tried to get little Guido to bless them before selling them in the hospital gift shop."

"And what did Guido do?"

"Gave Eddie a sermonette on simony, and Eddie backed down, sort of. He's now selling the stuff without the blessing. I hear that he's had a souvenir stand built nearby so that the 'pilgrims' can make their purchases on the spot. Needless to say, all major credit cards are accepted."

"Good for Guido! I never thought he'd have the testicular fortitude to refuse Dr. Edward Cronin."

Father Dan had never before heard the Boss use such vivid anatomic language.

"Your Excellency, start eating before your food gets cold."

"I'm not hungry, Danny. You can have my sandwich if you like."

13.

The single window in Tom Rowley's office looked over the lawn that separated the research wing from the executive offices across the courtyard. The power plant's yellow brick chimney was visible in the distance.

Taking in the view, he saw the lights go on up in Eddie Cronin's office.

The lab was a quarter the size of his office on the other side of the locked door. It was originally a supply room, and the hospital still had it listed as such on its master plan. Not even Eddie Cronin had an inkling that Tom had converted the space into a state-of-the-art laboratory.

He had been outfitting and updating the place for years, doing the carpentry himself and bringing pieces of equipment section by section from home.

He used the lab only on nights and weekends when he could be assured of privacy, so that people like Claire Mulcahy wouldn't be asking questions. One day she'd pointed to the special keypad lock on the door and asked what was inside.

When he told her that he was protecting his research papers from plagiarism, that seemed to fit her perception of Tom the Eccentric, and she stopped asking.

After slipping on a mask and gloves, he removed his culture plates from the incubator and placed them in the biological safety cabinet.

The first plate was a surprise. The cultures should have been greenish gelatinous specks at forty-eight hours, each the diameter of the head of a pin, lined up in neat rows. Instead, the plate was covered with a thick film of translucent material. The other plates were equally impressive.

He worried that his tularemia cultures had been contaminated by rapid-growing invaders, but to the naked eye, the material had the characteristic greenish-blue coloring and moist surface of the real thing.

To rule out a contaminant, he smeared a drop of the material on a slide and applied a stain. Under high power, a sea of identical organisms, tiny plump rods with only a dusting of pink from the stain, filled the field. He backed away abruptly, striking the refrigerator behind him in the cramped space—while the enormity of what he was seeing sank in.

He had a pure culture of millions of Francisella tularensis organisms, and no idea what had caused them to multiply so rapidly.

He looked at the plates again, just to be sure he wasn't hallucinating, when something else hit him. The pale green-blue cultures were—he was sure of it—the same color of Our Lady's gown out there on Leo Mulcahy's window.

He thought back to Monday morning, so angry at first that he wanted to smash the window with a brick, when the Blessed Mother smiled back at him.

Now, with the plates the color of her gown, the Virgin Mary was giving him the real explanation and sending him a signal to proceed.

All he had to do was dry the little buggers out, and he'd be in business.

"Weaponizing" his tularemia would be a simple matter. Since his little friends would be dispersed only a short distance in closed spaces, they wouldn't require any modification to make them hardier. It wasn't as if they were going to be dropped from an airplane at forty thousand feet, where they'd need to withstand big-time environmental stresses. Add to that the fact that they were so powerful that a dose of just ten would infect a healthy adult.

He shifted his weight off the bad hip by leaning against the refrigerator a minute, and when the pain eased, he started the final chore of the evening.

After cutting filter paper into a dozen strips, he spread a layer of the bacterial culture on one side of each with a lab spatula and laid them side by side in the safety cabinet to air-dry. They reminded him of coffins lined up in a cargo hold.

He stood back to survey his handiwork. Thousands of little pink rods made up this beautiful, iridescent mass. It was hard to believe that they were direct descendants of the bug that had infected his first patient twenty-five years earlier.

For years, he'd added increasing concentrations of antibiotic to the cultures, making them so antibiotic-resistant that only industrial-strength doses could kill them off.

His homegrown tularemia had become super-bugs.

Along the way, another problem had cropped up. The more antibiotic-resistant the bacteria became, the harder they were to grow. He tried every trick in the book to keep them going, but it was beginning to look like his long line of tularemia organisms was about to die of starvation or old age.

Until this latest surprise.

By morning, the bacteria would be dry enough to pack into the delivery vehicles, ready to do their work.

Finally he removed his protective gear and exited through the double safety door back into his office. He looked at the clock above his bookcase, next to the Purple Heart. Then he popped another Percocet and packed up for home.

14.

One of the worst parts of J. J.'s job was waiting for one of Spike Birdsong's calls. Eddie Cronin and his executive committee held their weekly meeting every Wednesday night in Eddie's office, and later it was J. J.'s job to give his boss, Spike, a summary of the wiretap.

Tonight's meeting had been hilarious. Eddie, fixated on the "miracle" on the window at the doctors' office building, told his inner circle that in no time the hospital would build a shrine around it and make gazillions.

He hated waiting for these late-night calls that Spike liked to call "debriefings." Waiting could take up to hours. Of course, the minute J. J. would try to do something else, Spike would call.

While waiting, he thought back to his first dinner with Spike, outside Mobile. That was the night he learned he wouldn't be lugging around drug samples forever. J. J. Rideout would be going places.

Spike waved from a booth as soon as J. J. appeared. He was a few minutes late, and Spike looked pissed. Spike had little patience for people being late, even though he kept people waiting all the time.

"I almost sent out a search party, ol' buddy."

"Sorry, Spike. I made a couple of wrong turns."

"I reckoned you'd already discovered this joint. Hottest servers this side of N'awlins."

J. J. soon discovered what Spike was talking about. The waitress towered over him, wrapped in the franchise's signature miniskirt and a skin-tight top emblazoned with a large pelican. Its eyes were spread apart just enough to accommodate the double O of "Roost" stenciled across her chest.

While she swiveled across to the bar for their drinks, Spike got down to business.

"You got the official 399 tutorial. Now I'll tell you the important stuff. You know that it's a pill that helps a guy get an erection."

"That's about it, Spike."

"Now I'm gonna tell you about two other thing this itty-bitty capsule does," he continued, after taking a drag on his cigarette and

blowing a couple of smoke rings. "It's also a birth control drug, and—get this—it makes your ding-dong bigger!"

"Wow! What about the number 399?"

"Ah, shit, J. J., we made that up! I bet you thought we tested 398 other drugs first. Nope, it was the first. Beginner's luck, I guess."

Spike's call to his cell roused J. J. from his reverie.

"Let's hear the latest bullshit, ol' buddy."

It took J. J. only a couple of minutes to summarize the ninety-minute meeting for his boss. As usual, Eddie had done most of the talking, but he was upbeat for the first time J. J. could remember. It was a whole new ballgame, was the way Eddie put it. With the discovery of the Virgin Mary on the window, Saint Kay's would make a fortune, and Eddie and friends would be free of J. J., Spike Birdsong, and American Pharmaceutical Enterprises—and their blackmail.

Spike laughed drily. J. J. could picture the sneer on his boss's face.

"Horse's ass! We have those guys by the balls, and some funny-colored window ain't goin' to change that. Do you remember my little trip up there last winter?"

J. J. wasn't likely to forget.

Spike had requested a meeting with Eddie and the Executive Committee to discuss a "mutually beneficial" business arrangement. A stenographer would not be necessary, he added, since the information would be confidential.

Eddie had no problem with that, since his committee never kept minutes anyway.

Spike started his talk with a description of AP 399's magical powers, adding that it wasn't quite ready to be marketed. Obviously knowing his audience, he predicted that the drug would be promoted only as an erectile dysfunction drug, since contraceptives were "against some religions, especially up north." The "size issue" he added, would be "tricky to advertise" but would spread fast enough by word of mouth.

He then walked over to one of the committee members, Andrew Pinkham, an old friend of Eddie's, and shook his hand.

"Mr. Pinkham, I hear you're called The Vitamin King in these parts. How many of them health food operations you got up an' runnin'?"

"Twelve outlets in Massachusetts and two in New Hampshire so far," he said proudly.

"That brings me to one last piece of news about AP 399. It's a natural product, not a drug. Who knows? Maybe we can partner up sometime."

Afterward, Spike gave a PowerPoint presentation of all twenty-three drugs in APE's product line while J. J. passed out samples.

"I know I can be candid with you, gentlemen. Our products are no better than our competitors', but no worse either."

Spike looked around to make sure he had everyone's attention.

"From what I hear, we're making this offer at an opportune time."

He nodded to J. J., who passed manila folders around the table.

"As you can see, we're aware of the empty retirement fund, the overdue loans to banks, and your profit-sharin' arrangement, personally run by my new friend Mr. Pinkham. If this information got into the wrong hands …"

He stopped there, and the only sound in the room came from Eddie clicking his ballpoint.

"Don't worry, Eddie. J. J. will pick up the files and," he said, pointing to the state-of-the-art console behind the desk, "feed them to your personal shreddin' machine. It'll chew those suckers up like a hound dawg at a barbecue."

There were no questions.

On the way to the airport the next morning, Spike had one more assignment for J. J.

"Tell Eddie that AP 399 will be ready much sooner than we expected. And yeah, tell him to call it Triple Play from now on."

15.

Heading back from the funeral home along Charles River Drive, Kitty pointed out a steep hill at a sharp bend in the river.

"Did Bridget ever tell you about the Mount, Buzzy?"

"The Mount?"

"Sorry. That's the nickname. Mount of Olives. You know, the school."

"Sure. Bridget calls it Eunice's third child."

"She *was* involved in getting it started."

"Weren't you a student there, too?"

"Yep, for twelve years. I was in the first class that graduated."

"On the way up from Woonsocket yesterday, we talked a lot about your mom, as you can imagine … and Bridget mentioned Mount of Olives. Eunice is still a mystery to her, and Bridget wanted to hear more about the place. Have you kept up with what's going on up there?"

"Oh, yes. I guess I never told you that I'm on the board."

"That's news to me, and I'm sure Bridget doesn't know."

"Buzzy, I have an idea. It would involve you doing me a big favor."

"Shoot."

"I'll give her a tour. That way she might get a better idea of the school, and it would give us a quiet place to just talk. Could you watch the kids for an hour or so?"

Minutes after getting back, they had everything arranged, and the girls were on their way.

After the last turn of the driveway, the Piersall "mansion" stood before them.

"Pretty for a reform school," Bridget said.

"I can see why'd you'd say that, but it wasn't anything like that, even when I was a kid. When it came to religion, though, the teachers could be a little rigid. The truth was the truth, and that was it. There was a so-called 'deposit of faith' that you simply had to accept. In fact, my favorite teacher, a young nun, was suddenly 'transferred' for encouraging us to ask questions."

"Where did she go?"

"I could never find out."

Once out of the car, Kitty led her sister through a wooded area to the playing fields, where they could get the best views.

"What about the Mount now? I bet it's different with you running the place."

"I'm only a member of the board, Bridget."

"You know what I mean."

"It's a good school. We're getting kids into top colleges. But we had a crisis a few years ago when a student committed suicide. He shot himself in that little patch of woods by the ball field."

Bridget turned and looked back.

"We just walked through there."

"Of course there was an inquiry, and the kid's parents came close to suing the school."

"Were you involved?"

"We both were. I was already on the board by then, and Eddie knew the boy's father from the hospital. When Momma heard the story, she cried and cried. I don't think she ever got over it."

"What a nightmare!"

"It was, but it made us do some major soul-searching."

"And?"

"We brought in a consultant and ended up firing a couple of teachers, but that was only the start. It's taken years, but the school is a much more open and diverse community today. And the kids are encouraged to ask all sorts of questions."

"Did they ever find out why the boy killed himself?"

"He was bullied."

"Is that the whole story?"

"No. He was bullied because he was gay."

"Oh my God!"

"And the Catholic teaching—"

"I know all about the teaching! Kitty, do you love my Brian?"

"You know I do, Bridget. I adore both your boys."

"Kitty, my Brian is gay."

Now that the ice was broken, Kitty let her sister in on her latest worry. Archbishop Quilty, the trustee chair, had convened a special meeting of the board for Saturday. Rumor had it that he'd be announcing an "audit" by a committee of bishops from out of state—to be sure that with all its openness, Mount of Olives hadn't lost sight of "fundamental Catholic teaching."

"I'm worried sick, Bridget. The Mount has come a long way since that terrible day when the boy killed himself. This 'audit' could turn back the clock and destroy everything we've achieved."

16.

The archbishop filled both cups from the carafe that Sister Philippe left when she cleared the table.

"What now, Danny?"

No one on the face of the earth would have dared call 275-pound Father Dan Skerry *Danny* before he went to work for the archbishop. Not even his mother! He'd never forget his first day of work. The Boss started calling him by that name in the first hour, and the new secretary was afraid to object. So it stuck. And it was only a matter of time before the chancery staff was calling him Danny Boy behind his back.

"You need to see the window yourself. The sooner the better."

"Okay. Let's get over there around sunrise to beat the rush. I doubt that Eddie Cronin will be prowling the hospital grounds at that hour."

"No problem. I'll ask Joe to pick us up at 5:30."

"Get some sleep. I know you need more than I do."

"Thanks, Archbishop. See you in the morning."

"Before you turn in, Danny, see if you can locate Professor Mears down at the seminary. I need to talk to him."

Father Richard sounded like he'd been waiting for the call.

While clearing the table, Father Dan heard the archbishop say, "Richard, could you drop by for a little brandy? Good. Father Skerry will be at the door to let you in."

17.

Vincent Mulcahy would be the first to acknowledge that he was a stick in the mud, but after twenty-eight years of widower-hood, he was entitled. He set his own schedule, the only accommodation being to Echo, and to a lesser extent Frank, who spent at least one night a week at the house.

Still, he hadn't imagined that sharing the house with Portia would be so difficult.

As he thought about it, though, there was something more than his daughter's mere presence that set him on edge.

First, she seemed too comfortable being back at home, as if she'd been away for a brief vacation. It was as if her anger toward him after Maddy died, her disappearing act, and her years of silence never really happened.

Then there was the way he'd find her looking at him. He'd look up from what he was doing to find her staring at him.

After supper, Portia joined her father on his walk out to the point to check the weather instruments. The rain gauge measured

0.84 inches, all from the cloudburst that interrupted lunch, and he marked the amount in his notebook.

They both tried to jumpstart a conversation but had trouble sustaining it, reminding him of tennis players unable to get a volley going. For the moment, at least, they had run out of things to say.

Portia finally went up to bed, still complaining of jetlag.

From his seat at the kitchen table, he could tell that she was still awake long afterward. He didn't need perfect hearing to sense her padding, barefoot, from room to room. He pictured her opening drawers and closets, nosing around.

Later, Vincent took the dog out for her obligatory walk and waited from the yard for the lights on the second floor to go out before going back inside. Then he listened at the foot of the stairs, just to be sure.

Finally confident he wouldn't be disturbed, he lifted the bundle of letters from California out of his desk drawer and began reading them again in chronological order.

18.

Late as it was, Father Richard Mears was fully dressed in case the summons from the archbishop came. Since the tremor was forcing him to spend more time on buttons and shoelaces lately, it was the only practical thing to do.

When the call did come, all he needed to do was click his Roman collar in place.

On the short walk up the hill from his quarters to the residence, he passed Cardinal O'Rourke's mausoleum, which caught the moonlight like a haunted house in an old movie. Once meticulously cared for, it had fallen into disrepair.

O'Rourke had planned his interment in detail. He decided to be buried under a small chapel on the hillside between the seminary and the residence, two places where he had spent most of his career.

That was the official story, accurate as far as it went.

There was, however, an unofficial story, which was still circulating fifty years after the old cardinal died, handed down from generation to generation of seminarians.

Eyewitnesses reported that at dawn the morning after the funeral, trucks arrived on the scene. Soon the burial vault was covered with several feet of concrete, insuring that his remains would repose right there on the hillside for eternity.

Years later, Father Richard researched the unofficial story of the cardinal's gravesite but found no documentation to back it up.

At the crest of the hill, Father Richard could see Father Dan Skerry standing in the driveway, waiting for him.

"Just getting a little air before turning in, Professor. I think the moonlight enticed me outside—or perhaps all the ghosts."

The main entrance to the residence sat inside the elaborate porte-cochere. He pictured Cardinal O'Rourke arriving in the back of his Rolls Royce, his priest-chauffeur coming around to open the door for His Eminence and his beloved poodle.

No wonder the old cardinal wanted to be buried nearby.

Archbishop Quilty was waiting for him in the paneled reception room on the second floor. Father Richard had been in that room dozens of times, but only once before alone with the archbishop. On that occasion, the Boss had sought his advice regarding a strangely shimmering stained-glass window.

The sofas and easy chairs placed about the room could easily have accommodated a dozen people. Softly lit bookcases filled with memorabilia lined the walls. On one wall was a spectacular watercolor of Mount Chocorua, flanked by birches. Father Richard knew that the archbishop himself had painted it years before.

"Have you visited the White Mountains, Professor?"

"When I was a seminarian, we climbed Chocorua as part of a retreat. You must have done it too, Archbishop."

"Oh, yes. On my first climb, I understood why the Native Americans considered it a holy place."

"Did you ever climb it again?"

"At least a dozen times, Professor, before my joints started acting up."

One bookcase displayed materials from the pope's visit in 1979, including pictures of the outdoor Mass on Boston Common, conducted in a heavy rainstorm. One of Father Richard's colleagues referred to it as the "Monsoon Mass."

The archbishop caught him giving the bookcase a glance.

"What were you doing that day, Professor?"

"I stood with the crowds watching the pope's motorcade pass. By then, the rain had stopped." He gestured to the avenue outside the large window, as a late trolley rolled slowly westward on the Green Line. He couldn't help noticing the TV trucks lined up along the road.

"That night, the Holy Father slept right across the hall. Perhaps you've seen the plaque on the wall outside."

"I have, Archbishop. Earlier that day, I watched the Mass on TV, comfy and dry in the faculty lounge at the seminary. What were you doing?"

"I was out there on Boston Common, assigned to hold an umbrella over the head of the pope's secretary. That's what monsignors do. I got soaked and have the video to prove it."

Father Richard looked out the window again. "It looks like the media has you in their crosshairs, Your Excellency."

"That's the reason I asked you over. As I mentioned on the phone, we're planning to visit Saint Kay's at dawn."

The archbishop motioned Father Richard to the chair beside him. Two snifters on the coffee table were already filled, and beside them stood a bottle of Courvoisier at the ready.

"I assume you've seen the window."

"Of course, Archbishop. You know I wouldn't miss it."

"Another hoax?"

"I'm not sure, Archbishop."

"The case of the shimmering stained-glass windows was a doozie."

"I was thinking of that just as I came in. It was a doozie, all right, but it had an easy answer."

"Not at the start, Richard. You should give the fellow credit, using a portable laser like that."

"I do. Not as much for the laser as for the ingenuity. He stayed blocks away, kept changing locations and targeting different windows of the church, and, best of all, climbed trees in the neighborhood to do his work."

"So the Saint Kay's case doesn't have an easy answer?"

"Not for me. I've never seen such a window. The colors are vivid, and with a little imagination, you can see a human shape up there. I looked at it from every angle, but of course I couldn't actually touch the window from the outside."

"Did you go inside?"

"Oh, yes. Leo Mulcahy's secretary let me have a look from inside the office, but it looked and felt perfectly normal. But there's one other thing. I did a little research."

After he explained the grotto and the Virgin Mary's promise to return, the archbishop looked unimpressed.

"The geographic connection is intriguing," he responded, pouring more brandy into their glasses. "But I'll need more than a historical footnote to convince me that we have a miracle on our hands."

The conversation drifted to other topics until the archbishop glanced at his watch.

"Thanks for coming over, Richard. I hope I have a better feel for what's going on in the morning."

"I'll be praying for you."

19.

Eddie Cronin was still sitting at his desk, doodling, when the grandfather clock chimed midnight. Although it was a high-end knock-off, not the antique it pretended to be, it looked impressive enough.

Eddie had a whole sheet of a legal pad covered with whorls, g-clefs, stick figures, hangmen's nooses, five- and six-pointed stars, and question marks, as he thought about his miraculous window.

With his management skills, he'd have no problem transforming Saint Kay's into the biggest Marian shrine in North America. Admittedly, there wasn't much competition. Saint Anne de Beaupre, outside Quebec City, hadn't kept up with the times and was losing market share. Kitty and her mother visited a few years back when Eunice could still travel, and they found the same dusty, old crutches lying around the church that they had seen when Kitty was in high school. As for Our Lady of Guadalupe, pilgrims were scared off by pickpockets and muggings. As he could have guessed, the Mexican authorities were too inept and corrupt to get a handle on the problem.

The window would be the focal point of the pilgrimages, with a state-of-the-art chapel built around it. The remainder of the medical office building would house the shrine's administrative staff.

Of course, Guido would be history. Eddie would need to replace him with a charismatic young priest, like the ones leading those huge congregations on TV. It wouldn't hurt to make the guy sexy either, but not too sexy.

The whole complex would require a total upgrade, starting with the infrastructure. New roads would be needed, with a couple of state-of-the-art parking garages, hotels, restaurants, and gift shops. There was enough land on Hospital Hill to accommodate all of this, since the old monastery behind the hospital needed to come down anyway.

The hospital itself would be transformed. The new paradigm would be "miracle," and it would infuse the work at the hospital with a new spirit. With that in mind, he'd ramp up the adult and pediatric oncology services and create a new kind of cancer hospital, one with a soul.

The profits would be incalculable.

Eddie was doodling again, only now crosses and dollar signs, when his private line rang.

He hoped that the archbishop had come to his senses and was calling. A midnight call would not be unusual from that insomniac.

It turned out to be the next best thing.

"Eddie, it's Corinne. My sources tell me that Archie will be in your neck of the woods around dawn."

"I knew he couldn't stay away from our prize window for long. Meet me here; let's say around 5:30. I'll have breakfast sent up from the kitchen."

Eddie decided that the trip back to Sycamore Hill to get four hours of sleep wasn't worth the trouble. He'd settle for a few Zs on the office sofa instead.

20.

Tom Rowley dragged himself out of bed, since he had no intention of lying there, worrying. He could do his worrying upright as well as flat on his back, he figured, and could get some computer work done as a bonus. The only downside was that his hip would start to ache again after a few minutes in the chair, but a little pain was preferable to a totally wasted night.

In the dark, he nearly tripped over the packing boxes from Faneuil Movers still taking up the center of his living room and made another silent promise to unpack.

When he and Helen broke up, he never dreamed that they'd become modern-day pen pals. It started during one of their meetings at the lawyer's office. She asked him matter-of-factly if he had an online name and laughed when he told her it was "tularedoc."

"I should have figured that out myself. That little germ has been the only object of your affection all these years."

Soon she was sending him articles from all kinds of way-out periodicals and names of some weird-sounding websites. Only a librarian could know that such stuff existed.

Early on, she forwarded Second Amendment stuff for the most part. The Brady Bill people were making a lot of noise at the time. Imagine disarming the American people! What about our Second Amendment rights? The next thing, they'd be outlawing baseball, for Christ's sake. That was one area where he and his ex saw eye to eye.

But the material Helen sent him about the survivors' network was much more interesting … and that was when he began writing back.

The Internet turned out to be the perfect way for them to communicate. They could think before writing and edit their messages before sending them off. No more words said in anger and haste. If only they could have dealt with each other like this when they were married, they'd still be together.

After logging on, he found a one-liner from "faneuilbookworm," sent minutes before.

"How are the cultures?"

He was planning to share his good news in the morning, but now that she was awake, he instant messaged her.

"Glad you asked. Enough bugs on the plates to kill hundreds. Any more targets in mind?"

She got right back.

"We already have enough on our plate."

Just like Helen, he thought, *always playing with words.*

THURSDAY

1.

The Boss wore his simplest clerical garb. The only indication of ecclesiastical rank was the gold chain of his pectoral cross worn diagonally across the front of his black vest.

He looked rested and ready to go.

Father Joe, however, looked bleary-eyed. If anybody needed sleep, this superannuated adolescent did.

Father Dan had instructed Joe to use one of the seminary maintenance trucks in place of the Marquis. The reporters camped out across the street from the archbishop's residence would be on the lookout for the limousine with its hard-to-miss low-numbered plate. If they took notice of the truck at all, they'd figure the maintenance guys were going out for early coffee.

The Boss sat up front with Cowboy Joe, while Dan pushed aside a pair of pruning shears and sat in back.

"I believe this is called 'riding shotgun' in some circles," the archbishop offered.

"They won't report the truck missing, will they, Joe?" Dan pictured a roadblock and police with guns drawn.

"Nah, I left a note for the super." Father Joe Maguire was one of these guys who acted like he'd never left his college fraternity house, let alone Saint Luke's Seminary, although he was now four years ordained.

There was next to no traffic. A few people stood at the bus stops. Hotel, hospital, and restaurant workers with early shifts, Father Dan imagined. At an overpass near Faneuil Center, he noticed an encampment of makeshift tents under the trees. There seemed to be homeless everywhere these days. They were probably comfortable now, but in a few weeks, they'd be shivering in the late October chill.

At Hospital Drive, a line of TV trucks, satellites attached, stretched all the way up the hill. They reminded Dan of a science-fiction movie where radio-telescopes picked up messages from outer space.

Cowboy Joe drove at the speed of a brisk walk. He must have understood that one word from the Boss, and he'd be packing his bags for a church in the far western suburbs with about fifty Masses per weekend.

Joe was about to grab one of the clergy spaces in the Saint Kay's garage when Father Dan put a hand on his shoulder.

"Whoa. Security will be all over a truck parked here. Go up a level."

The grounds were quiet. A guy in a uniform that read *Northeast Security* stood outside the garage. Although he didn't appear to notice the three priests as they walked by, Father Dan caught him speaking discreetly into the microphone on his shoulder—and saw a pistol on his hip.

In case a pilgrim or two had trouble finding the window, cardboard signs with arrows and *Marian Apparition* in gothic letters were placed at ten-foot intervals on the walkway. *Saint Katherine's Medical Center* was printed at the bottom of each sign, in case someone forgot where he was.

On a traffic island in front of the hospital lobby stood the kiosk. It was wood-framed, with glass on all sides and a pointed red-shingled roof. At the front, under a sign reading *Souvenirs* was a window like those at a movie theater or a bank. He wondered how early they opened for business.

They made their way single file, with Father Joe walking point, the archbishop sandwiched in the middle, and Father Dan bringing up the rear, where for the first time, he concentrated on what was about to happen.

He'd been simply too busy watching the Boss, watching Cowboy Joe, watching that security guy, to prepare himself. Up to this point, he had thought about the apparition as a logistical problem, a public relations matter, a political headache, and possibly a security threat to the archbishop.

All those concerns had kept him from the fundamental question. What if this was something more than a bizarre chemical reaction or a hoax?

Seconds later, they found themselves in front of the window. With first light just striking the building, Dan was impressed. The bright reds, greens, yellows, and blues in one window on the second floor were more vivid and arresting than anything he could have anticipated.

But that was all he saw.

Standing there, he thought about all the faithful who were flocking to the window. Many were seeing something more compelling and, yes, more miraculous, and he was comfortable with that.

"People see what they want to see," he said to himself.

Then he remembered his job description. He was there to protect the archbishop—period. Everything else was a distraction. Once that sunk in, he got back to work, surveying the scene. The other windows of the building looked blank and uninhabited, and the grassy area under the window was deserted. Mementos—pictures, notes, children's toys—were scattered on the ground beneath a tree. After that, he checked the roofline, just to be thorough, and saw no activity.

Meanwhile, the Boss stood there, head bowed at the usual angle for prayer. He could always tell when the Boss was praying, because he would tilt his head just so, but this time an important detail was different. The Boss always closed his eyes when praying, but now his eyes were wide open.

A quick look was usually all he needed to read the Boss's mind, but now he couldn't tell whether the Boss was concentrating on the scene or simply staring off into space.

Father Joe, though, was an easy read. He looked terrified.

2.

Turning over in bed, Tom Rowley felt a twinge in his left deltoid, just below the shoulder.

The booster, he thought, when his arm gave out another jolt. He had given himself the tularemia vaccine ten days earlier. He had no idea at the time if he needed it, but it had been taking up space in the lab freezer for years. He'd injected himself with the first dose years back, when he first got interested in tularemia, and had kept the leftover vaccine.

The swelling took about a week to resolve, but the injection site was still tender.

He'd never written down the date of the first dose but remembered that Helen and Tommy went out to her parents' summer cottage at the time. The little guy had to have been about seven, about the time Tom began to worry how he'd turn out. Tommy had shown no interest in sports, in spite of balls, gloves, skates, and pucks under the tree each Christmas. Worst of all, he threw a ball just like a girl.

He gave himself that first injection while they were away so Helen wouldn't see the nasty skin reaction that it would cause and ask a thousand questions. Happily, the skin reaction was milder this time, but the pain was just as bad.

A buddy from the Fort Detrick days had sent him a vial of the stuff just before they stopped production. The guy knew about Tom's early interest in tularemia (and how he was screwed by the CDC). The vaccine was 100 percent effective, but it took between twelve and fifteen days for the body to mount an effective antibody response. Since the incubation period of tularemia was only five to eight days, the vaccine was useless if given after exposure. No one really knew how long the vaccine was protective, because no one ever studied the matter.

The Fort Detrick people eventually lost interest in the vaccine because they were strictly in the business of preparing for a biologic attack and weren't about to pay for a scientific inquiry that didn't promise a quick payoff. Once Detrick ceased production, Tom figured that another government agency would pick up the ball. But nobody did.

As far as he was concerned, this was a typical bureaucratic snafu. The vaccine, now discontinued, provided ideal protection for Tom Rowley and the shrinking number of pure scientists who the government didn't give a shit about.

Now that he thought about it, the Blessed Virgin herself got him to inject that last dose of vaccine, exactly a week *before* she appeared at Saint Kay's. The vial had been sitting in the back of his refrigerator for years, forgotten. There was no other way to explain his sudden urge to locate it.

Then came Monday morning, when she smiled directly at him from Leo Mulcahy's office window. The signal was clear: she was thanking him for heeding her advice, and she was giving him the final okay for his battle plan.

At any other time, the prospect of visiting Mount of Olives Academy would have kept him up all night, but thanks to Our

Lady, he slept like a baby and awakened feeling like he'd logged ten hours.

He was ready for his reconnaissance mission.

3.

The archbishop stood motionless for an eternity before flashing Dan the ready-to-leave signal. The signal was subtle but unmistakable, and it had gotten them out of an endless number of groundbreakings, wakes, testimonial dinners, and the like. He'd flip his left thumb upward, as if he were hitchhiking, but only for a second. Father Dan missed the thumb sign in his first weeks as secretary but quickly caught on.

They were silent as they retraced their steps back to the garage, with Father Joe in the lead again. He set a dignified pace but looked like he'd break into a sprint at any second.

Dan knew that he'd never make sense out of what he'd just seen without serious time for reflection and prayer. That said, he was satisfied with the visit. Commandeering the maintenance truck was a brilliant tactic, and showing up at sunrise, while the press and Eddie Cronin were fast asleep, was creative.

In fact, he was still patting himself on the back when he suddenly saw big trouble ahead.

Corinne Caruthers was waiting for them at the entrance to the parking garage, on the very spot where he'd seen the security guy earlier. At her side were a cameraman who Dan recognized from past encounters, and Cronin himself.

It was a full-scale ambush!

"Danny, I'm not ready to talk to them now," the archbishop whispered.

The camera was rolling, and Ms. Caruthers was speaking into her handheld mike. "Here comes Archbishop Sebastian Quilty, who has just had a firsthand look at the 'Faneuil Miracle.' Would you share your thoughts with our viewers, Archbishop?"

The Boss kept on walking while Father Dan improvised.

"The archbishop has just visited the window and will be making a statement later today. Please excuse us."

He could see the challenge in the newswoman's eyes. This was not going to be easy, but he had his orders. He took the archbishop's arm while Father Joe picked up the pace.

When Dan brushed past the group, his shoulder must have sideswiped the mini-cam being thrust into the archbishop's face, because the moment they reached the garage doorway, Joe still in the lead, he heard the crash as it landed on the pavement.

That was when they broke into a run.

Once in the truck, Joe jammed it into gear and floored it. They flew out of the parking garage, tore down Hospital Drive, barely missing a school bus coming in the other direction, and ran the red light at the foot of the hill.

No one complained about Joe's driving. Actually, the only sound Dan heard besides the screech of brakes was the archbishop's heavy breathing.

4.

Tom kept the TV on after downing his juice and coffee so he could watch Corinne Caruthers report the Church's latest atrocity up at Saint Kay's.

It didn't surprise him in the least that the archbishop's bodyguard got violent. Those guys up at the chancery were sanctimonious assholes but had no problem sneaking around like common criminals when it served their purposes. If they got caught in the act, they'd go for the kill like a cornered animal.

The sex abuse scandal showed everybody that.

He shaved at the kitchen sink just in case there was more to the story, but Channel Six just kept replaying the videotape of the archbishop and his bodyguard committing their assault and battery.

Then it was time to go.

It had been seven and a half years since he last took the winding drive up to the school.

He decided against parking in the main lot where people might start asking questions and cruised into the upper lot, behind Pope Pius XII Auditorium, where he found a spot behind a couple of yellow school buses.

"Typical," he said to himself when he looked at his watch. He was a good ten minutes early. As Helen used to put it, he was always early, she was right on time, and Tommy was always late.

Instead of sitting in the car, he decided to walk through the wooded area separating the playing fields from the school. Over dinner, Tommy would entertain his parents with a story about the "copse," as his teacher called it.

The sunlight filtered through the maples and birches in full leaf. Was this the same patch of woods? Where were the police cars, lights flashing, and the yellow crime-scene tape strung around the leafless trees?

"Doctor, I know this will be very hard, but I need to ask you to make an identification," the detective said quietly. He was dressed in a business suit, unlike the other police officers who stood around stiffly in uniform. The guy could have passed for a bank vice president, except for his deep-set, sad eyes that had seen too much of this kind of thing.

The horror of seeing his son, his only child, lying there on the snow-covered ground quickly turned to fury when he saw the boy's hand clutching Tom's own .45 in a death grip.

He turned toward the driveway when her car rounded the last turn and watched it glide into a spot in the lower lot.

You could set your clock by her. You always could.

No sooner out of her car, she was ready.

“Here’s the master plan of the building, Tom. Ready for the guided tour?”

5.

The archbishop was still chewing a couple of Rolaids when Father Dan switched on the *Today Show*. But instead of Katie Couric, the all-too-familiar face of that Caruthers woman stared back at them.

The announcer intoned, “We interrupt the *Today Show* for breaking news from the site of the ‘Faneuil Miracle.’”

Ms. Caruthers was standing at the precise location of their encounter one hour earlier. Dr. Cronin stood a few steps back, not flashing his trademark grin for a change.

“Already strained relations between the archdiocese of Boston and the media reached a new low this morning when a member of the archbishop’s staff attacked a Channel Six cameraman. If we can zoom in on the pavement here, you’ll see a pool of blood.”

Dan could make out a dark spot, a blemish on the pavement, but certainly no “pool.” He walked over to the TV to get a better look. There was no way of knowing *what* it was.

“I didn’t attack anybody.”

“I know, Danny. I know.” The Boss gripped his secretary’s forearm in a rare physical display of emotion.

“Larry Lang, a member of our TV family for the past decade, was injured in the attack and is now being evaluated in the trauma center at the Saint Kay’s Emergency Department. We will pass his condition along to you as soon as we get word.”

The archbishop never looked paler.

“Archbishop Quilty made an unannounced visit to the Miracle

Window before sunrise, and our crew caught up with him as he was leaving. Before the archbishop could answer any questions, his bodyguard, the Reverend Daniel Skerry, struck Larry, threw our video equipment to the ground, and fled with the archbishop and another priest, who remains unidentified. In another bizarre twist, they sped off in a truck used for maintenance at Saint Luke's Seminary. Fortunately, Larry's video survived the attack. For the record, Father Skerry is said to weigh twice as much as our cameraman. As the saying goes, he should pick on someone his own size."

Seconds later, a video of the encounter appeared on the screen. Dan was impressed once again by how much a videotape of a scene can differ from the scene itself.

The segment, about fifteen seconds long, showed the three churchmen approaching the camera, Caruthers's question to the archbishop, and Dan's response. This was followed by a flurry of blurred images, a voice, probably the cameraman's, saying "What the (bleep)," and then blackness.

"Danny, please turn off the TV." The Boss sounded exhausted, as if he'd finished officiating at three back-to-back confirmations.

"Archbishop, the big question is who tipped these people off?"

The Boss remained silent, and from the way his head was tilted, he could have been praying.

"Danny, I agree that there's a leak somewhere, and that concerns me. But there's a bigger question."

"Yes, Your Excellency?"

"Just what were we seeing on that window?"

6.

Father Guido awakened to the *putt-putt* of lobster boats exiting the harbor and lay there listening to the sounds getting fainter. He thought about the passage from the gospel he'd read to Tommy Rowley when the boy talked about being a priest.

> As He was walking along the Sea of Galilee he watched two brothers, Simon now known as Peter, and his brother Andrew, casting a net into the sea. They were fishermen. He said to them, "Follow me and I will make you fishers of men."

After breakfast, he waited until Leo's office went off their answering service and Veronica would be at her desk. He was already overdue for a visit to Leo to begin with, and both his blood pressure and blood sugar had to be in the stratosphere with all this stress. Of course, the extra slice of toast with Marilena's homemade peach preserves he just consumed would push the glucose up a little more, but he wasn't calling for a routine appointment.

He couldn't keep the FedEx, the garage, and the rest of the story to himself a moment longer. He needed Leo's advice.

Veronica never failed to put the person on the other end of the line at ease. Leo was lucky to have her.

She could make bad news seem only half-bad. He could hear her sigh when she told him that Leo was on vacation and wouldn't be back until after Labor Day.

"Could Dr. Nalbandian help? I know he'd be happy to see you later today."

Father Guido knew that Harold would be stretched without Leo, but Veronica would squeeze him in anyway. With her at the desk, the patient schedule quickly sprouted double-books and add-ons. And since she hadn't mastered the scheduling software that Harold had installed, she would scribble the extra patients' names on the margins of the daily printout without entering them into the computer.

He simply couldn't tell Harold about what happened. He'd wait for Leo to get back.

Veronica must have picked up on Father Guido's uncharacteristic silence.

"You know, Father, Dr. Mulcahy hasn't left for Maine yet. He and Mrs. Mulcahy delayed their vacation on account of Our Lady's appearance. I'm sure he'd talk to you on the phone."

Guido knew that a jury would acquit Leo for justifiable homicide when Veronica did things like this, but she could get away with it.

"When you do hear from him, I'd be very, very grateful if he could call me. I'm in Gull now, but I plan to take the nine thirty boat back. God bless you, Veronica."

Father Guido's phone rang five minutes later.

"Hi, Father, what's up?" Leo sounded like it was just another day at the office.

7.

The archbishop and Father Dan spent what was left of their morning on strategy.

First off, Dan was to call Rome and arrange for the Boss to speak with a high-ranking prelate serving as a member of the Congregation for the Doctrine of the Faith about the apparition. Of course, he already knew what their response would be.

"You're there. You've seen it. As the local bishop, you make your own statement. Don't compromise yourself by being too definitive, but above all, avoid scandal to the Church."

Next, he was to draft a statement, arrange for the archdiocesan TV guys to videotape it at the residence, and get the video and the written text distributed to the local media. Dan suggested that they consult the archdiocesan lawyer first. One question for him would be whether they should acknowledge the incident with the camera man or ignore it.

The Boss agreed.

Dan hoped that attorney Gene Autry was in town.

Autry had succeeded his uncle as the archdiocesan lawyer years earlier. In those days, the archdiocese was a simple operation with lots of compliant parishioners and priests who rarely made any trouble. Gene did mostly probate and trust matters then—little, old ladies leaving their savings to the Church, as well as larger bequests, like Mount of Olives—all pretty straightforward. Autry was also the Saint Kay's counsel. The hospital was much smaller in those days, and life was much less complicated, when doctors were revered almost as much as priests.

Autry was a problem because everything had grown too big and too complex for him to handle, but the archbishop refused to consider a change.

Dan suspected that Autry knew too much to be eased out.

The archbishop was reluctant to hold a live news conference, and Father Dan agreed. A taped statement was definitely the way to go.

Then there was the issue of the leak. The list of people who knew about their sunrise trip to Saint Kay's was mercifully short.

He jotted down the list: Archbishop Quilty, himself, Father Joe Maguire, Father Richard Mears, and possibly Sister Philippe. None of them seemed likely.

Just to be sure, he called Father Richard at the seminary.

"No, Dan. I've talked to no one, in person or on the phone, since I left the residence last night. No, not even Frank Mulcahy. In fact, you're the first human I've spoken with since I said good-night to the archbishop."

Archbishop Quilty's schedule was already overloaded, the norm after being away. He was slated to meet with a delegation of Bolivian religious women at eleven, host a business lunch with his auxiliary bishops at noon, attend Eunice Rafferty's wake at five, and give the keynote address at a Knights of Columbus dinner at the Freedom Trail Hilton at seven. He also had two office appointments with archdiocesan priests, at least one of whom was planning to request a leave of absence.

The rest of the week was equally jammed.

"Let's cancel the auxiliaries and get Lou Fannon to fill in at the Knights. He'll jump at the opportunity to get a free meal and hobnob a little. But remind him to read my speech word for word with no ad libs. Any screw-up, and he'll be the next bishop of Green Bay. The Vatican has been looking for someone to go out there, and he'd fit the bill nicely. For a man who worships the sun and detests football, northern Wisconsin would be genuine purgatory."

Auxiliary Bishop Fannon had been a boyhood pal of the late Cardinal Campion and was rumored to be a charter member of the late cardinal's poker group. Just after arriving in Boston, Archbishop Quilty, voiceless with a bad case of laryngitis, made the mistake of asking Fannon to read his commencement address at Saint Ignatius College. Fannon delivered the speech in its entirety but added a few flourishes of his own.

After reading a line in which the archbishop urged the graduates to "reach out not only to the poor and disenfranchised, but to those of different cultures and beliefs," he removed his reading glasses a moment and made it clear that he'd been sent to read the archbishop's prepared remarks, not to endorse them.

From that day on, Fannon was put on a strict regimen of confirmations, ribbon cuttings, and standing in for the Boss at funerals.

It was little wonder that Lou Fannon's nickname was "Loose Cannon."

"I can duck the Knights tonight but not the awards dinner on Saturday. Danny, you know the Youth Outreach Banquet on Saturday is one of my favorite nights of the year."

"Mine, too, Archbishop."

8.

When Kitty brought her mother's blue silk dress over to the funeral home, she asked Michael Mooney about displaying pictures.

"There'll be room for all the pictures you want. We'll be putting Eunice in the parlor at the front of the house. We could squeeze half of Faneuil into that room if we had to."

Kitty and Bridget spread hundreds of prints out on Eunice's dining table at Cosmas House. Eunice was featured in most of them, dressed for all occasions—in her Christmas dress, her Easter hat, her tennis attire, her bathing suit, and even in her Jackie O sunglasses and pillbox hat.

Thumbing through the pictures, Kitty couldn't understand why there were no pictures of her sister. Bridget must have been reading her mind.

"You're not going to find many pictures of me, Kitty. I have to tell you that when Richie and I were about to elope, I went through the pictures and took mine out."

"Why would you do that?"

"Spite, I guess. I knew that Momma wasn't too happy with me and would be even less so when we ran off."

"What does that have to do with the pictures?"

"I guess I wanted to make a clean break."

"Where are the pictures now?"

"I kept them for a while, and then I burned them."

"You have to be kidding."

"No. One day, I doused them in lighter fluid and torched them."

"Why, Bridget?"

"I'm not sure. I was pretty mixed up at the time. Richie had taken off by then, and I was alone with two-year-old twins."

9.

Waiting for Father Guido to arrive, Leo stood at his office window.

Cousin Frank had stood at that same window the day Harold and Leo moved in and identified the church steeples jutting out of the horizon.

"There's St. Paul's in Cambridge, and then to the right, is that St. Catherine of Genoa in Somerville? I think so. Leo, hand me the binoculars so I can be sure." He worked his way deliberately, north to south, identifying every steeple and ending up at Gate of Heaven in South Boston.

Leo checked the view from his window whenever he got the chance.

While on hold with a pharmacy or listening to an overly long litany of symptoms from one of his "worried well," Leo would scan the cityscape and feel the tension drain away. Soon he learned to use the window to settle himself down before phoning someone about an unexpected death, or before having a heart-to-heart talk about an ominous test result, while the patient who was about to get the bad news sat anxiously in the exam room across the hall.

Seeing Boston stretched out before him allowed him to step back a little, to gain some perspective before getting engulfed in his next crisis.

On 9/11, he stood there stunned, trying to imagine the chaos in New York while he gazed out at his paradoxically peaceful city.

Then he turned his attention to his old friend, Father Guido. Veronica was right, as she was practically all the time, when she suggested he call the priest.

Guido sounded terrified on the phone.

10.

Vincent had slept more fitfully than usual, awakening half a dozen times during the night by sounds coming from Portia's room. At dawn, he gave up and stood by the bedroom window with its view of the point, Squimset Harbor, and Boston on the western horizon—remembering.

He was determined to keep his daily routine exactly the same. Somehow, if he didn't change a thing, Maddy would magically reappear and take up right where she'd left off.

While getting dressed, he gazed out the bedroom window as he had done every morning since they moved into the house, still newlyweds. From up there, he could look all the way out to the rocky point and beyond. A lobster boat chugged south out of Squimset Harbor, leaving a wake that picked up the earliest morning light. Meanwhile, the Boston high-rises transformed themselves from bejeweled fantasies to gray hulks on the horizon.

First light was his favorite time of day. He never tired of studying the landscape as it steadily lightened, allowing indistinct objects to sharpen their edges, second by second.

Just then, an unusual movement caught his eye. The swing under the big spruce the kids called the Christmas tree was moving.

He had never seen the swing make such huge arcs before. Whoever was on it (by now, he could make out a human shape) was pumping furiously, calling on every ounce of energy. He wondered if the rider would be thrown off by centrifugal force or if he would propel the swing over the top, making a 360.

Before it got light enough for him to see well enough, the voice gave him his answer.

His daughter began singing at the top of her lungs as the swing brushed the lower limbs of the huge tree.

"Jingle bells, jingle bells …" was all he could make out.

Barefoot, Vincent ran down the stairs and out into the yard. She kept singing, even louder if that was possible, while he grabbed at the swing as it swept by, slowing it down little by little at each pass.

"O'er the fields …"

Finally, Portia jumped off without giving him a look and ran out to the point, still singing.

Instead of pursuing her, he marched back to the house and slammed the door shut.

Little did he know that she'd leave minutes later and be out of his life for the next twenty-eight years.

He snapped out of his reverie at the sound of Portia's bedroom door opening, followed seconds later by the spasm the old pipes always made when the shower was turned on.

As the minutes went by, Vincent, in the kitchen by then, worried about how much hot water was left in the tank. Still, the longer she was up there, the more time he had to prepare.

He had spent a good hunk of his professional life conducting cross-examinations. The trick was to be well prepared, but a lot of lawyers didn't understand that simple fact. Preparation meant poring over reams of documents and committing the tiniest details to memory. Then, in the middle of a deposition or a trial, he'd look for an inconsistency ("You described the man wearing a red sweatshirt in previous testimony. Now which was it, red or black?"). Such an opening didn't materialize every day, but when one did, he'd be on his way to winning the case.

Portia wasn't the usual witness, of course, but he needed answers, and cross-examination—in some form—was the only skill he had.

Just like the old days, he'd done his homework. He started by rereading her letters from California and then studied photo albums he hadn't touched in years. Meanwhile, he worked on recalling details like his daughter singing from the swing so many years before.

She hustled into the kitchen before he knew that the water had shut off.

"Good morning, Daddy. Yesterday's breakfast filled me up so well that I'll just stick with coffee for now."

Once she sat, he took the chair opposite and got started.

"Sleep okay?"

"Sure did. What's up, though? You look serious."

Masterful, he thought. With one word, she'd gotten the upper hand. Vincent was sure he didn't look "serious," but that didn't matter. He pictured his daughter in the courtroom—if only their lives had turned out differently—demolishing a witness.

Changing his strategy, he carried the photo albums to the table.

Maddy loved to take pictures. Actually, she'd be the first to say that she didn't take "pictures," only "snapshots." She didn't know the first thing about the inside of a camera, exactly how lenses worked, or what shutter speed meant—and she didn't care.

She took a Kodak "Brownie" along on their honeymoon, and around the time Frankie was born, Vincent gave her a "Hawkeye" for Christmas.

What she might have lacked in technical knowledge, she more than made up for in enthusiasm. She never went anywhere without her camera. Of course, she took the usual "event" shots at birthday parties, First Communions, and weddings, where everyone else was snapping pictures. But she didn't put it away after that. She had her camera ready every hour of every day.

Maddy's snapshots were special because she had a way of sneaking up on her subjects and clicking away before they knew what was going on. That way, she got some spectacular candids.

She was taking a roll of film over to a photo lab in Squimset every week. When Vincent and his brother were starting out, money was so tight that he almost asked Maddy to cut back. He was so glad he didn't.

Maddy spent hours arranging her snapshots in albums and captioning each one in her precise, parochial-school cursive.

"Frankie and Portia making a snowman
Feb. 20, 1960."

"I found your mother's photo albums, Pumpkin. I haven't touched them since—well, for years."

Portia, coffee mug in hand, came around the table and sat next to him.

"What fun! Let's take a look."

11.

Leo led Father Guido into his office, offered him a seat, and pulled up a chair beside him. He couldn't recall his doctor looking so worried.

"Leo, are you okay?"

Leo knitted his brow.

"Guido, you just told me about having 'a near-death experience' on the phone, and now you're asking if I'm okay? I'm fine, but I'm very concerned about you. Can you tell me what this is about?"

"I'm all right now, honest."

The priest handed him an envelope.

"This was waiting for me when I got to Gull yesterday. Take a look."

Leo read the three pages slowly. Since Guido had told him all about Kevin Sheehan and Tommy Rowley during previous appointments, Leo needed no explanation. But when he got to page three, the one with Guido's own death notice, all color drained from his face.

"What a nightmare! Were you alone when you read this?"

"Yes, Leo. Marilena was at work."

"Unsigned, I see. Any idea who would send you such a thing?"

"None."

Guido then told Leo about going to the garage, taping the hose to the exhaust, and getting into the driver's seat.

"But I came to my senses before turning the key in the ignition."

"Guido, had you ever considered suicide before?"

"Never."

"How about now?"

"No, Leo. I can't imagine doing such a thing now."

"What made you change your mind when you were in the garage?"

"I finally realized that taking my life would be an admission of guilt. I'm not guilty."

"I know that, Guido. I know it as well as you do. But you must promise me something."

"Anything."

"If you ever feel suicidal again, even for a minute, that you'll call me immediately."

"I promise."

Guido then described making it back to the house, getting a chill, getting under a blanket on the recliner, and seeing the Virgin Mary in his picture window.

"The Blessed Mother saved me from myself yesterday afternoon."

Near the end of the visit, Leo took Guido's blood pressure, once in each arm. Then he exited the room and returned seconds later with another blood pressure cuff and checked each arm again.

"What a nice surprise! Your pressure is absolutely normal for the first time in years! And it's real. First I thought the pressure cuff was broken, but the pressure is the same with the second cuff. I expected to increase your blood pressure medication today, since it was still on the high side at your last visit. Did you increase the pills on your own?"

"No, Leo. I'm taking that little yellow pill, you know, shaped like a little shield, every morning at breakfast. Twenty milligrams. You gave me the samples."

"I guess it just took a little longer than usual for the medication to kick in."

"Could the blood pressure come down for other reasons?"

"Like what?"

"The experience down in Gull changed me, Leo. I feel clear-headed and energized for the first time in ages. I believe that's why my pressure is better."

"You're going to make me a believer yet, Father."

"I'd like that."

The priest paused as he got up to leave.

"By the way, how are your roses doing?"

Leo smiled.

"My best year ever! New blossoms have been popping out since around Easter. With them starting so early, I expected a short season. But the bushes are still so weighed down by the blooms that I'm clipping them every morning and giving them away to neighbors. And I don't ever remember such a fragrance. It's as if someone sprayed our whole neighborhood with perfume. As you can imagine, Claire is thrilled to have fresh roses on the kitchen table every morning. She tells everyone that I have a green thumb, but to be honest, I have no idea what's gotten into them. I'm using the same fertilizer as always, and I haven't changed the way I do the pruning, mulching, and watering. It's kind of a mystery. What made you ask?"

"The rose is Our Lady's flower. The Blessed Mother's appearances are often marked by the rose's fragrance. Perhaps she's sending you a signal."

"Father, I'm the last person on earth she'd be interested in. It's no secret I've taken her name in vain more than once."

"Come on, Leo. You know that Our Lady doesn't waste time preaching to the choir."

Leo stood as the priest collected his things.

"Guido, would you object if I held on to these 'documents' for a few days? I'd like Claire to have a look."

Without a moment of hesitation, he handed Leo the envelope.

12.

Leo punched in the combination on the door of the doctors' lounge and let himself in. It was noon, and the place was jammed. He squeezed into a seat between Tom Rowley and Avery Smythe, the chief of psychiatry.

Harold, seated at a table nearby, gave him a wink and resumed talking to Nina Nichols, by far the most attractive member of the staff. It was hard to imagine Nina, an orthopedic surgeon, all one hundred pounds of her, hammering away at those total hip replacements. Nevertheless, she had become the go-to person for hips at Saint Kay's and was giving the orthopedic big shots downtown a run for their money.

Tom Rowley and Avery Smythe greeted their colleague.

Smythe watched Leo struggle with the cellophane encasing his sandwich.

"It's a blessing you're not a surgeon, Leo."

"Claire tells me that all the time."

"I thought you were on vacation," Tom said, addressing his bowl of chowder.

Leo shrugged.

"It's hard to take off in the middle of a mass hallucination, especially when it's centered on your own office window," Avery wheezed, the next forkful of pasta poised in front of him. "Leo doesn't want to miss the excitement, any more than you or I do. Right, Tom?"

Without answering, Tom got up from the table to refill his coffee.

"Tom's having a lot of trouble with the apparition," Avery said, after making sure his colleague was out of range. "All this religious stuff can shake a person up, especially when they've been traumatized like him. He really hates the church."

"It's no secret that I'm no fan, either."

"I know, Leo. Vietnam and the plane crash had to test your faith. It's a lot easier for a guy like me. My folks were atheists from the start, so I didn't have to worry about religion as a kid. I didn't lie awake worrying about burning in hell every time I thought about girls, the way you probably did. So when something like this—apparition, or whatever you want to call it—comes along, I don't get all lathered up. I can just sit back and watch."

Tom returned to the table.

"You and Claire should be in Maine," Tom said.

Leo feared that Tom wanted Claire to come back to work, since he was totally lost without her.

"We'll stick around until the excitement dies down. I can't leave Harold alone right now with our office so chaotic. With a little luck, we'll get out of town next week."

"Look, Leo, if Claire gets any ideas about coming in, tell her to forget it. She might be tempted to catch up on paperwork or give me a hand. She needs a vacation."

That was the last thing he expected Rowley to say.

"Should I hide her keys?"

"No need. I changed the locks. She'll get a new set when she gets back."

Avery Smythe gave Leo a subtle shrug of the shoulders. Leo recognized the gesture. Whenever the chief of psychiatry was faced with a difficult clinical question, he'd do just that.

13.

Eddie Cronin took advantage of a break in his schedule to thumb through his new copy of *Road and Track*. Now he had all his car magazines (*Car and Driver*, *AutoWeek*, *Motor Trend*, *Car Audio and Electronics*, *Truckin'*, and *Lowrider*) mailed to the office. Kitty had been getting on his case about how much time (and money) he was spending on the cars, and the magazines' arrival at Sycamore Hill every few days only gave her more ammunition.

For as long as he could remember, he loved cars.

His old man adored anything on four wheels and spent hours tinkering with his Chevy. It was a 1955 Bel Air convertible, the first small block V8 the company made. By the time Eddie was ten, Ed Senior had taught him how to change the oil, check the tire pressures, and clean the spark plugs, and he paid him a couple of bucks every week to polish the exterior and vacuum out the inside.

Once Eddie got his license at sixteen, he started bringing wrecked cars home and rebuilding them.

For total relaxation, nothing else in the world could match getting under the hood and fine-tuning the carburetor or rolling underneath on his creeper to check the drive shaft. Just a couple of weeks before, when one of those crunchy-granola community activists quizzed him about the financials at the board meeting, he escaped to the garage as soon as he got home and simonized his two-tone Vette until his blood pressure came back to normal.

When Eddie felt the world really closing in, it was time to hit the road. Getting out on the Mass Pike and cranking up to eighty was a great way to let off steam. The speed limit on the Pike was sixty-five outside the city, but you could usually go ten to fifteen miles over the posted limit and the staties would look the other way. But like all rules, there were exceptions. An overly zealous trooper, usually just out of the academy or one of the increasingly common females, would nail him on occasion. Still, after a particularly trying day, he'd cruise out to the New York line and back just to unwind. He chalked up the resulting insurance surcharges as just another business expense.

For the moment, Eddie liked the jet-black Dodge Ram with its oversized tires and the Mazda ZFX the best, but he tried to give all his cars equal time, like demanding children.

One of the great plusses of Sycamore Hill was the old barn in back, hidden from the main house by two rows of mature upright yews. He converted it for his dozen cars and three bikes as soon as they passed papers. With the addition of wiring invisible to the casual observer, the yews provided near total protection. The last thing he needed was to have a drunken department head from his Christmas party stumble outside to take a leak, discover the garage, and babble to one of those tight-sphinctered morons on the board. The electric shock, not enough to leave a mark or alter the heart rhythm, was potent enough to scare anybody off.

Although it was an extravagance, Eddie's garage was puny compared to one on the West Coast he'd read about where one of those late-night comedians custom-built a megastructure, housing eighty cars and sixty motorcycles!

Right now, the garage was at capacity, with all the nooks and crannies jammed with work benches, while shelving for tools and spare parts filled all available wall space clear to the rafters.

It was time to expand.

Expansion would be quite simple, since the land behind the old barn was empty and flat. There would be plenty of room to line up a dozen additional bays behind the present ones, as well as an updated bedroom and dining area.

For the time being, however, he could do little more than thumb through his magazines and dream. He didn't even dare take the first step of getting the hospital's architectural firm to make some sketches.

All would have to wait until the apparition paid off. Then he'd own the most spectacular private garage this side of Beverly Hills.

He was scanning an article about vintage T-Birds when the intercom buzzed. Gert started talking before he could say "yes" or "hello."

"Don't blame me if you're late at Mooney's." Then she was gone.

He checked his Rolex and decided that five more minutes wouldn't hurt. The less time spent looking at his Eunice today, the better.

He went into the lavatory, and after taking a leak and applying spritzes of cologne to the usual areas, he looked straight into the mirror.

"My mother-in-law was my biggest fan," he told the surprisingly middle-aged man looking back at him. Instinctively, he smoothed the longer strands of hair over the thin spots.

Eddie tried to give Kitty the engagement ring on Christmas Eve. Eunice had invited him over for Midnight Mass, and he arrived a little early. When he and Kitty were alone in the family room, he made his move. Kitty held the tiny package, in silver paper with a crimson ribbon, embossed with the logo of Boston's most prestigious jewelry store, but made no move to open it. From the solemnity with which he handed it to her, she had to know what it was. He didn't get down on one knee and actually propose, but Eddie was hardly the get-down-on-your-knee kind of guy, and actually asking her to get married wasn't his style either.

"Is this an engagement ring?"

"Uh-huh."

"Eddie, I need time to think about this. I'd rather not look at it yet."

She handed the box back gingerly, as if it might explode.

Eddie felt like he'd just been told he had three months to live and had better get his affairs in order. But before he could compose himself, the door swung open, and there stood Eunice in her favorite Christmas dress, red with faux ermine at the collar, cuffs, and the hem of her skirt. She looked like an anorectic version of Mrs. Santa Claus.

Edward stuffed the little box into his pocket.

Early the next morning, he was in the middle of a great dream about becoming a cardinal when the phone rang.

"Eddie dear, sorry to wake you. Kitty and I had a chat after you left last night. If I were you, I'd offer her the ring again. I don't think you'll be disappointed."

After breezing by Gert in the outer office, Eddie made his way to the garage where his midnight-blue Mercedes SL 500 roadster was parked. In the morning, he'd had no problem making the decision to use it, since it was Eunice's favorite—and its color made it appropriate for mourning. A minute later, he caught sight of Corinne Caruthers in front of a Channel Six truck, talking to a cameraman, probably backup for the guy who Father Skerry pole-axed in the morning. Eddie waved as he cruised by, but she pretended not to see him. Once past them, he looked in the rearview mirror. Corinne had walked out Hospital Drive and was pointing in his direction while her companion aimed his mini-cam at the Mercedes.

14.

Leo Mulcahy took a long look at Mooney's from across the street.

Mooney's was an institution. Every Catholic family from Faneuil (including many who had migrated to the suburbs) brought their loved ones to Mooney's for their final "public appearance," as his Uncle Vinny liked to put it. Up Main Street a couple of blocks south of Saint Brendan's Church, it had been a family business from the beginning. Michael F. Mooney was the fifth generation to operate the home since his great-great-grandfather, Michael I., set up shop for the growing Irish immigrant community surrounding the Faneuil Stockyards in the 1880s.

Leo studied the building. At its core was a nineteenth-century home, most obvious from its upper floors. The two windows on the third floor, side-by-side under the peak of the roof, had rounded tops popular at that time. It looked like a Civil War daguerreotype of a home turned into a field hospital, with the wounded lying on cots in tents filling the front yard.

At ground level, the original entrance had been replaced by a modern, glass-enclosed entryway. And to the right rear, a newer L-shaped wing separated the front and back parking areas. Leo could just make out the loading dock at the end of the L, hidden behind a cluster of rhododendrons.

He thought back to the evening he exited the building from that wing. He was attending the wake of a patient who had died unexpectedly. Although he had only known the gentleman for a year or so, they really hit it off. They both had been army medics, Leo in Vietnam, and his patient in World War II.

Leo was standing in line to give his condolences to the family when the patient's widow spied him. She spoke up immediately, loud enough to be heard down in Faneuil Center. "There's that quack Leo Mulcahy, the man who killed my husband!"

Before he knew what was happening, Eiko Mooney gently took him by the arm to a side door and led him through the new L-shaped extension out to the parking lot.

"You can never predict what grief will do to a person," she said, as she ushered him to safety.

"Believe me, Eiko, I know."

Claire was already in line, waiting for him.

"Is Father Guido okay?" she asked.

"Like a new man. I expected his pressure to be sky-high, but it was 120/80. I don't understand it."

"Maybe he lost some weight."

"Nope. Up three pounds. He brought some papers with him."

Claire looked puzzled.

"He had a close call, but he's okay. I'll explain later."

15.

When the cameras got rolling, the archbishop started off just fine.

"Beloved brothers and sisters in Christ, I am grateful for the opportunity to speak to you about an event taking place at Saint Katherine's Hospital in Faneuil. A window at the hospital has drawn the attention of thousands, both in person and through the media. Many of you have seen the window. Some see an image of Our Blessed Mother the Virgin Mary, while others see an impressive display of light and color."

He went through that first paragraph flawlessly each time.

The second paragraph was where he stumbled.

"Earlier today, I had the privilege of visiting the window. I approached this event as I hope you would also—with humility and prayer."

At this point, he stopped cold on his first two tries. He didn't cough or clear his throat or anything like that. He just stopped.

Dan couldn't believe what was happening. The Boss was an excellent speaker, whether reading a text or making extemporaneous remarks. It was true that before any speech he needed to do one last dry run in front of a mirror. More than once, Dan would enter a hotel men's room to see the Boss standing before the row of washbasins, notes in hand, soundlessly moving his lips.

But that wasn't the problem here.

The Boss had been in and out of the john a couple of times beforehand.

The prepared text went on to read "To fully understand what I saw will require further prayer. Meanwhile, the fact that this event is attracting so many of the faithful is a sign of God's favor upon us. The Church rejoices in this event, whatever its meaning."

After the second failed attempt, the Boss sat back and took a sip of water. One of the cameramen rolled his eyes while a couple of others whispered to each other.

Then he straightened up and looked directly into the lights.

"Let's try it one last time."

He took a deep breath.

"Earlier today, I had the privilege of visiting the window. I approached it as I hope you would also—with humility and prayer."

Using no notes, he continued.

"No doubt many have visited the window with genuine religious feeling, but I see no miracle here. This event, whatever its cause, has been seized upon by those who seek to profit by it. It has been turned into a circus.

"Therefore, as your bishop, I urge all of the faithful to avoid the spectacle at Saint Kay's. Instead of getting caught up in the hype, let us focus on the Church's core mission, the sanctity of human life at all stages, peaceful resolution of conflict, care for the poor, the sick, and the marginalized—and most important, our Savior's message of tolerance and redemption."

The lights dimmed as soon as the archbishop finished, and the camera guys wasted no time getting their stuff packed up.

Dan felt blindsided. Never before had the archbishop abandoned his text. Never had he spoken so forcefully. And never before had he said something so controversial.

How could the Boss be so sure? The window at Saint Kay's might or might not be a miracle, but calling it a distraction and a circus was way out of bounds.

The symbol of the bishop as shepherd came to mind. This time, instead of tending to his flock, he may well have caused a stampede!

He thought about his predecessor, Frank Mulcahy, out there at Saint Gabriel's and wished that he too was a former secretary with only a parish to worry about.

The archbishop looked clueless. As if he hadn't singlehandedly invited an insurrection from the pews, the Boss pointed to his watch.

"Now we've got a wake to get to, don't we, Danny?"

Cowboy Joe was waiting at the wheel of the archbishop's black Mercury Marquis. The limo was appropriately impressive, but its license plate, 40, gave it added cachet.

Father Dan had heard all kinds of rumors about how Massachusetts 40 ended up on the archbishop's limousine. He didn't know much about "number plates" in other parts of the country, but in Boston, a low number was a sign of status and prestige. In fact, the low-numbered plates had a name coined exclusively for them, "affinities."

A few months earlier, Father Dan had accompanied the archbishop to a confirmation outside of the city. After the ceremony, one of the parishioners pointed to the license plate.

"Father, do you have any idea how the archbishop got that number?"

"I think it was given to one of his predecessors as a gift."

"The way I understand it, old Cardinal O'Rourke lobbied pretty hard to get that number, and my guess is that he had that particular number in mind. As you must know, the number forty is full of religious significance."

"I can think of Noah's ark and the days and nights Jesus spent in the wilderness."

"You're only scratching the surface, Father. I'm an engineer over at Minuteman, working on guidance systems."

Dan was aware that the defense contractor was the major employer in that part of the archdiocese.

"As you can imagine, I work with numbers all day long. You'd think that by the time I got home at night, I'd be sick of numbers."

"Yes, I think I would."

"Actually, numbers are my hobby, too. Especially religious numbers."

Dan didn't like the way the conversation was headed. Perhaps the guy was freaked out spending each day calculating payloads and trajectories for ICBMs and needed to compensate. He was into numerology, first cousin of astrology.

Who needs God when you have the numbers?

He glanced at his watch again. Where in hell was the Boss? They were already running late.

"The Old and New Testament are packed with references to the number forty. Moses spent forty days with God on the Mount, for instance; the number of days Christ remained on earth after the Resurrection; the forty days and forty nights of the Flood; and of course, the forty days God gave Nineveh to repent."

"Of course."

"And you know about St. Swithin's Day, don't you, Father? And the origin of the word quarantine?"

He was really getting wound up when the archbishop appeared and gave Dan the familiar "let's get out of here" sign.

Dan's favorite license plate, by far, belonged to Gene Autry. When

Dan asked him what the plate on his Jaguar, BITSA, stood for, Autry looked at him as if that was the stupidest question he'd ever heard.

"Although my namesake and I are not related, at least as far as I know," he said, "I'm trying to honor him."

Dan was still puzzled.

"'Back in the Saddle Again,' his greatest hit. You priests ought to get out more."

They made it to Mooney's by five o'clock and, after prayers at the casket, were ushered to the head of the receiving line by Eiko Mooney, who introduced the family. The archbishop greeted Kitty, whom he knew from the Mount of Olives Board of Trustees, but had never met Eunice's other daughter and her husband from Rhode Island. Eunice's niece and nephew from Cleveland were also on hand. Father Guido stood quietly behind Kitty and nodded in greeting.

Dan scanned the room, just to be sure, but Eddie Cronin was nowhere to be seen.

The grandchildren, Kitty's eight kids and her sister's twin sons, were not in the line but sat quietly in the back of the big room, the boys ungainly in their jackets and ties, and the girls with eyes red from crying. One of the littlest, a girl about two, blew a kiss at the archbishop.

Dan had brought up Eddie Cronin in the limo on the way over. He was worried about a confrontation and asked the Boss his thoughts.

"I haven't given that any thought, Danny. I guess I should have, but what with all that I was doing today—"

"You might want to consider what to say when you meet him."

"Danny, I'll let you do the talking. I'm sure you can handle it."

While the Boss was talking to the grandchildren, Dan asked Eiko Mooney the obvious question.

"Oh, yes, Dr. Cronin. He was standing here next to his wife when he motioned me over. He needed to make an urgent telephone call. I had my son take him to Michael's office for some privacy. You and the archbishop had just arrived."

Father Dan kept waiting for the thumbs-up signal, but it never came. Finally, he broke into a conversation the archbishop was having with Eunice's twin grandsons—something about holograms.

"Your Excellency, I'm sorry to interrupt, but you'll be late for your next appointment. We need to be going."

Eiko Mooney led them out the back exit, where Father Joe had parked the limo at the loading dock, out of sight behind some shrubs.

He had the engine running.

"Father Joe, instead of heading back right away, I want you to run inside and get Father Guido. Father Dan and I will wait here."

Dan wanted to object, but the Boss didn't give him a chance.

The young secretary was told to look for a tiny, roly-poly priest, bald, with a fringe of gray hair.

"Kinda like Friar Tuck?"

With that, Joe trotted inside, as if he'd been to Mooney's a hundred times.

The rookie secretaries got to know the layout of the funeral homes pretty fast.

In no time, he was back with his quarry. He opened the door so Father Guido could join the archbishop in the backseat before stationing himself outside.

"Thanks for coming out here, Father. I wanted to have a minute with you, privately. Oh, don't mind Father Skerry there in the front seat. I told him to switch off his hearing aid."

Guido looked like a defendant before the judge, awaiting sentencing.

"I want you to know how very proud I am of you."

Guido didn't react.

"I've learned that you handled a difficult situation with great skill."

Still no reaction.

"I'm referring to your response to Dr. Cronin's attempt to commercialize the apparition and your refusal to bless the materials he planned to sell."

"Oh, the simony issue, Your Excellency."

The archbishop smiled. "Exactly. You showed great courage standing up to him. As you know, he can be a bully."

"But in his heart, I'm sure he is a good man."

"I'm not so sure about that, Father Guido."

From his seat, Dan peeked through a gap in the shrubbery where a long line was forming on the sidewalk.

"There is something I want you to know, Father. And I expect you to keep this information confidential."

"Of course, Archbishop."

"I'll be petitioning Rome on your behalf, to be elevated to the rank of Prelate of Honor. We used to call it Domestic Prelate. Every time I turn around, Rome changes the name."

"Do you mean Monsignor, Archbishop Quilty?"

"Yes, Father. The simony business is a minor consideration. I'm making you a monsignor in recognition of your life's work, bringing the gospel message of love and hope to the most desperately ill among us. The paperwork should be completed in a month or so. They move slowly in Rome, especially in the summer."

This was all news to Dan. As a rule, the Boss would discuss such a decision with him before moving ahead, and the preliminary paperwork would already have been submitted before informing the candidate.

"Now I'm sure you want to get back inside to be with the family."

"Yes, Archbishop."

Joe was holding the door open for Father Guido when a commotion on the sidewalk got Dan's attention. People were clearing a path for something. Then he saw it. A Channel Six truck with a likeness of the Caruthers woman on its side and a satellite dish on its roof lumbered into the parking lot.

Joe must have seen it too, for without a word, he jumped into the driver's seat, put the limo in reverse, and turned sharply into the lot from behind the shrubs, missing the TV truck by inches—all the time with his free hand on the horn. Miraculously, the crowd on the sidewalk moved out of the way again, and #40 blended into the line of traffic heading in the direction of the residence.

16.

Eddie was impressed. Eunice lay there like she was just taking a nap. But it was not just that. So often he'd seen undertakers mess up the lower face, jaw, and neck, but her jaw line was perfect. In life, her jaw had been her most distinguishing feature.

Kitty once said that her mother had a "chiseled" jaw, and, strange as that sounded, he agreed. He was also grateful that Eunice hadn't passed the trait down to her daughter.

When arguing a point, she would lift her head so that her jaw would be at her opponent's eye level. Then there was no question that Eunice Rafferty would get her way.

Everyone in the room started buzzing about the archbishop's arrival when Eddie pulled Eiko Mooney aside to tell her he'd been paged and needed to make a phone call in private. Up to then, he had every intention of greeting the entourage from the chancery, especially since they would be on the defensive after this morning's encounter. Now he wasn't so sure.

Eiko had ushered him into her husband's private office and told him to take all the time he needed.

After making his phone call, Eddie took a look around. The office's only window was covered about three-quarters of the way up with one of those shutter-like wooden blinds that allow some light in at an angle but permit complete privacy. The walls were covered with the expected certificates, awards, and plaques. "Faneuil Chamber of Commerce—Business-Person of the Year—1999," "United Fund—Meritorious Service," "Saint Brendan's Church Restoration Fund—Benefactor," and so on.

Eddie looked for Mooney's Saint Katherine's Hospital Trustee Plaque. Then he remembered.

Michael Mooney showed up at Eddie's office without an appointment. As a rule, Gert sent such visitors packing, but she genuinely liked Michael. Apparently he had been helpful after a sudden death in her family years back.

Once inside Eddie's office, Mooney wasted no time getting to the point.

"Window dressing's one thing. That's what being civic-minded gets to be most of the time. But I have no intention of becoming party to a criminal enterprise."

By the time Eddie could respond, Mooney was already outside, wishing Gert a nice day.

His Trustee Plaque probably ended up in the trash within the hour, along with empty bottles of embalming fluid and other refuse Eddie preferred not to imagine.

He sat at Michael's desk biding his time until he heard somebody leaning on the horn out in the parking area. He adjusted the blinds just in time to see the archbishop's limo make an end-run around a Channel Six truck and take off.

He had no choice then but to rejoin Kitty for a minute before getting back to Saint Kay's.

17.

Father Richard Mears wasn't exactly a regular at the Faneuil branch of the Boston Public Library, but he showed up frequently enough to be recognized. In fact, when Helen Rowley saw the priest enter the lobby from the vantage point of her desk, she hurried over to greet him.

She wore a well-tailored white blouse with a high collar and a gold brooch. Her hair, unnaturally black, was pulled back severely. She could have posed for a nineteenth-century tintype of a preacher's wife, or the preacher himself for that matter.

"Hello, Professor. I know you never come in here just to browse. What can we do for you?"

He got right down to business. "I wondered what you have for Boston newspaper archives from 1859 and 1860."

He was not surprised by her response. Anyone else would have scurried off to look up the information.

"I'd start with the *Boston Evening Transcript* and the *Advertiser*. Then if you want to get the Church's view of things, take a look at the *Catholic Intelligencer*. There's also a handful of limited circulation papers that might be helpful. I can link you up to our archives at the main library, and you can download whatever you need."

"From the way you came up with the facts, Mrs. Rowley, a computer might be superfluous."

"Thanks for the compliment, Professor, but my brain is crammed with reference data, the stuff a good librarian needs. I don't have room for much else."

Within minutes, he was at a computer terminal.

She stayed with him a little longer than he expected, no doubt checking on the tremor. He could feel her looking over his shoulder, making sure that he still had enough agility to work the keyboard.

It made him think back to the day Leo Mulcahy made the initial diagnosis.

"There's one bit of good news, Father. This is a 'resting tremor,' the type that goes away when you move. An 'intention tremor' is far worse. With one of those, the more you move, the more intense the shaking. Simply lifting a cup of coffee to the lips can be a nightmare."

At last she told him to "just yell" if he needed any assistance and excused herself.

The apparition had been on his mind nonstop since Monday and was cutting into his sleep. This was unlike anything he'd ever investigated before. The nineteenth-century grotto dedicated to the Virgin Mary was on a hill, he knew. If that hill was the one now occupied by Saint Kay's, the window could be a fulfillment of her prophecy.

Even then, with Tuesday dawn breaking and the squirrels cavorting beneath his window, something didn't "smell" right. Much of his life's work depended on hunches—the "feel" or "smell" of a problem. His conclusions were always based on hard fact, but the "hunch factor," as he called it, was critical.

Something was telling him he was on the wrong track.

On Wednesday night, Archbishop Quilty listened carefully but wasn't impressed.

Increasingly skeptical himself, he had come to the library to dig up more information on the grotto.

He also felt rushed. After a few hours' sleep, he'd struggle back to his desk as if every hour counted. All the while, he kept thinking about a recent conversation with his neurologist.

"I've done more research on my condition and need to clarify some things. Am I going to lose my marbles?"

The neurologist rocked back in his chair and put the tips of his fingers together, the way kids make a church and steeple.

"Father, you have a big advantage over most patients with this condition: you exercise your brain strenuously every day. I like the athlete analogy. The more you exercise, the more you'll maintain your muscle mass, or in your case, brain function."

"What are the odds? I've had this thing for three years now, and I'll be turning seventy in December."

"Most people with Parkinson's don't get dementia, but some certainly do. The accepted figure is 30 percent, but many think the number is higher than that. The odds do rise with age, especially after age seventy. Most often, the dementia develops after having the disease for ten years or so, but for some, it comes earlier. A few unlucky people actually get the dementia before the tremor and the rest of the physical findings appear."

"Will the medications help prevent this dementia?"

"No. They only help with the physical part of the condition."

"So you agree with the 30 percent?"

"I wish I could, Professor." Then he stopped rocking. "But recent data suggest it's higher, nearer 50 percent."

Since then, he felt that his brain tissue was being eaten away by the Parkinson's, neuron by neuron, every day.

Scrolling though the August 1860 *Catholic Intelligencer*, he saw the word "grotto" glide by, but by the time he took his finger off the keyboard, it was gone. Going back, it took him several minutes to locate the word again.

It was an eyewitness account of the apparition by one of the pilgrims. Most of the account was similar to the one he read earlier in the *History of the Boston Archdiocese*, but one additional detail stood out.

"From the front of the grotto, we could see the River Charles meandering serenely through the meadows at the foot of the hill."

He pushed his chair back, pulled off his glasses, and wiped them with his handkerchief, while his heart raced as it always did when he made an important discovery.

Then he reread the passage to make sure he understood.

There was no such view of the Charles River from Hospital Hill, which sat a good mile south of the river's closest point near the Cattle

Drive restaurant. He wasn't sure quite how Hospital Hill looked in 1860, but it certainly didn't get whittled down like Beacon Hill, whose entire top was carted away to help fill the Back Bay. Still, the hundred-foot hill would need to be three times higher to provide the panorama of the Charles described in the old newspaper story. Even then, you'd have needed binoculars to get a decent view.

The description reminded him of the Charles he'd seen from Mount of Olives Academy on Tuesday afternoon, the day he met up with the security guard in the golf cart.

Once his heart settled down, he began working his way through the other accounts, taking notes as he went along. He found another mention of the Charles being visible from the hilltop, but it was so similar to the first that it probably came from the same source.

He was about to call it quits when a report buried inside the *Boston Evening Transcript* caught his eye.

The grotto had been accessible by a carriage road, described as "steep and winding" with a "sharp turn" just below the summit.

The present road up Hospital Hill was short and straight, and from what he could see, any other route from any direction could not have been any steeper or winding, even 150 years back.

Once again, he recalled his walk up to the Mount on Tuesday. The road up the hill was so steep and winding that he almost gave up.

He pushed back from the screen and tried to review what he'd learned. The evidence that had him so excited early Tuesday wasn't holding up. From what he now knew, the grotto was not on the site of the medical office building, or even on Hospital Hill.

He'd made a historian's fundamental mistake—making facts fit a preconceived notion.

Helen Rowley was nowhere to be seen when he got back to the library's lobby. Just as well, because he was too worn out to chat. He'd get some rest, and tomorrow he could start over.

18.

Father Dan instructed Joe to detour onto side streets so they could enter Little Rome through the rear gate near the abandoned tennis courts. The last thing they needed was another confrontation with the press.

By now the archbishop's statement would be headline news. Channel Six and the others would be promising the "expanded coverage" at six o'clock, and if anyone could get an exclusive with the archbishop, that channel would win the ratings game.

He was not surprised to see two big cruisers flanking the rear gate, but the archbishop looked shocked.

"What are they doing here?"

Father Joe braked and powered down the window.

"Good afternoon, Archbishop Quilty." It was a state cop Dan recognized from the height of the abuse crisis, when the Boss was under police guard. "We thought you might come back this way."

He then turned to Father Dan.

"The media contingent has doubled out front, and I hear a good-sized demonstration is getting organized."

Dan prayed that the archbishop wouldn't ask why.

"There's no practical way for us to cordon off sixty acres—"

"Sixty-four," the Boss interrupted.

"Thank you, Your Excellency. That would make the task all the harder. Instead, we will be manning the entrances and patrolling the grounds. We've spoken with your housekeeper, Sister …"

"Sister Philippe."

Dan pictured himself sealing the Boss's mouth with duct tape.

The cop nodded deferentially. "We asked Sister Philippe to lock all the windows and doors, close the curtains, and expect three of my men to be staying overnight, one on each floor."

With that, he waved the limo onto the grounds.

19.

Portia and Vincent spent the rest of the day looking over the photo albums.

They started with the wedding album. Portia remembered the rainy afternoons when she'd take that oversized leather volume from the living room bookshelf and sit on the carpet cross-legged, with the open book between her knees. She'd pretend to be the bride and imagine the solemn ceremony, dancing at the reception, and the excitement as she and her new husband left on their honeymoon.

The photos, black-and-white with crenellated borders, were as familiar to her as if she'd looked at them only weeks ago.

She'd forgotten all about Father Mal, but the more pictures she saw, the more she recalled. Her mother was Father Mal's biggest booster, telling everyone that he married them, baptized their children, and, "God willing," would do her funeral (which he did). He appeared in the photos of the wedding itself, of course. What she'd forgotten was that he was in most of the other pictures as well, usually in the back, almost but not quite out of range. He was all over the Vets Club at the reception and even appeared in the shot of the newlyweds waving from their car, festooned with crepe paper and a *Just Married* sign. In that one, everyone including the bride and groom were waving, but Father Mal just stood in the shadows, watching.

They attacked the albums chronologically, watching her and Frankie grow up, and her parents age. Maddy the photographer was seldom seen but did appear at most important events.

"She'd trust me with the camera once in a while," her father said while opening still another album.

They buzzed through the earliest albums quickly, since they were filled with the usual crib, playpen, and stroller pictures.

After that, things got more interesting. Several pages were filled with pictures from a cousin's wedding where she'd been the flower girl. Then there were lots of birthday parties with friends she had totally forgotten. Some she remembered right away, but others would have been totally lost without Maddy's captions.

Vincent brought another stack of albums to the table after lunch. The top one, unlike the others, had an inscription of the cover.

Portia's First Holy Communion, May 7, 1964
Saint Lawrence Church, Egg Rock

"I gave your mother a new camera at Christmas—an Instamatic—and she couldn't put it down. And remember, Pumpkin, she was a Sunday school teacher at the time, so she was always around."

Inside, again in chronological order, were shots not only of the Mass itself, but of the preparation for weeks before the event—buying the dress, etc.—and then breakfast in the church hall afterward, and Portia and the other kids outside playing tag, still in their First Communion best.

She pointed to a picture of a rack of identical white Communion dresses. "I remember that! That's Rogers and Sanborn's in Squimset. They carried hundreds of dresses and suits for the boys—white, too, but all with short pants. They looked so silly! But for my veil, we had to go to a store that sold religious goods over in Salem."

"Dorgan's."

"That was it! An eerie place, with all kinds of altar pieces on display. They had one of those sun-burst gizmos. You know, where they put the host inside, and everyone prays."

"Monstrance."

"Right. And I remember they had a mannequin of a priest all dressed up in the front window."

Again, Father Mal was in just about every group of pictures.

Under the heading *Dress Rehearsal*, Father Mal was inspecting the kids all lined up in the center aisle of the church.

Portia laughed. "There I am in the front row. The reason I'm there is that I was the shortest. Shortest first, tallest last.

"Father Mal looks like a general inspecting the troops."

When Portia looked at the picture again, she snapped the album closed and stood.

"I'm going out for a walk."

"Echo and I could join you."

"No. I need to be alone."

20.

Helicopters hovered overhead. There must have been a half dozen of them, some whirring westward toward the archbishop's residence and others heading back east toward Saint Kay's.

Claire looked up from the passenger window, worried that they'd collide.

"Don't worry, Claire. They're in formation."

The whirring was only a distant hum by the time they reached the lights at McKinley Circle and crossed into Muddy River.

Leo switched on the TV in the kitchen the minute they got into the house. Then he pulled a bottle of wine from the fridge.

"We're going to need this."

Leo was, as Claire put it, a "mega-surfer." Remote in hand, he tried to avoid repetition, commercials, and "human-interest stories" that took up so many of the newscasts. He just wanted the "facts."

Each of the local anchors must have been standing only a few feet apart, since the view behind each of them, with the trolley tracks, the stone wall, and the archbishop's palazzo up on the hill, was identical.

They all played the archbishop's statement at the top of the hour.

Afterward, they all showed the crowd milling around. Signs and banners were sprouting up by the second. Three big ones were being pumped up and down in front of the cameras.

Don't Mess with the Blessed Mother!
The Faneuil Miracle is For Real!
Quilty Can Go to Hell!

Claire finally put her foot down.

"Settle on one, Leo, or I'm confiscating the remote."

He picked Channel Six, since it was planning "continuous coverage" instead of breaking for the network newscast.

Corinne was hard at work as always.

"Archbishop Quilty is under police protection at his residence tonight. If you look behind me, you can see that the window shades are down and the curtains pulled. He did attend a wake in Faneuil earlier but sped away before our crew could ask him any questions. Now we'll take you over to the Miracle Window for the latest there."

A woman who could have passed for Corinne's younger sister stood in front of Leo's building, with little to report.

Leo switched the TV off, and they sat, watching the twilight deplete the garden of its colors.

Too much was happening for them to start talking right away.

Claire thought back to when she first saw the window on Monday. Awestruck in the morning, she was disgusted by evening.

She imagined the archbishop going through the same change of heart, but of course she had no way of knowing. Anyway, he got it right. The window was a distraction and a circus and was being exploited for the wrong reasons.

Her mind drifted back to her childhood.

A gold-framed picture of the Blessed Mother hung over the buffet in their dining room in Bangor. Paul claimed that wherever you sat, she was looking directly at you. Under her gaze, they did their homework at the big table each evening.

Likenesses of the Virgin were everywhere at Sainte Jeanne D'Arc School—inside and out.

Claire and the ten other girls sat on the auditorium stage for the Legion of Mary induction. It was a big affair, with the hall filled with proud families. The state chaplain for the Legion came up from Portland and gave a talk entitled "Our Lady's Submission."

"Our Blessed Mother," the priest explained, "teaches us about submission. She accepts the will of God without question. She is never upset. She is never angry. She is never rebellious."

Claire didn't give the priest's message much thought until her best friend, Aimee, called it brainwashing. Another time, Aimee pointed out a portrait of the Virgin, fair-skinned and blondish.

"We're talking about a Jewish woman from the Middle East. There's no way she could look like that."

As she got older, life got more complicated.

Her brother, Paul, was killed senselessly. As a nurse, she watched people suffer through no fault of their own. By then, it was getting pretty hard to see how a loving God could exist.

Then a cute medical student named Leo Mulcahy walked into that emergency room in Portland. It was obvious to her on that very first evening she met him that he was smart, hardworking, and caring—and sure of himself the way only people who've been tested by life can be.

He had come to take a patient upstairs, an old man with pneumonia. She'd thought back to that nameless, disheveled gentleman many times over the years.

"Claire, honey, a penny for your thoughts."

"Remember your first patient up in Portland?"

Leo smiled. "The prophet."

"When Frank came up from Boston to help marry us, I told

him about the old fellow in the emergency room. Know what Frank said?"

"Tell me."

"God put the man there for a reason."

"I wish I could believe that. I really do. But the fact that I don't believe it doesn't make me love you any less."

Claire gave him one of her lopsided smiles.

"I know that, Leo. And I don't love you any less for not believing."

Claire got up to fix supper.

"You promised to tell me about Father Guido."

Leo gave her the lowdown on the FedEx, the near suicide in the garage, the nap, and the appearance of the Virgin in the picture window in Gull.

Then he told her about the office visit. Guido's blood pressure was down, as he'd told her earlier. But there was something else he couldn't quite put his finger on.

"A new self-confidence is the best I can do."

He handed her the FedEx and excused himself a moment.

Minutes later, he returned with a vase of roses. "Guido asked me about these and wasn't at all surprised they were flourishing. He was sure the Virgin Mary was sending me a message."

"Where's the sarcasm?"

"I don't believe any of what he said, of course, but I respect his feelings."

After the meal, Claire laid the three pages of the FedEx side by side on the table and read them slowly a couple of times. By then, her mind was made up.

"Leo, we need to go to Saint Kay's tonight."

"Rowley changed the locks."

"He says a lot of things that just aren't so."

Leo didn't look enthusiastic.

"You know what a night owl he is. We'd probably walk in on him."

"You could call Pat Kaminski. His guys could let us know when the coast is clear."

"Okay, Claire. I'll call Pat. If your plan can help Guido, I'm in."

"It's not a plan, Leo, just a hunch."

Leo looked at his wife.

"Sweetheart, are you okay?"

"I'll feel better when we learn the truth."

21.

Gert called in an order for Chinese and told the woman at the Panda Parlor Take-Out that she expected the food to be dropped off at 8:00 p.m. sharp at the executive offices.

"Tell your little driver that Dr. Cronin expects the food to be hot this time. I don't mean spicy hot, but hot as in the opposite of cold. The stuff you sent over last time hadn't seen a stove for hours. And make sure he brings plates and utensils for six—and plenty of paper napkins. That moo shi pork gets sloppy. Chop, chop!"

Then, before locking up her desk for the night, she made one last call.

"Quiet, Philippe! I'll do the talking."

22.

The archbishop peeled off for his private chapel as soon as the priests got in the door. Several minutes went by before he reemerged, ducked briefly into the restroom, and then slipped into his private office and shut the door firmly behind him.

Sister Philippe had switched on the table lamps. Father Dan thought back to what his grandmother had told him about the blackouts during the war.

"The shades had to be pulled completely tight. If the air raid warden saw even the tiniest chink of light, he'd issue a citation."

She wasn't talking about London, but Boston. Boston never got bombed, of course, but for a while they thought it would happen.

Now, Little Rome was about to have its own *Blitzkrieg.*

The Boss stole into the room without a sound. In fact, Dan didn't know he was sitting there until he spoke.

"Danny, we need to talk."

"Where do you want to begin?"

"Let's start from the present and work backwards."

"Okay. How about your statement? You sure surprised me."

"I surprised myself, Danny. Until the last minute, I had no idea what I was going to do. That's why I excused myself twice to practice alone before the taping began."

Dan nodded.

"Well, I stood before the mirror, trying to read the script, and had just as much trouble as I had later in front of the cameras. I thought of calling the whole thing off, but that would have caused such a stir. So I convinced myself that I'd be okay once the cameras were turned on. Well, I was wrong. Do you remember when I sat a minute after the first two tries and drank some water?"

"Sure."

"The strangest thing happened. The text of my revised statement appeared before my eyes, in the same type as the original statement—in those extralarge letters from your word processor. I'm not making this up, Danny."

The archbishop glanced at the curtained window for a second, as if he could see the crowds outside.

"The only conclusion I can draw is that the Holy Mother herself was letting me know that the 'apparition' at Saint Kay's is a fraud."

Father Dan pointed toward the street. "What about the backlash?"

"I'm not worried. We're on the right side of this."

"I hope so."

"Before I forget, make a note to call Frank Mulcahy in Salem and ask him to see me here—tomorrow."

Dan was wondering what that was all about when Sister Philippe appeared out of nowhere, announcing that the TV coverage of the demonstration had been interrupted by a news flash. A line of severe thunderstorms was coming in from the west. Tornadoes were a possibility. She wanted to know whether the archbishop should take shelter in the basement.

Smiling, he slowly shook his head no.

Just then, Dan heard a loud thunderclap. He parted the curtain a few inches and saw it was already raining heavily.

"Look, Archbishop, people are running for cover."

"See, Danny. I knew things would turn out okay. Sister Phil, what's for supper?"

23.

Vincent had the TV on when Portia returned. He'd been checking the Weather Channel every ten minutes because of a squall line speeding in from the northwest. Boston was already getting hammered, but it looked like Egg Rock would be spared. He was also watching the Boston skyline from the windows. They were getting vivid lightning with some beautiful "shazaam" cloud-to-ground bolts every couple of minutes.

"Wow, Pumpkin, we're seeing the storms three ways at once. It doesn't get any better than this!"

"The crickets are making a racket out there, Dad. When I was a kid, the sound made me so sad."

"No wonder. You don't hear them until the middle of August, and by then you were thinking about going back to school. Your Uncle Walter was an expert."

"On crickets?"

"On everything. Geology was his passion, but birds, bugs, flowers, fish—all interested him. He told me I could have the weather, but he managed to stick his nose there, too."

"So do they rub their legs together to make that sound?"

"It's not their legs rubbing together; it's their wings. Late summer is mating season, and the sound is the guys looking for mates."

"Figures."

"The most interesting thing, though, is that you can calculate the temperature by counting the sounds. Count for fifteen seconds, add forty, and presto, you have the temperature in degrees Fahrenheit."

"So they slow down as it gets colder. That's sad, too."

"I found something else while you were out. It was in your mother's things."

Vincent handed his daughter a silver cup.

"We gave this to you when you were a baby. It's called a christening cup. It was a tradition to give this to each newborn, but I don't think folks do that anymore. Frank must have had one, too."

"I see my name on the front, but what's that on the back? A poem?"

"You know how you got your name, don't you?"

"I don't remember ever being told, but we read *The Merchant of Venice* in high school, and everything clicked—Portia acting the lawyer and all that. We never talked about it because so much was going on then. I actually read the play again awhile back at the urging of my therapist. I was trying to understand who I was."

"Read the back. It's a quote from Portia in the play."

She put on her glasses.

The quality of mercy is not strained.
It droppeth as the gentle rain from heaven
Upon the place beneath. It is twice blest:
It blesseth him that gives and him that takes.

Portia held the cup in both hands a moment. Then without a word, she gave her father a kiss on the forehead and ran upstairs.

24.

Pat Kaminski instructed his men to keep an eye on Dr. Rowley's office, just as Leo requested, and once Rowley cleared out, he got a call from the head of the night shift.

At the hospital, things turned out just as Claire had predicted. The key to Rowley's office worked fine.

While Claire went through Rowley's desk and file cabinet, Leo took a look at the Purple Heart in its glass case. On the night Leo came back from Vietnam, the family threw a welcome-home party. That was when Uncle Vinny told him a story about the Purple Heart.

During my war, the government manufactured two hundred thousand Purple Hearts for the casualties expected from invasion of the Japanese home islands. Then came Hiroshima and Nagasaki, leaving this huge surplus of medals for the ground attack, which never happened. Most are still in storage, but I can see the day when they'll be cranking out more of them.

Claire brought a file folder over and placed it on the desk in front of him. It was labeled "FedEx" in block letters.

"He labels everything," she commented.

There were a half-dozen pages inside. On top were the obituaries of Kevin Sheehan, Thomas Rowley Jr., and Father Guido himself. They appeared identical to the ones in the FedEx delivered to Guido.

Next came three more sheets of paper stapled together. The first was a scientific paper entitled, "An Improved Vasectomy Technique," by Bruce Gilchrist, MD. It was followed by a short quote from the papal encyclical *Humanae Vitae* on page two, and an article from the *Mobile Morning Messenger* from 1965.

Last in the group was a copy of an op note for a vasectomy, filled out by Gilchrist personally by hand. The patient was Edward Cronin.

At the back of the folder were some copies of FedEx order forms.

Claire photocopied everything quickly and placed the file folder back in the cabinet exactly as she had found it.

"So far, so good," she said as she pulled a piece of paper from her pocket.

"What's that?"

"Oh, I jotted down a couple of potential combinations for the keypad. I'd love to get into the 'inner sanctum.'"

"Didn't you ask him about it once and get nowhere?"

"Yep. Remember, he told me he kept his research papers there, away from plagiarizers. But judging from the gowns, gloves, and masks he has stored here …"

She opened the bottom drawer of the file cabinet.

"It has to be a lab."

"How did you come up with your combinations?"

"I'm only guessing, Leo, but I think the combination is a date. Most are. Usually dates we carry around in our heads."

She entered some numbers on the keypad and waited. After each sequence, she tugged on the handle, but the door didn't budge.

"May I see the paper?"

"Sure, but they're just the dates of what Tom must consider important—birthdays, dates he'd know by heart, his birthday of course, that's the first one, Helen's, and Tommy's. I even managed to look up his parents', just in case. None work."

"What about the day Tommy killed himself?"

"Darn! I should have looked that up."

"It's right here on the obit you copied, 12/27/94."

Claire punched in the numbers, and the door swung open silently.

It looked like a miniature micro lab, with the usual paraphernalia crammed into the closet-like space. The incubator had a glass door, allowing them to see petri dishes arranged in neat piles. There were no "research papers" to be found.

However, a book lay open on the lab bench. It was a typical lab notebook, just like the ones Leo used in medical school—with hard-backed faux-leather covers and pages lined not only horizontally, but also vertically, making it easier to make charts and graphs.

Without a word, Claire stepped back into the office to turn the copier back on, and Leo followed with the notebook.

Twenty minutes later, they had copied every page and returned the notebook to its exact place on the lab bench, doused the lights, and locked up.

This time Raymond Stanton acknowledged them with a friendly wave when they walked through the lobby on their way to the garage.

25.

After Gertrude's phone call, Sister Philippe still needed to turn down the archbishop's bed and get the breakfast table set up for the morning.

Then she could sit with a cup of tea in her favorite chair in the back of the pantry. It was the perfect hideaway, where no one could see her when the door from the dining room opened. And it was blessed with its perfectly placed little window overlooking the carriage entrance to the residence.

Once settled, she'd give Gertrude's message serious thought.

To see Gertrude today, it was hard to imagine her, a willowy seventeen-year-old, walking into the old convent down the hill from Little Rome on the day the new postulants arrived.

It had been only a couple of years since Philippe had made her final vows, and this was the first time she was given the responsibility of mentoring one of the young would-be nuns.

Gertrude lasted barely three months. Philippe helped her pack her bag the week after Thanksgiving, and she never thought she would see Gertrude again.

Years later, however, she got a phone call at the residence from her old mentee, who sounded distraught. Her son (Philippe didn't know until then that Gertrude was married, had a child, or anything else) had been admitted to Saint Kay's and somehow managed to climb out a window and fall into the courtyard a year before. After a day on life support, he died. Philippe remembered the archbishop talking about the incident at the time, especially since the hospital president was worried about a lawsuit. There was also a little article she remembered seeing in the papers, but she never made the connection.

"I know we haven't spoken in years, but I remember how kind you were to me in the convent, and hoped I could speak with you."

There was no way that Philippe could refuse.

It turned out that Gertrude was working at Saint Kay's by then, so their first meeting was over coffee in the hospital cafeteria. The poor girl said she had no one to talk to. She and her husband, the boy's father, had been having a rocky time as it was, and their son's terrible death only made things worse.

Philippe listened sympathetically but finally asked how Gertrude located her.

"Your sister."

Philippe's sister had worked at Saint Kay's some years back, and Gertrude's first position at the hospital was in the same department. Philippe's name had come up in conversation, and Gertrude made the connection right away.

It wasn't long before Gertrude enlisted Philippe's help. Over another coffee, she said that her boss, Dr. Cronin, was interested in getting a heads-up each time the archbishop planned to visit the hospital. Cronin wanted to be on hand day or night, even if the archbishop preferred to keep his visit secret.

When Philippe hesitated, Gertrude changed her tone.

"I'm sure you'll help out when I mention the little problem your sister had at Saint Kay's."

Philippe knew that her sister had been fired from the hospital finance department without warning but was never told the details. From what Gertrude said (and backed up with documents she'd brought along), Philippe's sister had diverted some insurance payments to her personal bank account. The hospital decided not to prosecute, to avoid publicity, but Gertrude was prepared to send copies of her documents to her sister's new employer and the IRS.

Philippe had no choice.

"Okay, Gertrude. The archbishop usually tells me where he's going, and if he doesn't, I usually overhear him and Father Skerry making plans."

She felt like she was digging this deep hole, so deep that she could see stars, whole constellations from the bottom, in spite of it being the middle of the day. And every time she'd give Gertrude information, the hole got deeper.

But on the phone tonight, Gertrude didn't ask for information the way she always did. Instead, she gave Philippe a warning.

"Make sure you keep Boss Quilty from visiting Mount of Olives on Saturday. I'm not going to tell you why, so don't ask. I don't care if you put knock-out drops in his orange juice, tie him to a chair, or crown him with one of your cast-iron skillets. Just don't let the old boy go up that hill."

The archbishop was a stubborn man. Take the thunderstorm earlier in the evening. When she suggested taking shelter in the basement, he brushed her off.

Then she remembered that the archbishop and Dan were making plans to attend a meeting at the Mount of Olives School on Saturday.

She'd keep her ears open.

26.

Claire cleared the kitchen table and put on a pot of decaf before they got down to work.

The first three pages of the copied file were identical to Guido's FedEx, so they turned their attention to the rest.

Gilchrist's paper on vasectomy was the usual dry recitation one would expect from a urology journal. The bottom line was that he'd devised a faster and safer method for performing the procedure. Leo remembered hearing about the paper when Gilchrist was hired.

The quote from the papal encyclical was brief and pointed.

"Equally [with abortion] to be condemned, as the Magisterium of the Church has affirmed on many occasions, is direct sterilization, whether of a man or a woman, whether permanent or temporary.

"Similarly excluded is any action which either before, at the moment of, or after sexual intercourse, is specifically intended to prevent procreation ..."

The old newspaper article told about how Alabama country folks had known about the properties of the extract of boiled sugarcane root for generations. It was especially beneficial for men, who found "renewed vigor and vitality" with regular use.

The last sheet was a FedEx invoice, containing three names and addresses: Father Guido della Chiesa in Gull, Dr. Bruce Gilchrist in Metro West, and Mrs. Katherine Cronin at Sycamore Hill.

"Leo, I'm so frightened. Should we call the police?"

"No. The police could do only one thing."

"What, dear?"

"Arrest us for breaking and entering."

The newspaper article from Alabama didn't fit in. Then Leo reminded Claire that American Pharmaceutical Enterprises (APE), the company that Eddie Cronin made a deal with to stock the Saint Kay's formulary, was headquartered in Mobile.

"Either it's a coincidence or—"

"No, Claire. Rowley learned that Eddie had made a deal. I bet it's a new drug that will make him a lot of money."

Next they looked over the pages Claire had copied from the notebook on Tom Rowley's lab bench. Rowley had inscribed the front page in neat block letters:

F. TULARENSIS DATA

Date and time were carefully noted in the corner of the pages, packed with columns of numbers. Leo didn't understand everything but recognized bacterial growth curves and drug resistance data. This went on for twenty or so pages until they came to the entry dated just three days earlier, on Monday. The entire page was filled with a remarkably accurate sketch of the image on Leo's office window. Leo stopped turning the pages and looked up.

"It looks like this religion stuff is catching."

"Leo, I feel like such a dunce! My own boss was doing all of this right under my nose, and I didn't catch on."

On the very next page, they found another sketch depicting a diagram of a building, with a corridor and rooms marked "kitchen" and "conference room." It was otherwise unlabeled.

They looked at each other and shrugged. It looked like nothing at Saint Kay's or any other place else they could think of.

"Leo, you need to speak to Guido."

"It's too late now."

"He's got Eunice Mulcahy's funeral in the morning."

"When there's a quiet moment in the next couple of days, I'll sit down and tell him. But first we need to figure out what else to do with this stuff. What good would it do to tell him right away?"

"None, I suppose."

FRIDAY

1.

Over breakfast, Claire told Leo that she'd had a dream about her brother, Paul, during the night.

"Not surprising, I suppose, since it's his anniversary," said Leo as he looked out the kitchen window. Leo had a theory that anniversaries take on an added power because of the angle of the sun.

"Run that by me again, dear."

He explained that the *lighting* of every August 19 is the same, as long as you're on approximately the same latitude. And lighting has significant evocative power.

From where they sat, the sun was barely above the neighbor's garage roof, the light reaching only the tallest roses at the back fence, while the big magnolia in the middle of the lawn was casting a shadow for the first time in months.

The morning the soldiers arrived looked much the same.

Claire was having breakfast with Mom and Dad when they came. The Beauregards didn't see the official car pull up because the kitchen was at the back of the house. So it turned out that the neighbors knew about Paul before they did.

She ran to answer the doorbell, thinking it was her friend Aimee.

Two men stood there in their olive-green uniforms with gold buttons. The older one had rows of multicolored decorations on his jacket, and the younger one only one or two. Their polished black shoes shone in the morning sun while they stood before her, hats in hand.

The only sound was birds singing in the trees.

Before Claire could utter a word, she sensed her mother behind her.

"Oh God, not Paul. Blessed Mother, no, no, no."

In those first years after Paul was killed, Sainte Jeanne D'Arc in downtown Bangor was jammed for his anniversary Mass. Since their parents both came from large families, innumerable aunts, uncles, and cousins Claire barely knew showed up. Her father closed the market, and all the employees were expected to attend. Most of them remembered Paul, who worked there on school vacations and summers, starting out as a stock boy and check-out clerk, finally rising to the evening manager before he left for basic training.

In those years, the pews overflowed with classmates, buddies from the football team, and many of his teachers.

Last year, a total of eight people showed up.

2.

Father Dan had already gone through the newspapers and was working on the crossword when Archbishop Quilty strode into the dining room.

He hadn't seen the Boss walk with such energy and authority since he became secretary. When he knocked on the archbishop's door, as he always did at five-thirty, he didn't know what to expect. Thursday had been such a nightmare, with the dawn incident at Saint Kay's, the archbishop's off-the-cuff statement for TV, Eunice Rafferty's wake, Father Joe's acrobatics behind the wheel, the protestors, the police guarding the residence, and the storm.

He half-expected the archbishop not to answer, but the voice behind the door was strong.

"I'm all set in here, Danny. Did you reach Frank Mulcahy?"

"Yes, Archbishop. He plans to be in Faneuil on other business today. I asked him to come at ten."

"Good. See you downstairs after prayer."

The archbishop had put up with rheumatoid arthritis for years. He loved to tell the story of how his affliction began hours after he held the umbrella for the pope's secretary during the Holy Father's visit to Boston, twenty-three years before.

From then on, he kept the problem under control by popping a handful of aspirins every day.

But the morning after learning of his elevation to archbishop, he awoke with a high fever and was so stiff and sore that he could barely get out of bed. Overnight, his arthritis, always a nuisance, had flared into a serious medical issue.

"I guess God doesn't want this assignment to go to my head," he joked at the time.

His knees and hips froze, making it impossible to walk any distance without a cane, and soon all the joints in his hands and fingers stiffened and swelled. Over time, fine movements like buttoning his shirt or tying his shoes became almost impossible.

He confronted these obstacles with zippers and Velcro and the constant attendance of Father Dan, who added the titles of valet and personal care attendant to his job description.

Most people outside the archbishop's inner circle wouldn't have picked up on his disability, had it not been for Holy Communion. The arthritis had no effect on his sermons or speeches, and when he celebrated Mass publicly, other priests and altar servers did most of the physical work. He only had to lift the chalice and the host at the moment of consecration, bow and genuflect a couple times, and he was done. He did all that at half speed, but no one seemed to notice. Or if they did, Dan thought, they'd be gratified that the archbishop wasn't rushing through the most solemn part of the liturgy.

As for other ceremonies, such as ribbon-cutting and cornerstone-laying, the archbishop did little more than show up anyway. Father Dan, of course, remained at the Boss's side, ready to assist with a shovel or a pair of scissors.

The distribution of Holy Communion was the big problem.

The simple process of picking an individual wafer out of the ciborium, holding it up in front of the person about to receive, and placing it in the person's cupped hands or on their tongue became a struggle.

Masses at which the archbishop officiated slowed to a crawl.

Lines for Communion became inordinately long and slowed down the entire liturgy. Things got so out of hand at the cathedral that the rector instructed his ushers to move the faithful into the shorter lines in front of others who were distributing Communion. Complaints about this practice grew, and one unhappy worshiper told a reporter that she was "man-handled" by the cathedral staff and was consulting an attorney.

Leo Mulcahy increased the archbishop's steroid dose and started him on a round-the-clock aspirin regimen. When even those stepped-up measures didn't make a dent in his symptoms, Leo referred him to a rheumatologist, who started once-monthly infusions of a brand-new medication.

The effects were dramatic. Within days, he was walking without a cane for the first time in years. He was told that the medication could affect his immune system, but he wasn't worried. Danny himself would bring an occasional cold or stomach upset back from their travels and pass it on to Philippe and the rest of the staff, but the Boss never came down with anything.

Shortly after the second infusion, Father Dan walked into the Boss's study to find him at his easel.

"My fingers are coming back, Danny. See, I can actually hold the brush again!"

The archbishop had been painting all his life, and when he

graduated from high school, he came close to choosing art school over the seminary. He explained his decision to pursue Holy Orders this way: "As a priest, I could always paint on the side, but as an artist, I could never be a priest on the side. This way, I have the best of both worlds."

His talent was obvious to anyone walking into the residence, where his work graced the walls of his study, the large sitting room where he entertained guests, the formal dining room, and the guestrooms.

Father Dan's favorite was an impressionist-style watercolor of sailboats on the Charles that hung above the Boss's desk.

Sister Philippe had already left the carafe of coffee, a glass of orange juice, and his pills at the archbishop's place, while his daily ration of raisin bran, a pitcher of skim milk, and his bowl awaited him on the sideboard.

"What's in the papers, Danny? We gave them plenty of ammunition yesterday."

After yesterday's excitement, Father Dan made a point of looking at the newspapers first thing. He was downstairs so early, in fact, that he, not Sister Philippe, brought them in from the doorstep.

"They're holding their fire, Archbishop. They both printed your statement on the front page, and the Early Bird News on Channel Six used the tape of the statement as its lead story."

"Any editorials?"

"None. No editorials, no op-ed pieces, no opinion whatsoever."

"I threw them off stride, Danny."

"I'll say."

"What about the so-called assault?"

"The papers are downplaying it. One has one line about us 'bumping into' the TV crew buried on page twelve, and, believe it or not, the other totally ignores it. I figured the Early Bird News would be running the tape of our confrontation, but after leading off with your statement and broadcasting another remote from the window, they moved on to weather, sports, and entertainment news."

The archbishop pointed in the direction of the street.

"They're still out there, aren't they?"

Father Dan nodded. The demonstrators, scattered by the thunderstorm, never returned. But the TV trucks remained in place, ever vigilant.

While the Boss downed his pills, Dan scanned the papers again, making sure he hadn't missed anything.

Unlike the sex abuse scandal, the Boston papers had different views on the Virgin Mary story. The high-brow *Transcript* reported everything tongue-in-cheek, to the point of putting the word apparition in quotation marks every time they used it, whereas the *Traveler* seemed a shade more open to the possibility that a genuine religious event could be taking place.

Until now, both papers agreed on one thing: people couldn't get enough of the story. Not a lot had changed since Monday—she was still up there on that office window—except that the crowds had gotten larger each day. In order to keep their readership happy (and sell more papers), both featured lots of pictures and interviews with visitors, clergy, and self-styled experts.

Father Richard Mears, probably the only true local expert on such phenomena, was barraged by requests to be interviewed but repeatedly declined.

In the Friday edition, the story was still on page one of the *Transcript* but had fallen below the fold for the first time all week. The story still had the blessing of the *Traveler*'s management, however, taking up the entire front page of the tabloid.

In addition, the *Transcript* was planning an "in-depth" report, comparing the Faneuil Miracle to Lourdes and Fatima for its Sunday Arts section.

The archbishop suppressed a small belch with his napkin. "What ever happened to the old-fashioned Religion Section?"

Father Dan added that the *Traveler* was not to be outdone.

It planned to publish the results of its "scientific" telephone and Internet survey on miracles, also in its Sunday edition.

"Where do you think they'll put their report, Danny? On the sports page?"

The archbishop walked over to the massive mahogany sideboard (a gift from one of the late Cardinal O'Rourke's admirers), gazed at the cereal bowl for a second, and shook his head.

"I can't face another breakfast of twigs, no matter what Leo Mulcahy says."

He turned back to his secretary.

"Danny, do you drink skim milk?"

"No, but I suppose I should."

"Don't. It's a quality of life issue. I always get a chill every time I taste the stuff, and lately whenever I look at it. I don't know the science, but skim milk is colder by far than ice water. Maybe they use dry ice. Take my advice, Danny, and wait a couple of years before switching, because by then researchers will be warning that twigs and skim milk cause cancer. I can see it coming."

He ambled over to the kitchen door and eased it open a few inches.

"Sister Phil, could you fry a couple of eggs sunny-side up for an old admirer?"

This was met with a girlish giggle from the other side, and then "Of course, Your Excellency. Have a seat, and I'll get them ready."

While his favorite breakfast was being prepared, the Boss got back to business.

Father Dan recounted the essential stories in the papers while the archbishop worked on his eggs and the two slices of buttered toast that Sister Philippe had added as a "bonus."

"By the way, Archbishop, Bishop Fannon's speech at the Knights of Columbus dinner last night was a big hit. The *Transcript* reports that he brought the audience to its feet with a story about some nuns getting lost at Disneyworld."

"That was your joke, Danny, the one I used at the Conference of Women Religious in the spring. It fell flat then."

"An open bar can do wonders."

The boss was still bent over his plate when Sister Philippe reappeared, letting out a torrent of "franglais." The only words that Dan was sure of were "telephone" and "Sarto," but that was enough.

Giuseppe Sarto was the papal nuncio—the pope's ambassador to the United States.

The archbishop nodded to Sister Philippe, downed the last of his eggs, and darted out of the room. Seconds later, Dan heard the door to the Boss's office shut firmly and the lock click to the closed position.

3.

At breakfast, Portia announced that after the Paul Beauregard Mass and lunch, she'd be visiting an old friend.

Vincent couldn't understand how she'd kept up with acquaintances from twenty-plus years back when she barely communicated with her own family, but he was happy for her. Apparently the friend worked not far from the Cattle Drive—close enough, Portia added, that she'd be able to walk there from the restaurant. The friend would take her back to Egg Rock later on.

"Is this a friend from before you left home?"

"No."

"What does he or she do?"

"She's a librarian."

"So you know her from work?"

Portia shot her father a look he knew well. He'd seen it hundreds of times from people he questioned in depositions and trials … and even in his own clients, when he sought out personal information. It was a stare, eyes opened wide for a second, saying you've crossed the line, and you're not getting anything else out of me if I can help it.

"Yes. We've corresponded but never met."

"Okay. Did you work on a project together?"

"No. Libraries are all interconnected by computer these days. You get all kinds of requests to borrow materials, that kind of thing."

"So you got acquainted through the Internet?"

"Dad, you make it sound unsavory."

"I think you're overreacting."

"And I think you're asking too many questions."

Vincent finally changed the subject.

"Frank will drop us off at Saint Kay's to see the window while he's at another appointment."

"I'd like that. What did Frankie say about the window? Does he think it's a miracle or a hoax?"

"He didn't bring it up, and I didn't ask."

"It sounds like you're easier on him than on me."

4.

Kitty, Bridget, and the younger kids stood at the top of the steps watching Eunice Rafferty's casket being carried into Saint Brendan's. The men of the family served as pallbearers, with Eddie and Buzzy at each end, and the children, John, Lawrence, Ambrose, and their cousins, Sean and Kevin, at the sides.

Saint Brendan's was filled to capacity, reminding Kitty of the very same church on her wedding day. This time, too, there were lots of unfamiliar faces, no doubt friends and colleagues of Eddie's she'd never met.

Without warning, Irene broke away from her mother to join the pallbearers, but Bridget caught up with her before she could disrupt the procession.

Eunice had to be smiling down at that moment.

Kitty thought back to her own wedding, which almost never happened.

Eddie Cronin and Kitty Rafferty were having an unorthodox courtship. Eddie had limited time off from his residency at Saint Kay's that summer and divided his free time between his two passions, cars and the Church. Kitty was welcome to come along if she wanted. And she did.

They spent a couple of weekends at the formula races down at Lime Rock. Actually, Eddie watched the races, and Kitty watched Eddie. While the cars whizzed around the little track, Eddie jumped up and down like the other fans and seized her around the waist and twirled her around a couple of times after his favorite car won.

At the Checkered Flag Motel, they slept in the same room for the first time. Kitty thought that it was fine to share a room since it meant saving money, but Eddie assumed that sharing a room automatically meant sex. He started hinting around and even mentioned that he had brought along "some protection."

That's when they had their first argument, which Kitty won.

Eddie used most of his remaining time off that year working on his old Chevy or taking Kitty along to some church event. Being a religion major, she expected these outings to be more to her liking than car races, but she was mistaken. The boyish enthusiasm Eddie displayed at the track didn't carry over to his dealings with the church.

Somebody was sending Eddie a copy of Cardinal Campion's weekly schedule, and he made it to any event where he'd have a chance to hobnob with the cardinal. They even went to the cardinal's birthday party in a big tent behind the residence on a beautiful July afternoon. On the way in, Eddie pointed out Saint Luke's Seminary at the foot of the hill.

"What's that over there, Eddie? A chapel?"

"It's a long, sad story involving a great churchman who's been forgotten."

Eddie took her to the cathedral in the South End the week before she was due back at college, and after Mass, the rector greeted Eddie like an old friend and gave the couple a guided tour.

Kitty was astounded by how much Eddie knew about the cathedral and its place in the history of the archdiocese. She had taken a seminar on Boston church history junior year, but she was no match for Eddie and the monsignor. They walked around the handsome church trading anecdotes while Kitty admired the stained-glass windows.

Over dinner in the St. Botolph Hotel dining room (a favorite of Boston priests), Kitty told him how impressed she was. They shared a bottle of wine, and Kitty, knowing that she could get tipsy on just one glass, had three.

"How did you find time to learn all this church history?"

"I have a confession to make, Kitty. I spent a few years in the seminary. The rector was one of my professors."

Kitty couldn't believe that she hadn't figured that out on her own.

"Eddie, we've been dating for months, and I find this out now?"

"I wasn't sure how it would go over, Kitty. Some women consider ex-seminarians damaged goods."

"You know, Eddie, you're much more lovable at the races."

"This church stuff is really part of work."

"What do you mean, Eddie? You're a doctor, not a priest."

"Kitty, honey, I plan to stay at Saint Kay's—"

"I still don't understand."

"I intend to be the president of Saint Kay's, but I'll never get the job without connections. And the most important connections are inside the most political operation of them all, the Church. The best way to be an insider is to know all the inside stuff, even if it's mostly trivia. By the way, do you remember that little chapel you pointed out at the cardinal's birthday party?"

Kitty nodded.

"That's Cardinal O'Rourke's gravesite. Do you remember who he was?"

"Sure. Boston's first cardinal."

"And the creator of Boston's most powerful political machine."

She began to laugh, first just a snicker, and then louder and harder than she had since she was a little girl. It must have been the wine catching up with her. She laughed so hard that her eyes watered and her stomach tightened up. People at other tables started to stare. Still she couldn't stop.

"What's so funny?"

"Eddie, dear, with all your obsessing about 'inside stuff,' trivia, and power, you've forgotten the basic gospel message."

With that, she started to giggle again—and began feeling sick to her stomach.

"Blessed are the meek, Eddie, for they shall inherit the earth."

"You're drunk, Kitty. We're out of here."

Father Guido celebrated Eunice Rafferty's funeral Mass. Eddie had lobbied hard to get the archbishop to attend but had to settle for Auxiliary Bishop Fannon. Fannon did as little as possible, sitting motionless in his seat throughout the Mass.

Eddie had parted from the other pallbearers and settled into the space beside Kitty in time for the first reading. When she looked over at him, he was glaring at the bishop with that flushed look he'd get just before blowing his top.

Everybody knew that Fannon was Boston's designated funeral bishop, dispatched to every send-off the archbishop could wiggle out of. It made perfect sense, since Fannon was by far the most senior member of the hierarchy, and most likely to have his own obsequy soon enough.

In fact, the staff up at the chancery referred to a proper Boston passing as "having your Fannon moment."

The only time Eddie looked at her was at the Sign of Peace and when they left their pew for Communion. Then, without a word, he slipped out of the pew to rejoin the pallbearers during the final prayers.

Kitty had selected "Lift High the Cross" for the recessional. Eunice had always sung that hymn like a football fight song. She had no tolerance for "recycled Protestant hymns" like "Amazing Grace" and "A Mighty Fortress is Our God" by, of all people, Martin Luther, and she reminded everyone that before "all those Vatican reforms," those non-Catholic hymns were never sung in church.

And it was through Eunice Rafferty's efforts that you'd never hear "drivel" like "Kumbaya" or spirituals like "Were You There?" up at Mount of Olives. Some Christmas carols really set her off, too. She had nothing but contempt for "It Came upon a Midnight Clear" and "O Little Town of Bethlehem," written, as she let everyone know, by a Unitarian and an Episcopalian. For her, "The Little Drummer Boy" was only a step further on the road to perdition.

"That's why we started going to Saint Brendan's in the first place," she once told her daughter. "And that's why we started our school, to end the 'watering down' of the true Church."

After Father Guido's last prayer, the Commendation of the Dead, the pallbearers gathered in front of the altar. Only Eddie was missing! When Michael Ichiro Mooney took his place at the end of the casket, she figured Eddie's back was acting up again.

Eddie or not, she couldn't have engineered a better exit for her mother. With the procession working its way down the center aisle and out the big doorway into the sunshine, the soloist belted out Eunice's favorite hymn, and everyone in the church joined in.

"Lift high the cross, the love of Christ proclaim, till all the world adore His sacred name."

Outside, cars were lining up for the trip out to the cemetery. Each had a little black pennant attached to its antenna, with *Funeral,* in yellow letters.

Eddie reappeared and looked at his watch before clearing his throat. He always cleared his throat when he was about to say something he knew his wife wouldn't like.

"Kitty, I've got to get back to the hospital."

"Now? What about the cemetery?"

"Now," he called over his shoulder as he hurried over to a car she hadn't noticed before, idling on the other side of the street.

"That husband of yours really is a son of a bitch," said Bridget, as she watched her brother-in-law jump in.

He barely had the door closed when the car sped away.

5.

Father Dan refilled his cup and paced the room.

He was being frozen out.

After the archbishop's disastrous run-in with the press in the first months he was in office, he relied on Father Dan for just about everything. Their "symbiotic" relationship (Frank Mulcahy's term) became stronger in those early days, as the Boss's rheumatoid arthritis worsened. Dan was with him 24/7, and he believed that the Boss's physical dependence brought about dependence in other areas.

Frank noted during one of their periodic dinner meetings that Dan was the Dick Cheney of the archdiocese, wielding unprecedented power. Dan laughed Frank off, of course, but knew his predecessor was right.

He was writing the Boss's speeches, choreographing his appearances, taking his phone calls, and often speaking in the Boss's name without clearing it first. He even knew the location of the safe, hidden behind the big watercolor in the Boss's office.

Yes, the safe. For reasons Dan couldn't fathom, the archbishop insisted on keeping Father Mal's diary there, instead of destroying it. It had been mailed anonymously, and the Boss shared its contents with Dan soon after receiving it.

One night, the mother of a boy named Tommy Rowley confronted the Boss and Dan at his booth in the Cattle Drive. Before Dan could get rid of her, she told Quilty of her suspicions about Father Guido molesting Tommy and causing his suicide. The Boss had no choice but to agree to look into things and get back to her. Of course, there was no way the Boss could tell her the truth—that Mal was the molester, and Guido was innocent—because questions about the Father Mal cover-up would be sure to follow.

Back at the residence later that evening, the Boss told Dan to find Philippe and send her into his office. From what Dan could hear, the Boss had her open the safe, since his fingers were giving a lot of trouble at the time. After she departed, the Boss invited Dan inside and showed him the diary. In it, Mal chronicled his sexual exploits in detail, adorning the narrative with marginal sketches. The entries about the Rowley boy were especially graphic.

So Archbishop Quilty and Father Dan did the only thing they could do.

They remained silent.

The Boss shared information selectively. Over time, he showed Dan other items from the safe but not everything. And who was to say that there weren't other hiding places?

Dan knew that he'd been told part of the story, but the day could come when he'd be held responsible for all the sordid details. As weak and dependent as the archbishop appeared, he was a crafty man.

Just then, the Boss came out of his office, carrying a business-size envelope with his episcopal seal in the left upper corner.

"Danny, I need you to hand-carry this letter to Eddie Cronin, put it in his hands yourself, and tell him that you've been instructed to await his reply, in writing. By the way, we'll be having a houseguest on Sunday."

Father Dan was not in the mood for another surprise.

"Archbishop Sarto, the papal nuncio," as if Dan didn't know who Sarto was, "will be flying up from Washington."

6.

During the ride into town, Portia tried to get Frank's take on the window but got nowhere.

At Saint Kay's, they had no trouble finding their way, since that was where everyone was headed. You had to be living under a rock not to know the details. Not being a "believer" in any sense, she figured the apparition was either a hoax, a weird chemical reaction, or a colossal publicity stunt. Vincent filled her in on the hospital president, Eddie something-or-other. Apparently Frankie had dealings with the guy when he was the archbishop's secretary—and considered Eddie an overly ambitious, ethically challenged publicity hound. The guy was on TV nonstop and was clearly relishing the attention. It would make sense that this Eddie character cooked the whole thing up.

That's why the window itself was such a shock.

It's not like she had some religious conversion. She was way beyond anything like that.

The window was shimmering with vivid colors, and once her eyes adjusted, she could make out a humanlike form. Possibly it was a woman and child, but she quickly decided that she made that connection because of all the hype. A humanlike form was the best she could do.

As for Portia, deciphering the message was not a priority. *Feeling* was the important thing, and she felt more comfortable, more relaxed, and more serene than she had for years. The sense of well-being she had made her realize how inadequate her therapy and medications had been.

7.

Dan was waiting for Frank outside the entrance to the residence.

"Did the Boss get around to telling you what this is about?"

"Nope. Your guess is as good as mine."

"Will you be there?"

Dan shrugged. "Negative. He's flying pretty much solo these days. This will be strictly one-on-one."

"Say a prayer."

Since Quilty was smiling when Frank entered the office, he figured it wasn't going to be bad news—and he was right.

"Thanks for coming over, Frank. I'm going to ask you a big favor."

Frank was beginning to think that "bad news," at least in the conventional sense, might be better than what he was about to hear.

They sat in leather armchairs at the window.

"We've known each other for years, and I hope you know how much respect I have for you—especially the way you made the transition from Little Rome here back to parish work. The people in Salem love you. But I imagine you have some nostalgia for your days here."

Just then, Sister Philippe slipped in silently with a carafe of coffee, winked at Frank the way she did back in his secretary days, and exited quickly.

"Don't worry, Frank. I'm not inviting you back. I wouldn't do that to my worst enemy. In fact, I'm doing the opposite. I'm inviting myself to Salem, to be a senior priest at Saint Gabriel's. Don't worry. You won't be losing any staff. I'll be in addition to, not instead of."

Frank wasn't sure he understood.

"Let me repeat, Frank. I want you to remain pastor of Saint Gabe's, and I'll be there to assist. No one I know is a better pastor than you, and I want to learn from you. I know it's an unusual career move, but it's not unprecedented. Before making this decision, I thought of moving into the monastery for keeps, but that would be simply throwing in the towel. I want to make a difference.

"Everybody knows that I've been on the fast career track all along—and that I actively sought out my promotions. I spent most of the year after ordination at Saint Eulalia's, the same place you broke in, and those months were the only time I really felt like a priest."

Frank nodded.

The archbishop poured coffee for the two of them.

"You know a lot about the archbishop's job, since you worked for Cardinal Campion for—have I got this right—ten years?"

"Wow! You're very close, Archbishop. Nine years, seven and a half months."

"You might as well get used to calling me Sebastian again, like the old days, before I … I got to be important."

"I'll try."

"Well, Frank, when I was named archbishop, I expected to be able to follow my own conscience, to make decisions on what I believed was right or wrong, but that rarely happened.

"I needed to fine-tune every statement to pacify multiple groups. The 'faithful,' as you know very well, are not a monolithic group thinking in lock-step, and thank God they aren't! The 'faithful' are made up of individuals with different ideas about what being a person of faith is. Then there is the church leadership—here as well as in Rome—and they can be hard to read. That's not all. Anything you say will be analyzed and criticized by the political establishment, the press, and other religious leaders.

"I've spent too many of my days being a paper-pusher, spin-master, and a lightning rod. That leaves little space for what the archbishop should be doing—being a spiritual leader. I know that others—and I could name a few—could be very successful in the position. I simply haven't been a good fit."

"Parish work has its disappointments, too."

"I'm ready for that, Frank. Nothing turns out exactly the way you expect."

"Amen."

"That brings me to the window. Have you seen it?"

"I came into town on Monday to have a look."

"And?"

"I chickened out. I stood there a long time, but I couldn't pull it off. I guess I was afraid of what I'd see."

"I don't know what I'd have done in your shoes, Frank, but I had no choice. But it worked out. Otherwise, I'd still be playing it safe—and we wouldn't be having this conversation."

The archbishop paused while a trolley made its way noisily along the tracks outside the residence.

"The window crystallized what I was feeling about my life—what I was just talking to you about. The instant I looked at it yesterday morning, I saw no miracle. To make matters worse, whatever it was, a random chemical reaction or an outright fraud, it was being exploited for financial gain and notoriety—and creating a scandal for the Church."

Eddie Cronin's name remained unspoken, but it didn't matter.

"You see, Frank, I have been too timid to say what I thought, too afraid of the reactions I was sure to provoke. Then, yesterday afternoon, when I tried to read a prepared statement about the window, a statement that really said nothing, I had a moment of clarity—an epiphany. I am convinced that the Holy Spirit guided me to the right decision—to reject not only the window, but all the damage it was doing.

"Paradoxical as it sounds, my rejection of the so-called apparition has strengthened my faith. As soon as I finished making the statement, I had my mind made up to be a real priest. Suddenly my wishful thinking became a concrete plan. That's when I asked Dan to give you a call. We'd been giving Salem some thought anyway. For some time, our plan had been to suppress Saint Monica's but keep it as a chapel of Saint Gabe's, with you as pastor for the whole city. Having me come on board will work perfectly, since you'll have more to do. Perhaps you could send me over to do their 'golf Mass.' You know I'd slow the pace down a bit."

Quilty looked directly at Frank to make sure he was listening carefully. Apparently satisfied, he continued.

"I want to learn how a parish really runs. I want to celebrate Mass for people who really know me. I want to live a life of service. I want to visit the sick, hear confessions, marry people, celebrate funeral Masses. I want to share others' moments of joy and sadness, as a friend and counselor. I want to live out my faith in God and the gospel. And, Frank, I'm asking you as a brother priest to help me do that."

Frank didn't give a damn about protocol or etiquette when he reached over and squeezed Quilty's hand.

"You can count on me, Sebastian. The only problem I foresee is how you'll want to be addressed."

"Father Sebi should work."

8.

Paul Beauregard's picture sat on the easel outside the chapel. It was a twenty-by-thirty blow-up of a snapshot he must have sent home.

Tom Rowley was pleased that it was in black and white. The detail was sharper than you'd get with color, especially with the technology they had back in the sixties.

His own color shots from that era were blurry to begin with and quickly became discolored.

Paul was seated on a box stenciled "fuzes," smiling shyly. He was dressed in fatigues and wore a camouflage-covered helmet with a small Magic-Markered peace symbol inscribed on the front. A helicopter was sitting on the tarmac in the background. It was a Huey, officially the UH1, easy to ID with its stubby nose and the diagonal pitch of its rotor blades. The kid was probably about to fly out to a firebase to rejoin his unit. Or maybe he was going on R&R.

Tom planned to ask Claire if she knew.

The young soldier had Claire's jaw and cheekbones, but the eyes, nose, and mouth were inherited from other parts of the Beauregard gene pool. In spite of all the props, the kid looked like an imposter, auditioning for a school play.

Tom was sure that Claire had put the portrait in the lobby without permission. He couldn't imagine Guido approving.

Guido wouldn't take a piss without checking with Eddie and the archbishop, in that order, he thought.

The hospital chapel was nearly full when he slipped into the last pew. From his seat, he could see Guido spending a moment up front with Claire, Leo, and the kids before getting into his vestments and beginning the noon Mass.

Claire had left a message on his answering machine. He feared that she was itching to get back to work, but she never mentioned it. Instead, she invited him to Paul's anniversary Mass.

"You never knew Paul, of course, but I thought in light of your both being over there …"

He expected more, but her voice just trailed off, and she hung up.

This was his first time inside a church since Tommy's funeral. The appearance of the Virgin Mary and the inescapable conclusion that she was guiding him made him think hard in the last few days about returning to the fold. In fact, Claire's message was further evidence of the Holy Mother's influence; if she hadn't appeared, there would have been no Mass and no invitation.

The pattern was obvious if you cared to look.

There was an empty seat up front, which he assumed was being held for Eddie Cronin. Everyone knew that Eddie attended noon Mass regularly and had a seat more or less reserved in the front row. One time, a newly hired administrator sat in Eddie's place, and Gert gave the guy a little page about the matter as soon as the Mass ended.

Eddie wouldn't be there, of course. No one would expect him to come from his mother-in-law's funeral.

He was surprised at how familiar the liturgy was and had no trouble standing and kneeling at the appropriate times. Things that are beaten into you as a child stay with you for life.

An elderly man and younger woman, perhaps father and daughter, presented the gifts.

Communion posed a dilemma. He decided beforehand that he should not go up, that he needed one long and thorough confession and absolution before receiving the Eucharist. But when the entire chapel stood and lined up, he changed his mind. He decided that sitting alone while the others "received" would make him stand out.

He cut the line on the right side of the aisle so he could receive the host from Leo's brother, Frank Mulcahy, instead of Guido.

At least Mulcahy *looked* like a priest.

Afterward, the crowd poured into the hospital lobby where the family had stationed themselves beside Paul's picture. The arrangement made the long-dead soldier look like part of a receiving line.

Claire introduced Tom to the couple who presented the gifts. "This is Leo's uncle Vincent and cousin Portia. She's Father Frank's sister."

The old man seemed affable enough and gave him a strong handshake. The woman was plain looking, forgettable if it weren't for the chunky Navajo necklace she wore.

"Dr. Rowley, is your wife a librarian?" she asked unexpectedly.

"My ex, to be exact, but yes, she's a librarian right here in Faneuil. Do you know her?"

"We've never met," Portia answered, before turning away to take another look at Paul Beauregard's portrait.

9.

Frank's meeting with the archbishop ran much longer than he'd expected, giving him no time to speak with Vincent and Portia before Paul Beauregard's Mass.

Pulling out of the hospital garage, he pointed a finger in the direction of the MOB.

"What did you see, sis?"

"I don't know, Frankie. I need time to sort out my feelings."

"And you, Dad?"

Vincent was silent a moment.

"A con job, pure and simple."

Claire had reserved one of the Cattle Drive's function rooms, the one on the far side of the big horseshoe bar, with a fine view of the Faneuil Marina and the Charles River.

Frank had been in the restaurant so often in the past week that he wished they offered frequent-flyer miles. When he walked in, he half expected to see Gert Kleindienst sitting in a booth, working on another manhattan.

At least this time his role was clearly defined. He was to say grace.

He'd had plenty of experience with the bittersweet gatherings following a funeral or memorial service. The easiest, and rarest, were spontaneous celebrations of long and happy lives, but many were awkward affairs, especially when the deceased died young or tragically. As he looked around the room at the guests for Paul's memorial luncheon, he thought of one he attended during his first priestly assignment, years before.

Well lubricated at an open bar, family members got into a fistfight that was broken up only after the police arrived. Young Father Frank spent the remainder of the evening accompanying the injured to the local hospital for X-rays and stitches.

The group gathered in the function room wasn't about to rumble, he knew, but it was an odd assortment nevertheless. He picked up bits of conversation—baseball, the weather, vacation plans, but no mention of Paul. It would be his task to remind them one more time of why they were gathered and then let them get on with their lives.

While lunch was being served, he stood, and the other guests shuffled to their feet.

"Eternal and loving God, help us honor the brief life and brave sacrifice of your servant Paul, and help us remember the sacrifice of countless other men and women whose service is forgotten in the hectic pace of our daily lives. We beg you to help us make decisions that will protect the Paul Beauregards of our generation, both on the battlefield and upon their return. We pray for their families and loved ones. And in the name of your son, the Prince of Peace, we pledge ourselves to end the folly of war and seek peaceful solutions to our conflicts."

He then raised his hands over the table.

"Bless us, O Lord, and these your gifts, which we are about to receive from your bounty.

Through Christ our Lord. Amen."

Over the meal, the conversations picked up where they'd left off.

10.

Tom found himself seated beside the woman with the Navajo jewelry, the one who knew about Helen but had never met her.

The woman asked him about his work and seemed to understand when he spoke about the more technical aspects of what he did.

"You must be a medical person."

She could have been a Navajo shaman, he thought, laying hands on the dying, mumbling incantations to their gods.

"I don't have any formal medical training, but I read a lot, being a librarian and all. I'm particularly interested in the biological basis of emotional disorders."

She was beginning to sound like someone who had undergone too much psychotherapy.

"I believe you wrote a paper on the contagion theory of homosexuality … how 'deviant sexual behavior' itself could spread through the population like an epidemic."

He was stunned. He did write such an article many years back, for a throwaway journal that had long since ceased publication. He'd forgotten about it until she brought it up and wasn't even sure what he'd written.

"Where on earth did you find that old paper?"

"It popped up on a computer search."

He'd need to locate the paper in his files and ask Helen what she knew about this strange woman.

Leo tapped her on the shoulder. He had his college-age children with him, and they shyly greeted this aunt they had never met. The boy stood there, looking like he'd die of boredom.

As Tom watched the little drama unfold, he could not recall one minute of the seventeen years, five months, and twenty-two days of Thomas Rowley Jr.'s life when he looked bored.

11.

That hideous woman was sitting outside Dr. Cronin's office when Father Dan walked into the executive area. Her desk was positioned so close to the door to the inner sanctum that all she needed to do was lean over a few inches to speak to her boss—or block any undesirable from entering.

Give her two more heads, he thought, *and she could be Cerberus guarding the entrance to Hades.*

He wondered if this creature had any kind of a sex life and immediately checked himself. It was only a little after noon, and he had already added two items to the list for his spiritual advisor: his anger toward the archbishop, and now these bizarre sexual thoughts.

"I'm Father Skerry—"

"I know," she interrupted. "The TV star. You've made quite a name for yourself around here, Danny Boy."

He refused to take the bait.

"The archbishop has instructed me to hand-deliver a letter to Dr. Cronin. Is he available?"

The woman looked like she'd enjoy barbecuing the priest for lunch, on a long spit.

"Give me the letter, Father, and I'll see that it gets to Dr. Cronin as soon as he's free."

He pictured her holding the oversize envelope in those fingers with the long curved nails, over a steaming tea kettle, and then reading the contents.

"The archbishop ordered me to hand-deliver the letter to Dr. Cronin *in person* and await his reply."

After staring at Dan several seconds, she motioned the priest to a leather loveseat. It was crisscrossed with large brass tacks that indented the surface so severely that the diamond-shaped areas between them bulged to the point of bursting, and its color, somewhere between crimson and fire-engine red, reminded him of a creature recently skinned alive.

At last, in a voice more gravelly than ever, she said, "I'll try to find out whether the doctor can see you. Read a magazine or something."

He imagined that she could provide some graphic ideas for "something" before he thought about his spiritual advisor once again.

In an instant, she disappeared into Cronin's inner office.

12.

Vincent felt drained. He had picked at his food and worried that he was coming down with the flu.

As he thought about it, though, it was Paul Beauregard who killed his appetite, the countless Paul Beauregards. He thought back, as he always did at times like this, to Okinawa. They were bombing the heck out of the Jap mainland by then, but everyone was talking about the inevitable ground assault—with street-to-street fighting, Kamikaze-like resistance, and a million American casualties.

Then Truman had the guts to drop atomic bombs on Hiroshima and Nagasaki, and the war was over in days.

He arrived on Okinawa after the long battle for control of the island ended. Until then a B-29 radioman with thirty-five bombing runs over the Japanese mainland under his belt, his luck changed. He would still be a radioman, only now on the ground. His assignment was to obtain data—basically temperature, wind direction, velocity, and barometric pressure—from other stations throughout the Pacific. The weather team then transferred the information to large maps and tried to figure out where the fronts were.

In the end, their forecasts were accurate less than half the time.

He made a habit of getting out on the runway to watch over guys strapping themselves in, all smiles, before giving the ground crew a thumbs-up. Many never came back, of course, but the ones who bothered him the most went down in weather his group failed to predict.

In October, about a week before he shipped out to the States, a monster typhoon veered off its expected course and slammed into Okinawa with over one-hundred-mile-an-hour winds. Vincent spent hours lying in a trench while debris whizzed overhead.

The damage was total, but he knew things could have been worse. If Truman had not dropped the atomic bombs and war had not ended, they would have been in the middle of the Japanese land invasion, and the typhoon could have cut supply lines and communication, endangering the entire mission.

Vincent knew that he needed to talk to Frankie about his little prayer at lunch. That line about the "folly of war" was way off base. It brought dishonor on Paul Beauregard and the millions of other men who served their country. Like it or not, war was a reality. He really hated it when anyone, his own son included, who hadn't put his own life on the line made such sweeping statements.

Frankie was waving the white flag of surrender.

Things were no different now than they were in the war … only the enemy is different.

With the world full of terrorists, haters of our way of life, bringing down innocent people in airplanes, crashing into office buildings and killing thousands, how could his own son be so blind?

No wonder he felt like shit.

After the lunch broke up, Frank spent a few extra minutes with Claire, while Vincent and Portia went outside to look at the steers. The life-like Texas longhorns had adorned the entrance to the restaurant since the day it opened. Portia got a kick out of them when they drove into the lot earlier and wanted to get a closer look.

If Maddy were there, he thought, she'd be snapping pictures.

Portia walked up to the fiberglass animals and looked one in the eye. She seemed in no rush to leave.

Vincent considered bringing up Portia's friend the librarian again. If he heard right, she was the ex-wife of one of Leo's colleagues at Saint Kay's. Interesting, he thought, but not worth another confrontation.

Instead, he moved on to the next best thing, the apparition.

"Are you still sorting out your feelings about the window?"

"Yes. By the way, what did you mean about it being a con job?"

"Eddie Cronin has taken a little chemical reaction between two panes of glass and hyped it into a religious miracle. It's as simple as that."

"That's what I was telling myself—*before* I saw it."

"Now you've drawn another conclusion?"

"I'm not 'concluding' anything. I had a feeling of *purity*."

"Go on."

"She was pure, unworldly, unencumbered by all the pettiness, meanness, selfishness, greed that we experience every day."

Portia gestured.

"Just look around, Dad. Look at the crappy world we've built for ourselves."

"A parking lot in the middle of Faneuil isn't the nicest place, I'll agree—"

"But the whole world is getting just like this—overcrowded, noisy, polluted. I'm just saying that the image up there on the window, whatever it is, is pure and uplifting."

Just then, Frank emerged from the restaurant.

"We can drop you off."

"No thanks, Frankie. The library is only a few blocks from here. The walk will do me good. And, Dad?"

"Yes, Pumpkin?"

"Don't wait up."

13.

As the meeting between Eddie and his executive committee wore on, Cronin looked more and more pissed off. J. J., the only invited guest, knew the look. Eddie's cheeks were more flushed and the nose even redder than usual.

From what J. J. could piece together, the board had just reviewed the annual audit of the hospital's books before he was invited in. In the past, the auditors had barely glanced at the hospital retirement fund and the trustees' profit-sharing plan, but this year, they gave these accounts a careful look. In their report, the auditors went so far as to cite "inconsistencies," "deficiencies," and "puzzling omissions."

Apparently, a new chief auditor was assigned to Saint Kay's, and he hadn't been briefed on how to proceed.

Autry, the hospital lawyer, was trying to spin things by saying that "no one was alleging misappropriation of funds, falsifications, or fraud." Nonetheless, he raised the possibility of suing the auditors for malpractice. Although none of the board members looked as incensed as Cronin, they all looked pretty glum.

From the looks of Autry's suit—Italian cut, meticulously tailored—he must be pulling in a nice hourly fee. But what a ridiculous name! He should have had it changed years ago. J. J. couldn't understand why the guy would allow himself to be called Gene Autry, whose namesake was a goddamn singing cowboy.

Just as Autry was finishing up, the office door opened silently, and Gert slipped into the room.

"I need to have a word with you privately, Dr. Cronin," she said as she eyed the other participants in the meeting as if they were trespassing.

The next thing J. J. knew, he, Gene Autry, Pinkham, the health food magnate, and that doormat Gilchrist were being herded into the little washroom. And the final indignity was hearing Cronin turn the key in the lock.

Suddenly, J. J. felt he had to take a leak but decided that he'd sooner let his bladder burst than be put at a disadvantage by relieving himself in front of those other guys.

But his bladder problem got resolved right away. Gilchrist the urologist announced he needed to "take a whiz" and proceeded to do so. J. J. was surprised that a professional urinary tract expert of his stature didn't use the term "void" or "micturate." Then, before J. J. could get in line, Autry announced that he needed to use the "head," and Pinkham got in line behind him. When J. J. finally got his turn, he could think about other things besides the sharp, tingling sensation at the tip of his penis. Maybe everything else would turn out okay, too.

The captives turned their heads toward the door when they finally heard the key turn again.

"Sorry to keep you in here so long, gentlemen. An urgent matter has come up, and I'm going to ask you to leave the office by the back exit. J. J. knows the way and will lead you out."

With that, Cronin closed the door and turned the key in the lock once again.

When J. J. pushed back the towels to reveal the Alice in Wonderland door, the other guys laughed.

Obviously sharing J. J.'s literary sophistication, Autry exclaimed, "Where does this go, to a fuckin' rabbit hole?"

J. J. squeezed through first. He was getting better with practice. Maybe his occasional workouts at the gym were paying off after all.

Autry had a little trouble getting his long, angular body through, and it looked for a moment that he'd leave an arm or a leg behind, but he made it. Pinkham appeared to have no problem, and shrimpy little Gilchrist also made it with ease, closing the dollhouse door behind him.

As he waited for the others to exit, J. J. looked down and was pleased that no one was on the service road to witness their flight. He was also reassured by the cool feel of the little brass key that he pulled from his pocket.

Like a squad leader, he led his recruits quickly over the fire escape toward the safety at the bottom where they'd be hidden by the pine trees.

Then the unthinkable happened. He must have caught the heel of his new Cole Haan loafers on the metal step and lost his balance. He hadn't broken the shoes in yet, and he wasn't used to the extra height of the heels. He had a fleeting image of the salesman saying how "athletic" the built-up shoes made him look, while he was trying to regain his balance. He was finally able to correct himself to avoid falling flat on his face, but he lost his concentration for a second, and the key tumbled out of his hand and fell thirty feet to the ground below.

"Shit, guys, that was the key to the gate at the bottom of the stairs."

14.

Kitty was furious. Until Eddie sped away from Eunice's funeral, she had been just numb. Now she agreed with her sister.

Eddie Cronin was a son-of-a-bitch.

Father Guido kept the burial service mercifully brief. It was getting hotter by the minute, and the air was dead still. But during the committal prayers, Kitty couldn't think about her mother anymore. Eddie monopolized her thoughts.

They served catered sandwiches and coffee back at the house, and Bridget was able to shoo all but immediate family out of there by two o'clock.

The twins left for Rhode Island soon after that. Bridget was pleased that Brian was going to stay with his brother overnight in Providence before taking the train back to New York.

Finally, the au pair piled the kids into the minivan for ice cream, and Kitty, Bridget, and Buzzy sat in the empty kitchen.

Bridget had an idea. Actually, she and Buzzy had been talking about it since they arrived.

If they were ever going to find out what Eddie was really up to, they should get into the garage and have a look around. It shouldn't be much of a problem to pull off, she added, because Buzzy's education on the streets of Woonsocket included "gaining access to unauthorized places."

"And I think you told me there's a safe. Well, Buzzy has had some experience in that area, too."

Kitty pictured the thing, an ancient free-standing model on tiny wheels that must have weighed a ton. Eddie picked it up at a foreclosure auction years before. They had to use the services of three Saint Kay's maintenance men and their truck to get it transported to Sycamore Hill.

She'd never seen Buzzy look flustered before.

"Wait a second! I wasn't the only kid in town to get lessons, and I never robbed a bank or anything."

Kitty looked at her sister.

"I can't say I'm not tempted."

"We'd be in and out in a few minutes, and no one would be the wiser."

Afterward, Kitty was shocked that it took her so long to decide.

"Bridget, I just can't do something like that. I couldn't look the other way while you and Buzzy broke in, either."

"Are you sure?'

"Yes, Bridget, I'm absolutely sure."

15.

Frank got free of the Faneuil traffic and headed east along Charles River Drive to the turnpike entrance. Once they were settled into the flow of traffic on the pike, Vincent tuned in the all-news station to check the weather forecast.

Tropical Storm Arthur was a hundred miles off the Carolina coast. It had actually "lost some of its punch," as the announcer put it, with top winds of sixty-five miles per hour. The National Hurricane Center expected the system to track north for the next few hours, before colliding with a high-pressure zone over the Delmarva Peninsula and getting pushed out to sea.

"It should only be a problem for North Atlantic shipping," the fellow concluded before breaking for commercials.

"That's good news for the summer fair, Frankie. I was afraid you'd get rained out."

"I guess my prayers were answered."

"Speaking of prayers, Frank, I didn't think much of your prayer at lunch."

Frank took his eyes off the road a moment and looked at his father.

"I think we've had this discussion before. You seem to think that when I criticize war, I dishonor those who fought. Nothing could be further from the truth."

Vincent looked out the passenger window without saying a word.

They passed the airport, the Dawes oil tanks, and the big rotary just south of the Sachem River Bridge before Frank finally broke the silence.

"What have you and Portia been talking about?"

"I'm afraid I've been doing most of the talking."

"Has she talked about her life in California, her work, her friends?"

"Not really, Frankie. Actually, not at all, now that I think of it. Has she told you anything?"

"No."

After dropping his father off at the house, Father Frank drove on to Saint Gabriel's, saddened by the reminder that he and his father disagreed about so much that they long ago ceased having any meaningful conversation.

16.

The one-page letter from the archbishop caught Eddie by surprise. At worst, he'd anticipated a suspension with pay, "pending the resolution of legal issues" or some such rhetorical crap.

Instead, it read: "I, Edward Cronin, MD, resign as president of St. Catherine's hospital, effective August 19, 2002, at 4:00 p.m." Below the one sentence was a signature line, and affixed to the sheet was a Post-it note in the archbishop's hand: "Please sign immediately and hand over to Father Skerry." The archbishop was the chairman of the hospital board in name but had never attended a trustees meeting. So the letter was perfectly legal—but totally absurd.

Not signing was one of the easiest decisions Eddie ever had to make. And as he handed the envelope back, he informed the archbishop's bodyguard, messenger boy, speechwriter, and personal attendant exactly where, anatomically, he could stuff the document.

Before Skerry could reply, Eddie was out the door of his office, past Gert, who stood open-mouthed but silent for once beside her desk, and speed-walking down the stairs to the lobby and the parking garage. For an instant, he'd considered taking the fire escape, but for all he knew, those idiots J. J., Autry, Pinkham, and Gilchrist were still out there.

He made it back to Sycamore Hill in seventeen minutes, the best possible time considering the Friday afternoon traffic. Most drivers got out of the way of the Hummer when he loomed in their rearview mirrors. He had to use the horn only a couple of times.

Pulling into the driveway, he congratulated himself on his record-setting commute. Then, while waiting for the garage door to open, he caught a glimpse of his daughter, Irene, before she disappeared from her perch on the kitchen window seat.

17.

Portia worried that she wouldn't recognize Helen right away, since all she could go on was the e-mail description.

"I'm five-four with jet-black hair, which, I admit, gets a little help. I'll be wearing a light green blouse with a high collar."

Portia didn't have to worry. As soon as she stepped into the library lobby, a woman fitting that description got up from her desk to greet her.

They had worked out the details of their get-together in advance. After walking over to Helen's place to pick up the package, they'd stop somewhere for a drink before driving up to Egg Rock to drop Portia off.

Helen's apartment sat on a pretty side street a few blocks from the library. It was so crammed with books that the living room walls were barely visible behind the bookshelves. And there were smaller shelves in both the kitchen (holding dozens of cookbooks) and the bathroom. "That's where I keep short stories, quick reads, and humor," she commented as she showed Portia around.

The most stunning room, however, was Helen's office, occupying the second bedroom. In one corner was one of those modular computer desks that looked constructed from old milk cartons.

It held the computer and monitor and dozens of cubbyholes filled with papers.

But the computer desk took up only a small area. The rest of the room looked like a teenager's bedroom. Posters of rock bands and basketball players lined the walls. The bedspread was covered with a pattern of alternating baseballs, bats, and mitts. Even the bedside lamp sported the logo of a local sports team.

"This is Tommy's room," Helen said proudly. "Not in a literal sense, since he never lived here, but it's pretty much what it looked like in our old house. Take a look at this."

Helen stepped aside to let Portia see a gilt-edged picture frame resting on the dresser. It held what looked like a letter on fancy stationery, with a crimson seal at the top.

"It's his early acceptance letter from Harvard. He must have received it the day before he died."

18.

After giving the Hummer's finish a once-over with a chamois, Eddie exited the garage. Buzzy's Range Rover with its Rhode Island plates was still parked by the kitchen door. With the funeral over, he'd hoped that his in-laws would be on the road to Woonsocket by now.

He could hear the kids letting off steam as he walked by the family room. Above the din, he could make out the au pair speaking slowly. Her German accent gave her words extra authority.

"Irene, stop. Stop this instant."

Kitty was seated alone at the kitchen table, looking like she'd been crying. Bridget was nowhere to be seen.

"There are plenty of tea sandwiches left over."

She pointed to the center island, its granite surface nearly obscured by cardboard boxes from the local caterer.

He felt himself clear his throat, and Kitty looked up.

"The archbishop has asked for my resignation."

Kitty didn't change her expression.

"There must be more to the story, Eddie. Sit down and tell me."

He grabbed a couple of sandwiches, ham salad he thought but couldn't be sure, and some coffee and took a seat.

After a couple of bites, he was as ready as he ever would be and told her about Father Skerry and the letter.

"Did you sign it?"

"Hell, no."

"Does that mean you're still the president?"

"I doubt it. I'm sure he fired me once his flunky Skerry got back to the residence with the unsigned letter."

"Why?"

"Why what?"

"Why were you the CEO of Saint Kay's this morning and the ex-CEO tonight?"

"I don't know exactly."

"I have an idea, Eddie. I bet the archbishop got wind of your little operation last week. That would be enough to finish you off."

"Who told you about it?"

"First off, you come into the house limping and not talking quite right. Then you're downstairs getting ice from the kitchen. I knew something was wrong, but I couldn't figure it out. Then I got a FedEx on Monday."

"Unsigned?"

"Yes. It was only one sheet, a handwritten op note from your pal Gilchrist."

"Gilchrist?"

"I don't think he sent it, but who cares?"

"I care."

"Then, I'm sure you'll recall Tuesday morning when I happened into the powder room, and you were coming out of the shower."

"I remember."

"Eddie, the worst part of all of this is that you didn't tell me."

"I wanted to protect you."

"I'm your wife, Eddie, and believe it or not, I still want to be your wife. But it's past time for you to tell me the truth. Can you think of any other reason that the archbishop fired you?"

"Asked for my resignation …"

"Let's face it, dear, you were canned."

"I've racked my brain, Kitty, and can't come up with any other explanation. If only the church were more open-minded about birth control, I'd still be in charge. And the tragedy is that I was about to put Saint Kay's on the map, once and for all."

"Eddie, I have to go upstairs. Come up when you're ready. We can talk more then."

"Okay, Kitty."

Once he heard his wife on the stairs, he jotted a quick note, saying he'd be spending the night in the garage, and tucked it under her placemat. Then he got up quietly and eased the door shut behind him. While unlocking the door to the garage, he glanced back at the house to see Irene, back at the window seat.

19.

The path up to the football field was about a yard wide, just narrow enough to allow the treetops on each side to cover it completely from above. Understandably, there was barely light enough to see the path though there was still an hour until sunset. Tom had packed the flashlight for the work he needed to do inside the building, but it would also come in handy on the way down. Without the light, he could easily trip on a root or slip on a moss-covered rock after dark. He was glad he chose his Vietnam jungle boots, which would be less prone to slipping and were high enough to protect him from twisting an ankle. They fit perfectly, and the red stains from the clay soil along the Cambodian border gave them added authenticity.

He knew that walking down the driveway would be suicide. The golf carts that security used were so quiet that he'd have no warning and would be caught in the middle of the road.

He speculated on how much sex went on in these woods. It looked like a perfect combination: peak adolescent hormone levels and plenty of places to hide.

At the top of the hill, he kept to the tree line as he circled the football field. The white goal posts stood out sharply against the darkening sky. He thought back to the field at his high school, with the scrimmages in the early New Hampshire dusk. There were Saturday games with marching bands, cheerleaders, and the people spilling out of the stands after a win over the next town on a chilly Thanksgiving morning.

Football, like war, builds character.

If Tommy had understood that simple fact, things might have turned out differently.

Exactly as he'd been warned, the security vehicle was parked in front of the administration building with its mini-headlights on.

"The security guy arrives at 7:15 and takes between ten and twelve minutes to walk around the mansion and Pius XII Auditorium, checking all the outside locks. I've never seen him enter a building. Between 7:30 and 7:33, he should get back into his golf cart and head down the driveway. He returns between 8:35 and 8:40. I haven't seen him deviate from the schedule for three nights running."

From behind a tree at the top of the parking lot, he watched the watchman emerge from the back of the auditorium. The fellow didn't exactly look like Sherlock Holmes. Instead of using his eyes, actually patrolling the area, he walked with his head down. When he crossed in front of the cart, Tom had a momentary glimpse of him, silhouetted by the headlights. He wore a Walkman and was bobbing his head in time with the music. Tom could have been doing cartwheels in the parking lot, and the boy wouldn't have noticed.

The security cart had probably not quite made it to the foot of the hill by the time Tom pulled on a pair of plastic gloves, unlocked the door, and punched in the six-digit code he'd been given to disarm the security system.

After a short walk by the deserted kitchen, he was in the hallway leading to the administrative area of the school. The door to the trustees' room was unlocked, just as he had been told it would be.

The utility closet at the back of the room contained the air-conditioning unit. Its door opened silently with a gentle push, and he smiled when he saw the strip of masking tape that had been carefully placed over the latch.

The air handler for the air-conditioning system sat at the back of the closet. It was one of the older models, taking up twice the room of the new one he recently had installed in his office at the hospital.

He laid out his equipment on a small table in front of the unit. The multiple pockets of his fatigues easily accommodated the flashlight, his prefit face mask (hepa, with a p-100 filter), two pair of purple Nitrile gloves, a Phillips screwdriver, a pocket knife, a spool of wire, and his custom-made culture chamber. The chamber resembled the kind you attach to your garden hose to dispense fertilizer.

He had the lid off the unit in seconds and trained the flashlight on the outflow tract of the air handler. After changing into the gloves, he fit the mask snugly around his nose and mouth, making sure there were no leaks. Next, he bisected the rubber hose, inserted the ends of the culture chamber, and secured the ends of the hose to the chamber with 25-gauge stainless steel wire.

He knew that Kitty Cronin did not like to walk into a cold conference room and requested that it not be precooled for the trustees' meetings. Instead, she'd ask the custodian to switch on the air conditioner after they got started. That way the room would not overheat during the meeting, and the chance of a trustee or two nodding off would be minimized.

At a previous trustee meeting, the custodian had made the mistake of turning on the AC early, and she made a fuss about it.

Tom pictured the Mount of Olives Academy Board of Trustees sitting around the polished conference table when the AC kicked in. In seconds, they'd be inhaling that first beautiful inoculum of Francisella tularensis. They'd go on talking as if nothing had happened. In fact, they'd be fine for a couple of days.

Then the fun would begin.

It would start like a case of the flu, with muscle aches, fever, and just feeling lousy. People don't usually get the flu in the summer, even late in the summer, but no one would be sharp enough to pick up on that. Meanwhile, Tom's little bacterial friends would be happily replicating in their victims' lungs. Soon there would be a dry cough, then a little shortness of breath, but by the time they decided to see a doctor, their lungs would be packed with tens of millions of tularemia organisms. And with a head start like that, even the best antibiotics would have trouble making headway.

He felt sorry for the custodian, the kitchen worker who'd be serving coffee, and any other innocent who'd enter the room. They were sure to get infected, too, but you had to expect some collateral damage in this kind of operation.

Everybody in the conference room would suck in a hefty dose of Tom's favorite microbe, but Archbishop Quilty would be at an added disadvantage because his immune system had been screwed up by the arthritis medications. The others would fight the bacteria with their armies of white cells and antibodies, giving them a chance of recovery. But Quilty would be opening the gates for the enemy without firing a shot. Even if he was lucky enough to get the right antibiotics, he'd be in deep shit.

Tom thought back to Monday morning, when the Virgin Mary first smiled at him from the window, endorsing his plan. He made the sign of the cross in gratitude.

After checking his watch, he repocketed his tools, and in less than two minutes, he was able to strip off the masking tape, lock the closet door, reset the alarm system, and secure the outside door behind him. Before scooting across the parking lot for the safety of the woods, he made sure that security hadn't made an unscheduled visit. Then he stayed low, the way you would if the Vietcong were hiding, ready to pick you off with their AK-47s before you reached the tree line. Once safe, he found he had enough moonlight to scurry around the ball field and onto the path before using the flashlight again.

Long before the Northeast Security golf cart made it back up to Mount of Olives on their next patrol, he was back in his apartment, putting a Hungry-Guy Fried Chicken Dinner in the microwave.

20.

On the way to Cambridge, they drove past the Cattle Drive, where the lights were coming on and the parking lot was filling up.

"Early-bird special," Helen commented without looking up from the road.

Soon they were on a bridge separating Faneuil from Cambridge.

"Here's the border crossing."

Faneuil's gas stations, taverns, diners, and barbershops were replaced by boutiques and bistros as soon as they crossed the Charles.

"Tommy used to say that grills were good, and bistros were bad, but I'm sure he would have developed a taste for life over here."

Helen had found a space in front of a movie theatre featuring its "Annual Bergman Festival." The restaurant (Helen's "absolute favorite") was in the basement.

The last time Portia picked up a drink (except for that cute little bottle of Chardonnay on the plane) had been at the library's Christmas party back in December, when after a few trips to the punchbowl, she got into an argument with her boss about book bindings, of all things. Her boss was partial to vellum while Portia preferred red morocco.

Helen ordered daiquiris, and Portia cautioned herself to go slow. An argument was the last thing she'd need if she wanted to get Helen's package to Egg Rock, safe and sound. Right away, Helen launched into a lengthy indictment of her ex-husband. There had to be something about two women sitting together over drinks that made such a conversation inevitable. Helen seemed happy to do the talking, which suited Portia.

If Helen could be believed, Doctor Thomas Rowley was a louse.

He'd been a gun enthusiast since Vietnam. Early in their courtship, he showed her his Purple Heart, which he had mounted in a clear plastic box and kept in his office. He was wounded outside his medical station rescuing one of his men, according to a typed affidavit that he let her read.

Years later, at the time of their impending divorce, her attorney did a background check and learned that Tom had never even served in the military. Instead, he had been granted a deferment for work on a classified defense project at a government laboratory in Maryland.

"What about the Purple Heart?"

"No problem. You can pick one up at an army surplus store, and I bet you can find dozens on eBay these days. Then he must have typed out a phony affidavit, giving a detailed account of his actions."

"How can you work with the bastard?"

"Partly because the lawyer came up with other biographical details that Tom never talked about. He was not your run-of-the-mill draft dodger. While at Detrick, the lab in Maryland, he did something truly heroic. There was an accident involving a highly lethal biologic agent. From what I understand, a container of these very dangerous bacteria spilled inside one of the high-security labs, exposing several technicians. They were immediately quarantined, and Tom, who had not been exposed himself, volunteered to enter the quarantine area to provide medical care for the victims. Apparently, three or four became very ill, and one died. He stayed with them, shut off from the outside world, day and night for three weeks. He never received an official award because of the secrecy of what they were doing, but he was a hero nonetheless."

"Why didn't he ever tell you?"

"I asked him only after the lawyer found out. He hadn't told me, he said, because he couldn't be in two places at once. It's a pity that he preferred the fantasy of Vietnam to the reality of Maryland—where he was really a hero."

"You said it's 'partly' because of his exposing himself to danger like that. Is there another reason you can work with him now?"

"All I can tell you, Portia, is that my desire for justice trumps everything else."

Portia took a little sip and waited for Helen to continue.

"When Tom and I split, I vowed never to speak to him again. Losing my son was a nightmare, but it was only the beginning. Tommy was dead only a month when I discovered that Tom was having an affair. The woman was a respiratory therapist at the hospital, who had the good sense to find a position out of state once I found out."

Helen, who had looked so calm and controlled until now, was methodically ripping her cocktail napkin into tiny shreds.

"We didn't say a word to each other for years, but then we began exchanging e-mails ... Second Amendment stuff at first. Tom and I disagreed about just about everything, but we both believed in the constitutional guarantee to bear arms."

Portia, who had never touched a gun in her life, didn't like the sound of this. And Helen picked up on it.

"It's only natural that we'd feel that way, since my father was a policeman and Tom was brought up in the country, where hunting is a way of life. After a while, the e-mails got more personal. He made the point that if we had been able to communicate dispassionately, with time to think and tone down the rhetoric before blurting things out, we might have saved the marriage. As far as I was concerned, all the e-mail in the world wasn't going to fix our marriage."

"I understand that."

"When Tommy used Tom's own weapon to kill himself, he was sending his father a message."

Helen waved the waitress away when she approached the table.

"Tommy was probably gay. I have no actual proof, and I don't think for a moment that he voluntarily acted on his impulses, if he had any. What I do know is that a priest molested him and that the staff at Mount of Olives and the Archdiocese of Boston chose to ignore the obvious."

Portia must have looked puzzled, because Helen paused.

"Do you know anything about the Mount of Olives?"

"I'm no biblical scholar, but isn't that where the Sermon on the Mount took place?"

"No, but that's another matter. I'm talking about a school that sits on a hill a short way upriver from the Cattle Drive. It's a parochial school. Both Tom and I were in favor of our Tommy going there, not because we were particularly religious, but because we felt he'd get a good education. And he did."

"Remember, I saw the letter from Harvard."

Helen gave her the briefest of smiles.

"Tommy was being harassed by other students. An incident took place around Thanksgiving of his senior year where other boys tripped him in a hallway and made fun of him. Students and teachers saw what happened, but no one stepped in; no one supported my son when he was humiliated like that. In fact, from what I could learn, no one even acknowledged that it happened."

"Did Tommy tell you about it?"

"No. But how could he? That would have opened a whole can of worms. And I think he was especially fearful of confiding in his father, who had announced to the world that he was a big-time war hero."

"How did you find out?"

"I received an anonymous note. I think it came from another student, but I never tried to find out. Then I made some inquiries."

"You still despise Tom, don't you?"

Helen nodded.

"My ex-husband had strong ideas about manhood. From time to time, he let his son know that he didn't measure up."

"How?"

"By making fun of him. One night at supper, Tommy announced that he'd gotten a part in *Macbeth*. Not the lead, but Duncan the king. Instead of congratulating him, Tom …"

She paused.

"… started to laugh. Now Tom Rowley is not the laughing type. I remember his exact words. 'Phew, I thought you were going to be Lady Macbeth.' The kid just sat there, wounded, and Tom didn't seem to notice."

"Ouch!"

"Tommy was always trying to appease his father. You saw his room. He chose the sports motif more for Tom than himself. But Tom never backed off."

"How did you learn about the priest?"

"No one ever told me outright, but no one had to. The chaplain at the Mount of Olives spent a lot of time with Tommy soon after he enrolled at the school. It seemed that every week or so he'd be having another appointment with Father Guido—that was the chaplain's name. He's still active at Saint Kay's."

"I just met him a couple of hours ago, a little roly-poly kind of man."

"That's the guy. They even visited Saint Luke's Seminary together. Tommy would tell me all about those appointments and the seminary visit. It seemed he'd talk to me about everything then. I didn't make much of it at the time, but right after the seminary visit, Tommy clammed up. He no longer talked about the priest but didn't share much else either. I kept asking him about school, friends, and so forth, and he'd give me reluctant one-word answers. I chalked it up to adolescence. I can remember feeling so weird when I was that age that I hated to talk to my family about anything. I just figured it would pass, the way those things usually do. But it didn't. Looking back, it's clear that something happened to Tommy when he was spending all the time with the priest. After he died, the cause and effect became clear."

Helen hesitated before continuing.

"Guido molested Tommy, but that's not the whole story. His alpha-male father still doesn't understand how much damage he did, and I don't expect he ever will. Once we started communicating again, I tried to get Tom to face up to his role in Tommy's death. And do you know how he reacted? By accusing me of being an unfit mother! As for Guido, he knows exactly what he did to Tommy but doesn't have the courage to admit it."

She looked at Portia directly.

"Then the sex abuse scandal came along, confirming what I already figured out on my own. Priests were abusing boys right and left and getting away with it. Their superiors knew but didn't lift a finger. Their desire to protect the Church's reputation overrode all other considerations—even the death of such a promising seventeen-year-old boy. Guido was the perpetrator, but higher ups like Quilty were equally responsible."

Helen paused a moment before signaling for menus.

"Do you remember the hokey Western-style restaurant we passed on the way here?"

"Sure. The Cattle Drive."

"I learned that Quilty was planning to have dinner there one night, and I confronted him about what Guido did to Tommy. Before his bodyguard got rid of me, Quilty promised he'd look into it, but guess what? I never heard a word from him. There I was begging for him to take action, and he blew me off."

Each settled on quiche and salad. Helen ordered another daiquiri before going on.

"Suicide is so much more than an unnecessary death. It sends out ripples of guilt and anger that can last for generations. Don't you agree?"

"You know, Helen, I'm a better listener than a speaker."

"That's okay, Portia. You've already been clear about how committed you are to our plan. That's all that counts."

By the time they got on the road to Egg Rock, the traffic had thinned out. The stretch north of the airport looked very different from the sprawl she'd seen from the taxi on Tuesday. With the oil tanks hidden in the darkness, they could have been passing parkland stretched out beyond the reach of the streetlights. But it was the Squimway further up the coast that was transformed. It could have passed for the stretch she'd known as a teenager. The old amusement park she and Frankie went to could easily have been hidden behind the splashes of neon along the road. Maybe it was the daiquiri, or the little package she held in her lap, but she felt like a senior at Squimset High again, with her whole life ahead of her.

As they drove over the causeway out to Egg Rock, Portia hoped that Vincent had taken her advice not to wait up.

Late as it was, she had one more thing she needed to do—alone. She needed to take another look at her mother's photo albums.

SATURDAY

1.

"Danny, are you awake?"

Although he was still coming to, there was no question that it was the Boss. Never in Dan's seven years as secretary had Archbishop Quilty knocked on his bedroom door. Something must be very wrong.

Before he could react, the Boss continued from the hallway.

"Stay in bed, Danny. I'm fine. It's just that I've decided to cancel the trustees meeting up at the Mount of Olives School. You'll need to give Kitty Cronin a call. Make some kind of excuse and tell her you'll get in touch about another date. That will give me time to push back a little. During the night, I kept thinking about the bishops who'd be conducting the audit. Those guys could turn the whole thing into a witch hunt. After the week she's had, Kitty will be relieved, too. See you downstairs for breakfast."

Dan eased his head back on the pillow and thought about how different his life had become since the archbishop went off-message in his press statement Thursday afternoon.

The Boss was totally his own man for the first time. And Dan Skerry was no longer a player.

2.

J. J. punched the clock radio and missed the "snooze" button by a mile, sending the plastic cube crashing to the floor. Once he became fully conscious, the throbbing of his temples and the dryness of his throat blotted out everything else, reminding him of what one of his army buddies referred to as the "bottom of the birdcage" feeling.

After the crew from Saint Kay's security and a locksmith from Faneuil Center got him and Eddie Cronin's other guests freed from the fire escape Friday afternoon, he walked over to the spot where he knew the key landed but couldn't find it. It was like one of those golf outings down in Mobile with the home office crowd. Those southern boys all played effortlessly while J. J. kept knocking the ball into the rough, or worse. Each time, he made a mental picture of just where the sucker landed, but he could never find it when he started beating the high grass with his iron.

Oh, yes, Mobile. He should have been on the phone last night giving Spike an update, but he went to the Cattle Drive instead and got shit-faced. At least he had the good judgment to turn off his cell and pager before downing his first Captain Morgan and Coke.

He had no idea how he got home, undressed, and into bed. Then there was the matter of his car, which could be anywhere. It took him half a day to find it the last time.

After a long shower, a gallon of orange juice, and half a stale bagel, he decided it was time to let Mobile in on the bad news.

But he was having trouble.

His cell phone was acting up. Every time he called the home office, he got a busy signal. After a dozen tries, he dialed the local number of a girlfriend he knew was out of town and got the same rapid *beep, beep.*

That left the computer. He used the Internet for routine communication with Mobile and checked it almost every day, even though he didn't get that much e-mail. He wasn't an Internet addict like some people he knew. He got the usual corporate bullshit about marketing bonuses, salesperson of the month, and "employee discounts" on crap no one wanted anyway, and he mailed whatever forms they needed back regularly.

Honestly, other than an occasional porn site he got off on, he didn't waste a lot of time online.

So he couldn't believe it when he saw that he had twenty unread messages! When he'd checked Friday morning, there was no mail except for the usual garbage.

After deleting the usual junk mail, he opened up the remaining nine in order, starting with the earliest. The first three were from Spike and were identical: "Tried to get you by cell and beeper but getting no answer. Get back to me ASAP. Spike."

That left six.

Next on the list was from Saint Kay's Public Relations: "Late this afternoon, the Board of Trustees announced the resignation of Dr. Edward Cronin as president of Saint Katherine's Medical Center, effective immediately. Mr. Andrew Pinkham, CEO of a well-respected health-food chain and a senior member of the hospital's board of trustees, has been named interim president pending a national search."

That piece of breaking news was all over the big screen at Cattle Drive while he was sitting at the bar last night. He had no trouble with "The Vitamin King" running a hospital when he was half in the bag, but was having second thoughts this morning.

Down to five.

Next on the hit parade was another message from his ol' buddy Spike: "Sounds like all hell is breaking loose up there, and you're AWOL, soldier. I'll have your ass in a sling if you don't answer, boy. S."

J. J. was down to four semifinalists. He pictured a beauty

pageant, featuring four luscious women strutting across the stage, practically bursting out of their swimsuits.

The first semifinalist was a message from "stkaysprez": "Come out to Sycamore Hill alone and meet me at garage at 11:00 a.m. today. Pull in behind the hedge in back and don't go near the house. ECMD."

J. J. smiled. From the look of things, Cronin would be in the market for a new screen name. He imagined the possibilities: "stkaysxprez," "crookeddoc," "felonydoc." The list was endless.

Before Eddie got fired, J. J. would have walked barefoot the twenty miles to Sycamore Hill. But times had changed, and he scrolled down to the next message.

It came from Corporate: "APE is proud to announce that the domestic sales have increased 22 percent in the last quarter …" Typical bullshit, since they had no foreign sales.

He pressed the delete button before reading another word.

And the runner-up for Miss America is …

Another message from Corporate: "It has come to the attention of the APE Board of Directors that one of our junior sales representatives, one Jeremiah Justinian Rideout, has been implicated in activities totally unknown to and independent of the company. Mr. Rideout was fired today, as soon as this information became known to the board.

"We here at APE are proud of our ethical, faith-based business practices. The Birdsong family is saddened that one of our team, albeit an entry-level employee, has tarnished our good name.

"We apologize to our valued customers and shareholders for this rogue individual's actions.

"Our CEO, Mr. Robbie Birdsong, has already contacted the Alabama Attorney General's Office and the Federal Bureau of Investigation to offer all the assistance we can in this painful matter. We in the APE family ask for your prayers at this difficult time."

J. J.'s mind filled with memories of Walter Reed, the *Frauleins* at Landstuhl, Spike, and the golf course in Mobile, all at once. The scenes formed a vivid collage, reminding him about people relating near-death experiences, watching their life pass before them like a newsreel on fast-forward.

He was down to his last message.

Miss America herself, crowned by her predecessor and proceeding regally out on the runway in an evening gown and high heels that defied all laws of physics. Bert Parks was at the microphone singing, "There she is …" while the audience went wild.

It was his ol' buddy Spike, checking in again, this time with a more formal communication: "Mr. Rideout: I have been informed of your rogue actions in Boston and of your termination by the board. I am, of course, shocked by the allegations. I regret the trust we put in you to represent the APE family in its quest to maintain the highest standards of ethical behavior, and I feel personally betrayed by your actions. I have contacted our legal representatives in Boston about this matter and have instructed them to ensure that you vacate your apartment, owned by APE, by Monday noon, August 22. A representative of our law firm will be present at that time to expedite your departure. All other property of the company, including the Lexus sedan, computer equipment, cell phone, pager, and the company credit cards from American Express and Visa, will be collected at the time of your departure. The cell phone and pager have been disconnected, and the credit cards have been blocked as of 8:00 a.m., Saturday, August 20. Lavern Birdsong, Vice President, American Pharmaceutical Enterprises."

Nice piece of ghostwriting, J. J. thought. He was sure that the words "standards," "ethical," and "expedite" weren't in Spike's vocabulary. Undoubtedly Spike helped with the text, however, since "Lexus," "American Express," and "Visa" were some of his favorite words.

His head pounding, J. J. ducked into the kitchen, pulled the bottle out of the cabinet under the sink, and poured himself three fat fingers of Chivas Regal.

That's when he heard the doorbell.

He hoped that whoever it was at the door would give up and go away, but after about the hundredth ring, he gave up. He wished he had one of those little peepholes that gave a fish eye's view of the front step, where the person waiting outside was scrunched down into a little pygmy.

"Who is it?"

"Gert. I need to talk to you, J. J."

When he opened the door a crack, she pushed it back the rest of the way, and in a flash, Cronin's secretary was inside, surveying J. J.'s little living room. After shoving a pile of old newspapers out of the way, she found space to sit on the sofa, snagged a cigarette from her bag with her skeletal fingers, and lit up.

"I hear you've got yourself in hot water, J. J. I came over to give you a little help."

She sounded almost motherly.

"I'll get right to the point. Let's take a drive out to Sycamore Hill and pay a visit to your pal Eddie. He's expecting you, and I'm coming along. Besides, you and I have a proposition for him, and I know he'll want to compensate us for our trouble. Who knows? If we're lucky, we'll get a tour of his beloved car collection."

Why not? Now that he, too, was unemployed, he had nothing to lose. Besides, Gert didn't look like she'd go away.

"We're going to need your supply of AP 399 pills. How many have you got squirreled away? And where?"

She looked around the room as if it were contaminated.

"Under the bed in the spare room. Twenty-five thousand total." He was glad that he had the foresight to stash a few bottles in a safe deposit box at the Faneuil Savings Bank for his personal use.

"By the way, we're taking your car."

"I'm not sure where it is."

She pointed a bony forefinger at the front window covered by a bed sheet serving as a curtain. "Right across the street, you lush. You parked in a handicap space and got a fifty-dollar ticket. Lucky they didn't tow."

They were all packed up and on Charles River Drive up by Mount of Olives when J. J. remembered to check the fuel gauge.

"Gert, I need gas. I'm almost on empty. And I'm low on cash."

"Don't you have a company credit card?"

"Two actually, but they've been inactivated."

"From the smell of your breath, you could probably piss in the tank and get us out to Worcester."

She smoothed out a five-dollar bill and placed it on the dashboard.

"That's all you'll need."

3.

Eddie had been holed up in the garage since Friday evening right after Kitty went upstairs. It was a relief to be away from her questions and that look of curiosity mixed with disapproval she'd mastered. And since he'd outfitted the place for the long haul, an overnight was no hardship. Actually, overnights made him feel like one of those mountain guys in Montana or Wyoming or wherever, living out in the country in a shack, refusing to pay taxes and ending up in an armed stand-off with the feds.

He'd stocked the storage area under the floor with about fifty gallons of bottled water and a dozen jars each of instant coffee, extra-crunchy peanut butter, and an equivalent amount of canned tuna fish. The free-standing freezer (a little sweetener for closing the hospital kitchen deal) was stacked with macaroni and cheese casseroles, English muffins, his favorite TV dinners, and three cartons of Klondike bars.

With his two restaurant-grade microwaves, refrigerator, and backup gasoline generator, also part of the kitchen deal, he could hide out there for weeks without breaking a sweat.

Besides, he loved sharing space with his vehicles. The aromatic atmosphere, with its blend of motor oil, rubber, and car wax, was an aphrodisiac. The masculine lines of the Hummer and the delicate, ladylike silhouette of his 1939 Mercedes roadster beat anything he ever saw in those skin mags back in college.

It was no surprise that the land line connected to the garage hadn't rung. It was unlisted, and no one except Kitty knew the number. And in his note, he'd made it crystal clear that she was to call only if World War III was underway.

He was up before dawn, hoisting the engine out of the old Studebaker, the coolest car in his collection. It was a '51 Champion Regal Convertible coupe, still strikingly modern for a fifty-year-old vehicle.

The Studie had been burning oil, and the compression was low in two cylinders. It was time to pull the engine for a rebuild.

Eddie had been planning this for months. It took that long to acquire all those hard-to-find Studebaker parts. He laid them out neatly across the back of his best workbench, and once armed with an original workshop manual for the Champion, he was ready.

Eddie could think of no better way to concentrate his energy. Twenty-four hours overhauling this baby, and he'd be ready for the other stuff.

Just as he reached for a wrench from his mobile toolbox, a quick but tiny movement, a flicker really, caught his eye. He turned to find his daughter, Irene, standing between his '67 Corvette and his prewar Lincoln Continental, studying him.

"Irene, honey, how did you get in here?" He was sure he'd locked the doors on both ends of the building.

Of course she didn't answer. She simply stood there watching, with those liquid brown eyes that looked too big for her tiny freckled face. Before Eddie could take off his work gloves to pick her up and give her a hug, she ducked behind the Continental and disappeared.

He scoured the garage for a sign of his two-year-old, even crouching under the cars carefully so as not to aggravate his groin problem. He didn't bother to call her name, because he knew she wouldn't answer. After checking every inch of the place, including the tiny restroom, he looked out the window through the opening in the hedge, and there she was, darting into the kitchen.

Eddie felt an urge to follow his daughter, go inside, and tell Kitty everything. He loved Irene, not more than his other children—but differently. He wasn't sure why exactly, but he had some vague notion that she was a part of him that was missing. Kitty once told him that he had no conscience. That wasn't true, of course, but if he was a little deficient in that area, Irene made up the difference.

Instead of following her, he walked back into the restroom, took a leisurely leak, and after checking himself in the mirror, combed his hair over the thinning areas. By then, he was ready to get back to the Studie, tethered to the hoist like a giant mobile in a museum. But as soon as he saw it hanging there waiting for him, he knew he couldn't continue.

Irene had broken his concentration. The car would have to wait.

What he needed to do was think about his predicament, and he did his best thinking behind the wheel.

Only then did he remember e-mailing J. J. during the night, practically ordering him to Sycamore Hill. If APE had anything to do with his being sacked, he'd find out. And if that line of questioning didn't work out, he'd make a pitch for a job with the company. Now both ideas seemed absurd, as they must have to J. J. when and if he read the message.

There was no chance in hell that J. J. would take the bait.

After washing up, he peeled off the jumpsuit. He owned half a dozen, all cleaned, pressed, and hanging in the closet next to the restroom, each sporting a different logo from the NASCAR circuit. This one was his favorite, emblazoned with a large checkered flag and *Bardahl* in yellow letters on the front.

After a moment's deliberation, he selected the keys to the Dodge Ram from the board where he had them all arranged by bay number.

By then, Eddie was ready to hit the road.

4.

While Kitty was hovering between sleep and wakefulness, she assumed that Eddie was in bed beside her, but the illusion didn't last. After waiting for him to come upstairs the night before, she'd finally gone to the kitchen and found his note.

From bed she could hear the house come to life downstairs. In the midst of the kids' voices and the usual kitchen clatter, she could hear Bridget and Buzzy getting things organized. They must have known that she'd crash sooner or later, and they were right.

The bedside phone rang, and she picked up right away, hoping it was Eddie. When Father Dan Skerry introduced himself, she assumed that the call was about Eddie anyway. Why else would the archbishop's secretary be calling, after what happened to Eddie yesterday?

But she was wrong.

The news that the trustees meeting at the Mount would be

cancelled was the first good news she'd had all week. She was so overwhelmed that she nearly broke down.

"Thank him, thank him," was all that she could say.

Immediately she called the trustees and managed to get Pat Kaminski at Saint Kay's, since Northeast Security needed to be in the loop. Up until now, she thought, Eddie would have taken care of that detail.

When she finally made it downstairs, Bridget and Buzzy were busying themselves with the breakfast dishes while Irene stood on the window seat, looking out at the summer morning. The au pair had herded the others into the basement playroom, where Kitty could hear excited voices and furniture being moved around.

As she poured her coffee, Kitty saw Irene jumping up and down excitedly. A second later, a car turned sharply into the driveway, and from the screech of the brakes, she could tell that the driver had been traveling too fast to make the turn easily. As aggressively as Eddie drove, he'd never make a mistake like that.

A tank-sized white sedan, one of those Japanese luxury models with a touch of gold on its trim, whizzed by the kitchen window and disappeared behind the bushes up at Eddie's garage.

5.

J. J. had never seen the Cronin estate in daylight before. The one night he visited months earlier gave him no picture of how big the spread was. It had to cover three or four acres. The house was a classic white center-entrance colonial with a semicircular drive, reminding him of Mount Vernon, where he'd taken one of his girlfriends from the Walter Reed days. To the right, another driveway led past the kitchen in the back of the building, where an unobtrusive *Deliveries* sign was staked into the ground. At the end of the driveway sat an old barn, also white, converted into a garage. Behind the garage, J. J. could see a large meadow with a pond in the middle.

He wondered how much Cronin's mortgage was … and how soon he would be defaulting on it.

Before he could pull the Lexus into the parking space marked *Visitors*, one of the automatic doors purred open, and a black SUV with oversized tires started backing out. It looked like an entry in one of those monster car races J. J. had seen on ESPN during a slow sports weekend.

Once Cronin saw that he had company, he eased the car back into its bay. A minute later, he came outside to greet them.

"I was going out to run some errands, but they can wait." He looked at J. J. "I didn't think you'd show up." Then the cartons on the backseat caught Cronin's eye.

"Let me pull the Ram out again so you can park the Lexus inside."

Cronin offered Gert the chair by his desk, but she shook her head no, and J. J. dropped himself into the seat clumsily, aware that the chair bounced once or twice when he did so. Meanwhile, Gert reached into her bag and pulled out a cigarette and was about to light up when Cronin held up his hand like a traffic cop.

"Fire hazard," he said.

She didn't respond verbally but made her displeasure known by crumpling the cigarette and tossing it into the wastebasket.

"J. J. and I have a proposition for you, Eddie."

He and Gert hadn't exchanged more than a dozen words after her wisecrack about pissing in the gas tank, and to be honest, silence was the thing he needed most until the pounding in his temples eased off.

Whatever "proposition" she was talking about was her baby, and he was not the father.

"By the way, Eddie, we're all unemployed."

Clearly, Cronin wasn't used to the first-name stuff.

"Yep, I was canned about an hour after you. A security guy, a kid really, marched into the office, demanded my keys, and escorted me out of the building. I could only grab my bag and a few magazines from the top of my desk. The rest of my personal belongings will be available if I want to pick them up next week. It was humiliating. Everybody knows what's going on when you're taken away by security."

Cronin glanced at J. J.

"I got my sendoff from Mobile this morning, by e-mail."

Gert looked impatient. "Here's the deal, Eddie."

6.

Seconds after Vincent backed the old Buick out of the driveway, Portia hurried up to her room and lifted a plastic bag out from under a pile of bras and undies in the bottom drawer of her dresser. She read once that the police always began a search with the bottom drawers of desks and dressers, where most objects are hidden, but the police weren't her concern. Her father was. And from what she'd witnessed over the past few days, Vincent Mulcahy would die a thousand deaths before rooting through his daughter's underclothes.

She calculated that a walk on the beach would take the old man and the dog at least an hour.

She could take her time.

Using more care than probably necessary, she set the bag on her bed and unzipped it. Inside was the hazmat stuff, gloves, mask, etc., and the delivery vehicle. Rowley had encased it in bubble wrap, reducing the chance of leakage to almost zero. The delivery vehicle was actually a miniature bellows. Instead of blowing air into a dying fire, this model would release a dose of deadly bacteria. As she held the bellows in both hands, she thought about how things got to this point.

It was a slow morning at the engineering library, and when it got slow, Portia would surf the Net.

The site looked interesting: The Faneuil Survivors' Club. Its homepage featured an artist's rendition of Boston's new suspension bridge with the caption "Building a bridge between survivors and families."

She was drawn to the name Faneuil because her brother Frankie attended the seminary and her cousin Leo worked at Saint Kay's Hospital, both Faneuil institutions.

She was drawn to the survivor part for obvious reasons.

Portia closed the dresser drawer and carried the bag downstairs and out to the yard.

The rocky point jutting out into Squimset Harbor looked tranquil in the morning sun, giving no hint that the weather was about to go downhill. The weather station sat on open ground, about halfway between the back door and the big spruce. The instruments were housed in a wooden box, about two feet on each side, painted white, standing on four legs a couple of feet off the ground. A small door took up one whole side, and it and the other three sides were made of louvered wood, much like a window shutter. A rain collector was attached to the back of the structure, far enough away to escape the run-off from the station's tiny pitched roof.

Portia knew that her father would be out there to check the barometric pressure as soon as he got back.

Unwrapped, Portia knew the bellows would be only three and a half inches long. Like the reservoir for the AC at Mount of Olives, the bellows was the handiwork of one of her engineer friends from the university. Actually, it wasn't an act of charity on the friend's part, since she received fifteen crisp one-hundred-dollar bills for her trouble. The third delivery vehicle didn't require engineering. It was a perfume dispenser bought at a department store.

Portia knew it would take only a couple of minutes to hide the bellows inside, behind the bulky hygrometer. Connected by a thread to the door, it would release its contents the next time the door was opened.

Vincent would get a hefty dose of the bacteria in seconds, and with his hearing like it was, he wouldn't notice the whoosh as it emptied its payload.

Afterward, she'd have no trouble removing the evidence and throwing the spent bioweapon into Squimset Harbor with no one the wiser.

From what Helen said, he'd show no ill effects for days, but he'd be fighting for his life in less than a week.

She paused a moment in front of the weather station and looked out beyond the big spruce at Squimset Harbor, with the Dawes shore on its far side, and the Boston skyline in the distance.

The view brought her back to her last day in Egg Rock, when she was seventeen and about to leave home forever.

There were already streaks of light in the sky beyond the lifesaving station. It was hard to believe that her last night in Egg Rock was over so quickly. A few drags on a joint usually slowed time to a crawl, but the night had flown by anyway.

The swing hung limply on its ropes, attached to the big spruce she and Frankie always called the Christmas tree.

She didn't need to pump hard to get the swing going, and that weird empty feeling you get in the back of your thighs when the swing makes its descent seemed to be heightened by the drug. It had to be the sexiest feeling in the world.

She started singing, increasing the volume with each arc the swing made. She was amazed it took so long for her father to turn on the light upstairs.

The swing must have been taken down long ago, but she was pleased to see that a loop of rope survived, a memento wrapped around the long horizontal limb.

Vincent marched out on the lawn in his bathrobe and stuck out his hands each time the swing's ropes flew by, grasping at them for a second, slowing her down little by little.

Finally, she jumped off and was about to run to the beach when she caught a glimpse of his face in the early light and saw the tears. She had never seen him cry before, not even when her mother died.

As she turned away, she heard him say the thing she had wanted to hear for so long.

"Portia, I love you. Please don't go away."

But she had already made her plans. It was too late to turn back now.

She walked past the weather station, glanced at the tree again with its remnants of the swing, and made her way to the pier at the end of the point. There, before she fully understood what she was doing, she tied the bellows, still wrapped in its plastic cocoon, to a stone and flung it as far as she could. A second later, all she could see was a ring-shaped wavelet expanding from the point of impact on the placid surface of the water. It reminded her of the times she and Frankie found the flattest stones on the beach and skipped them across the surface of the harbor when they were little.

Before the old man and the dog could get back, Portia carried the hazmat bag upstairs and hid it again beneath the bras and panties in her dresser drawer.

7.

Gert looked her former boss squarely in the eye.

"Eddie, you don't know how lucky you are!"

Before he could come up with an answer, she went on.

"Do you have any idea why I came to Saint Kay's in the first place?"

She didn't wait for a reply.

"My son—"

"You have a son?"

"For Christ's sake, Eddie, shut up!"

He sat back and listened.

"My son was a patient in your lovely hospital and jumped out a window. They had to hose down the courtyard after they carted him away."

"I remember the incident but had no idea …"

She gave him another look, and he stopped in midsentence.

"I rushed to the hospital as soon as I got the call. Father Guido headed me off in the lobby and took me to a little room near the chapel. I was hysterical by then, and he tried his best to comfort me. But I was with him only a couple of minutes when that stuffed shirt Avery Smythe came in to give me the bad news. I have to say that Guido did the best he could, and Smythe was sympathetic enough I guess, but he was so pompous, it was hard to tell. But the guy who showed up with Smythe, your lawyer-buddy Autry, was a cold sonofabitch. He shut down the conversation and ordered a nurse to take me down to intensive care to see my son. Autry must have warned everybody to put a lid on it, because after he showed up, nobody said two words to me."

J. J. had never seen Gert on the verge of tears before.

"You know, Eddie, you never asked me how or why I came to Saint Kay's. Of course I wouldn't have told you the truth, but I can now. I needed a job, and when I saw an opening in the Saint Kay's medical records department, I jumped for it and got hired. It involved adding diagnoses and upgrading the diagnosis codes enough to increase the insurance payments, but not too much—or the hospital would be fined for fraudulent billing. But that kind of thing is right up your alley, Eddie, so I don't need to elaborate. Then, miraculously, a position in the president's office opened up, and I saw the stars lining up in my favor."

J. J. felt like a fan at a boxing match, watching the former champ stagger from a nasty left hook.

"Right off, I found out as much as I could about you. You'd be surprised how much. I have detailed information, with documents to back everything up, about the cash you diverted from the retirement fund and the kickbacks you pocketed from the high bidder for the hospital kitchen, and the percentage you skimmed from the Saint Kay's malpractice fund. I also have a pretty good idea how much hospital money you pissed away at those casinos down in Connecticut. But you really got in over your head, Eddie, when you got into bed with those sharpies from Alabama, J. J.'s outfit."

She gave J. J. a glance and went on.

"I know a lot about your personal life, too. How you got Dr. Gilchrist to tie your tubes offsite in that bungalow you bought at the bottom of Hospital Hill, so that the archbishop, who probably wouldn't know the difference between a spermatic cord and a cord of firewood, wouldn't be on to your little game. All the while you decided to keep your wife in the dark, as if she were some kind of a moron. By the way, the only really smart thing you ever did in your whole life, Eddie, was to marry Kitty Rafferty—a sweet, loyal, and endlessly patient lady—and you're too damn stuck on yourself to see it."

Instead of looking back at Gert, Cronin gazed out over his collection of cars. But J. J. knew he was listening to every word.

"Finally something strange happened to me. The more research I did on you from my desk right under your nose, the clearer it became. Dr. Edward Cronin wasn't the evil genius I assumed he would be, the guy who killed my only child. No, Eddie, you're too stupid to be genuinely evil. You're pathetic. Revenge sounded good when I started, but it lost its allure. So I abandoned my plan. Do you have any idea how I was going to get even?"

He looked at her as if he saw her for the first time and shrugged.

"I was going to poison you with your perfume, the crap that you buy by the gallon, the cologne you spray all over your ugly little body every time you step into your private powder room. Did anyone ever tell you that you smell like a pansy with that stuff? I'm told that after you got a load of the bugs in that spray bottle, you'd end up taking your last breaths on one of those ventilators downstairs in intensive care, just like my boy, after they told me his brainwaves were flat. They got his father and me to sign the papers, and they pulled the plug."

By the time she was finished, Gert looked like she needed a cigarette more than anything else on earth.

"Eddie, I'm going to have a smoke one way or another. I have no problem stepping outside for a couple of minutes. I'm sure you don't give a goddamn if Kitty or the rest of the clan over at the plantation see me in the driveway taking a few drags."

"You can smoke here," he said quietly.

8.

Father Frank was able to grab a few minutes alone in his study at Saint Gabriel's before the summer fair got underway. Out the window, he could see Miss Shanahan having a pow-wow with the rest of the church volunteers.

He closed his eyes and prayed.

"Heavenly Father, please give me the tools I'll need to deal with the challenges you've set before me. I see Your Hand in Sebastian Quilty's decision to come here. Give me the wisdom and humility to guide him in Your Name.

"Give me the patience I need to communicate with Vincent, understand Portia, and help Leo find peace.

"Most of all, give me the strength to minister in the name of your Son, even at those times when I'm filled with doubt."

Just then, his phone rang.

"Yes, Jane."

"I have your sister, Portia, on the line. She knows you're real busy with the fair but says that something's come up that can't wait. Father, I could see you really needed a few minutes of quiet. I'm sorry."

"No problem, Jane. I'll take the call."

Portia sounded upset.

"Frankie, I'm sorry to call like this, but I just discovered something important. Dad and I have been going through photo albums off and on for the last couple of days. I'd forgotten how many pictures Momma took."

"Did you find something that troubled you?"

Frank could hear his sister take a deep breath.

"Are you okay, sis?"

"Troubled me? Troubled is too mild, way too mild. This is hard, Frankie—really, really hard. I'll try to get to the point."

"Go slow."

"I know you have a lot to do …"

"Don't worry, sis. I'm alone in my study. Take your time."

"Do you believe in repressed memories?"

"I'm not sure. From what I've read, a lot of them that seemed real at the beginning turned out to be suspect or even frauds."

"This is real."

"Go on."

"She put together a whole album of my First Communion pictures."

"I remember that day."

"Funny, I really can't, but then I was only seven. One picture has me freaked out. I actually took a Xanax before I called."

Frank waited—and worried.

"There's this picture Momma took of me and Father Mal. I'm looking at the camera …"

"I remember. I stood next to her when she took it."

"Well, then, I was looking at Momma and you, I guess, but Father Mal was staring kind of sideways, at me."

"That makes sense, since you were the one being honored."

"Let me finish, Frankie. The look on his face brought something back, something awful."

Frank felt he should be remembering something but couldn't put his finger on it.

"The picture reminded me of a day—it must have been around the same time—when Momma dropped me off at the rectory after school. Another kid and I were supposed to meet with Father Mal, but the other kid didn't show up. I sat waiting in a small room with a table covered with a crocheted cloth and a crucifix on the wall. He came in and sat next to me and …"

"Take your time, sis."

"He started talking about something religious, I don't remember what exactly, but, maybe I'm making this up, but it could have been about the joyful and sorrowful mysteries. I can't be sure. Anyway, while he's talking along and without pausing, or slowing down or anything, he slips his hand under my dress and wiggles his fingers under my underpants, and …"

"You don't have to say anything else …"

"But there are a couple more things I have to say. He took my hand and placed it in his lap, making sure I felt his erection. Frankie, I'm not making this up."

"I believe you, sis."

"Frankie, I was only seven years old!"

He heard her blow her nose before continuing.

"And that's not all. Remember how Mom adored Father Mal, and Dad insisted I continue to get religious instruction from him, to make me more disciplined?"

"Yes, I remember."

"Finally I went. I put up a stink, but Dad didn't listen. You know how he would make up his mind about something, and the case was closed."

Frank wanted to tell her about how he and his friends had a "sixth sense" about the priest and avoided him. He never went to anyone about Father Mal because there was only a sense of uneasiness, nothing concrete. Even if he had spoken up, no one, most especially his mother and father, would have believed him. Still, if he'd said something …

Later, there were the stories at the seminary and the rumors that he heard after Mal died. It was his old friend Greg Tally who seemed to know more about this kind of stuff. He was with Greg the time he'd seen the two guys exit the orchard up behind old Cardinal O'Rourke's tomb back when they were in the seminary, their clothes awry.

Greg and Frank sat together at Father Mal's funeral. Bishop Fannon, a lifelong friend of Mal's, was the eulogist. Fannon, for all his faults, was an inspired speaker.

Father Mal had spent a seminary year in Rome, and it made a deep impression on him. "Not," as Fannon put it, "all positive." Coming as he did from a destitute family, he had trouble reconciling the vast riches of the Vatican with the Church's mission to the poor. He felt that the precious metals and jewels in every corner of Saint Peter's would better carry out Christ's message if at least some of them could be sold for charity. He was so committed, Fannon continued, that after a short stint assisting in a Boston parish, he spent two decades as a missionary ministering to the faithful in shanty towns in Bolivia. When he finally came home, he became the pastor of Saint Lawrence Church in Egg Rock.

As Fannon was winding down, Greg Tally whispered that the bishop had neglected an important biographical detail. "Saint Mal" was "an equal-opportunity pedophile" with a thing for both boys and girls. It hadn't been a "problem" down in South America, but when he got back to the States, people began to complain.

Frank wanted to tell his sister, right there on the phone, about the rumors but couldn't find the words.

"Sis, as I said, I believe you. Right now I just need to be sure that you're okay."

"I am, Frankie. I really am. I feel better just talking about it. And I still want to go to the fair with dad."

"Good. I'll be coming back to Egg Rock tonight."

"Before you hang up, Frankie, I need to tell you one last thing."

"Shoot."

"It's about me and Dad."

He pictured Gert, sitting in that booth at the Cattle Drive, lighting up another cigarette.

"Yes."

"I confess that I did come back to Egg Rock to get even. I was convinced that my father had ruined my life. When you and I talked that first morning, with Dad running around the kitchen about to whip up bacon and eggs or belgian waffles for us and finally taking the dog out for a walk, and later when you asked me about Gert, I wasn't telling the truth."

"That was Wednesday. Wednesday morning."

"You know, it seems like weeks ago, with so much going on since. I lied to you, Frankie, and I hope you can forgive me. Then, this morning, when I started carrying out my plan, I couldn't go through with it. I was already changing my mind before I saw the pictures of me and Father Mal. Something was telling me that I had the wrong guy."

"Of course I forgive you, sis."

"Looking back, I can't believe how long it took to change my mind. I was pretty messed up when I left home. You've seen the scars. It took years of therapy for me and my therapist to conclude that Dad had tried to molest me. I know it sounds crazy, but it made sense at the time. I guess it allowed me to focus my anger on someone other than myself. Dad and I did have an ugly scene soon after Mom died. I came home late from an evening out in Squimset, and he met me at the front door, very drunk and very angry. He was unsteady and sort of fell into me. I told him that he should have been dead instead of Mom, and he slapped me across the face."

"Dear God."

"Dad apologized right after I got back this week. He said he had never struck anyone in anger before or since and that he thought about what he had done every day."

"I believe that."

"So do I, Frankie. And I don't believe that he had any sexual intent that night. He was drunk and angry and grief-stricken. We had an ugly scene, but those things happen. The problem for me was that I had invested so much in this theory—this assumption—that it was an incredible struggle for me to walk away from it. Even with Father Mal staring me in the face. Am I making any sense?"

"Yes. You're a very brave woman, Portia."

"I love you, Frankie. See you in a couple of hours."

Then she was gone.

Frank looked out on the lawn again, just in time to see a couple of volunteers filling the dunk tank with cold water from a garden hose. Even being dunked sounded tolerable now that the truth was out.

9.

Gert took a couple of drags on her cigarette before setting it on Eddie's desk, lighted end a couple of inches from the edge. Then she rooted around in her bag.

"I brought along copies of some of my favorite documents, so you can see I mean business."

While Eddie shuffled through the papers, she picked up her cigarette again and flicked the long ash on the glistening floor of the garage.

"J. J. and I both know that you have been discussing AP 399 with a drug wholesaler in Montreal."

"Yes. He's a friend of Andrew Pinkham, you know, one of the trustees."

"Eddie, this is the last time I'll tell you to shut up. There is nothing you can tell me that I don't already know. The next time I want to hear from you, I'll ask."

She stubbed the cigarette out on the desk.

"Your Montreal connection wants to get his hands on the miracle drug. I guess there are lots of horny, impotent, poorly endowed guys north of the border, panting to get their hands on J. J.'s product. Here's the deal. J. J. and I need money. I happen to know that you have over fifty thousand in small bills here in the garage. Hand fifty thousand over to me, and we'll let you have all the 399s in J. J.'s possession—25,000 capsules—in return. All you need to do is take a little trip to make the delivery—and at four dollars a pop, you'll double your investment and take care of your immediate cash-flow problems … like the mortgage on Sycamore Hill here. And the best part is that you won't need to cross the border. Just a little road trip to Vermont and you'll be all set. He'll be meeting you at this lovely motel tomorrow evening. You could stick around for some quality hunting and fishing afterward if you like."

She handed Eddie a sheet of paper with the address.

J. J. had to give her credit. She had everything thought out and organized. Besides, twenty-five thousand could make his transition a little easier—if, that is, she'd be willing to go fifty-fifty.

"Okay, Eddie, your answer. Either it's a yes or we'll be handing the documents to Corinne."

Eddie looked surprised.

"Corinne, Eddie, your gal pal at Channel Six. Your choice."

"Yes."

"By the way, you might be interested that Corinne and I are friends."

By now Eddie looked more spooked than surprised.

They carried the AP 399 boxes into the garage while Eddie counted out the fifty grand in twenties and fifties.

10.

When Irene began jumping up and down on the window seat again, Kitty ran over just in time to see the big white car exit the drive and with a screech of brakes turn onto the street. The car slowed down enough for her to see a woman who looked like Eddie's secretary, Gert, in the passenger seat. The driver looked familiar, too, but she couldn't place him.

Then Bridget, who'd rushed to another window, announced that the driver was the man who had picked Eddie up at Eunice's funeral.

Kitty was finally ready to march out to the garage to confront Eddie when Irene got agitated again.

A shiny black SUV, with Eddie alone at the wheel, exited at a more dignified pace.

11.

Dr. Nina Nichols, in Harold Nalbandian's opinion the most attractive orthopedic surgeon in the galaxy, was waiting at the curb in front of Saint Kay's when he pulled up. In her pink party dress with its spaghetti straps, Harold could see that she'd be the hit of the archbishop's Youth Outreach Banquet.

"I was beginning to worry about you guys."

Geri explained why they were late. Just before leaving the house, Harold discovered that the lock on the kitchen door had been jimmied.

"Not a very professional job, either," Harold added. "It looks like somebody forced the door with a screwdriver."

Nothing appeared to be missing. The silverware and Geri's jewelry were untouched, and the cash that Harold kept in his study for emergencies was intact. Amazingly, about twenty dollars in small bills Geri had left on the kitchen counter was undisturbed as well.

"Maybe they were frightened off and never actually got into the house."

"I guess that's possible, Nina, but my gut tells me that someone was in there, going through our things, looking for something. In any case, I'm calling the alarm company on Monday."

He waited for Geri to make a crack about locking the barn door, but she held off.

12.

While the archbishop read over his remarks in the backseat, Father Joe sailed by Fenway Park at an easy seventy-five. They were just about at the spot where at least once a season, when the wind is coming in from the southwest and the humidity is just right, and the guy at the plate is in the zone—a homer lands on the highway.

"I believe the speed limit on the Pike is fifty-five, Father Joe," the Boss said quietly, as if talking to himself.

Joe eased off to sixty-five, and the Boss appeared satisfied.

Minutes later, they took the sharply curving off-ramp under the Prudential Tower and emerged smack in the middle of Back Bay, with its eclectic mixture of high-rises and brownstones.

Joe was still backing the limo into the space in front of the Saint Botolph Hotel when the doorman had the rear door open and was greeting the archbishop like an old friend.

"Welcome back to the Saint Botolph, Archbishop Quilty."

The archbishop was smiling as he put the folded sheaf of papers in the inside pocket of his jacket and emerged from the car.

Dan stood by while the Boss asked the doorman about his family—by name. Better than anyone he ever knew, the archbishop was able to file away the name and some biographical detail of everyone he met.

With no TV trucks parked out front and no reporters at the hotel entrance, it looked like Saint Kay's was keeping all the media hounds occupied. He'd been worried about confronting them here at the dinner, especially following the "assault" on the Channel Six cameraman and the outcry over the archbishop's statement.

But it was a Saturday night in August, and everyone, including the press, could use a break, he thought.

Once inside the ornate lobby, he could tell that the party had already begun. The combined boys' choir was warming up the crowd with "When the Saints Go Marching In" from the ballroom.

"Do you think they're referring to us, Danny?"

"Not if you're including Father Joe, Your Excellency. No saint would drive like that!"

Monsignor Jim Healy, the head of Catholic Charities, caught up with them. Tall, athletic, and charismatic, he was the highest ranking black prelate in Boston, and if the gossip could be believed, its next auxiliary bishop.

"We have a bigger turnout than last year, Archbishop, and last year was a record. I can't help but think back to the time I warned you that August was a bad time to hold any social event, but I sure got that wrong. Everybody is invested in this. You'll be happy to hear that the band and the choir went through two long rehearsals this week."

With that, the monsignor escorted the archbishop into the ballroom.

Immediately the crowd broke into applause, punctuated by cheers from the children. The band began "For He's a Jolly Good Fellow," and everyone joined in. Flash cameras flickered throughout the room.

The deep-pocket donors who were clustered around the bars and the hors-d'oeuvres stations turned toward the archbishop's party and joined in the welcome, clapping politely.

A huge banner draped over the stage proclaimed, *The Future of the Church.*

Walking a few paces behind the Boss, Dan was pleased to see the old man's shoulders relax. When stressed, the Boss could hunch his shoulders up to his earlobes.

Joining the archbishop on the receiving line were Monsignor Healy and Father Joe Maguire, whose job was to make the introductions. This would be Joe's first time in the receiving line, and he had asked Dan to stand nearby in case "I get into trouble."

13.

After seeing the archbishop and his secretaries head off in the limo, Sister Philippe sat in her corner of the pantry, going over her day.

The archbishop looked the happiest she'd seen him in weeks—no surprise, she thought, since he loved the Youth Outreach Dinner.

Philippe thought back to dawn, when the archbishop knocked on Dan's door to cancel the trustees meeting. In that moment,

Philippe's biggest worry—how to keep the archbishop away from the school—was wiped away. For all her faults, Gert always had her facts straight, and Philippe had taken her warning seriously.

So she sat, looking out at the old orchard and the roof of Cardinal O'Rourke's mausoleum further down the hill.

The pantry was her domain, and the privacy it gave her was still a novelty, even after so many years. Personal space simply didn't exist growing up in a farmhouse with five brothers and two sisters. But the convent outside Quebec City, with its barnlike dormitory and communal showers, made the family home seemed like a castle.

She knew that she'd established herself that first Christmas in the residence when Frank Mulcahy, Cardinal Campion's secretary, gave her the perfect gift and offered to install it right away. *Chateau Philippe.* She looked up to see the back of the sign still hanging from the ceiling, exactly where Frank had secured it.

It was natural for her to think of herself as Philippe, her name since she turned fifteen. She was baptized Mathilde after her mother's favorite aunt, but she despised the name as long as she could remember. In fact, the prospect of a name change was one factor in her decision to enter religious life.

Like all the novices, she was assigned her new name by the superior. Over time, she learned a bit about Saint Phillip Neri and was pleased to find that he was not a run-of-the-mill saint. He was something of an eccentric, who had an easy laugh and loved what we now call practical jokes. That fact made her think that the Holy Spirit was indeed involved in the assignment, since she was a bit of a cut-up herself.

Another reason she liked the name was because the town of Saint Philippe, only a few miles from the farm, was where her grandmother lived.

As the superior said more than once, "The Spirit works in very personal ways."

Indeed, the Holy Spirit must have had a hand in her improbable journey from a Quebec potato farm with its well and outhouse to Little Rome with its state-of-the-art everything.

The thought made her glance over to the computer on her desk.

There wasn't a single computer in the residence when she arrived, the same month that Father Frank started work as secretary. By then, there were probably dozens of computers at the chancery, partway down the hill to the seminary, but as far as Philippe was concerned, the chancery could have been on the moon.

One day, Gert and her soon-to-be ex-husband, Norman, dropped by, carrying a brand-new computer already containing a software program for managing the residence. When Gert saw the pantry with Father Frank's sign, she told Norman to set the machine on Philippe's desk. After a few sessions where he walked her through the programs for inventory, payroll, accounts payable, and so on, Sister Philippe became the computer expert of the cardinal's residence.

In his last session, Norman showed her how to navigate the Internet and send and receive e-mail.

"Oh, I'd never use that!" she protested.

Before she knew it, however, she was e-mailing her far-flung siblings, checking the Quebec weather, and scrolling through recipes on the Web—as well as keeping Gert up to date on the archbishop's schedule.

14.

Vincent couldn't understand what had gotten into Portia. From the moment he and the dog came home to find her waiting out at the weather station, he could sense it.

Up until then, she had been pleasant enough, and even her words were loving and familiar, with Daddy this and Daddy that, but something had been missing. Her eyes were part of it. She didn't stare at the ground or the horizon in an obvious way but just looked at him slightly off-center.

Then there were moments when he was working in the kitchen, checking his instruments, or playing with the dog, when he knew she looked at him so intensely that he felt almost violated.

This morning, he saw her eyes straight on for the first time.

Her mother's eyes.

He had forgotten how powerful and seductive Maddy's eyes had been.

Until now, she talked quite a bit, but real information was flowing only in one direction. She kept quizzing him about Egg Rock and the family, but she offered next to nothing about herself.

Suddenly, it was as if a dam had broken, and all the information she'd been holding back poured out.

On the way up to Salem for the summer fair at Father Frank's church, she told her father about the day she left home.

"My friend Laura from Squimset High borrowed her father's car and picked me up early in the morning just as we'd planned. By then, you were back upstairs after finding me on the swing. She took me all the way into Boston and dropped me off at the Greyhound bus terminal, where I took a bus to New York. I didn't know a soul and really didn't know what was going to happen. I just needed to break away."

Vincent kept driving but wondered whether he should pull over.

"In Times Square, I met some kids who let me sleep on the floor of their loft awhile. I have to tell you that we were smoking a lot of marijuana then."

She looked over to him at this point, monitoring his reaction. He must have looked calm enough because she forged ahead.

"I was so stoned that when I learned about Uncle Wally's and Aunt Patty's plane crashing, it made no impression."

By then, he wondered whether silence might have been better than this gush of information after all.

She went on to tell him about waitressing in New York when her money ran out, traveling cross-country, sleeping on the benches of bus stations, the drunks, the guys trying to pick her up, her stay in Santa Fe, and her arrival in the Bay Area.

If she spared any details, he couldn't imagine what they would have been.

Cruising through North Squimset, the sky grew darker by the second. Finally they crossed the bridge into Salem, where the Saint Gabe's steeple was a welcome sight.

"Tell you more later," she whispered when Leo and his gang from Muddy River greeted them in the church parking lot.

By then, the sky was packed with ominous billowy, black-bottomed clouds racing in from the ocean, but the winds at ground level, on the Saint Gabriel's lawn, were calm. After a word with Frankie, who was watching the dunk tank get rigged, they checked out the fair on their own. Wally dragged Leo, Claire, and his sister, Francine, over to the line forming in front of the Whammo cars while Vincent followed Portia over to a booth where a woman was selling miniature lighthouses.

In minutes, the atmosphere turned a sickly greenish gray, a color Vincent remembered from his two hurricanes, in Egg Rock and then in Okinawa, both when he was a boy.

By the time Portia had moved on to a booth featuring starfish and sand dollars, he had his transistor radio out of his windbreaker and raised to his ear.

"Listen to this, Pumpkin. They just changed the forecast. If today's weather people were the old-fashioned kind, meteorologists instead of entertainers, they would have stepped outside the studio and changed the forecast hours ago."

The moment she raised the little box, wrapped in a dozen elastic bands to her ear, a sudden gust blew napkins and paper cups off the picnic tables.

15.

Dan had stationed himself a couple of feet behind Father Joe, just in case. So far, Joe seemed to be handling the receiving line well, introducing the guests to Monsignor Healy, who in turn handed them over to the archbishop. Joe's job was to keep things moving. Otherwise, as Dan had told him earlier, "We don't eat."

Without warning, Joe dove to his left, behind the monsignor, tackled the archbishop, and pirouetted in a kind of somersault before they both landed on the floor. Dan heard the shot while they were in midair. It was loud and unmistakable. He had never been that close to a gunshot, ever, and if he'd been quizzed beforehand about what it would sound like, he probably would have been concerned that he'd confuse it with a balloon popping. But there was no question what it was.

He could see men in tuxes and women in evening gowns ducking for cover.

The choir was between numbers and stood on the stage, frozen in time as if posing for a group photo.

Then came the blood. Not just a little ketchup, like you see in the movies, but it seemed gallons of the stuff on the floor where the archbishop and Joe were lying.

Before Dan could react, Dr. Nichols, the orthopedic doc at Saint Kay's and Dr. Nalbandian, Leo Mulcahy's partner, converged on the spot where the two men were sprawled.

"Somebody get me a belt before this guy bleeds to death!" the woman doc yelled.

Half a dozen belts from a half-dozen pairs of pants appeared simultaneously. While the doctors worked on Joe, Dan stayed with the archbishop, who was sitting in the pool of blood. He was getting checked over by a couple of other doctors he recognized from the hospital. The big guy, who had to weigh even more than Dan, was a shrink.

The archbishop was grimacing in pain, and from the way he was clutching his right arm, he might have broken it when he fell.

"It looks like you didn't get hit by the bullet," one of them said.

"Thanks to Our Heavenly Father and Father Joe Maguire," the archbishop gasped. "God gave our boy a great set of reflexes."

It seemed forever before the police arrived. By then, word spread through the crowd that a priest had fired from the balcony and then calmly walked out an emergency exit before anyone could react.

Dan decided not to share that information with the Boss while they waited for the ambulance.

16.

Cousin Frank waited gamely while a freckled ten-year-old in an oversize New England Patriots shirt aimed the hard rubber ball at the bull's eye under his seat. Behind him stretched the longest line by far at the fair. And why not, Leo thought. A mere twenty dollars gave anyone (under sixteen) three chances of hitting the bull's eye, thereby releasing the seat from its moorings and sending Father Frank into the water.

The dunk tank had been a Saint Gabe's tradition (and significant money-maker) for as long as anyone could remember. However, Frank had had enough. Over their monthly dinner, he'd told Leo that he omitted the tank from this year's plans. He calculated that in his six years as pastor, he had been aimed at about three thousand times, for a total (at the old rate of ten dollars for three throws) of ten thousand dollars. With the ratio of about one dunking for every one hundred throws, he managed to get doused about five times a year.

And he spent most of each summer dreading it.

Unfortunately, Frank went on, Matt Houlihan noticed the oversight. For years, Matt and his son, John, would drive up to just over the New Hampshire line and pick up the tank from a cousin in the rental business on Friday afternoon and take it back on Sunday … for free. Assuming that Father Frank had simply forgotten, Matt took care of securing the tank for another year. So thanks to Matt Houlihan's vigilance and willingness to lug the apparatus back and forth in his truck, Leo's cousin was a sitting duck for another year … all for the sake of Saint Gabriel's and its bottom line.

Frank doubled the price to twenty dollars in hopes of reducing demand, but the line was longer than ever.

Leo caught himself praying for the ball to miss, and it worked. The kid's three throws were wildly off the mark.

All the while, Frank, God bless him, smiled as if he couldn't imagine a more congenial place on earth than that flimsy chair dangling by a rope over a tub of not very warm water.

Leo was so distracted that he didn't hear his cell until Claire pointed to it with her finger and her eyes at the same time, in that cute way she had.

Harold was on the other end. He and his partner intruded on each other's weekend only if there was no alternative.

"Leo, I'm calling from the Saint Botolph."

He remembered that Harold and Geri were going to a high school awards night at the hotel. Geri's school was slated to get a prize.

"Somebody just tried to shoot the archbishop right here in the ballroom. Father Joe Maguire pushed Quilty away and took the bullet himself. It looks like Quilty's got a humeral fracture from hitting the deck. You can imagine the pandemonium. Father Joe has a good-sized lower extremity wound, and it looks like part of his femoral artery got blown away. He lost a shit load of blood before Nina got a tourniquet on him. It's doing some good, but we're taking turns applying manual pressure. Joe's wide awake and trying to make jokes, but while they were loading him on the stretcher, he asked to see you. As if things aren't crazy enough, they're saying that the shooter was a priest."

It took Leo only a minute to tell Claire and Frank about the call—and another minute to sprint for the car. When he looked back, Frank was already off his perch and running into the rectory with Claire.

17.

The fair-goers rushed into the rectory to watch the updates on TV. It was hard to believe that the crowd that had been having such a good time outside minutes earlier could become hushed, so reverent. Claire noticed two women up front holding rosary beads.

The TV sat in the "parlor," a large room next to the rectory's entrance. Its large screen looked out of place in the midst of the overstuffed chairs and religious pictures on the walls.

Channel Six was chronicling the events with a split-screen. Corinne Caruthers was speaking from in front of Saint Kay's while a male reporter awaited his turn at the entrance of the Saint Botolph Hotel.

"We're following another breaking news story this evening. Donna Kent from Storm Team Six reports that the tropical storm off the New Jersey coast has strengthened into a category-2 hurricane and is bearing down on us. Get used to the name Hurricane Arthur, because from what Donna is saying, Arthur's going to make a name for himself."

Claire noticed that Corinne was prepared to ride out the Storm of the Decade in a thousand-dollar Burberry trench coat, neatly cinched at the waist.

She reported that "both victims of this senseless crime at a downtown hotel" were en route to the hospital, and the "assailant" was still "on the loose," and wrapped up by urging viewers to stay tuned to Channel Six for the "very latest on these breaking stories."

No mention was made of a priest doing the shooting. With all the excitement at the hotel, Harold probably got it wrong. A priest taking a shot at the archbishop seemed too bizarre—even for a week like this.

That's when she thought about the copies they'd made of Rowley's FedExes and the lab book, sitting innocently on the kitchen table back in Muddy River.

She stepped into the restroom, away from the blare of the TV, and dialed Leo's cell.

18.

Kitty spent the evening in front of the TV in the family room. Buzzy and Bridget ducked in every few minutes to see if she needed anything, and the kids appeared one or two at a time but soon got bored and took off.

She tried to pray for Father Joe and the archbishop but was so stunned that she could only stare at the screen. When they switched to the remote at Saint Kay's, it seemed so odd not to see Eddie front and center.

Eddie had been on her mind since Irene alerted them to his departure from the garage, right after Gert and the man who looked familiar took off. And from where she sat in the family room, she could see the garage through the window.

He hadn't come back.

They flashed a photo of a Father Maguire on the screen, and Kitty recognized him—from someplace. Then it came to her. He'd been the priest who hustled Father Guido out of Mooney's during Eunice's wake. He looked younger in person, with a full head of red hair, cowlick at the back, and freckles.

"I'm really sorry to barge in on you, Mrs. Cronin, especially at a time like this. We were about to leave the parking lot when the archbishop thought of something and asked me to bring Father Guido outside to speak with him. I imagine their meeting won't take long. Then he can come back to join you. Please forgive the intrusion."

Father Maguire's picture was most likely a formal ordination portrait. He could be dead by now—she shuddered at the thought—and here was this young man who looked so full of life just two days earlier, staring sternly at the camera in a Roman collar that looked pasted on.

After a quick update on Hurricane Arthur ("It's bearing down on the coast with all its fury") and a flurry of commercials, they switched to a series of old news clips of Archbishop Quilty, starting with his installation at the cathedral five years earlier.

With no news likely for a while, Kitty saw her opportunity. She'd left notes she'd prepared for the trustees meeting up at the school. With the meeting cancelled, Eddie fired, and the archbishop nearly assassinated, her access to the school—and those notes—could be cut off at any time.

She found Buzzy in the basement playroom watching a *Star Wars* movie with John and Lawrence.

"I need a favor."

"Anything, Kitty."

"I'm going up to the trustees' room at the Mount to pick up some papers."

"It's stormy. I'll give you a ride."

"It's okay, Buzzy. I've driven in worse. Besides, the storm is going to come ashore north of here. Tell Bridget I'll be back soon, and if Eddie shows up or calls or anything, call me right away."

"Be careful."

19.

The going was slow. It was rainy and windy enough, but Leo was seeing nothing like the "alerts" on the car radio suggested. There were no fallen trees or street flooding—not yet anyway. Instead, the traffic was bottled up every few blocks with long lines of cars at convenience stores and gas stations. It looked like half the population of the North Shore was out, stocking up on candles and other emergency supplies, and topping off their tanks.

He was on the Squimway, midway between Salem and Boston, when Claire called.

She was concerned that the papers from Rowley's office should be in the hands of the police, after all. After hearing her out, he agreed. The shooting changed everything. After visiting Father Joe at the hospital (if he got there on time), he'd pick up the papers from home.

20.

Tom Rowley's hip was killing him—and he was more ticked off than he could ever remember. If Quilty hadn't chickened out and called off the trustees' meeting at the last minute, they'd be in the clear.

And the tularemia organisms would already be multiplying in the old bastard's lungs.

The best course of action would have been to lie down, ice his hip, and wait for the pain pills to kick in.

But if someone stumbled on the bioweapon up at the Mount, Tom Rowley would really be in some serious shit. He gathered up the tools, flashlight, and mask and changed into his camouflage and jungle boots. His wide-brimmed safari hat was the only addition to Friday's wardrobe.

Without Hurricane Arthur, neither their escapade at the hotel nor this return trip to the Mount would have gone well. The thick cloud cover made the early evening much darker than normal, and the rain diminished visibility even further. He slipped into the woods below the school un-witnessed.

The ball field was covered in white. His immediate reaction was snow. So much for pattern recognition, he thought, when he realized he was looking at thousands of sea gulls instead of an August blizzard. He was curious about what tipped them off and made them leave their nests miles away to take refuge here. He circumnavigated the flock carefully, and they stayed put. A few eyed him suspiciously, but the rest were oblivious.

At the edge of the parking lot, he got a glimpse of the taillights on the security vehicle as it took off down the driveway.

He punched in the code at the service entrance, walked by the deserted kitchen, and quickly made his way along the hallway leading to the administrative area just as he had done a day earlier.

He didn't notice the tiny sliver of light coming from under the door of the trustees' room. In fact, he was so elated to find the door still unlocked that he didn't realize the room was totally illuminated until he he'd pushed it half open.

Then he saw her. Kitty Cronin was seated at the head of the long table. Thankfully, she had swiveled her chair away from the door toward the windows and was talking on the phone.

Because of his hip, he had given up running, let alone speeding up a little to catch an elevator at the hospital. But just as Kitty turned and said, "Who's there?" he slammed the door shut with a bang and broke into a sprint back along the hallway, past the kitchen, and out into the parking lot. He dispensed with any attempt to hug the tree line this time and simply tore through the wooded area and crossed the ball field directly, scattering scores of surprised gulls in the process.

By the time he reached the trail, he was convinced that the police had been alerted, and patrol cars were already speeding up to the school. He listened for sirens as he descended as fast as the slippery rocks and his hip allowed, but all he could hear was the rain and wind in the trees. Only when he reached the street and headed back home did he resume a normal pace. The hip pain was the worst ever, and his limp had progressed to the point of his dragging his left leg behind at every step. Still worried about the police, he made the rest of the walk home over back streets.

He could hear his answering machine bleeping before he got the door unlocked. There was one message—from Helen. It was about his last chore of the night.

"You'll find the package for Guido on the kitchen counter," she had said, adding that she'd be waiting at his apartment when he got back.

21.

Kitty spoke as soon as she heard the door open.

"Who's there?"

She turned in time to glimpse a figure in a camouflage jacket and wide-brimmed hat before the door closed again with a bang.

"Are you still there, Kitty? What in God's name is going on?"

"I'm okay, Father Guido, but I think I surprised an intruder."

"Lock yourself in while I get one of the ER nurses to call security and the police."

"I think I'm safe. Whoever it was made a lot of noise running down the hall and is probably long gone by now."

"I'll stay on the phone until someone gets there."

Kitty kept the phone to her ear as she opened the door a few inches, pressed the latch, and closed it again.

She could hear Father Guido speak to someone on his end and then say, "One of the nurses just made the calls. Is the room secure now?"

"I opened the windows to cool the room off when I got here, but they're closed now—and the door's locked."

She could hear someone speaking to Father Guido in the background.

"Hear that, Kitty? They've stabilized Father Joe, and they're rolling him down to the OR. You see, my dear, everything is going to be just fine."

22.

They managed to get Saint Gabriel's tucked in for the night in record time, and by then, Vincent had the old Buick by the door, lights on and engine running.

Frank eased his father into the middle of the front seat next to Claire, while the kids and their aunt Portia shared the back.

"I hope we make it across the causeway in time."

"We can always come back here if it's flooded, Claire. Saint Gabe's has plenty of spare rooms."

"And plenty of skeletons in the closets," Portia said quietly.

Exiting the empty parking lot, Frank gave the big tent one last look just as the strongest gust yet threatened to loose its moorings and send it airborne.

23.

Eddie Cronin knew something about dealing with pressure, but nothing before ever came close to this.

As the pressures in his life evolved over the years, so did his methods of coping. The Rosary did the trick for a while during his seminary days, and a few drinks took the edge off back in college, but neither method stood the test of time. He finally had to reach back to his childhood, before the days of booze or prayer, to find a foolproof coping mechanism: his love of cars.

No, the pressure was never anything like this. In less than a day, he'd lost the only job he ever wanted, he hid out from Kitty, the only person who really mattered to him, and he'd been blackmailed by his personal secretary and her new friend, a cheesy drug rep.

The loss of Saint Kay's hurt the most. Here he was, barely twenty-four hours out of his job, and his hospital lands the PR extravaganza of the century. The apparition was only the beginning. The hospital had already been on the verge of being the go-to Marian Shrine in North America.

And that was before the assassination attempt on the archbishop. Now with Quilty and the heroic Father Joe Maguire being treated at Saint Kay's, the branding could be complete.

A special place, blessed by a miracle, where medical miracles occur every day.

He could taste it. The TV networks would be waiting in line to interview him, and the investors would be waiting in the wings.

Gert was smart all right. He'd already given her lots of

responsibility, but her performance this morning—not only the blackmail, which was backed up with meticulous documentation, but the plan for him to meet the Canadian distributor with the pills—was very impressive. If things had turned out differently, he'd be creating another VP slot at Saint Kay's just for her.

He ruled out the Pike. He'd have no trouble navigating the slick roads, but with these conditions, the speed limit on the Pike would be lowered to fifty or perhaps forty—and the staties would be all over the place.

So he decided to stay local.

After passing Walden Pond, invisible in the rain and darkness, he turned onto Route 2 and headed west. He slipped his favorite Gregorian chant discs into the player but kept the volume down, just to set the mood. The rain out here was not nearly as heavy as it was in Boston, and there was no wind to speak of. Still, people were staying in. Instead of the usual Saturday night traffic, there was only a trickle of cars.

He'd visited Walden only once, with Kitty during their courtship. They used to talk about going back, walking around the pond again, but never got around to it.

Still, he assumed that they'd be back one of these days, talking about Thoreau, who lived in those woods, and about civil disobedience and nonviolence the way he and Kitty did that spring afternoon.

The traffic lights were slowing him down, but he knew that the road widened west of the Concord rotary, and then he'd let 'er rip. He could feel the Ram's eight-cylinder engine strain under him like a race horse fidgeting in the starting gate.

Soon he saw lights beyond the trees up ahead, reflecting off the low clouds and seemingly magnified by the rain. He was still trying to figure out what was out there (a shopping center? A small airport?)

when from around the next curve the walls and guard towers of the state prison loomed before him, bright as day.

How could he forget? He'd visited Concord once as a seminarian, assisting the chaplain with Mass in that shabby auditorium that smelled of stale cigarettes and disinfectant, with the inmates lining up quietly for Communion in their gray prison jumpsuits with DOC stenciled on the back.

He had been asked back more than once but always found an excuse.

Amazing he was thinking straight at all. Since the archbishop's goon Skerry barged into his office with the resignation letter Friday afternoon, he hadn't slept.

After Gert and that little greaseball J. J. finally took off, he went back to the safe to be sure that he had really given them the fifty grand. But that was nothing compared to the last few hours, driving around in the rain, when he couldn't be sure whether he was awake or dreaming.

He took another look at the prison lighting up the night and realized for the first time that he, Dr. Edward Cronin, would be living right here in his very own cell, peering through bars at the lights and the guard towers.

It was so obvious.

Eddie visited Sister Annunziata, his old high school teacher, at a nursing home south of the city. She was barely recognizable until she spoke, but her voice was just as commanding, and her mind just as sharp as he remembered.

"They call this a geri-chair. At first I thought it was named after someone named Jerry, like Jerry Lewis perhaps, but no. Geri is short for geriatric. The chair is ingenious. You see this tray, Eddie, and how it's attached to the arms? It actually serves two purposes. One, it's good for resting your elbows, holding up a magazine, or supporting your lunch, that kind of thing. The second purpose is more sinister, and that's where

the name 'geri' comes in. It keeps you in your place. If I had any intention of getting up, walking around the room, going to the bathroom, forget it. They tell me it's for my own safety, in case I do something 'geriatric' like wandering off the reservation."

After asking him about his career, his family, and all of that, she looked down at the geri-chair again.

"Another reason they keep us locked up like this should be obvious. If I could, I'd fling myself out the nearest window."

"But—"

"I know what I'm saying, Eddie dear. I taught religion for forty years, and if anyone knows the catechism, I do. And I believed every word I said. You were there, and you know that."

We are stewards, not owners, of the life God has entrusted to us. It is not ours to dispose of.

"But when you're faced with no option but another day of captivity, you change."

Once he cleared the rotary, he let the Ram's V8 engine come to life, fast-forwarded the CD to the "Gloria," and cranked up the volume. A mile or so farther west, at a sharp turn on the road, he remembered the day he followed one of those tankers that bring milk down from Vermont. It must have been speeding back home, empty, when it failed to make the turn and crashed through the guardrail and down an embankment, killing the driver.

He unfastened his seatbelt and concentrated on how important it would be to lay down skid marks just before he crashed through the barrier, so that it would look like a foolish mistake of speeding on a dark road in a storm and missing a turn.

If it looked like he tried to stop, the accident reconstruction team might give him the benefit of the doubt, and Kitty would collect the life insurance.

One thought consoled him. Enigmatic little Irene would watch over her mother and in the end turn out to be Edward Cronin's finest achievement.

He'd cranked the Ram up to about eighty-five when he heard a siren and saw flashing lights in the rearview mirror. At the same time another cruiser swung onto the road ahead of him.

The stereo was pumping out a Gregorian chant just as he intended.

Gloria Patri, Filio, et Spiritui Sancto: Sicut erat in principio, et nunc et semper, et in saecula saeculorum.

Like one of the professional drivers at Lime Rock maneuvering around a wreck on the track, Eddie deftly skirted the cruiser and sliced through the guardrail at ninety-plus.

Airborne in his favorite vehicle, the monks' assuring voices filling the space, he felt pretty damn good—considering.

24.

Just inside the emergency room, Leo nearly collided with Nina Nichols, wandering around in a daze, her pink party dress splattered with Father Joe's blood.

She looked like Jackie Kennedy in Dallas.

Harold shook Leo's hand and told him that they just rolled Father Joe up to the OR. He was hemodynamically stable but had been pretty shaky earlier. Nina and Harold rode in the ambulance with Joe, taking turns using the heels of their hands to keep the femoral artery from spurting, while two EMTs poured Lactated Ringers through large bore Angiocaths in both arms.

On the way to the hospital, Harold was afraid that Joe would arrest at any second, but Nina kept talking to the young priest about the Ignatius College football team and their upcoming season. She even managed to get Joe to laugh with her stories of the new players meeting the team doctor for the first time and finding out that it was a woman!

The archbishop was still being worked on in Major Med, the mini-ICU in emergency. The "old boy" (as Harold put it) made a stink when they got out the scissors and cut away every stitch of clothing, but after one of the senior nurses warned him to "Cool it, Father," he kept quiet.

The staff was worried about an MI, since he was nauseated and his pressure was only ninety over sixty when he arrived. However, his pressure came up quickly with fluids and pain meds. Serial EKGs remained normal, and two sets of enzymes were flat.

X-rays showed a clean midhumeral fracture, requiring only immobilization.

Since an MI was the greatest worry, the cardiologists planned to keep him overnight in their unit downstairs as a precaution.

Harold pointed in the direction of the "family room."

"You know how teeny that room is, Leo. Well, there must be fifty priests jammed in there, praying for Father Joe and the archbishop. Wanna take a look?"

It was a standard waiting room, with the expected molded plastic chairs, well-worn magazines in a rack on the wall, and the ubiquitous TV mounted high in one corner. Leo had been in there only a few days back, on Tuesday. That was where Kitty Cronin and Father Guido had waited for him to come in and make it official that Eunice had died.

Cousin Frank's buddy Father Richard was leading the group reciting the Rosary, while Father Dan Skerry stood outside the door, like a bouncer at an after-hours bar.

He thought back to a recent conversation he'd had with Claire. She was putting her rosary beads into her handbag before leaving the house on an errand.

"Do you really think you'll need those at the supermarket?"

"Leo, dear, the beads are my business."

"I respect that, Claire, I really do. But I can't see how they can be useful."

"Leo, you can't see because you're too pissed off. You can't get over Vietnam and the plane crash. Prayer gives me peace and strength. And do you know what I pray for most of all?"

"Tell me."

"For you to overcome the anger so you can feel the serenity I feel."

Leo listened from the doorway while the priest and his flock prayed, and he found himself carried along by the sing-song repetition of the Our Father, Hail Mary, and Glory Be prayers. Father Richard stood up front, reciting each prayer's opening lines, and his congregation finished each prayer in perfect unison. And the longer Leo listened, the more he envied them.

The *rhythm* of voices lent additional power to the prayers that he had never appreciated before. The voices fused into an independent force with a heartbeat of its own.

He was reminded of the piano lessons on the old upright in the living room of the old house in Egg Rock. Before he was ever allowed to play his first note, the teacher would pull the metronome out of her bag, place it on the piano, and set it in motion.

Yes, the prayers were metronomic.

One thing was clear. Without Nina Nichols and Harold jumping in the way they did, Father Joe would have croaked right there on the floor of the Saint Botolph Hotel ballroom. But there was no harm throwing the Rosary in for good measure.

And he had to admit that the Rosary made him feel better.

"Placebo effect," he whispered. The religious equivalent of a sugar pill.

Just then, he remembered Rowley's papers sitting on the kitchen table back in Muddy River. He told Harold he'd be back soon and made for the car.

25.

After hearing Helen's message and making sure the package was where she said it was, Tom downed a couple of Percocets and stretched out of the sofa. He was able to doze about twenty minutes before willing himself awake, an old trick from his years of medical training. Refreshed, he changed into his hospital garb, put the package under his raincoat, and walked up the hill to Saint Kay's.

Hospital Drive was even more congested with news trucks than anytime all week. The shooting had to be the news event of the year, probably the only thing that could drive the Virgin Mary off the front pages.

Just as well, he thought. A truly religious event had been twisted into a kind of folk festival. People were trooping up to Saint Kay's to be a part of the action for an hour or so, buy a souvenir or two, and go home. It had become a recreational activity, like cruising the mall or playing miniature golf.

The pity of it was that by appearing in that window at Saint Kay's, the Blessed Mother was sending a message to the world—and no one was listening.

After dialing Guido's number from the lobby and getting no answer, he took the stairs behind the gift shop up to the chaplain's quarters. The old master key slipped into the lock, and the bolt fell back with his first turn. Like an army ranger behind enemy lines, he moved silently and efficiently, getting in and out of the little man's apartment in less than thirty seconds.

From there he went directly to the ER, where the staff would fill him in and could vouch for his presence later on. Just as he had hoped, a couple of nurses were taking a break while housekeeping was trying to put the trauma room and the Major Med back in order. A pile of plastic bags, some colored bright red to signify hazardous waste, already sat outside the room.

From the way they were talking, Nina Nichols was the hero of the evening, and the archbishop was a pain in the ass.

Then he made his way over to the MOB and found the place deserted. In spite of the darkness, the rain, and the wind, the Blessed Mother remained beautiful, magically catching the distant light of the parking garage.

Without really thinking about it, he got on his knees right there on the lawn in front of the window, near the bouquets, cards, and messages left behind. The Hail Mary he learned in Sunday school came to mind.

Hail Mary, full of grace,
The Lord is with thee.
Blessed art thou amongst women
And blessed is the fruit of thy womb, Jesus.
Holy Mary, Mother of God,
Pray for us sinners,
Now and at the hour of our death.
Amen.

He could feel her smiling.

On his way home, he saw one of those yellow school buses with St. Luke's Seminary stenciled on the side. Young men in clerical garb filed off quietly.

The nurses had told him about a bunch of priests praying in the family room. He had no idea what they'd do with this second wave.

He saluted the seminarians and recognized one he'd seen at the hospital, most likely rotating through its chaplaincy program. The guy looked Tom up and down, and must have seen the knees of his trousers soaked through. Would any of them believe that he'd been on his knees outside on this stormy night, praying to the Blessed Mother?

If these priests-to-be would take a minute to visit the Blessed Mother out there in the rain, they'd see why.

Helen greeted him at the door, and for the first time in years, gave him a kiss. Not quite one of those passionate kisses from the old days that would always get his juices flowing, but not a peck on the cheek either. She kissed him full on the lips and lingered there a few heartbeats.

"I already called the tip into the police."

"Not from here, I hope."

"Of course not, silly. I used the pay phone outside the library."

He was glad to hear there was at least one working pay phone in Faneuil Center. With all these cell phones, old-fashioned pay phones were becoming an endangered species.

Crazy as it might seem to others, the surviving pay phone could have been the work of the Blessed Mother.

It fit the pattern.

26.

Leo always felt jittery when the house was empty. The rooms seemed larger, more echo-y than when Claire and the kids were around—as if he were trespassing on someone else's property.

Cup in hand, he sat down next to Rowley's papers, which were sitting in neat piles exactly where he had left them on the kitchen table Thursday night.

He was gulping the last of the tea when the phone rang. Harold was on the other end.

"Leo. As if things couldn't get stranger, I just heard some terrible news. Eddie Cronin was driving one of his muscle cars up on Route 2, missed a turn, and crashed through a guardrail. Witnesses said he was flying, and I hear that he was already dead when the police got to him."

"Wow! Poor Kitty! I'll be back to the hospital in a few minutes. I need to show you what Claire and I found in Rowley's office."

Leo grabbed the papers and headed to his car. He pictured Eddie tooling out Route 2, trying to believe that Eddie, the consummate driver, had miscalculated somehow.

27.

The police were polite and reassuring. They believed that whoever opened that door was a common thief. There had been similar break-ins in homes at the foot of the hill. Kitty's de-briefing was short but would have ended even earlier had Pat Kaminski not added a few questions of his own.

She gathered up her belongings, and Pat accompanied her to her car.

"Whoever it was is in the next county by now, Mrs. Cronin, so there's no danger. Usually the biggest problem up here is rabbits eating their way through the flowerbeds. Last summer, they started gnawing the wires for the sprinkler system, and we needed to get the whole thing replaced. Actually the sprinkler people weren't sure if it was rabbits, squirrels, or chipmunks. They dug up the flowerbeds, of course, but also the patch of lawn in front of the Saint Pius statue and the ball fields. They finished the work on the first day of school."

He seemed to have forgotten that she was up there every day, checking their progress.

"After coming face to face with a robber, it's normal to be shaken up. So I'll walk to the parking lot with you, just to keep you company."

Just then, Pat's phone bleeped. He turned away to take the call and then walked out of earshot.

When he came back, she knew something was very wrong.

"Kitty … I mean Mrs. Cronin, we need to go back inside."

Minutes later, another policeman and Father Guido arrived, and Father Guido looked as downcast as he did on Tuesday, when she sat in that claustrophobic room with the TV mounted on the wall, waiting to hear about her mother.

"It's Eddie," he said quietly. "Eddie is dead."

To be honest, she wasn't surprised.

28.

Harold sat in one of the lobby chairs and studied the papers. Leo knew that his partner was concentrating because he kept playing with his mustache—a habit Leo first noticed when they were interns together. Whenever a patient posed a difficult diagnostic problem, Harold would unconsciously roll the ends (his mustache was bushier then) and then flatten them out.

Harold was giving these documents every ounce of his attention.

"We need to get this information to the police, but let's not get you and Claire arrested for breaking and entering. The tip has to be anonymous."

"That's what kept us from handing them over before."

Harold spied Pat Kaminski chatting with the woman behind the information desk and motioned him over.

"Pat, could we sit down in your office and go over some papers?"

They waited while Pat read the papers at his desk and placed them in an envelope from the drawer. Leo was amazed that he had no questions.

"I don't understand all of it, but I don't need to."

Then he stood up and stretched.

"You have nothing to worry about, Dr. Mulcahy. It will be passed along as an anonymous tip, no questions asked."

29.

J. J. knew they lucked out. He and his new friend Gert walked into the Cattle Drive on a Saturday night about an hour before closing and found two empty places side-by-side at the bar.

That's about as lucky as you can get!

After their tête-à-tête with Eddie, they'd checked out the neighborhood around Sycamore Hill for a while, and Gert, bless her little black heart, coughed up a twenty so they wouldn't be worrying about the gas gauge every five minutes.

They had lunch at a burger joint he knew about on the road back into town. Double-thick shakes were the joint's claim to fame, and deservedly so. He didn't understand how she could get by with salad, coffee, and smokes, but that was her problem. Besides, she was paying.

After lunch, they stopped at a package store in Watertown for bourbon, vermouth, cherries, ice, and more cigarettes. Cherries and ice always cost triple in a liquor store, but Gert, with her wad of dough, didn't give a shit. Finally, they stopped at a convenience store where she picked up a couple of magazines.

By the time they got back to his place, he needed a nap, but Gert didn't seem to mind. She needed to run "some errands," she said, and took off in the Lexus. That was fine with him, since that way she could give the American Pharmaceutical Enterprises official vehicle one more outing before it got repossessed. And if she got into a little fender-bender, it was no skin off his nose.

That was why they didn't really get down to drinking and planning their next move until it was already dark.

He'd been worried about the way they were going to split up the money, but not until they were pretty well settled in with their manhattans did he dare bring the subject up.

"Sixty-forty," she answered.

That didn't sound too bad to him, so he nodded.

"But you're not getting your cut until we get all our business taken care of."

"Business? What business? We're both unemployed."

"I'll tell you tomorrow when we're both sober."

Since he didn't feature getting into an argument, he nodded again.

Gert, believe it or not, was getting sexier as the night wore on. But when he made a move, she looked irritated. Around then, she suggested they move the party down to the Cattle Drive.

So he handed her the keys to the Lexus, and off they went.

The bartender knew both of them, of course, and brought Gert a manhattan on the rocks without asking. But before he mixed J. J.'s usual Morgan and Coke, J. J. spoke up and ordered a manhattan, too. Bad idea to mix drinks this late in the game.

They were showing ESPN baseball highlights on the big TV, but J. J. had to close one eye to keep from seeing two of everything.

He must have been more blasted than he thought.

Then he had the bright idea of getting back to why he wasn't getting his share of the sixty-forty split right away. Gert pretended she didn't hear at first, but when he kept at it, going so far as saying that she was stonewalling him—well, she lost it.

Without warning, she grabbed a bottle of Miller Lite the guy on the other side of her had just set down and thrust it, neck first, into his chest. J. J.'s balance wasn't the greatest to begin with, so that was all it took to send him off the stool and headlong to the floor.

After that, everything was even more of a blur. The cops were there in no time, and next thing he knew, he and Gert were in the backseat of a cruiser on their way to Station 14 up by Saint Brendan's.

To make a bad situation all the more pathetic, the motion of the police car got his stomach going, and he barfed all over his three-hundred-dollar shoes.

SUNDAY

1.

Father Guido couldn't recall a more momentous night. It felt like a whole week had been squeezed into the eight hours since he'd heard about the shooting during the Red Sox game.

As hospital chaplain, he'd brought word of a death to people hundreds of times and knew that if that task ever became routine, he'd better be looking for different work.

Kitty had lost neither a child nor a spouse of sixty years, but telling her about Eddie's death was very hard. Driving back to the hospital after Bridget and Buzzy took her home from the Mount, he tried to figure out why.

Some things were obvious.

Only his sister, Marilena, was more important to him than Kitty. On Tuesday, he'd sat with Kitty in that little room at emergency and told her that Eunice, who'd been spunky as ever an hour before, was dead. And here he was a few days later, telling her that Eddie had been killed in a car crash. Telling a stranger that she'd lost her mother and her husband in a few short days would be difficult enough, but Kitty was his best friend.

But there was more.

During their phone conversation earlier in the evening, she'd told him something he expected (and dreaded) to hear for some time.

She'd been thinking of leaving Eddie.

She'd made no concrete plans and had told no one else yet, but she'd had enough.

Later, after hearing about Eddie's accident, she asked him an impossible question.

"Guido, could he possibly have known?"

He was afraid she'd be asking that question over and over for the rest of her life.

The ER was already in full Saturday night/Sunday morning mode by the time he got back from the Mount. The casualties from the bars began trickling in around midnight and peaked between 2:00 and 3:00 a.m. Often this overnight shift would process triple the muggings, slips and falls, and psych emergencies of any other night of the week. And tonight was no different.

At one point, the police brought in a fellow the nurses recognized as a drug rep at the hospital. He'd apparently become boisterous, fell from a barstool, and needed to be checked out. Guido heard that once the X-rays came back negative, the police took him to the station for booking.

It wouldn't go well for the poor fellow's job to spend a night in jail.

The evening supervisor was on the phone, trying to locate any nurse who could come in. Nobody from the North Shore would be making it, because once the storm cranked up, it downed hundreds of trees and blocked all access to the city beyond the harbor tunnels and the Tobin Bridge. Most of the 3:00 to 11:00 staff would be pulling double if not triple shifts.

Leo Mulcahy had been lucky to get back into town, he thought, as he pictured the rest of the Mulcahy clan stuck out there in Egg Rock. He said a prayer for their safety.

Faneuil had gotten off easy. A good-sized rainstorm was about it, with less wind than you'd expect from a run-of the-mill nor'easter.

Marilena called the ER at one point, reporting that the South

Shore was untouched and that she was safe at the beach house in Gull.

"Get some sleep, Guido."

He told her he'd try.

Once Nina Nichols got into her scrubs and began working on the archbishop's arm, she perked up. When they heard from the OR that Father Joe was out of danger, she smiled for the first time, and later on, when Guido was in the middle of something else, he heard her musical laugh in the background and knew that she was really coming around.

At one point, he saw Dr. Rowley speaking to the nurses, but he was gone before Guido had a chance to say hello.

Leo and Harold were in and out of the emergency room. Leo needed to get the cardinal's suite emptied and ready for the archbishop but was getting an earful from the current occupant, the owner of a famous downtown eatery, recovering from a gastric stapling procedure.

"Eddie guaranteed that the only person who could bump me would be the pope or the president of the United States—so Quilty doesn't make the cut," the restaurateur argued, before adding a remark about the sex abuse scandal.

Finally Father Dan and Pat Kaminski dropped by the cardinal's suite for a chat, and the fellow changed his mind.

Harold called it a "good cop, bad cop situation."

With Father Joe and the archbishop settled in, Leo came back to the ER to have a word with Guido. Leo called it "a private matter," so they went into an empty office and closed the door.

Leo handed back the FedEx he'd borrowed and told Guido about the visit he and Claire had made to Rowley's office, where they found copies of the three obituaries sent to him in Gull.

Guido tried to put this news in perspective. He understood that three obituaries, and one fictitious at that, could hardly be compared to the attempted murder of the archbishop and a sudden death of the hospital president.

Of course, that was only because the FedEx hadn't been successful.

He felt angry—not the flicker of irritation he'd feel from time to time—but full-blown pound-your-fist-on-the-table anger. He was surprised and upset by its intensity. He'd seen his share of angry people over the years—some angry at the Church, some angry with a spouse or other family member, some angry with themselves, and some simply angry about everything. Eddie Cronin, red-faced, dismissing him in the gift shop after Guido refused to bless the souvenirs came to mind. Guido knew how fortunate he was to have been spared that emotion. He had to reach back to his teenage years to recall getting really furious at Marilena, but, as so often is the case, he had no memory of what he'd been angry about.

He feared that Leo could see him shaking, and he was so unhinged that he forgot to ask how the family was coping up in Egg Rock.

Under normal circumstances, he would never have had such a lapse.

After Leo left, he headed outside to visit the Blessed Mother. Mary, he knew, could calm him.

The rain had stopped, but the wind was starting to pick up. The lights from the parking garage barely made a dent in the darkness and lingering fog in front of the MOB, but he could still make out the outline of Our Lady.

He bowed his head and silently thanked Mary for all that she had allowed to happen since her arrival on Monday. Giving Father Joe the courage to risk his life was only the latest of her blessings. The familiar passage from John's gospel ran through his head: "Greater love hath no man than this, that a man lay down his life for his friends."

Still shaking, he thought back to Wednesday afternoon, when his delightful boat trip to Gull turned into a nightmare. He pictured the FedEx envelope slipped under the door, the death notices centered neatly on the three pages stapled in the upper left corner, and the lime-colored garden hose taped to the car's tailpipe … and how the nightmare came to an end with the Blessed Mother herself, smiling down at him from the picture window.

Standing before her, he prayed out loud.

"No matter what he might have done, please, Blessed Mother, please intercede with your Son to grant the soul of Edward Cronin eternal peace. And watch over Kitty, whose long ordeal is far from over."

He recalled the pictures of Kevin Sheehan he'd cut out of the yearbook and the session with Tommy Rowley that he terminated out of cowardice.

Then he finished his prayer.

"Grant me the strength to overcome my anger and forgive my accuser. Amen."

The wind picked up suddenly, rushing between the hospital buildings and tossing around the cards and other mementos left below the window. The gust lasted only a few seconds and ended with a loud "crack."

A limb from the old tree nearby had snapped off and struck the window full force before falling to the ground.

He turned back to the window and for a second thought he was looking at the wrong one. No, he had the right window all right, but it was now dark, identical to the others.

In the past few days, he'd worried about how sad he'd feel when the Virgin Mary would no longer be out here to visit.

Now she was gone, but he felt no sadness at all. She had come, done her work, and moved on.

He blessed himself in gratitude.

2.

It was the most spectacular dawn that Vincent had ever seen. The sky remained clouded-over except for a ragged opening at the horizon a few degrees south of the lifesaving station, just large enough to accommodate the rising sun. Golden rays streamed horizontally across the property, reminding him of one of those Renaissance religious paintings.

During the height of the storm, he feared he wouldn't see another morning. The highest speed he recorded was 89 mph, right before the anemometer blew off the roof, but a short time later, the winds really cranked up, the house shook even more violently, and the lights went out. That was when he was sure the hurricane had spawned a tornado and that the pressure gradient would suck the windows out.

He and Frankie herded everyone into the pantry, where the house was structurally strongest.

His grandniece, Francine, broke the tension by getting everyone to sing ballads even he remembered.

"Someone's in the kitchen with Dinah
Someone's in the kitchen I know o-o …"

They camped out in the pantry until the winds relaxed around four. Amazingly, they dropped from hurricane force to calm in seconds, as if someone had closed a door in a thunderstorm. By then, everyone was so exhausted that they trooped upstairs to catch some sleep. Everyone, that is, except him and Echo.

The dog had actually ridden out the storm under the big four-poster bed in Vincent's room and carefully worked her way downstairs just as the others were heading up.

In the predawn stillness, the two of them sat by candlelight in the kitchen, listening to the waves breaking over the point.

At first light, a little before five thirty, the old man and the dog made their way outside in time for sunrise. With the yard littered with branches and large limbs, their wet leaves still attached, Vincent took every step with care. The last thing he needed was a fall. Claire would come running outside to give him first aid.

"Uncle Vinny, I think you broke your hip," she'd say.

The old dog, however, was fearless as she moved smartly through the debris. The arthritis that made the stairs so challenging seemed temporarily cured.

The large spruce between the house and the point, the tree that Vincent and Maddy festooned with lights every Christmas, had toppled, crushing Vincent's little weather station on the way down. As he picked his way around the fallen giant, he was dwarfed by its root system, ripped out of the soil to a ninety-degree angle.

It resembled the propeller from a B-29.

3.

Leo awoke to the aromas of coffee and bacon wafting up from Geri's kitchen. In a dream, he had been in an emergency room where hundreds of patients were being processed in a mass casualty situation. The place looked vaguely like Saint Kay's but had some features of the mini-hospital at Phuoc Vinh. An endless line of wounded filled the facility, some American, some Vietnamese, some military, some civilian.

At first, the kitchen noises blended into the action. But when his brain couldn't account for the breakfast smells, he came to.

It took him a few seconds to reorient himself, as it always did when he awakened away from home. Looking at the unfamiliar shape of the guestroom window, he worked his way back through the last few hours.

Father Joe was at his baseline by the time Harold and Leo left the hospital. Father Dan had heard the young priest ask for a pizza after coming out of anesthesia and pronounced him "the same old Joe," and the nurses were thrilled that he was peeing "like a fireman."

They needed four hours of OR time to get the kid's femoral artery patched up, giving him five units to make up for the blood loss.

Guido took the news about Rowley quietly and asked no questions, but he looked shaken. Leo had the feeling that Guido needed time to himself and excused himself quickly.

Outside, they got a glimpse of the seminarians filing into their buses, with Frankie's friend Father Richard in the lead.

Finally awake, Leo sat on the side of the bed and dialed Claire's cell.

He had gotten through to her from Saint Kay's around midnight. They were all back at the house in Egg Rock by then, and the power was still on.

"At least for now," Claire had said.

He tried again around two, and an automated voice said, "We're sorry. The party you are trying to reach is out of the area."

Geri and Harold were finishing breakfast went he got downstairs.

Geri looked upset.

"The police were here, Leo. I'm surprised you slept through it."

Saturday evening, Harold had decided not to call the police about the jimmied door, because nothing was missing.

That was before Geri made her discovery. Unable to sleep, she searched the house thoroughly to see if anything had been stolen after all.

"I was going through Harold's closet when—*blammo*—I saw that the priest outfit, the one he'd worn to the hospital costume party, was gone. It was behind his sport coats, with other stuff he never wears," she said, giving Harold one of her looks, "stuff he should have gotten rid of years ago. Harold thought of the hotel gunman right away, and I wasn't far behind. The police got here five minutes after I called."

"What did they say?"

"Nothing, but they looked the house over and took notes."

The TV was tuned to the Weather Channel where their in-house hurricane expert, white-haired and professorial, was describing Arthur as "a small but intense category-2 hurricane, pulling away from the Massachusetts coast and bearing down on Nova Scotia." On a map, he indicated how the Massachusetts North Shore was heavily damaged, but Boston and points south escaped. The coastal towns got the worst of it, from "the little hamlet of Egg Rock" at the southern edge of the impact area to the "exclusive enclave of Squimset Neck" to the north. Doppler suggested tornadoes at both locations, and they were hoping to get experts on the ground by nightfall. On the north side of Little Egg Rock, homes built on the steep cliffs had toppled into the ocean below.

4.

Vincent saw that the dock had washed away, leaving pilings that looked lonely without the two-by-sixes that had connected them.

The house had stood up well. Some shingles were gone, and a big limb had badly dented a gutter. His anemometer, which he heard strike the roof on its way down, was nowhere to be seen, leaving only one of its four metal struts as a reminder.

The downed spruce and his weather station looked like his biggest losses.

He pulled a pair of binoculars from his windbreaker and took a deep breath before surveying the rest of the damage.

Pivoting northeast, he saw no traffic on the small causeway

between Little and Big Egg Rock. No trees were left standing on the south side of Little Egg, and most houses had major roof damage. He shuddered when he thought of the cliff-dwellers hidden from view on the north side.

Turning to his right, he was relieved to see the lifesaving station at the south end of the causeway standing, but two-thirds of its steep, shingled roof was missing, exposing the upstairs rooms as if they were in a doll house. The lookout tower, an elongated pyramid on its southeast corner, had vanished, as had the adjacent building that housed the lifesaving row boats in his father's day.

He doubled back to get another look at the causeway because something didn't look right the first time. Sure enough! A chunk of land the length of a tour bus was missing, and water was flowing freely between the Squimset Harbor and the open Atlantic. No wonder he didn't see any traffic on the road. Big Egg Rock was now geographically alone, and the natives who referred to the peninsula as an island were now literally correct.

Only then did he notice the silence. His hearing, like his other senses, wasn't as sharp as it once was, but something was definitely missing. He looked up to find the morning sky, usually alive with swooping, shrieking gulls at this hour, empty, and marveled at how these creatures anticipated the big storms and fled to the mainland.

Echo barked until she had Vincent's attention. The dog had all kinds of barks: the sharp angry bark when another dog dared to walk in front of the house; the long, drawn-out "woof" to get back inside on a cold winter morning; and this, a shorter woof sound, repeated as long as necessary to get Vincent's attention. She was rooting through fallen branches and made sure he was watching.

There was the anemometer, all in one piece.

5.

The Saint Kay's lobby was bustling with reporters and police when Leo and Harold arrived to check on their patients.

Raymond Stanton saw them and walked over.

"What a week! On Monday, the Virgin Mary appeared, and this morning, she's gone."

"What do you mean, 'gone'?"

"Wind blew a limb from the old tree smack into the window, and the image disappeared. Now it looks like all the others again. Walk over and take a look for yourselves."

Camera crews were jostling each other in front of the window, once again as nondescript as the others in the building. The only remaining evidence of something out of the ordinary was the huge shrine on the lawn below it, which had tripled in size since Leo last looked. The feet of thousands of pilgrims had reduced the grass to a muddy mess, with bouquets, pictures, messages, and religious objects water-logged and scattered about. Incongruously, a giant Teddy bear, at least two feet tall and wintergreen in color, stood at attention in the midst of the rubble, soaked and forlorn.

Leo was reminded of one of those roadside shrines that pop up after fatal car crashes. On a recent trip to Egg Rock, he'd come across such a display, Teddy and all, near the dog track.

Harold peered at Leo from over the tops of his glasses.

"I don't know what to make of all this, but if I were Eddie Cronin's replacement up there in the penthouse, my first order of business would be to get the grounds crew out here with a bunch of rakes and trash bags. The sooner Saint Kay's gets back to normal, the better."

Rounds went smoothly. The archbishop was asleep in the cardinal's suite, snoring loudly while Leo went over the chart. His vital signs were rock solid, and his EKGs and blood chemistries were normal.

Leo let the archbishop sleep, since he'd accomplish nothing by waking the man up to tell him that he was doing well.

Next door, Father Joe was watching a *Tom and Jerry* cartoon on mute, so as not to disturb Father Dan, who was dozing in a chair.

Joe clicked off the set, and Leo settled himself on the side of the bed.

"You did a very brave thing, Father Joe."

"You know, Doc, I didn't have time to think. Just instinct, I guess."

"I can understand that."

"Did you hear that I had dinner with your cousin Frank a few weeks ago?"

Leo shook his head.

"Dan arranged it. We went to the Cattle Drive, and Father Richard joined us. We put Sister Philippe in charge of the Boss for a few hours. It was one of those secretarial get-togethers, where they compare notes on the care and feeding of archbishops. Anyway, I told Frank you were my doctor, and he filled me in about your time in Vietnam."

Leo smiled and got up to leave.

"Wait, Leo, please, and hear me out. What you just said about my being brave may or may not be true, but it means a heck of a lot to me—because it came from a guy who knows what he's talking about. Thanks."

6.

Father Richard was in the middle of his morning prayers when he heard a knock on the door. It wasn't the usual polite sound one of his fellow priests or one of the seminarians would make. He got out of his chair as quickly as he could before whoever it was broke the door down.

It was a policeman in uniform with "questions."

He invited the officer to sit, but the fellow just stood there as if he hadn't heard. He was so tall that the professor feared his head would scrape the ceiling. Although he was younger than most of the seminarians, he took in the room with a worldly look of suspicion and contempt.

"Can you tell me where you were between seven and nine o'clock last night?"

The fellow had opened a small notebook and was already scribbling before the professor could answer.

"Right here in my room. I ate supper downstairs at 5:30 with a few of the other faculty and came directly upstairs afterward."

"Did you see or speak to anyone after you came back up here?"

"Not until the rector called to tell me about the shooting and ask me to come to the hospital."

"What time was that?"

"Around ten I think."

"Can anyone vouch for your being here between seven and nine?"

"I saw no one."

"Not even in the john?"

"No. There are only two other priests on this floor right now. Most are away on vacation. I didn't see a soul between supper and when I went downstairs after the rector's call, to take the bus to Saint Kay's."

"Did you make or receive any telephone calls besides the one from the . . ."

"Rector. No."

"Did you e-mail or receive e-mails from anyone?"

"I guess I'm stuck in the last century, since I haven't figured out how to e-mail yet."

The policeman's expression didn't change.

"Do you have any travel plans?"

"No."

"Stay in town in case we have more questions."

"Is this related to the shooting last night?"

The boy ignored the question and left the room, closing the door firmly after him.

Alone again, Father Richard looked down at his hands, which were shaking more than he ever remembered.

7.

Geri still had the TV on in the kitchen when Harold and Leo got back from the hospital. The announcer was giving an update on the shooting.

They sat and listened.

The police had issued a terse statement that the investigation was "ongoing," but no arrests had been made. The two "victims," Archbishop Quilty and his secretary, Father Joseph Maguire, were both in "fair" condition at Saint Katherine's Medical Center. In response to a reporter's question, a police spokesman "could not confirm" that the shooter was a priest.

"I guess not!" Geri added.

The scene switched to a reporter standing in front of the cathedral downtown.

"This is the biggest gathering since the pope visited Boston twenty-three years ago. Loudspeakers have been set up for those who cannot get inside to participate in the Mass. We've been told that Auxiliary Bishop Louis Fannon will be the principal celebrant."

The camera panned the crowd in front of the cathedral's huge doorway, zooming in on a woman wearing a black shawl, in tears. Police were everywhere.

"And this just in. Sharpshooters are positioned on the roofs of nearby buildings in case of further violence."

After a break for the previous night's lottery numbers and a couple of ads, the scene switched to Saint Kay's. There was Corinne Caruthers, still plugging away.

"As we have been reporting to you all morning, our beloved Archbishop Quilty and his heroic secretary, Father Joseph Maguire, are in guarded but stable condition. But there is a startling new development here on the hospital grounds. The image on the window, thought by many to be of the Virgin Mary, disappeared after being struck by a tree during the storm. The window itself appears to be intact, but the image is gone. During the past week, it has attracted thousands of the faithful and the curious. Many are wondering if some kind of a permanent shrine will be erected on the site. We are trying to contact Auxiliary Bishop Fannon for his reaction and will pass it along to you as soon as we can."

A photo of Eddie Cronin then filled the screen.

"In another bizarre twist," Corinne continued, "Dr. Edward Cronin, who resigned as president of Saint Kay's on Friday, was killed in an automobile accident last night. At this time, the police are releasing few details. However, we are told that he was alone, and no one else was injured."

After another break, the newscast switched to the hurricane.

The storm had caused major damage on the North Shore, but considerably less south of the airport. Search and rescue teams were at work both at Little Egg Rock and Squimset Neck where dozens were missing. The pilot of a traffic helicopter over Squimset reported that power lines were down, and roads were blocked by fallen trees.

Harold reached for the phone. "I better check on the *Nerses*."

He was on the phone with the Faneuil Landing Marina for only a minute. One improperly moored skiff got loose and was recovered intact a short distance downstream. Otherwise, there was no storm damage. They were expecting a typical summer Sunday.

Geri spoke up. "With the roads blocked …"

"And no power up there …" Harold continued.

"And the *Nerses* undamaged …"

Leo was thrilled.

Harold turned to his wife.

"How much time do you need, Geri?"

"Only a few minutes. Let's take the generator. Who knows when they'll get their power back?"

Harold nodded.

"And we'll pack up three trays of lasagna from the freezer. That should be enough for lunch."

Soon Geri had the car filled with Styrofoam boxes containing all manner of food and drink.

"I just hope we don't sink, dear."

Geri shot back, "Harold, the first mate knows exactly what she's doing."

Backing the *Nerses* out of the marina, Harold bore little resemblance to the white-coated doctor Leo had known for years. The wraparound shades, cargo shorts, and boat shoes made him look like an ad in *Sailing World.*

Turning downstream, they cruised in front of the Cattle Drive on the river's edge. Its parking lots were empty, giving the *faux* longhorns a few hours of downtime.

On a hill in the background sat Mount of Olives Academy, its windows reflecting the morning sun.

"My biggest worry with buying a new boat was the bridges," Harold commented, as they approached their first obstacle, the graceful brick span connecting Harvard Stadium at the eastern edge of Faneuil to Cambridge.

"That's the Eliot dead ahead, with the Anderson and the Weeks footbridge another mile downriver. They're all okay in the clearance department. But it's the three others further downstream that are tight. I actually looked at a Viking Convertible before settling on the Cabo Express. She was four to five inches taller than this baby and would have literally scraped under the other bridges, especially with high water."

"And we have high water today, Harold." Geri climbed up to the cockpit with a carafe of coffee and three mugs. "How many inches did we get overnight?"

"I heard three downtown, four and a half at Logan, and close to a foot up in Gloucester."

"What about Egg Rock?" Leo asked.

"I'm not sure, but you'd probably be close if you split the difference between Logan and Gloucester."

"That makes eight inches!"

Harold smiled at his wife and turned to Leo.

"You know, partner, it's really important to take a basic scientist along on these voyages. Like Darwin on the *Beagle*."

They encountered few other vessels. In front of the Harvard houses, a handful of oarsmen in single shells glided by as if the *Nerses* didn't exist, but they exchanged waves with the crew of another pleasure boat near Magazine Beach.

8.

Echo deftly detoured around the downed limbs to greet Portia.

She looked close to tears.

"The Christmas tree! I suppose there's no way it could be righted."

"I doubt it."

She looked back at the fallen spruce.

"Do you remember the summer after Mom died, the morning I was on the swing, singing?"

"Very well."

"Do you remember what I was singing?"

"It sounded like 'Jingle Bells,' but the words didn't seem right."

"It was—or at least the tune was. Frankie and I would sing carols all year round swinging under that tree. It was always the Christmas tree for us."

"I talked to Frankie about it after you left home. I hoped that you were singing a new version and that he could get me the record."

"Why would you do that?"

"I guess it seems silly, but I thought it might provide a connection to you."

"I made up the words."

"That's what Frankie said. He said that you two were always improvising."

"Do you remember the lyrics?"

"Not really. I thought you were trying to say good-bye, but I wasn't sure."

Portia still looked like she was fighting back tears when she began to sing. Not loud enough to wake the neighbors (and the dead) as she had long ago, but softly, only for her father.

"Jingle bells, jingle bells, jingle all the way, oh how hard it is to ride so very far away."

"You still remember the words?"

"Sure. I've sung them to myself every day since I left home. Want to hear the rest?"

Vincent nodded.

"O'er the fields I go, dying day by day."

"If I only knew what I know now."

"Me, too, Dad."

9.

Father Guido had stayed at Kitty's side at the Mount until Buzzy and Bridget arrived to take her home. Before he left them, he asked if he could visit Kitty later, after she got some rest.

"Oh, yes, please come, Guido."

It was near midnight when they got back to Sycamore Hill—too late to tell the kids. Just as well, she thought, since she needed time to absorb the news. She crawled into bed but didn't doze off until dawn.

After breakfast, they herded the kids into the playroom downstairs.

On Tuesday evening, the children had all reacted to Eunice's death quietly. There had been plenty of tears for Grandma, but everything was low key, controlled.

This time was the exact opposite.

The moment Kitty told them about Eddie's death, they reacted. Lawrence, who at fifteen questioned everything, asked her bluntly if she was sure. John joined his younger brother with questions of his own, and in no time, they were all talking at once. Some, in tears, begged her for better news, while others just stared at her.

They were making her feel as if she'd made a very sick joke.

"Yes," she said, "I'm sure he's dead."

Then the room erupted.

One of the boys started it by throwing a soccer ball across the room with such force that it sent a framed picture crashing to the floor. At that point, everyone joined in, kicking toys, upending furniture, screaming obscenities.

These were supposed to be the Cronin kids, the children she loved so, but she didn't recognize these people.

She stood there, unable to budge.

Finally Buzzy ran into the middle of the room, yelling, while Bridget and the au pair physically restrained the worst actors.

It was all over in less than a minute, but by then, her basement looked like a crime scene.

Still paralyzed, she felt an embrace and looked down to find Irene with her arms around her mother's knees, her big eyes wide open.

Kitty scooped her daughter up and headed to the stairs.

10.

Frank poured himself a cup of coffee and joined his father at the kitchen table. While he'd been touring Egg Rock with the kids and some neighbors, Vincent had managed to get the gas stove going and threw some breakfast together.

Trees were down everywhere, blocking streets and bringing down power lines. Yards and basements were flooded from the heavy rain and the spill-over at high tide. Roofs were torn off. The lifesaving station took a big hit, as Vincent had seen with the binoculars, but the structure looked sound.

The golf course was a lake, Eighty Steps Beach was covered with enough kindling to fill every fireplace in town for the entire winter—and its iconic wooden staircase, Leo's favorite, had been blown away.

Everyone was touring the devastation, Frank continued. Egg Rockers were friendly to begin with, but the storm seemed to bring even the most withdrawn citizens out of their shells.

But this was no party!

Everyone lost something, and the helicopters hovering over the north side of Little Egg kept the whole town on edge.

"Dad, the Vets Club really took a hit. The roof is gone, and all the windows are blown in."

"Well, that's good news!"

"How can you say that? You love the club."

"The insurance, Frankie. Don't you see? The insurance will pay for a complete renovation. For years, we've been paying for every kind of catastrophic insurance imaginable. Now it's time to get our money back."

11.

East of the Mass Ave Bridge, the *Nerses* and her crew entered the Charles River Basin, where the river widened dramatically, separating Cambridge from Boston's Back Bay and Esplanade by a good half mile.

They were skirting a flotilla of sailboats when Leo recalled how the basin froze solid for weeks one winter. He was in college then and joined the nonstop party the ice-bound river made possible. Many a night, he and his roommates packed up their skates and took a bus down to the embankment in front of MIT to play hockey. People came to figure skate, and there were campfires along the riverbanks where you could warm up. Beer and girls were in abundance. Everyone seemed to understand that such ice was an anomaly and took full advantage of it.

It was as if both the ice and this carefree time of their lives could melt away at any moment.

Geri watched while he tried Egg Rock on his cell phone again, but the system was still down.

"Don't worry, Leo. We'll be in Egg Rock—what do you think, Harold? In an hour?"

"A little less if there's no traffic at the locks."

The *Nerses* made it through the locks in short order and dropped six and a half feet into Boston Harbor, with Old Ironsides standing guard at her berth in Charlestown.

After clearing Old North Church, Harold opened up the throttle. In minutes, they were in the middle of the harbor on a southeast heading, with the high-rises of the financial district to the starboard, and the airport coming up on the port side. At fifteen knots, the sultry air of the Charles was replaced by a comfortable breeze.

There was no hint that a storm had passed through during the night.

Harold pointed to a buoy, red with white markings. "Here's where we do a hairpin turn." Just then, a huge jet made its approach to the airport, coming in from the west, over Castle Island, so low that Leo felt he could reach up and touch its wheels.

Harold got his cruising speed up to twenty knots, rounded Deer Island, and headed northeast for the Mulcahy house in Egg Rock. The moment Leo felt the wind and salt spray head-on, Geri tossed him a hooded sweatshirt.

From then on, Egg Rock got bigger by the minute, and Leo concentrated on the larger of the two islands, where he grew up and, with luck, Uncle Vinny's house still stood. About halfway across Squimset Harbor, Harold pointed to a patch of darker water in front of them.

"Seal Rocks ahead, our last obstacle."

When Leo was little, seals actually sunned themselves on the rocks at low tide, but he hadn't seen them for years. He wondered what had driven them away.

Geri handed him her binoculars. "You should make out the house with these."

"There it is! I see people gathered on the point."

Leo was waving like a little kid.

12.

The chapel was packed to overflowing again. On Saturday, when only half the pews had been filled, Guido thought that things were finally getting back to normal. He told Sister Agneta then that even miracles become routine after a while.

But the shooting brought the crowds back.

He summoned one of the hospital telephone operators, who he knew was a Eucharistic minister, to assist with Communion. Good thing he did, since she was forced to break the host in quarters just to cover the folks in the lobby.

Dr. Cronin's place in the front pew center was the only empty seat.

Right then, Guido decided to order a commemorative plaque.

In Memory of
Edward Cronin, MD.
Daily Communicant

He'd have it ready for a memorial Mass and invite Kitty.

Greeting worshipers afterward, he felt the familiar throb in his legs and pictured his big lounge chair upstairs.

At the end of the line stood a heavyset man in an ill-fitting business suit.

"Excuse me, Father, are you Guido della Chiesa?"

The man flipped his wallet open to show Guido a Boston Police Department badge.

"I need to have a word with you, in your quarters."

"It's not about my sister, is it?"

"No, Father."

If Marilena was okay, nothing terrible could be wrong. He

wondered whether this had something to do with the FedEx. Or Kitty. Or Kevin Sheehan. Or Tommy Rowley.

Once upstairs, the detective asked the priest to account for his movements from six o'clock on Saturday night.

"I came up here for the ball game about six thirty."

"Did you have company?"

"Heavens, no. I never have company here. With all that's happened in the Church, how would that look?"

The detective looked impassive.

Guido continued. "During the ballgame, the guy who does the color mentioned the shooting, and I changed the channel to get a news report. After a while, I went down to the emergency department, because I expected them to bring the archbishop and Father Maguire to Saint Kay's."

"May I look around?"

"Of course, but I don't see …"

The detective had already stepped into the priest's bedroom. "Were you wearing this black suit last night?"

"Let me see that. That's not mine. I've never seen it before!"

"Father, I'm going to have to ask you to come with me."

Guido pulled his shoes back on while the detective spoke into his walkie-talkie. "We're upstairs. Bring a bunch of evidence bags up with you."

"May I call my sister?"

"You can do that from the station, Father."

13.

Helen Rowley couldn't get Papa out of her mind all morning. The odd thing was that she didn't really think about him for months at a time. He and her mother split when she was ten, and after that, she spent every other weekend with him. Then, during her junior year in college, he hit a tree on his way home after a night out and died instantly.

On those weekends, at least in the early years before she had better things to do, they practiced at his rifle range.

Once in a while, Papa would tack up an "hombre," as he put it, instead of the standard bull's-eye. He'd saved a stack of them from his days at the police academy.

"Make it a head shot, Helen."

She had worried that Tom would resist her coming along. Maybe the kiss helped make up his mind or calling him "silly" for the first time in years helped. And just maybe, since he'd failed to retrieve the tularemia cylinder the night before, maybe he understood that she would keep him from screwing up again.

The Northeast Security golf cart was exiting the drive when they parked in the river lot below the Mount. Then they took the foot path up to the school.

Up on the hill, she waited outside Pius XII Hall, and when he returned minutes later, he patted the bulge in his pocket and smiled. Mission accomplished.

They marched single file through the patch of woods near the ball fields, him in the lead, so he had no warning, nothing to worry about.

A few feet ahead of her, he resembled the "hombre" her father used to tack up on those special occasions when she was a kid.

"Hey, Tom!" she exclaimed. As he turned his head to see what was wrong, she got him an inch or two in front of the right ear, and he fell without a sound.

Tom was a lucky man. He didn't have to go through the torment her son experienced, and that made her feel like the kindest, most merciful of executioners.

She wiped Tom's handgun off with his own handkerchief, placed it squarely in his right palm, and closed his fingers around the grip. Only a dunce would think this was a suicide. The entrance wound was well positioned, but only a contortionist could angle the bullet's trajectory like that. Then again, maybe she'd luck out with some sloppy police work. Back in the rifle range days, her father told her endless stories of dumb cops, corrupt cops, cops who messed up simple crime scenes. She hoped some of those guys were still around.

Finally, she extracted the cylinder from Tom's jacket so as not to disturb the body. Looking at her watch, she was pleased to find she still had twenty minutes until the next patrol. She simply needed to cross the ball field, descend through the woods, and return to the car.

As Tom always said, he could set his watch by her.

14.

The boys secured both ends of the *Nerses* to the remnants of the Mulcahy pier. Geri gave everyone in sight her trademark bear hug, while the others carried the cargo to the house.

The Egg Rockers had been totally cut off and were hungry for news. Besides having the cell phones go down and losing power, Vincent's transistor radio gave out soon after they returned from the fair. And he had no fresh batteries.

Geri found Vincent and Father Frank getting the generator hooked up.

"When I saw you all out there on the point to greet us, I got an idea. How about saying Mass? You'd never guess, but we have the oldest altar boy in the Western Hemisphere to assist you."

Frank looked up, screwdriver in hand.

"Yes, Father. Harold was an altar boy, the kind of kid who'd have the sacramentary opened to the proper prayer at the right moment, and he'd hold it up so the priest could actually read it, and he'd never look like he was daydreaming."

"Did you know Harold back in his altar boy days?"

"Heavens, no, Father. I was still in diapers! His mom and his uncle Nerses told me all about it, though. Later on, I actually saw him in action. Harold got permission from the priest to assist at Uncle Nerses's funeral and did a great job."

"Look, Geri, make the assignments. I'd be honored to have Harold as altar server, but we'll need lectors, and music would add to the occasion. Get everybody in on this. Invite the neighborhood. I don't care if folks haven't seen the inside of a church in years—or ever, for that matter. Today is big tent day."

15.

Sister Philippe was waiting in the foyer. Father Dan could see that she'd been crying.

"The archbishop and Father Joe are both going to be fine, Philippe."

"You must be starving. I'll get you some lunch."

He didn't have the heart to tell her he'd just put away a stack of pancakes at the hospital cafeteria.

"Bishop Fannon is waiting for you in the archbishop's office. He said you'd undoubtedly be calling, but he'd save you the trouble. I suggested that he wait in the parlor, but he insisted on the office."

Dan imagined Fannon going through the Boss's desk.

"I'd better see the bishop. Then I'll eat."

Incredibly, Fannon *was* sitting in the Boss's chair when Father Dan entered. Perpetually tanned, he looked like an aging movie star. He appeared so comfortable, it was as if the archbishop were already dead and buried.

"How is the archbishop, Father?"

"Out of danger. He should be discharged in a day or two."

Fannon nodded solemnly. He didn't bother to ask about Father Joe.

"When will he be able to make decisions?"

"The doctors have given him pain medication, Bishop, but expect him to be alert enough to be working from his hospital bed by tomorrow."

Fannon nodded solemnly again.

"When should I visit?"

"He wants to wait until he's back here before seeing anybody."

"Even his second in command?"

"That's the way he left it."

"I came right over because I'm sure you could use some help, with Quilty incapacitated and all."

Father Dan knew he had to give Fannon something to do.

"We need to put out a statement about the condition of the archbishop and Father Maguire."

"Why don't you write out a draft and we can craft a final version afterward?"

Dan typed out a paragraph stating that Archbishop Quilty broke his arm but was comfortable, and that Father Maguire underwent surgery for a gunshot wound to the leg. Both men were out of danger and expected to make a complete recovery. In a second paragraph, he thanked the people of Boston for the outpouring of affection and asked everyone to keep them in their prayers. At the bottom, he typed, "Most Reverend Louis Fannon, Auxiliary Bishop, Archdiocese of Boston."

"That seems acceptable, Father, as far as it goes."

"Do you think something should be added?"

"Since this is an official document, I would add 'Vicar General and Moderator of the Curia' to my name."

Technically, Fannon was correct, having been given those titles by the late Cardinal Campion, but the titles implied that he was the archbishop's right-hand man.

Too exhausted to put up a fight, Dan typed in the additional information.

"Anything else you wish to add, Bishop Fannon?"

"No, Father. That should suffice. Since Quilty's getting better so fast, I guess there would be no need to state that I will be temporary administrator."

Both knew that such a designation could be made only by Rome or, in a crisis, by the papal nuncio, the Vatican representative in Washington.

"I agree, Bishop. I'll print this, and you can sign."

"I brought along some of my stationery, with my seal …"

"I respect that, Your Excellency, but I think it would look more authoritative on the archbishop's letterhead."

"Okay."

Once Dan had ushered the auxiliary out of the residence, Sister Philippe's chicken salad and iced tea were waiting for him on the dining room table.

For many, conflict and anxiety would kill an appetite. Being an exception to that rule, Dan dug in.

16.

Father Guido was led into a small room with a table and three chairs. It looked like one of those interrogation rooms he'd seen on TV.

The detective was joined by an older man, who introduced himself as Captain So-and-so and looked friendly enough.

"I just got a call from an old friend of mine, Pat Kaminski, your head of security over at Saint Kay's."

A young officer entered the room carrying a priest's outfit in a clear plastic bag. He whispered something about the forensics being completed.

"Father, Pat mentioned that you have an unusual physique and that it might be instructive if you tried the suit on for size."

Guido thought of Leo's many admonitions to lose weight.

"Don't be embarrassed, Father."

The jacket must have been three sizes too small. After squeezing one arm into a sleeve, there was no way he could maneuver the other arm anywhere near the opening.

The captain smiled briefly.

"By the way, Father, do you keep the door to your quarters locked?"

"Yes, always."

"Can you think of anyone who'd want to cause you harm?"

"No, no one I can think of."

"Detective, drive the good father back to Saint Kay's. After that, drop in on Pat Kaminski. He told me he'd be at the hospital all day. Maybe he'll have some idea how the suit got into the chaplain's quarters.

"And, Sergeant, get me the officer who fielded the call about the priest's outfit."

17.

Frank always had his "Mass kit" in the trunk of the car. It looked like a briefcase and contained everything he needed: chalice, candles, paten, and bottles of wine and water. A small overnight bag held his alb, chasuble, and stole.

Someone once saw him getting the "kit" out of his car and said he looked like a traveling salesman.

He thought a minute before responding.

"Come to think of it, that's a pretty accurate job description."

He decided to hold the Mass out on the point. Clouds were thinning and looked like they would burn off.

Sam and Francine carried away the fallen branches while Frank and Leo raked. Then they carried the oak table out from the porch to serve as the altar while others scoured the house for chairs.

Echo stuck close to the work crew but kept out from underfoot.

Geri made the assignments. Harold, of course, was appointed altar server. Vincent and Leo would do the readings; Sam was assigned the Prayers of the Faithful; and Claire and Geri would bring the gifts of bread and wine to the altar. Portia was to be cantor, and Francine would provide the music on her flute, which she always had with her.

18.

During Mass, Leo watched the gulls arrive. Without warning, the snow-white birds filled the gray sky and swooped in huge arcs over the point.

The readings and assigned prayers went smoothly, and Harold assisted Frank flawlessly.

Leo had to hand it to Cousin Frank. With everyone playing a part, Mass was actually interesting for once.

It would have been hard to find a more ecumenical group. The neighbors who attended were culturally diverse. As for the family, the only observant ones, as far as he could tell, were Claire and possibly Geri. Some might have put Uncle Vincent on the list, but he knew his uncle was a pragmatist who did the church thing more out of habit and deference to his son's vocation than any strong beliefs. As for Harold, Portia, Francine, and Sam—they were all about as unreligious as he was.

Sam was openly contemptuous of anything religious (except in the presence of his mother), and Portia, from what he could see, was more the aging hippie type, who considered the whole world her church. Harold enjoyed the theatricality of the ritual, but that was about as far as it went, while Francine, his sweet daughter, had found her religion in music.

That left Frank, who now stood before them, apparently trying to gather his thoughts. Next up was the sermon, to Leo's mind the most important part of the Mass.

Frank's sermonizing skills were immediately put to the test when he took over at Saint Gabe's. Old Monsignor Flynn had been a kind and gentle priest by all accounts, but not an inspiring speaker. With Mass attendance at rock bottom, Frank saw those minutes where the priest speaks directly to his flock as a way to turn things around. If the people could expect a well-executed, provocative, and relevant sermon from him every week, they might come back.

Saint Gabe's still had a long way to go but not, Leo knew, for lack of good sermons.

Frank's theme, naturally enough, was the storm. He began by recalling the middle of the night when the house started shaking, and they took refuge in the pantry.

"For a while, I was really scared. Was it just me?"

Most who'd spent the night in Egg Rock shook their heads, and a few ran hands across brows as if to say, "Whew, that was a close call!"

He referred to the gospel story of Jesus and the disciples getting caught in a ferocious storm on the Sea of Galilee, how frightened they became, and how Jesus scolded them.

"'Why are you so frightened? Have you still no faith?'

"Hurricanes, tornadoes, earthquakes—they terrify us because our security is stripped away. In seconds, order is replaced by chaos, and we're exposed and vulnerable. But it isn't only acts of nature that make us feel that way. Chaos takes many forms. Wars pop up all over the globe; terrorism is an everyday thing; violence infects our streets; people get laid off; drugs are everywhere; families get torn apart. Then again, not all chaos is outside. We all deal with our own internal chaos. Not every minute, not every day—but we all do. Doubt, anxiety, despair, and anger can be personally chaotic—and scary.

"We've had more than our share of chaos around here this week—even when the soon-to-be hurricane was no more than a blip on the weather forecasters' radar screen. Looking back, I'd have to start with that mysterious window at a hospital in Boston. For many of us, it was no more than a curiosity on the evening news."

He looked at his audience and saw many smiling.

"But it affected others deeply. Some of us found it inspirational, and some of us found it unsettling, or 'chaotic.' Of course, the window was only the beginning of a crazy week. Now we have news of an attempted assassination, a fatal car crash, and—who knows what's coming next? What about family, friends, and neighbors in Little Egg and in the other towns?

"This has been a banner week for chaos."

Frank looked at his audience a second before continuing.

"The big question is how we deal with chaos. A nonstop anxiety attack isn't the answer, drugs and alcohol are poor fixes, and I don't think anybody wants to give in to despair.

"When things get chaotic, we look for things that comfort us. When our family was huddled together last night with the wind threatening to blow out the windows, I was comforted by our kinship and love for one another. And walking around the devastation in Egg Rock this morning, I took comfort from the way the townspeople treated one another as extended family.

"The comfort of others is very important, but it takes me only so far. That's where Jesus's scolding from the back of the boat comes in. I don't think he's saying, 'Sit back and relax.' That might work for the rare person whose faith in God is so strong that he or she is fearless—like the early martyrs of the Church. The rest of us struggle. I believe that the message from the back of the boat is *try*. Try to believe. That's where prayer comes in, and prayer—real down-to-the-basics prayer—is hard work. I pray for strength—strength to confront the chaos and not run away. I pray to understand—to understand why I'm here and what God expects of me. I pray I can forgive, since by forgiving I can rid myself of anger and guilt. And I pray for acceptance, for only by accepting things I can't fully understand can I find inner peace."

Frank sat in a chair next to the altar and, as if choreographed, the sun came out. Someone said, "Look at that," someone else started clapping, and then everyone joined in.

Leo couldn't tell whether the applause was for the sun, the sermon, or a little of each. Anyway, Frank pointed to the sky and shrugged.

"Believe me. I had nothing to do with this!"

After the laughter died down, he asked everyone to stand and join him in prayer.

"Loving God, give comfort to all the victims of the hurricane, to those whose fate we don't yet know and to those of us who anxiously await news. Please grant Archbishop Quilty and Father Maguire full recovery from their wounds, and watch over the Rafferty and Cronin families in their grief. Heavenly Father, allow us to accept things in this world that we cannot fully understand and help us confront the chaos around us and the moments of darkness in our own lives. And give us the tools to make this uncertain world a better place. We ask this in the name of the Father, the Son, and the Holy Spirit. Amen."

After the Consecration came the Sign of Peace, where everyone was expected to turn to people in adjacent pews and shake hands, saying, "Peace be with you." As a rule, most people go through the motions, while a few go overboard, greeting as many people as possible and waving frantically to all the others. Then there are always some who look like they would sooner die than shake a stranger's hand.

Geri took the Sign of Peace up a notch by giving both Frank and her favorite altar boy bear hugs.

Another exception was Sam, of all people. The techie, who made it clear that he preferred computers to people, was shaking hands like an alderman running for Congress.

Their enthusiasm was contagious, and everyone, including Leo himself, got into the act. At one point, he looked over at Frank, who stood before them smiling.

19.

Dan arrived at the cardinal's suite to find Archbishop Quilty sitting up in the "living room" while the nurse was tidying up his bed. The IVs were gone, but his heart monitor was still connected.

And his right arm was in a sling.

"You see they took the bags of fluid away," he said, "but they left this." He pointed to a small piece of plastic tubing attached to his forearm. "She can plug me in again, you see, if I 'go sour.'" He pointed back to where the nurse was still at work and lowered his voice. "I guess she thinks I'm pretty sweet right now."

Dan filled the Boss in on Fannon's visit to the residence, omitting the detail of the auxiliary sitting at the archbishop's desk. Then he handed over a copy of the press statement.

Quilty smiled.

"I bet the bishop was thrilled to hear about my speedy recovery!"

He gazed out the window at the Boston skyline a minute.

"Have you heard from the nuncio, Danny? He was scheduled to arrive today."

"No. With everything that's happened, I totally forgot about it. Philippe reminded me when I was leaving a few minutes ago. Should I call him?"

"No. Let's just hope he's changed his mind. He may have contacted Fannon."

"Bishop Fannon didn't mention it."

"That's the kind of information he'd keep to himself."

The Boss then told Dan about his plan to resign and join Frank Mulcahy at Saint Gabriel's.

"Wow! Has that ever been done before?"

"Bishops retire and reinvent themselves. Recently, the archbishop of New Orleans joined the faculty of the seminary down there. I don't know of any going back to parish work, but I bet it's happened. I'll tell you one thing, Danny—when Rome hears I want out, they won't stand in the way. And once they understand that my going to Saint Gabe's is part of the deal, they'll go along."

Dan never imagined that the Boss would flat-out quit, but as he thought about it, the move seemed to be a fitting conclusion to the week.

"When?"

The Boss pointed to the wires on his chest. "As soon as I'm in the clear, I'll make an appointment with the Holy Father and make my request in person. Of course, he'll need to choose a successor before I can follow through with the move. How about going to Rome with me, Danny? We can take in the sights again."

Things were moving a hundred times faster than Dan would have liked.

They were interrupted by a commotion and raised voices. Northeast Security had posted a guard on the other side of the door with strict orders, and the guy was doing his job.

"The archbishop is not allowed visitors."

"You obviously don't know who we are."

Dan opened the door in time to see Bishop Fannon and the tiniest prelate he'd ever seen pushing past the security man.

Dan greeted Fannon and signaled that it was okay.

"Father Skerry, this is Archbishop Sarto. He just got off the train from Washington. With the storm, he was afraid flights would be cancelled. We need to see Archbishop Quilty immediately."

"I'll tell him you're here."

"That won't be necessary, Father. He'll see us. You wait outside."

20.

Helen glanced at her watch again when she reached the car. She and Tom had been up there only twenty-five minutes, fewer for him since his earthly time stopped abruptly at the fifteen-minute mark.

She was pleased with her efficiency.

Until now, she'd planned to flee. While Tom was up in Guido's apartment during the night, she packed a bag of clothes, the plane ticket she'd bought online, cash, and credit cards. It now sat in the storage area under the floor of the trunk, alongside the spare tire.

But walking out of the patch of woods where she'd left him, she changed her mind. The police just might fall for the suicide idea, and as for last night, it looked like she and Tom had made a perfect getaway from the hotel.

Besides, she was too exhausted to make a run for it.

She would head home and take her chances.

Once inside the apartment, she undressed and checked her clothes for any stains or splatters. She found nothing, but to be on the safe side, she threw her jeans, top, and socks into the washer, adding a good dollop of bleach. Then she rinsed her shoes in the kitchen sink.

The shower was brief because she needed to lie down in the worst way.

She lay there, going over what made Tom's execution so inevitable. It began with his scheme to infect the archbishop during the trustees' meeting at the Mount. Strictly speaking, it wasn't Tom's fault the meeting was cancelled, but it was his plan, and he was responsible for it.

Anyway, Tom had his plan B, at the Saint Botolph Hotel ballroom. When he told her about it, she was skeptical, but they had gone so far, and now everything seemed to be falling apart. His plan B was the only thing left.

Portia had been a disappointment. Over their daiquiri and quiche supper Friday, the girl just sat there. Somehow she'd gotten the delivery vehicles engineered, but it was a stretch to think that this over-the-hill peacenik would have the guts to actually kill her father.

Gert was no peacenik, of course. But she was so erratic that she could change her mind at any second.

They had to do something that would work!

So when Tom got the Nalbandians' kitchen door pried open, it took her no time to find the priest's suit in Harold's closet.

They were almost as lucky at the hotel. The ballroom balcony was deserted, and the archbishop's receiving line was getting organized only a few feet below her. Hiding behind a large column, she had a perfect view. The back of Quilty's head, with the little purple cap surrounded by a fringe of white hair, was a perfect target.

But as she raised the pistol, a red-headed young priest must have sensed something, because he turned and looked up.

She was ready to fire, but the priest—only a boy really, about the age Tommy would be now—spooked her, and she hesitated. By the time she pulled the trigger, he was in midair, pushing the archbishop to the floor.

She knew she'd missed.

Tom was waiting for her just outside the fire exit, and before anyone could react to the alarm, he had her into the long raincoat with the high collar, and they walked arm-in-arm to the car. Anyone seeing them would imagine a happy couple out on a stroll on a stormy night.

Safely in the car, she told him.

"I missed Quilty, but I hit the kid."

Tom looked so angry that she thought he'd drive off the road. He spat out his words.

"I give you a straightforward assignment, and all the support you'd need—and you fuck it up! Annie Oakley, my ass! No surprise, I guess, since you're just being consistent. You know something? If you'd kept an eye on your son like any decent mother, Guido wouldn't have dared to … to touch Tommy."

They drove in silence until Tom brought up the two tasks remaining: planting the priest's suit in the right place and retrieving the bacteria from the Mount.

"Are you with me, Helen, or am I on my own?"

She tried to sound sincere.

"I'm with you 100 percent, Tom."

"Good. Because if you aren't, you're the one who pulled the trigger. Don't forget that."

By then, she knew that after completing their two tasks, she'd need to perform a third one, alone.

She finally fell into a deep sleep and didn't hear anybody come in—although she could swear she'd locked the door.

Someone was shaking her and calling her name. She opened her eyes to see two policemen standing by the bed. The older one looked just like her father.

Strangely, she was lying on Tommy's bed, with its baseball-themed coverlet.

On the table, next to the framed acceptance letter, sat the canister Tom had retrieved from the Mount.

When told that she had the right to remain silent, she surprised herself with her response.

"That's okay. I've got a lot to tell you guys."

21.

Just when Frank asked everyone to stand for the final prayers, he heard a droning sound coming from the Dawes side of the harbor.

Then he saw it. It was just a dark speck at first but grew quickly in the western sky. The sound grew louder, and the speck blossomed into a helicopter.

Earlier, he'd seen a chopper set down on the strip of land near the lifesaving station, but this one was headed right for the house.

This time, the helicopter slowed its forward motion and hovered over the point. On its sides, Frank saw the Massachusetts state seal and the words *State Police.*

Portia ran inside, with Echo at her heels.

The air was stirred up by the big rotor, and the sound was deafening. The pilot gestured with horizontal movements of his arms like an exaggerated breast stroke.

"Clear the way," he was saying.

Everybody retreated to the house, carrying chairs and anything else they could pick up. He grabbed the sacramentary and the chalice, Harold scooped up the rest, and they ran.

Leaves, twigs, and branches that hadn't been raked up were airborne again, and the table that had served as the altar was upended.

They barely reached the screen porch when the chopper set down and its roar gave way to a high-pitched whine.

Vincent led the police upstairs where Portia was filling the bathtub with steaming water. She held her laptop under the surface while singing "Jingle Bells."

"That won't do any good, Miss Mulcahy. Our forensic guys would have no trouble interrogating your computer if you left it in the tub all day. By the way, Christmas doesn't come until December."

As the police escorted her downstairs, she turned to Vincent.

"Daddy, I'm sorry. I made a terrible mistake."

Frank watched helplessly while his baby sister was led away.

21.

As soon as Dan saw Bishop Fannon out to his car and grabbed some lunch, he left for Saint Kay's to check on the archbishop. And once Dan's car disappeared down the driveway, Philippe sat down in her little office off the kitchen. She hadn't had much sleep and needed to get off her feet.

She'd spent most of the night in her office, watching updates on the little TV on her desk. Around dawn, she had carried the vacuum cleaner and duster up to the guestroom in case the papal nuncio still planned to visit. With the archbishop in the hospital, she didn't know what to expect, but she wanted to be ready in case.

Afterward, she stayed near the TV in the kitchen. Corinne, as usual, had been front and center during the night, giving periodic updates from the hospital. With all this uncertainty, Philippe imagined she could be out of a job any minute. If so, she'd be staying at her sister's house for a while.

Philippe's sister Therese was the only other member of the clan to come to the States. Her brothers stayed on the farm, and her other sister married a local and lived nearby.

Therese was already living in Boston when Philippe arrived. Her husband, a mechanic for Air Canada, had been transferred to Logan, and they were hoping to stay for a few years. Having her sister already settled made Philippe's adjustment to her new environment smoother.

Soon after Philippe's arrival, Therese gave birth to a baby girl. Philippe was proud to be chosen the child's godmother and thrilled when she learned the child's name.

Corinne Philippe Caruthers.

Philippe was getting sleepy when her phone rang.

"Hello?"

"Auntie Philippe, I hope I didn't wake you."

"No, no, Corinne, I was just thinking about you."

"More bad things have happened since last night. I feel like our world is coming apart—fast."

Her niece sounded more like a frightened little girl than a polished newscaster, but she was able to give her aunt the facts.

Gert had been arrested for drunk and disorderly conduct during the night and placed in protective custody.

Dr. Rowley had been found shot to death on the grounds of the Mount of Olives Academy, and Helen had been arrested for his murder.

Portia Mulcahy had been arrested at her father's home in Egg Rock.

There was no official word yet about the charges, but Corinne's sources said that Helen would be charged for her husband's murder, and Portia, for conspiracy to commit murder.

"And from what I'm hearing, Gert and Helen aren't holding back. They're telling the police everything they know, including their sources of information. And that would include us."

"What should I be doing now, Corinne?"

"What I'm doing, Phil—waiting for the police to drop by."

"What should I tell them?"

"I've contacted a very good lawyer to represent both of us. Say nothing until he speaks to you. In the meantime, prayers can't hurt."

Philippe had more than prayers in mind.

She found the tiny slip of paper with the combination on it

from its hiding place in her desk. It had sat there since the night the archbishop had her open the safe—the night she overheard them talking about that awful diary and how they had to be hush-hush about it. Then she walked into the archbishop's office. The safe behind the big sailboat painting above the desk opened on her first try.

She was amazed how full the safe was and worried for a moment that she'd never find what she was looking for. But right on top of a pile of papers sat a good-sized book with a red cover and "Diary" embossed on the front. On page one, "Property of Malachy Dunn" was written in flowing script.

After locking the safe, she carried the volume to the kitchen, slid it into a Ziploc usually used for leftovers, and hid it in the back of her big freezer.

Minutes later, she put in a call to Corinne. Luckily, her niece picked up right away.

"Yes, Auntie."

"Corinne, about the lawyer."

"Did he call?"

"No, not yet. Something happened here just now. I need to visit the lawyer immediately, and I want you to come along."

"Immediately?"

"It can't wait, not even until tomorrow. I made a discovery that you and he need to know about—and I have some evidence that will back up my story."

"I'll call him now."

22.

Fannon and the nuncio spent a good hour inside with the Boss. Dan had expected the door to open at any time and to be asked inside, but it never happened.

Actually the door opened once, and a private-duty nurse exited, barely acknowledging Dan as she sat down.

When they finally emerged, Fannon was smiling.

"Nurse, you better get back inside."

Then he turned to Dan.

"No need for you to see Quilty, Father. We tired the man out with communiqués and paperwork, and he's dropped off to sleep. Of course, his nurse is watching him like a hawk. An old pro, that one. I've seen her around the hospital for years. Specializes in VIPs, and she's a regular at our pro-life rallies.

"You'll need to get us back to the residence anyway, but give your friend Sister Philippe a heads-up before we leave. Both Archbishop Sarto and I will be staying and expect a bona-fide meal tonight. Quilty's soup and sandwich regimen won't be sufficient for our needs. Tell her that the papal nuncio is allergic to nuts and make sure she puts the best wine she can find on the table. But I'm getting ahead of myself. Before dinner, we'll need to craft another press release and make some phone calls."

Then, the instant the nuncio preceded them out of the suite, he stated the obvious.

"I'm in charge now, Father."

Dan drove while the bishops spoke quietly in the backseat. He headed for the lower gate by the old tennis courts to avoid the crowds, but Fannon broke off his conversation and ordered Dan to enter Little Rome by the main entrance.

"No need to sneak around anymore, Father."

As they passed a handful of demonstrators and a couple of TV trucks in front of the residence, Fannon rolled down his window and waved.

23.

Vincent's lights came back on minutes after the helicopter took off. Frank was in the kitchen and looked into the other rooms to make sure everything was up and running. By then, everyone's cell phone was ringing.

His first call was from his assistant priest at Saint Gabriel's. As for "damage," the tent had blown across the road, and folding chairs were scattered over the lawn—but that was about it. He reassured his assistant that they were all safe before telling him that his sister was in a "legal situation" needing his assistance for a day or so. He signed off with a promise to get back to Saint Gabe's by Monday night or Tuesday morning.

He'd expected worse news. At the height of the storm, when they were singing songs in the pantry, he felt certain that the steeple, already in need of repair, had toppled.

Next he called Kevin Gallagher, the family lawyer. Kevin was shocked to hear the story, of course, and would drop what he was doing so he could find out what was happening to Portia.

Vincent announced that he was "perfectly fine" and that they all had "better things to do" than keep him company. This, Frank knew, was his father's way of saying that he needed to be alone. Since there would be no negotiation, he gave Geri the word, and she began packing up.

With good-byes around, the *Nerses* set off in time to get back to Faneuil by nightfall.

24.

While the nuncio was upstairs unpacking, Fannon led Dan into the archbishop's office, sat in the Boss's chair again, and motioned Dan to take a seat opposite.

There was no small talk.

"Archbishop Quilty will be taking a medical leave of absence," he said simply.

Apparently, the nuncio got the archbishop to sign a letter he'd brought along, and the Boss immediately requested transfer to the monastery where he'd been going on retreat for years.

"So, Father Skerry, first thing tomorrow, I want you to get hold of the abbot out there and get things arranged. Quilty should be ready to go by the middle of the week. He'll get all the rest he'll require out there. The medical leave will be open-ended, and from what we observed this afternoon, he may be staying out there permanently."

Dan made notes, as if he wouldn't remember.

"You'll be moving his effects out of the residence. Since he won't have space for anything but a few personal belongings at the monastery, and since he has no family, get his stuff into storage. I'll be moving in on Wednesday."

Dan was blindsided—again. A couple of hours earlier, he'd been blown away by the Boss's plan to resign and request transfer to Saint Gabe's.

Fannon arched his brow knowingly.

"I'm sure Quilty told you about his pipe dream of moving to a parish and becoming a 'real priest.' That showed just how unstable he is. Believe me, Father; your old boss finally gets it. He's unfit for any ministry at the moment."

"Old boss" troubled Dan, and Fannon seemed to pick up on it.

"Before I forget, Father, you work for me now. There will be no need for you to have further contact with the former archbishop. In fact, I forbid it."

Then, before Dan had a chance to absorb all that was happening, Fannon began dictating a press release out loud, speaking so fast that Dan motioned him to slow down while he scribbled away.

Because of "ongoing health problems" complicated by "recent events," Archbishop Quilty would "recuperate at a monastic community." Bishop Fannon (with the usual titles) has been named "apostolic administrator" and "asks for your prayers during this difficult time."

"Feed that to the press, Father Skerry. I told Philippe to have dinner on the table at six. We'll discuss your future then."

25.

The mood on board the *Nerses* was subdued. Claire sat quietly, but her facial muscles were tense enough to reveal her Bell's palsy. Leo knew that she wouldn't have much to say until they got back to the house in Muddy River. Even Geri, perpetually effervescent, was mute.

Leo welcomed the interlude.

The arrival of the police helicopter and Portia's arrest shattered the feeling of unity that the storm and the arrival of the *Nerses* had brought about. Everyone was busy with their own thoughts.

Leo stood side-by-side with Frank watching Egg Rock flatten out and blend into the horizon. He didn't envy Frank, who'd be entangled by Portia's legal problems, whatever they might be.

Frank finally turned.

"Well, there is some good news." He spoke quietly, so no one else could hear.

"Quilty."

"I don't get it."

"I was summoned to Little Rome on Friday to see the Boss. I didn't know what to expect, since I'd never been called in urgently like that before. Back when I was secretary, a call like that only meant trouble."

"I can imagine."

Frank surveyed the deck before continuing.

"Well, there was no 'trouble'—at least in the conventional sense. Quilty had two pieces of news. One, he's planning to resign; and two, he intends to come to Salem and live at Saint Gabe's. He says he's never had a chance to be a real priest, and he sees this as his last chance."

"You must have been relieved that—"

"I wasn't getting canned? Yeah."

"What a vote of confidence, Frank!"

"The news certainly gave me a lift. Look, you can tell Claire, of course, but that's it."

After they navigated the Charles River locks again, the mood on the *Nerses* lightened, and by the time they were cruising past Magazine Beach and the Harvard houses, Geri was back in form.

"Does anybody know the story about the Harvard professor who tried to walk on water? You don't count, Harold!"

They were throwing out the mooring ropes when Claire spoke for the first time.

"Leo, can you tell me why the trip back always seems shorter than the trip out?"

"No clue," he answered.

26.

Father Richard was trying to read when Frank Mulcahy knocked on the door to his room at the seminary. At first, he thought the policeman was back with more questions, but the knock was gentle and familiar, and he remembered Frank's phone call from Egg Rock.

He heated water for tea while Frank settled in a chair by the window. He'd never seen Frank look so drained.

Frank worked his way through the past couple of days chronologically, ending with the trip back to Faneuil on the *Nerses*.

He kept coming back to Portia. Her phone call on Saturday morning, describing Father Mal in grotesque detail, overshadowed everything else.

"That scene in the rectory, with Mal touching my sister like that, a little seven-year-old—I can't get it out of my head."

In their twenty-plus years of friendship, Richard had never seen Frank so overwrought.

"I kept picturing Mal while I celebrated Mass. It's a wonder I didn't get completely unglued, especially when that police helicopter dropped in on us. I figured they were after Portia even before they landed. Mal set off a chain reaction that no one can stop."

Frank went back to his meeting with Gert at the Cattle Drive, the evening he tried to match her manhattans with cups of coffee—and how Gert hinted that Portia was part of a conspiracy.

Just then, Richard heard a catchy little tune. It took him a moment to realize that Frank's cell was ringing. The call was from Kevin Gallagher, Portia's lawyer, who had just visited the girl in jail.

The only question Frank had came at the end of the one-sided conversation.

"So I can see her at nine tomorrow?"

Frank sighed after hanging up. "I think she's in capable hands."

"Frank, can I join you?"

"In the morning? Are you sure?"

"Very sure."

27.

Back home in Muddy River, Leo gave Claire the lowdown on Frank's new, high-profile senior priest.

She smiled. "We could tell that you two were having a private conversation. Did you notice how everybody on the boat gave you guys space?"

From upstairs, they could make out the mellow tones of Francine's oboe. The tune was joyful.

Claire began playing an imaginary woodwind, fingers flying.

"God love her! She's celebrating for Frank."

Claire listened a moment and turned to Leo.

"I learned something on the trip back, too. Not happy news, though. While you and Frank were talking, I joined Harold at the helm."

"I saw you."

"He told me something really creepy. He didn't remember it when the police were at their house this morning, but it came to him later, on the boat. Tom stopped Harold in the hospital some time ago and asked him if he still had the priest's outfit. He looked pleased when Harold told him it was still in his closet and said they should have another costume party soon."

The phone rang, and after picking up, Claire motioned Leo to the extension.

It was Pat Kaminski, who seemed rushed.

"Things are still buzzing here, Claire, so I'll get right to the point. Get Leo on the line if he's around."

"I'm here."

Dr. Rowley had been found shot to death at Mount of Olives School, "in the exact spot where his son killed himself. The police are calling it a suicide, but they're waiting for the medical examiner's report before anything is official. Father Guido is on his way to pay a condolence call on Kitty at Sycamore Hill. Guido doesn't know about Dr. Rowley's death yet, so I thought that if you two were to go out there, you might break the news to him and to Kitty."

Leo and Claire spoke at once.

"We're on our way."

Leo located the mysterious floor plan from Rowley's notebook and stuck it in his pocket on the way out the door.

28.

Kitty had spent much of the day in her room, staring at the four walls and thinking about Eddie and the kids until she finally dozed off late in the afternoon. She wasn't asleep more than a few minutes, however, when she was startled by the doorbell.

Father Guido was on the front steps when she looked out and was already having coffee with Bridget and Buzzy when she got down to the kitchen.

The priest stood and took Kitty's hand.

"What can I do?"

"There is something, Father Guido. Upstairs I was thinking about going through the whole Mooney's thing. Right now, I don't know how I can face another funeral."

"Michael Mooney and I go back a long way. I can give him a call—and with Bridget's and Buzzy's help …"

Bridget nodded, and Buzzy gave a thumbs-up.

"We can take care of everything."

"That would really help. But I need one more favor."

She sat a moment to get herself together.

"It will be more difficult."

"Take your time."

"It's about the kids. They reacted badly to the news."

"Badly? Violently is more like it."

"You're right, Bridget, violently. They started yelling and throwing things the second I told them about Eddie's accident. I could hardly recognize my own children. Now I understand how people were thought to be possessed. The playroom is a shambles. Could you speak to them, Guido? You've dealt with adolescents all your professional life."

"I'll do my best, Kitty."

Leo and Claire showed up minutes later, and after hugs and tears, Claire told them more disturbing news. Tom Rowley had been found dead at the Mount.

Kitty was beyond being shocked. Instead, she became hyperalert, conscious of every detail in the room. She found herself studying the details of the wallpaper's stylized strawberries, on vines and in bouquets—and wondered how on earth she could have chosen such a silly pattern. She looked around to see Bridget and Buzzy on the edge of their seats, ready to jump up and help in any way they could; Leo and Claire looking downcast, worried that they may have said too much too soon; and Guido, dear Father Guido, sitting calmly next to her.

She was ready to talk about her visit to the Mount the night before.

"Guido knows a lot about what happened, and Bridget knows a little. But," turning to Claire, "you two know none of this."

She'd put in a call to Father Guido from the conference room, and while on the phone, she was surprised by an intruder.

"Or the other way round. We were both surprised."

Leo pulled a sheet of paper out of his pocket and slid it over the table to Kitty.

"That's a floor plan of the building. How did you get hold of that?"

"We found it in Rowley's lab."

"It could have been him, but I didn't get much of a look."

Kitty looked at the paper again.

"That's the corridor, with the conference room right here," she explained. "And what's this, a closet?" One small, nearly square space off the conference room was highlighted in red. In the corner of the square were the letters AC.

"I never turned the AC on. The storm was almost over, and with the air outside so cool and refreshing, I cracked the windows open instead. After the business with the intruder, I took Guido's advice and locked the door and closed the windows again. But I left the AC alone even then."

Claire explained how she and Leo had gone to Rowley's lab and copied the notebooks.

Glancing at Leo for a second, she continued.

"Rowley planted the bacteria in the air-conditioning unit in time for Saturday's board meeting, but when the meeting got cancelled, he went back to retrieve the bacteria."

"To cover his tracks."

"Exactly, Kitty."

It took her a moment to understand how different things might have been.

"If we'd had the meeting, the whole board would have been infected. What would have happened to us? I know the archbishop isn't well and some of the board members are up in years …"

"There would also have been the staff, the people serving coffee and such," Claire added. "Or if it hadn't cooled off last night, you would have gotten a dose when you were up there alone."

Kitty thought about the Rowley family.

"Poor Tom! I know he tried to harm us, but to think that he shot himself up there in that little patch of woods where his son died … that's just awful. Helen must be beside herself."

"There's no end to the Tommy Rowley tragedy."

Suddenly, she felt as if a big earthen dam inside her was giving way and felt the tears, big fat wet ones, ready to let go. They'd been building since Father Guido had broken the news about Eddie.

When Kitty started to cry, Bridget handed her a box of tissues—but no one in the room tried to make her stop.

29.

The meal in the seminary refectory reminded Frank of the summer during his seminary years when he'd been a member of the grounds crew. Tonight was typical for August, with only a handful of faculty present, leaving many empty spots at one long table.

Conversation centered on the unbelievable past twenty-four hours.

Topic A, of course, was the shooting at the Saint Botolph Hotel, the archbishop's narrow escape, and young Joe Maguire's bravery. They all agreed that the shooter might have been dressed like a priest but was undoubtedly an imposter.

Frank wasn't so sure about that.

But the shooting only served as a warm-up for the latest intrigue—the future of Archbishop Quilty and who would become the next archbishop of Boston. Like any group of political observers, the professors were already looking ahead to who'd get picked for the big job next.

Frank didn't understand how they did it, but they were always up to the minute on what was going on behind the scenes.

They all agreed that Quilty was finished.

One professor said that he'd be willing to bet "a week of desserts" that Quilty had already been on a "Vatican watch list" for mismanaging the sex abuse scandal. Then, when he should have been diplomatic and noncommittal about the apparition at Saint Kay's, "he blew it" by calling the apparition a fraud.

"Indiscretion is the eighth deadly sin," added someone at the end of the table.

With Quilty out of the way, they started in on Fannon. A couple of the guys got a kick out of the auxiliary bishop waving from the limo on the evening news, and an ancient priest sitting across from Frank called it "Lou's fifteen minutes of fame."

Richard summed up for his colleagues while coffee was passed around.

Quilty would never see Little Rome again, Fannon would take over, pending a permanent appointment, and Father Dan would be exiled.

"The Church has plenty of Siberias for discredited archbishops and secretaries who know too much," he added.

Earlier, up in Richard's quarters, with Portia dominating his thoughts, Frank never got around to telling his friend about his meeting with Quilty.

So when he asked the obvious question, he felt that he had the edge on these guys for once.

"Where will the archbishop go?"

Richard was ready.

"Easy answer, Frank: his favorite monastery. He'll be on permanent retreat."

Looking up and down the table, Frank was dismayed to see the priests all nodding in agreement.

30.

Guido was settled into his lounger minutes after getting back to his quarters.

Dozens of images of the last day swirled around in his brain, but one stood out. He pictured Kitty, about to finally break down, stating the obvious: "There's no end to the Tommy Rowley tragedy."

Throughout the week, he kept feeling that there was a missing piece to Tommy's story, and now he forced himself to go over what he remembered once more.

Guido was doing double-duty at the time, filling in for the chaplain at the Mount who was on medical leave, while still working at Saint Kay's.

Tommy made an appointment to talk about the priesthood. They met several times, went on walks, talked for hours, and visited Saint Luke's Seminary together just before the school year ended. The next time they met, in the fall, in Guido's tiny office off the Saint Kay's chapel, he could barely recognize the boy. Curious and outgoing months before, Tommy appeared angry and withdrawn.

In the beginning, Guido took the change at face value. Tommy himself acknowledged he was gay, and Guido had personal knowledge of how the realization of that fact can affect a person.

But every day from then on, Guido blamed himself for not having the courage to reach out to the boy, and his guilt intensified after Tommy's suicide. Once in a while, he managed to put his guilt aside long enough to ask if something else had happened to Tommy Rowley that summer. As difficult as coming to terms with his sexuality had to be, Guido suspected that Tommy looked too traumatized for that reason alone.

Guido had gone over these memories countless times, but the "missing piece" never appeared. He was about to give up and try to get some sleep when a fresh idea came to him.

Concentrate on the last time he'd seen the "old" Tommy Rowley, the kid who wanted to be a priest.

They sat at the rector's table in the great oak-beamed refectory with its vaulted ceiling. As was the custom, one of the seminary professors gave a scripture lesson before lunch was served.

During the meal, the rector took an interest in what Tommy had to say and ended up inviting the boy back for another visit.

Guido sat between the rector and Tommy, and a fourth person sat at Tommy's other side.

Father Malachy Dunn.

Father Mal had been a missionary before becoming the pastor of the small parish up in Egg Rock. Over the meal, Mal entertained them with stories from "his" village high in the Andes. Like the rector, Mal took an interest in Tommy, and before lunch was over, he invited the boy to Egg Rock for a day at the beach.

Afterward, Guido heard rumors about Father Mal getting too "friendly" with children, but never, until this moment, had he given any thought to what might have happened between Father Mal and Tommy.

He had just switched off the light when the phone rang. The ER just had a DOA brought in, and the family was asking to speak with a priest.

He tried to imagine what the people he was about to meet were going through and said a prayer for them.

As for Father Mal, Guido chastised himself for making outrageous assumptions based on the flimsiest of evidence.

Besides, people in the ER needed a priest, and that was what really mattered.

31.

It was getting dark when Frank and Richard made it outside for their walk. They started up the hill, past Cardinal O'Rourke's gravesite and the old apple orchard where they could see the archbishop's palazzo ahead, its windows alight.

At the summit, they stood before the residence while Richard caught his breath, and were about to head back when light poured out into the porte cochere for only a second, as if a door had been quickly opened and closed.

"Wait, Frank!"

Dan Skerry emerged from the shadows.

"I was straightening up the kitchen when I saw you out here. Philippe went out with her niece right after supper. An urgent family matter, she said."

The three of them set out again, and once they settled into a comfortable rhythm, Dan chuckled and pointed in the direction of the seminary.

"I bet you and your pals have everything figured out, but let me give you the 'official' version—just for the record."

From what Dan said next, Frank's old seminary professors were still batting a thousand.

The archbishop would be moving into the monastery by midweek, and, if Fannon got his way, would never leave.

Frank tried to keep a lid on his emotions.

Richard kept the conversation going.

"Has Fannon discussed your future?"

"I was about to get to that. He and the nuncio laid out 'my future' over dinner."

Dan led them to a bench near the orchard.

"Fannon gave me two choices, military chaplain or missionary, and he wants a decision by morning. He made the usual noise about me being only on loan from the archdiocese and the choice being mine, but the message was clear. I was dialing your cell, Frank, when you two appeared outside Philippe's window."

Missionary? Frank pictured Father Mal in the Andes, doing the unspeakable.

"Did you ask why?" Richard continued.

"Sure, but you already know his answer."

Frank stole a glance at Richard. They both knew.

"The Holy Spirit."

"What about Joe Maguire?"

"Fannon didn't say it in so many words, but he mentioned 'Father Maguire's great service to the Church' and felt that 'the young man was destined to go far.'"

They noticed lights going out one by one in the residence while Dan continued.

"So, guys, what choice do I make?"

"I vote for chaplain. My cousin Leo's influence, I guess."

"And you, Richard?"

"Neither."

Headlights drew their attention to a pair of vehicles pulling up to the residence. A half-dozen figures emerged, and seconds later, the door opened, flooding the porte cochere with light as before.

"Better see who our company is. Thanks for the advice."

"Wait, Dan, have you made a decision?"

"Yeah, Frank. I'm getting out."

"Sounds like either choice will get you out of here."

"And neither, like Richard suggested. Out of the priesthood. I've had enough."

With that, Dan sprinted off to the residence.

Richard watched Dan disappear into the darkness.

"Frank, when Dan told us about the archbishop, you looked like you'd seen a ghost."

He told his friend about Quilty's plan to retire to Saint Gabe's.

"No surprise. He told me once that he would have been much happier just being a priest. Lots of the higher-ups say that, but he meant it."

"Why did he change his mind?"

"He didn't. Fannon and the nuncio gave him no choice. We know they have their methods of persuasion."

They walked back up to check on the visitors but recognized the vehicles after a few steps.

Two state police cruisers.

"This doesn't look like a social call."

"Wow! Who do you think they're after, Richard?"

"The nuncio's the only one in the clear, and that's only because he's out of their jurisdiction. But *what* they're after interests me more. That building is full of secrets."

As they started downhill, Frank looked at the nearly abandoned seminary dead ahead.

"I don't envy Dan, checking out like this. He's been too busy being a speechwriter, PR guy, and valet to have a clue about what the priesthood's all about. Lucky I stuck with it."

"Sounds like you thought about checking out, too."

"I did, Richard, once or twice. It never got that serious, so I didn't bring it up. I bet you've had your doubts."

"Never. I've got the perfect arrangement. All I do is I read, write, talk, eat, and sleep. Room and board are provided, and I have no night call, no difficult parishioners, no overdue fuel bills, and no fundraising to worry about. The seminarians still believe I know more than they do. What more could I ask for?"

Frank smiled.

"I did talk to my father about it once."

"What did Vincent say?"

"That I was born to be a priest."

"He got that right."

They walked in silence until they neared Cardinal O'Rourke's mausoleum, and Frank got talking again.

"What would the old cardinal say, Professor, if we could bring him back for a day?"

"We lost our way."

"Our moral compass?"

"Absolutely, Frank, but our common sense, too. The same stuff was going on back then. Some priests were too ambitious, some larcenous, and a few of them couldn't keep their pants on—just like today. O'Rourke would be shocked that we let the Church get so open and democratic that we can't keep our human frailties under control. He was a top-down manager. His word was law, and anyone who disobeyed was gone. He would have detested his successors, including your old boss. They've simply been too permissive."

Richard stopped in front of the gravesite before continuing.

"O'Rourke was no saint, but he understood 'scandal.' He came down hard on bad priests in order to protect the faithful and prevent scandal to the Church. The guys in charge today have it backwards. They think they can prevent scandal by protecting the bad priests and abandoning their victims."

He turned away and took in the property.

"Take a good look, Frank. Before you know it, Little Rome will exist only in the history books. The palazzo will change hands, the seminary will downsize and move, and O'Rourke's earthly remains will be carted away. I'll be history myself by then, but you'll see it happen."

"The house of cards."

"Yep, but you'll survive."

"You think?"

"People always need good priests. Once the housecleaning starts, the Frank Mulcahys of the world will be in high demand."

At the second-floor landing, Frank started for his guestroom.

"Get plenty of sleep, Richard. By the way, why are you so determined to come along in the morning?"

"To make up for some bad advice I gave a friend."

"I pushed Portia pretty hard, but she pushed right back. There was nothing more we could do."

The old professor gestured in the direction of the residence.

"Anyway, no sleep for me until I say my prayers. You know what I'll be praying for tonight?"

Frank stopped and waited.

"Justice."